May the victims of racial hatred and crime never be forgotten.

May the resources of the mentally disabled never be underestimated.

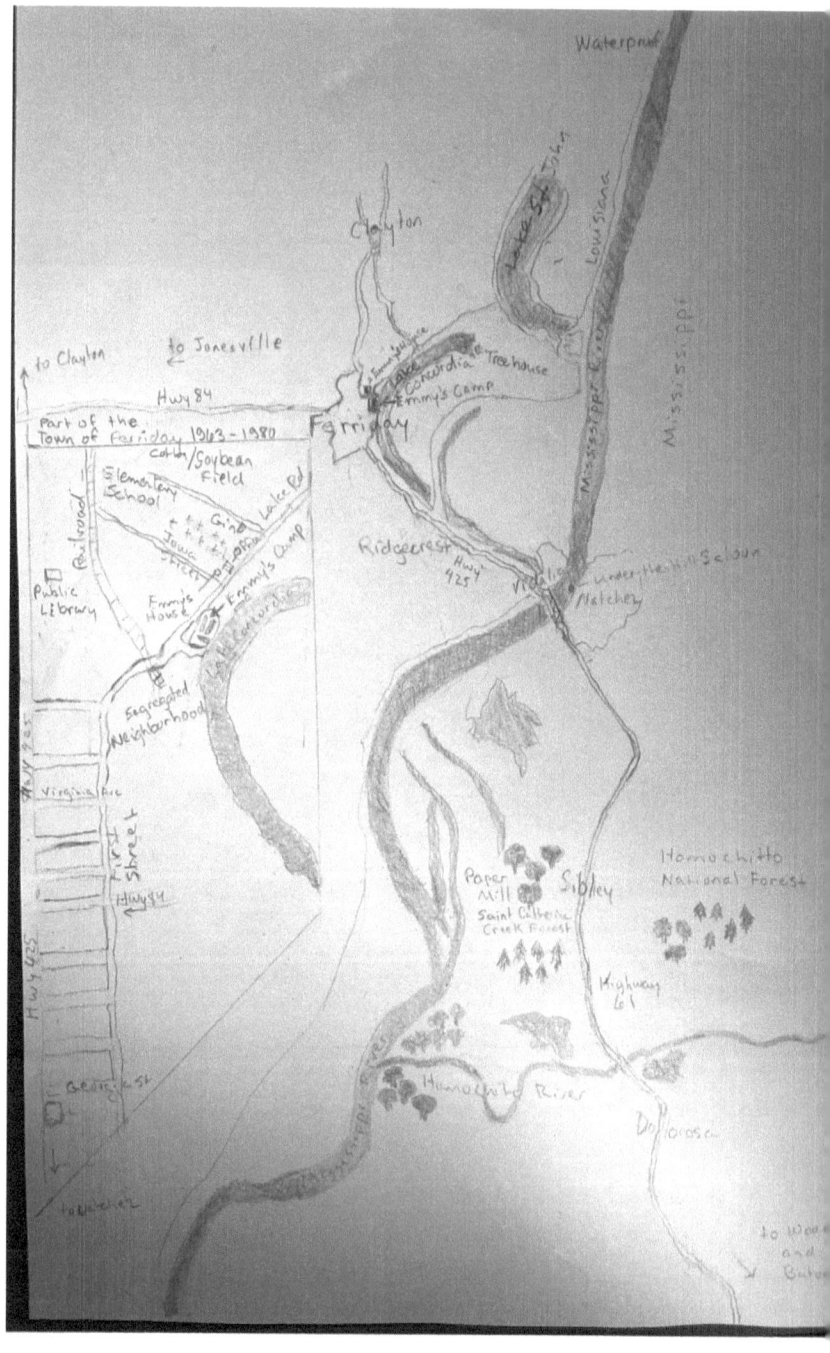

Deviling the Devil
US Copyright registration © May 2022
Barbara Bonneau
21000 Dijon, France
Austin, Texas
ISBN Kindle E-book 978-0-9884598-4-7
Paperback 978-09884598-5-4
The characters in this novel were first developed in *These Beans Have Too Much Salt*, and its previous versions under different titles
First publication under that title by Barbara Bonneau July 2015
Copyright © Barbara Bonneau 2015
First drafts/versions with mention of some of the characters
Copyright © for « Les Mains de Porcelain» 2004, translated by Barbara Bonneau (*Porcelain Hands*, 2005) and in 2007 called *Sweetbriar*, then *Sweetbriar Cajun*
White Light Yoga 2022
Some of this work was inspired by the research of the journalist, Stanley Nelson, editor of *The Concordia Sentinel*, Ferriday, Louisiana, and author of *Devils Walking*, 2016
Barbara Bonneau asserts the moral right to be identified as the author of this work.

Mentions to Kris Kristofferson and, Janis Joplin, "Me and Bobby McGee"
Mentions to Dave Brubeck "Blue Rondo à la Turk"
Mentions to the Carpenters, "Jingle Bells"
Mentions to Under-the-Hill-Saloon, Natchez, Mississippi
Mentions to The Beatles film Hard Day's Night
Mentions to The Beatles, Albums: *Rubber Soul, White Album, Let it Be*
Mentions to John Badham and John Travolta, *Saturday Night Fever*

Barbara Bonneau

Mentions to Elton John
Mentions to Freddy Mercury
Mentions to Willie Nelson, "Whiskey River"
Mentions to Joni Mitchell, "Both Sides Now", "A River"
Mentions to Bonnie Raitt, "Angel from Montgomery"
Mentions to John Sturges, The Great Escape
Mentions to Abel Meerpol, "Strange Fruit"
Mentions to Billie Holiday
Mentions to Donna Weiss and Jackie DeShannon, "Bette Davis Eyes"
Mention to Robert Aldrich, Bette Davis, *Hush, Hush Sweet Charlotte*
Mentions to Paul Simon, "Fifty Ways to Leave Your Lover"
Mentions to Ennio Morricon, "The Ecstasy of Gold"
Mentions to Oscar Hammerstein II, *The Sound of Music*
Mentions to Gene Roddenberry, *Star Trek*
Mentions to George Lucas, *Star Wars*
Mentions to Procol Harum
Mentions to Muddy Waters
Mentions to The Ramones "Rocket to Russia"
Mentions to Percy Sledge
Mentions to Bill Haley "Shake, Rattle and Roll"
Mentions to the Mamas and the Papas, "California Dreaming"
Mentions to Alfred Newman, "How the west was won"
Mentions to *Mad Magazine*
Mentions to Ada Blenkhorn and J. Howard Entwistle, "Keep on the Sunny Side"
Mentions to Neil Young, "Four dead in Ohio"
Mentions to Michael Jackson, *Thriller*
Toho *Mothra, Godzilla*
Mentions to Creedence Clearwater Revival, "Proud Mary"
Mentions to Robert Burns, "To a Mouse"
Mentions to The Three Penny Opera, "Mack the Knife"
Mentions to John Coltrane, Miles Davis, Weather Report, Jaco, Peter Erskin, Wayne Shorter, Elvin Jones, Hoagy Carmichael, Ella Fitzgerald, Nat King Cole
Mentions to Joaquin Rodrigo
Mentions to Charlie Chaplin, Buster Keaton, The Marx Brothers
Mentions to Hal Roach, *Our Gang*
Mentions to Haskell Wexler, *Medium Cool*
Mentions to Jerry Lee Lewis (1935-2022), "Great Balls of Fire"
Mentions Haney's Big House
Mentions to the National Association for the Advancement of Colored People (NAACP), CORE
Mentions to *The Natchez Democrat*
Mentions to *Wikipedia* and its millions of anonymous contributors

Deviling the Devil

by

Barbara Bonneau

Warning to readers. Please read with caution. To lend to the realism of the novel, this novel contains sexist, violent, racist language and scenes, other violence, including sexual violence, and disturbing mental images. In no way does the author condone in real life, what these fictional characters, some, members of the KKK, do or say.

We all were sea-swallowed, though some cast again, And, by that destiny, to perform an act Whereof what's past is prologue, what to come, In yours and my discharge.
William Shakespeare
The Tempest
Act 2, Scene i 245-248

Deviling the Devil

By the time she finished writing her anonymous missive, Waller's bullet riddled body had been cold a long, long time. She had some idea who had committed the murder, almost a generation ago. She knew the girl, now a full-grown woman, who had told the Klansman that Waller had flirted with her, and knew she had worked at Nettles' Truck Stop. Waller had worked at the paper mill in Natchez and was on his way home from his late-night shift. He had been dead for fourteen years.

She wrote her missive with the energy of the exalted. Sweat beaded on her forehead and she bit down until tiny dew-drops of blood appeared on her lower lip. Sifting through the old papers, she had seen something in *The Concordia Post* or *The Natchez Advocate* about an unsolved Klan crime. Now, she wanted to devil a man who worked at the plant. From childhood, he had been afraid of ghosts. His father, who her best friend had called a snake-faced venom spitting monster, wasn't around either. She couldn't kill him. Her mother had done that. But she wanted, she needed, to play some part in his punishment. It would give her back some part of the will to live her mother had stolen with the murder. His son would pay. She would make sure of that. He deserved it.

"Poison is a woman's weapon", said Mamere from the languid, low floating mist, waggling her long wispy toes between the cypresses' knees. "Why didn't your mother poison him? She knew how. No one would have guessed."

In the years since she had been hospitalized, Emmy had read many books from the library, including Sherlock Holmes and Agatha Christie. She couldn't remember if the killers who preferred poisons, were all women.

"Did you ever hear of *Miracle Kill*? Your mother used to use it on her garden before we knew about the dangers. Farmers sprayed it on crops, and municipalities fogged it from trucks to keep the mosquitoes down. By the look at some of the characters around here; I'm pretty sure it didn't just soften eggshells." She was pulling up her knee-high stockings, trying to hide her varicose veins, fighting to keep the humidity from *rhumatizing* the rest. It was too late for either. "In Roman and Medieval times, usin' unknown concoctions was a popular form of hospitality, available for enemies. Both arsenic and strychnine have always been easy enough to come by. Native Brazilians dip their arrows in *Stry-nos tox-i-fera*; before plantin' them in their neighbor's heart," she remarked. One way or another, they're welcomed, and takin' care of.

"Was the poison they used for dipping their arrows a sign of good manners or, was that just something added; for an extra measure of mean?" Emmy had turned to show her grandmother her dark, hard look, her head bending, her eyes looking past her brow.

Her grandmother shrugged off the silent accusation. "Conspirators fed *Mith-ri-da-ti-um* to ducks. Then, these royal birds were offered to the king, on silver platters, or at least ones made of pewter. It's hard to tell the difference in paintin's; especially when you only find them in the bookmobile's selection. Bless Mrs. Davis' heart. She couldn't tell a good book from a bad. Spent every penny the town gave her for whatever book came in the mail. A real sucker for romance stories, I'll say. In fact, if you want to know the truth, I sort of like those, even if they are always the same. You just can't read them one after another I suppose. Oh, well. I guess it it's better than just readin' one book, the same, over and over, the way some of these religious eccentrics do. Now what was I sayin'? Oh yeah. I'm tellin' you, used to be, revenge through poison didn't have to be a dish you served cold. French kings did it to their cousins. You know how they were forever hangin' around the courts. Didn't have much of a choice about it because Fleur de Lys Louis didn't want no dirty tricks played behind his back. Now Stalin? He kept his enemies close at the Kremlin for sure, unless he sent them away to the Gulag. Brezhnev probably keeps them in closets, like missiles. He can't just send 'em off to Cuba. He ain't Khrushchev you know. I know, I know," she said, raising an aged-spotty hand, ready for another one of her granddaughter's objections. "I'm a sucker for these stories and here, I'm skippin' a lot of generations, but all the same; why didn't your mother try somethin' like that?"

"Keep missiles in her closet?" questioned Emmy. Tonight, the memory of her grandmother was pressing hard from the other side. From there, she continued to rattle off her Latin and her two- bit knowledge of history from unverified sources. She had to voice her opinions just about everything with an unmistakable Cajun accent. This way of speaking, in itself, contributed to the fact that almost no one, outside southern Louisiana, listened. But she was right. Why had her mother murdered Harper in front of an audience? Was that a performance, an attempted suicide? Why hadn't she just used aspirin? She knew it caused hemorrhaging. *Undetectable,* if used right. She could have relieved Harper of his headaches in a less colorful fashion.

"The only thing I remember about Khrushchev, besides him being Russian, was from a parody of a Christmas song we sang in school. Fifth graders put the name of the Soviet leader in the song about Santa's leading reindeer, on account of their shiny noses. Probably older kids came up with the idea, before passing it down to us. Khrushchev's nose was compared to a guiding light. Did he drink moonshine?" she asked, as if her grandmother knew the answer to everything.

The young woman sat there holding her poisoned pen like a smoking gun. This wasn't her first attempt. Jeremy had already received one of her letters, and it wasn't the romantic kind. Could a pernicious letter lead the cops back to her? She wondered. "I would never poison anyone for real," she said. "Just in case, it would be better to cut and paste." Bent over her work, she thought about how the letters she was composing didn't reflect an Amy Vanderbilt-upbringing like the one in her *Guide to Gracious Living for Young Ladies*. "I wouldn't send a package of cat shit to the sheriff's office like Skizzum. Nothin' like that. She said got a kick out of it, but I wouldn't do that."

"I suppose you both believe wavin' a red flag in front of a bull will help you *Win Friends and Influence People*, too? This might not be a Dale Carnegie world, but you sure gotta try to stay out of trouble. Else be on your guard," said Mamere, pronouncing each syllable of the book's title as she eased down in a chair and took a folded fan from her sleeve.

Emmy waved her hand, dispelling her grandmother's words like smoke. "Skizzum is a blues musician. She doesn't worry about formalities outside chord arrangements. These days, I just prefer knockin' about words. I jest wanna help and wanna be heard." Like political pamphlets, at least these compositions would be read, and pondered. If the origins of her letters were attributed to someone else, this time, what of it? She hoped they would be attributed to someone else. Not just anyone, however.

To her mind, there were two ways of tormenting Jeremy. One, as his dead father's ghostwriter, assailing his son for his shortcomings, and another, through letters addressed to Klan members. From her way of looking at the picture, *ghost* was not an idle word. The word, *nègre*, the French word formerly attributed to a ghostwriter, also kept all of its verve, and, it wasn't without its reason for the Klan, or for her either. Even though she did not know if one of her ancestors had been reduced to enslavement, from her point of view, certainly on her mother's side, she shared something of her fundamental identity with Blacks who were tormented by the Klan. That was the thing with Emmy. When her words weren't abandoning their camps, these were stuck in the muck. Sometimes she peeled words like she did crawfish; dissecting these until they lost their vital substance, before thinking that she might be losing hers. She became transfixed, moored to a word she thought like herself: achromatic. With pallid skin, Emmy did not resemble her parents. Her color was drained as if she had been emptied of her origins by that monster, known to her only as Harper. She wondered what Skizzum would do.

Skizzum was her former best friend's older sister. She was the only person from Ferriday who had written to her at the psychiatric ward where she was sent after the fire, when she told her grandmother about her talking teeth. She was the only friend who had come to see her or help her after the imprisonment of her mother and the death of her grandmother; the only person who spoke to her about other places; Texas, Tennessee, New York, California, the Grand Canyon. Her best friend, Bee, had gone to college, become a doctor, and following a fellow student, married, moved to France, divorced, and now worked as a doctor for *Médecins du Monde*. During the last fourteen years, she had written one time. Not a card to invite her to her graduation. Not an invitation to her wedding. Not a word to simply tell her of her life. Emmy only received a post-card from a Red Cross camp somewhere in Southeast Asia, asking how she was doing, with no return address. When Skizzum came to see her,

Emmy at first thought the attention was motivated by a guilty conscious. "Wasn't she just looking for forgiveness for the snake-woman tattoo she drew on my back that caused so much trouble with my mother and the church?" But in a way, Emmy understood now, she was on a rescue mission...her own. Perhaps that is what Bee was doing as well. "After Harper, a conman if nothing else, we all needed rescuing," mumbled Emmy to herself, "but each of us mistrusted anyone who could have helped us."

She cut the letters from old newspapers her mother had kept. These had somehow escaped the flood and had sat, on top of furniture, all that time. Two copies of *The Natchez Advocate* had caught her attention. One held an article about Waller's murder in a 1964 edition, and the other, a 1966 list of Klan members from Concordia Parish and Southwestern Mississippi who had testified in front of the House Un-American Activities Committee. All had taken the Fifth Amendment more than two hundred times; every-single-time-a-committee-member-asked-a-question.

She clipped out the articles and saved them. She had the names now. Most of these men had worked at the paper mill in Natchez. Some punched the time cards at the Strong Tire Company. While wearing latex dishwashing gloves, and using tweezers, she cut letters from elsewhere in the journals and glued the pieces, like fragile butterfly wings, onto an old sheet of stationary. Her hands felt sweaty inside the gloves, which, for once, were her size. She was careful not to touch the pages with her fingers. Not once did she consider that there might already be prints on the pages. Not once did she consider who might have read these newspapers before she had. Copies of these fingerprints were stored somewhere in her mother's file, within the state penitentiary system.

Sardonic odors of time filled the air of the small trailer. Her mother had used it as an office, before the flood, before killing Harper, before going to prison, before all that had happened to her family. She picked up the files lying like a Fortune Teller's cards on destiny's table. Was there something in these documents? Had they predicted the future that was now the past? Why had her mother so uncarefully laid them? She knew about the Tarot. She believed what the cards predicted as they fell. Haphazardness was so unlike her mother. Not like she thought about the consequences every time, but she didn't leave well enough alone to come about as it might. No. Her medical files strewn over on a table? It was if after having predicated the future of her patients, they already predicted the following chaos.

Now the horses were all dead. It had been fourteen years since Emmy's fate had become random. Fourteen years since her teeth had talked. Fourteen years since her mother had been locked up. Returning the files to their cabinet would not straighten out the events or anyone's teeth. Nothing would stop her teeth from talking if they again so decided.

Emmy tied a rag like a scarf around the bottom half of her face to avoid inhaling the spores. She began to put her mother's records in the trash. Then she stopped. She opened the pages of what appeared to be a homemade catalogue of sorts, with recipes for herbal cures for both

14

people and animals. There were remedies for insect invasion, or tomato mildew, and so much more. Colorful botanical drawings of the medicinal plants, and biological diagrams of insects and other animals, both inside and out, seemed to come to life; though these were the stuff of mortuary portraits. Each species was designated by its Latin, Cajun, and English name. There were notes and drawings about surgical and birthing procedures for horses, goats, and sheep; cesareans and geldings, along with abscess removal and other minor surgeries. There were possums sporting their bivalent genitalia in graphic detail. The double dicks the kids laughed about at school were in fact true. Here the creatures were, both male and female, splayed open like the women in the pornographic magazine Bee had stolen from the gin watchman's coffee table and left under a pew at church. The images were numbered and lettered with terms of identification and descriptions, indicating the relevance of each organ. The writing was in her mother's hand and reprinted from a press of some sort. A vague memory of ferns and mushrooms wafted in her mind. She knew her mother would go into the swamp or woods on her horse; returning with hydrangeas, lilies, orchids, swamp irises, chanterelles, boletes, and even deadly amanitas.

Once, she had returned with a live baby alligator. Emmy remembered sitting on the floor playing while her mother photographed and drew the creature, already much bigger than a lizard. She called it Brutus. Emmy remembered that they fed it chicken scraps...before feeding it to the chickens. They'll eat anything. The gator had, of course, died one weekend while she was in Houma, visiting one of her aunts with her father. At least that is what her mother told her. They both knew they couldn't let the animal grow up in the house. It wasn't like a cat or dog, or even a bird. Nevertheless, there was a portrait of his insides, right next to his outsides, its scales finely drawn, its teeth sticking past its gums in a strange smile. Emmy contemplated the creature's deformed stomach. She wondered if it had really swallowed the paperclip that she had turned into a hook for her make-believe fishing pole. In another pile, Emmy found portraits, war-time photos, and a few landscapes; of herself as a baby, a few of her father and even one painted self-portrait of her mother. Emmy stared at the painting of the woman whom she remembered had a movie-star face.

Seeing her own portrait, remembering her former-self was kind of like looking in a mirror; there was a sort of truth to these before and after models of life, and its toll. She wrapped the catalogue and portraits with new newspaper to preserve them. She thought she should take the photos inside, and separate the ones stuck together if she could. She sighed. There was no use of thinking about how things could have, should have been. But she could still get angry about it.

Once she finished, she burned the scraps of wasted letters with the files of papers and animal records outside in an old oil drum while her grandmother watched from the porch with unrested eyes. Helena Plantation griots chanted from the earth's womb just twenty yards beyond; *Yé krik,* to which others responded; *Yé krak,* "Listen to yesterday's story." "We are cracking open the vault. Beware about tomorrow." The rhythms began, accompanied by a single Kora harp, *twing-tingle-ling-ling,*

16

twing-tingle-ling-ling; telling the story of generations of births and deaths, of how their African ancestors came to be enslaved, and brought to the Americas, two, three hundred-fifty years before. They came to build nations, died, and had been buried in a plot to become the foundation for generations of junked John Deere and International Harvester farm equipment. All equal in death. *Koute timoun yo. Koute timoun yo. Pran swem tèt ou. Pran swem tèt ou. Pa Fè sa, Pran swem tèt ou, Pa Fè sa, sa, sa,* warning, urging, pleading, "Listen child, Listen child. Take Care, Take Care. Don't do that. Take Care. Don't do that. That. That."

Emmy heard them, but her routine was now rhythmed with something other than their voices. She was reading her enemies' future. The transfixed block letters glared back at her with their bold, grim faces; their teeth unsheathed, their fists raised, ready to avenge, to rip apart the hearts of their antagonists. "They don't have to know about it, do they?" She turned to Mamere, but she was no longer there. To the griots she murmured, *Ou pral byento jwenn repo,* "you will soon find rest." She heard, and spoke in the broken Creole she had learned from her grandmother. Who knew what language the slaves had spoken to one another? Once in formation, the letters put their weapons aside, ready to take responsibility for hers. She wondered if they had an answer to her question, "what *is* justice?" *Ki sa ki jistis.*

Boneyard blues

I saw what you boys did down at Poor House Road. Y'all went all over that Impala. Man's face is gone. But his eyes still see. I know you workin' graveyards now.

This was the first of a series of messages brought up in the secret meetings. The calls and messages continued until there was another murder, and another, and another.

"This is devilment honey. It will lead to no good." Mamere found something wrong with anything she decided to do. Her skin prickled. At once she was irritated, and reassured, like when you have a rash, and, you know why. Nevertheless, sometimes, Emmy thought of her own deviling as Civil Rights' work. "The Klan hurt those people. They were our neighbors. Maybe our kin. I'm not talking about the slaves in the graveyard behind the house, but some of the Creole families who still live just across the Lake Road, next to the old camp. Some of them are still alive."

"You talkin' about the part of part of town Harper and them racists, and other pigeon-holers, call the *Chocolate Quarters*?" asked Mamere.

"Yeah," Emmy sighed. "Wouldn't stirrin' up trouble, between the Ku Klux Klan members, be like John Lewis' *good trouble in* Alabama?" Her grandmother shook her head in a slow sign of dismay.

Growing up in a cult had meant the understanding of a new order; seeing the world through Harper's warp.

Ordained by his own mystery, he was a man who came to them from nowhere. In spite of the twists and turns of his roadmap, he had led them to nowhere else. If *else* was a place; Emmy had never planned to go there. She had never planned anything about her life.

Thinking of outcomes came after her mistakes. When she made one, she held on to it like a treasure; keeping it like odds and ends in a jar, or on a shelf. She made things with them. When she needed money; she had things to trade. At least in theory. Fuck- ups were not much of a commodity in Louisiana. Not that these didn't happen. As with elsewhere, exchanging them required deep pockets; and not many people had that sort of vestment in the south. In nineteen seventy-seven; missteps were put in order by other means. With the new governor, who had learned from a powerful predecessor, in higher places, accounts were no longer settled by gunfire. Mistakes were exchanged, just like favors. Until one day, old laws settled these in no arbitrary fashion. But, was it enough to say that for now, until those ways of paying an eye for an eye, a tooth for a tooth, again became apparent to his constituents, Emmy among them, she did not much ponder over the gravity of her acts? Her mistakes could not be traded in commodities.

Hadn't the worst already happened? Hadn't the one person she thought had loved her turned out to be the person who hurt her the most? Hadn't his faults bubbled up to the surface with the stink of his rotting body? Didn't they ask themselves what led to his murder? Instead, people seem to feel that they must choose, must judge before the body falls.

After all, what was behind all the whodunit theories? Motive? Why a person was killed is secondary. *Who* is right, and *who* is wrong; the answers to these questions are the ones that matter. Yes, who? Since to these judges, Harper, a lay preacher, who, as a representative of Jesus on earth, was above the law and, as such, could do no wrong; he didn't seem like a person who needed killing. Nobody pursued the question as to what proceeded the first attempted murder. Nobody connected his detainment in prison for corrupting a minor with the shot. A polished speaker, with an ability to make a crowd laugh, he had said he forgot or didn't know. Of course, the turtles knew what a stinking character he was. They had been the first to find his body in the swamp, floating under his trailer. They made sure he wouldn't rise from the dead, not with a mind to call his own; not after they had finished unraveling his brains and swimming with them through the sewage.

For people of Ferriday, these judgments were like those pronounced by a gubernatorial candidate in the years to come; except with a colored slant. The only way a preacher could be found guilty, *post mortem*, was, if he had been found in bed with a dead White girl, or a live White boy. If the kid were Black, then the guilt would shift. The Black youth would be sent to death row. His guilt would be self-evident. There would be no cause for doubt in the minds of the jury, or the judge. People in Ferriday were like everyone else, forgiving on some counts, and fickle on others. For the White folks in Ferriday, dead Whites were always right; with any brains or not, that is to say, within the circumstantial evidence of their whiteness. There were no Atticus Finches whatever their teacher had said.

Between their preacher and her mother, the sentence was decided before the body was cold. Didn't she have a sinful interracial marriage? She had a deep voice. Was that undertone a tan? Could she have been part Negro? Part Indian? Did any of these Cajuns have a birth certificate? These were questions that the jurors asked with polite words in nineteen-sixty-three. The less cordial ones meant the same thing. Twelve men condemned her mother to the electric chair. Didn't they realize that the choice, if it was indeed that, was between a motherless victim and a decomposing corpse? Wasn't some measure of guilt considered? Some attenuating circumstances argued?

Instead having her back, the town turned theirs and hurried off down the track, racing about their lives. Their emotions were still caught up in a cloud of angry hooves over the dismissal of states' rights, galloping out of sight and being toted out as civil rights. Emmy wasn't one to bet on the nose, but you could see that many of the people who still held fast to their wagers, voted for the candidates who looked the most like them. The rest voted how they rode. That is to say, with the sheriff.

Wiping her brow with one of her father's old white handkerchiefs, Emmy stopped a minute to sip her lemonade. She noticed her trembling hands and looked down at her thighs poking out like toothpicks beneath her shorts. "Skin and ... bones. And bones." She said the word twice because she mistrusted it and wanted to lend it the consistence she did not elsewhere possess. Before her words had themselves become thin, she used to see herself as others saw her, as pretty, like her mother, with an angelic face. Now, on her best days, her saccadic movements and her weakened frame made her think of the characters of the first in the series of the *Silly Symphonies* Disney cartoon where skeletons dance to a whimsical percussion in a production featuring both horror and burlesque, constructing and deconstructing themselves like a box of Tinker Toys; playing with, and on, each other's bones. "What's funny about that? They couldn't get a gig together while they were alive?" she stifled a laugh about to breach; like a breath pulled back from the edge of Chaos. She scratched the back of her hand. Something was wrong with her skin.

Her focus shifted from her worries, to the rhythms, then to the idea of community. In Ferriday, as a child, she had played at school performances with other instruments. For the annual Christmas show, while "Somebody snitched on me," was belted out on stage at the Junior High Gym, and Jerry Lee Lewis watched from a first-row chair; she accompanied her classmates with the school's piano. Nearing the end, one classmate was so filled with emotion; he threw it up on the stage. She did not get to surprise the rocker, and the other parents, with his, "Great Balls of Fire". The curtain was closed. A mop and bucket came out, and the boy was whisked away with his father.

It was just as well. Ferriday wasn't ready to re-celebrate their famous son, or hear how their brains might be rattled with something other than a snake, or a *Bible*, especially not from a seven-year-old girl, singing it aloud, with or without the son of a local sun, in a Christmas pageant. "It must be hard to be the child of a celebrity," thought Emmy.

"So Skizzum's got some real gigs, playin' piano or guitar," said Mamere, standing again in the open doorway, looking at her fingernails, still red with henna, as if she could read her granddaughter's mind. This was not really a question, although she raised her voice a little at the end as if speaking French. She had known the whole time Skizzum had been to Woodstock, and what that event had meant to her. She had met a life-long friend, although her girlfriend, another famous musician from the south, had died young, from a heroin overdose people said. Emmy wondered if her grandmother, famous only in her family, still played dominoes, now, from her own bone yard.

Sound and fury

Emmy had not heard from Skizzum in a while. She knew she was busy, playing music in Nashville, performing like the artist she was meant to be. Emmy sometimes wondered if without Harper, without his church, without her mother's abandon, without the flood and ruin that followed, would she, too, have taken her harp to the performance level? Everyone had said that she had a beautiful lyrical voice, a voice that could sing opera. Did they mean the Grand Ole Opry?

Emmy loved music of almost all kinds. Cajun music rang out in her early memories, along with that of the Carter Family, Doc Watson, Hank Williams, Bob Wills and the Texas Playboys. Beyond the music itself, Emmy's world was a world of sound. Sound was in everything around her, in the whoosh and tinkle of the water, the rustle and rub of the leaves as the wind blew through the trees, the voices of insects, birds and other animals; but also, in the sound of movement, hands clapping, boards creaking, doors clacking, objects falling, and machines turning. She associated these with odors, not all of these pleasant, but in spite of this oddity, these enabled her to identify the source of sounds and to repeat these.

In music, with her grandmother's harp and Harper's xylophone, she had shifted towards classical themes, learning many pieces from listening to the radio. Once she and Harper went to Baton Rouge to see the circus where she heard a live performance of *Thunder and Blazes*. She memorized the notes as they stormed and whirred over and around the audience with their unmistakable perfume of popcorn and caramel apples.

Later, she learned that this military march they began playing with her mother's family in Ferriday had been adapted from Julius Ernest Wilhelm Fucik's piece. The harp lent a particular buzz to the brass as she accompanied the chromatic scales played by her uncles, and thought about how the musician's name rhymed with music. Mamere adored these new additions to the family repertoire and played along with bells. Encouraged by her grandmother, who said this music came from Irish *Travellers* (who spelled their name with two l's instead of just one); she learned Renz's *Circus Gallop* on a xylophone they made from scavenged pipes.

Emmy imagined leaving Louisiana for Nashville and playing in a band with Skizzum. Hadn't her friend suggested such? Emmy pondered an instant. She remembered the lightness of the breeze and the hum of the insects of the forest. These seemed to inhabit the makeshift stage with her as she played. She remembered how silky the air felt, moving between the strings and tickling her fingers like tender, cool gusts of wind lifting her hair. She remembered feeling that only these tough metal strings connected her to the earth and that if she stopped toiling and would let go, she would be lifted away like a cloud on the oily emanations of whiskey and turpentine. For an instant she let herself float away from the houses and the fields, across woods and the lake to the gypsy camp as she had in the past while she played the harp. She imagined again, being elevated on the air, like a bird, or a bee; flying up the Mississippi, then spreading out over the lakes, forests, and the Tennessee River until she found her friend's home in Nashville, guided by the iridescent city lights.

Skizzum would take her in her arms and hug her and make her forget that it was with that harp, on that day, on that stage, in front of everyone, among the aromas of cornbread and roasted meats, and the sounds of Clifton Chenier that Harper moved in with his hands, his face, pawing her and slobbering like an old dog, gobbling up a scrap of fresh meat under the table. It was then and there that he earned her trust through music. No longer did she hear the clicking of his tongue in time with the cogs clicking into place as he opted for moment when no one was looking, the moment where he would trick her, he would trick her, he would trick-trick-trick her...It was then and there that he had fooled her mother and grandmother into thinking that he was a responsible adult, capable of teaching and of caring, of caring, of caring...for the trusting child she had been. It was then and there he led her into the church late at night while her grandmother slept in her rocking chair and when no one else was around to save her. It was then and there that she realized that Skizzum was not with them anymore and that the other girls did not seem to be the object of favor by their preacher, and she was alone. All alone. It was then and there, then and there, then and there...She closed her eyes to blot out the memories.

Skizzum had been one of Harper's *Angels*. Graced with a smooth athletic build, with long dark chestnut curls, and brown eyes, Skizzum had a sibylline quality to her personality. It wasn't so much that she predicted what would happen; she teased the future out from its firmaments. Like a big feline, the ghosts of the future, stalked. These had been coming, coming, and at last, with Skizzum, they readied to pounce. Was it too much to say that she was someone who enticed horoscopes from the cosmos? Had she always been like that, or had the events that had happened, changed her?

Had Emmy been proud, like Skizzum had been, that she could obtain such privileges as to ride in front of his truck or car? Had she felt somehow that she was better than the other girls because he bought her fluffy-fine dresses, took her to restaurants, and to the beach? Had Skizzum felt uncomfortable, like she had, about trying on these dresses in front of him? Emmy had refused to change into her swimming suit with him in the same room, but all the same; he had crafted occasions where they had to stop on a roadside so she could relieve herself. She felt his presence as if he had been trying to watch when she pulled down her panties and squatted behind the trees, trying to avoid poisoned eyes and ivy. Emmy did not know if Skizzum had had these same experiences. She thought that Skizzum, like herself, had felt the burning red- face of shame. Avowals sparked and words fizzled. Emmy felt it now. Fourteen years later.

Harper had said some ugly things about Skizzum. He said she had "fornicated with the Devil," and that is why she drew the snake- woman tattoo on the younger girl's back. He said that Skizzum wanted to corrupt the younger girls, to steal them away from the church. He said the proof was the sixteen-year-old's out-of-wedlock's pregnancy. But, Mamere had said that Harper was the father of Skizzum's baby and that the baby had died. It was confusing. Emmy did not understand how all that could be true. She didn't think Skizzum was evil, not in a hellish manner. Or was she? At the time, Emmy was furious and hurt. "How could she have drawn the tattoo on my back? She knew it was nasty and knew I would get in trouble with my mother, my grandmother, and most of all, Harper," she remembered, as she cut another hissing letter with the scissors, slicing through her glove from both sides and drawing blood. Along with the snarl, the red droplets spelled anger. Revenge is a knife that points in both directions.

She would have to start over. But she *had* been in trouble. So had her mother. And it *was* Skizzum's fault. Bee's too, for suggesting it. Harper made her family pray all day on their knees, and, still on their knees, make their way up to the church alter with the rest of the congregation. He had made her confess in front of everyone and write prayers with a felt-tipped pen on colored cloth, torn from the borrowed skirt as she wore it, and hang it on a prayer tree outside the church. He said this was to expunge the tattoo on her back. And Bee was right; these tiny flags did look like underwear, flapping in the wind. She had laughed. Bee wasn't angry about her skirt. Emmy's skirt had been ruined too.

Emmy had felt lucky that day. Harper did not make her show the tattoo in front of the whole church to see. He said, "In the name of our Lord, take off that shirt so your mother can see the mark of the Devil, so that she can see and we will know how our Savior can see all, and has brought you before me today, for salvation." Time seemed to dangle with the T-shirt she held from one hand, while crossing her arms in a self-conscious defense against the intrusion, her tiny pubescent swellings beginning to point. Her mother said she was too young; her breasts weren't developed enough to wear a bra, but she hadn't been too young to be confused by the lack of decency of the situation. She had hung her head; staring at her white ruffled socks in the black patent leather shoes he had bought her. *Ballerines* he called them, showing off the little French he knew and the even less he knew about children's play clothes.

She had hung her head; engulfed by something greater than shame, something, which invaded her alignment with her words. She had hung her head; her sentences no longer hers, repeating the confession Harper imposed upon her like a smile on the mask of a sad comedian. She had hung her head as she confessed in front of the congregation. She had hung her head; after church, while he had made her mother scrub the tattoo as he stood there, making sure she rubbed her skin until it was raw and was what he called the color of sin. She had hung her head, while he admonished her, saying prayers. Why did he say that? What was wrong with the color of her skin? She had hung her head, as he told her mother that if she didn't want her daughter to be ruined like the dress, she would now have to do homeschooling with him and his kids. She had hung her head, while he said he didn't want her to suffer from the perversion of the other children in the public school. She had hung her head, and so had her mother, but it was her choice—after all. They had hung their heads as her mother listened to how she was free to choose how to raise her child. "But if you make the wrong choice, then you will suffer the consequences," he said.

She had hung her head as her mother uplifted hers, agreeing with Harper that she would do as he suggested to prevent the ruin of her daughter. "It was the freedom of choice thing that grabbed her," Emmy thought. "She couldn't risk what he said would be an abomination. Her mother had entrusted her own eyes, the only eyes she had ever had, the only eyes she had ever trusted, to someone who said he could see the glory, to someone who said that if she trusted enough, she should be ready to give up seeing what she had always seen to be true, so that she could see the *real* truth. The glory of God would reveal itself to her, before her own eyes as her daughter was sacrificed on the altar of shame." Emmy knew that Harper said things like that. He had said them to her as well.

Later, much later, Emmy learned the truth about her friend. The father of Skizzum's baby wasn't Harper after all. He was the Black boy, the first, who worked at the grain elevator. His name was Hiram. They all knew him, but not everyone knew his name. He had light brown skin, a warm smile, and laughing, almond shaped eyes. He weighed the small bags of pecans they gathered from the woods and wrote the weight on a slip of paper for the man at the cash register. They saw him walking home to the neighborhood beyond the woods or in a boat, fishing beyond the point. After the child's birth at a nearby hospital, she had given the baby up for adoption. She couldn't bear the idea that her mother would raise the child as a sibling. Her mother had not known the truth and still did not know. Skizzum said that she couldn't bear the lies another second. "That is where her path to alcohol began," Emmy concluded. "In those days, nothing else could have been done, but that didn't mean it didn't hurt. To give up her baby must have been awful."

Skizzum started hanging around a crowd that would slip beers to the younger kids. She put tucks in the lies about herself until these crouched low in her belly and she could no longer stand. Someone had to take her home. Sometimes it was a sheriff's deputy. Emmy wondered if these men drinking with her or taking her home took advantage of her adolescent vulnerability. Were these states of drunkenness worse than *Bible* boozing with Harper? Were the *Bible* drunkards the men encouraging Skizzum to take her wine elsewhere? Were they worse than Harper himself? Emmy pondered about her mother in prison, but more about the loss of something that all Cajuns treasured...their independence and their music. And although music was still part of their lives, the Cajun members of the cult gave up their personal style to Harper without a stance.

Skizzum had fought back and gained her independence. In spite of the health problems brought on by the whiskey, she had escaped from Harper. With her flight, she won something. Emmy thought she understood why people liked the blues, and some country music. There were stories about human sufferings, about life's hardships in those songs. She thought of Willie Nelson. "Whiskey River take my mind," he sang. Skizzum had sung this same song, begging for the amber liquid to take *care* of her, to make her forget. Was the alcohol worse than the treatments Emmy received at the Children's Hospital? Could alcohol or medical treatments replace one's lack of strength? Was what was deemed a moral weakness, a translation of parental love gone wrong? Emmy didn't want to think about it. She was still trying to forget. Different from Skizzum, and from her mother, Emmy didn't like whiskey. But she did wonder if drinking like that would help.

Emmy kept thinking in songs. This was something her grandmother had taught her by example. It was a way to remember; a way to think when your thoughts have been chomped, digested, dissolved, and diluted by someone who, for some reason, believes that they know better, that they are more deserving of their thoughts, and their ideas are more deserving than yours, so much more that you might as well forget you have any at all. Songs gave you something to hold on to. Harper wanted to control their thoughts and keep them confined like Emmy did with her mistakes. That is how he could control everything else about them. But they could still sing. Like gospel for Black people, Emmy's family held on to something through music that Harper could not destroy.

Skizzum too, sang of Joni Mitchell's cloud illusions from the song, "Both Sides Now". "I don't think I know clouds either. In a way, they help you forget," Skizzum said, watching the sky. "I'm a cloud-illusion magician. Half split open, a schism like my nick-name says, I have to work to create something in that wide open space where I let things go that I don't need anymore. Let's pretend to stitch clouds together, and rip them apart again, like cloth!" Like clouds, like her problems, she thought she could reduce the illusions she created to playthings; dividing, spinning, and shrinking them to nothing. In a psychiatric hospital where illusions were daily fare, when she visited, she enticed Emmy to remember good things, to forget her environment. She meant well. While she was least expecting it, Skizzum pulled her down on the floor and pointed at a herd of cellos roller-skating across the strip of sky encroaching the ward's window. Maybe she inherited this talent from her father, who Bee said was a fog- weaver.

"These aren't lies, but incursions to another reality," she said, her eyes kindling with the joint she had smoked. But her visions lacked sound. They lacked smells. And of course, you couldn't feel a cloud, no matter how billowy it looked. From Emmy's point of view, her friend's world was *skizzumed* into to compartments. She could start an argument or extinguish a fire. Neither concerned her much. "Why do empty spaces in my mind cause me problems?" wondered Emmy. For Skizzum, there was music, and there were soundless cloud-visions. Silent films that you loved with their piano accompaniments, when you had them. While Emmy was in the hospital, this cataloguing of illusions had helped her sort things out, but she thought there should be some kind of total feeling with the universe and the Skizzum perturbed her idea of oneness.

Emmy had the visions without the clouds, and could hear the percussion of the skates rolling, turning, and whirring on the parquet, as the cellos played "The Ecstasy of Gold" by Ennio Morricone from the film, *The Good, the Bad, and the Ugly,* and became horses stirring up golden or ferrous dust with the aromas of boiled coffee and burning pines. Sometimes Emmy wondered if clouding up part of what your mind knew, with the familiar forever chords of memory, into a forever blur of sunlight, was such a good thing. She didn't know if it was better to remember or to forget. Sometimes she needed songs. Sometimes she needed clouds. Both were helping her to get herself back together; to become what she could. "Can you could choose the memories you want to keep like picking through a pile of dirty laundry for something still clean enough to wear?" She asked her grandmother, who had taken off her stockings and was painting her toenails. "Memories are the only thing we really own," replied Mamere.

Paranoiac Punch

Emmy's grandmother was still trying to convince her to perform with Skizzum. "Maybe when I'm dead," Emmy scoffed. "Tribal drums are what brought me to this in the first place." She remembered playing gigs with her family and how the synchronicity of musical desire had given way to camaraderie of thought between the musicians. There was the transitory exaltation, the moment of pure joy, brought to each of them through their music. This was as bonding among the players as it was contagious to the audience. What would become of music if it all came from the radio itself? Would music be reduced to mechanical sounds, even if these could be beautified and strengthened? Wasn't there something that transitioned between the composer and the performer, the interpreter and the audience? Yes, *the*, that one, because every composer, performer, interpreter and audience was not the same. They did not create the same ambiance. Not that the radio couldn't produce an atmosphere, but it was all the same, still radio gas. Its only saving grace were the artful radio hosts, the interviews, and the music that was played. Radio waves were just oscillations of electromagnetic radiation. An emission was generated, and a receptor received. There was nothing artistic about a feat of engineering, however fascinating.

Emmy thought there was something special that was assimilated through artists, here musicians, and because of this moment of transcendence into another state of being, there were also risks.

There was the feeling of being transported into a trancelike state of sound and beauty. How long could the senses endure such an aesthetic elevation of the soul before this fascination of mere aerial vibration, under certain conditions, also lead to an entrapment by the performer, one that could hold both the musician and the spectator in mutual captivity? How long would they, could they waltz in step before one would consume the other? Must one of the two die to escape the hypnotic entwinement? Pull themselves from the fire? Looking down at her paper, she noticed a small patch of burning skin on her hand. "Have I been scratching it again?" she mumbled.

Thorns of anger crept up and began to throb in Emmy's temples and annoy her throat. Deviling the Devil gave her a mission, helped her to dispel old fears of annihilation when she played. Yet, it did have some disadvantages. "Will I rot in Hell for what I am doing?" She asked. Her concerned brow rumpled like cornfield furrows folding over behind a tractor. She turned towards the empty door. Emmy had been only eleven when the beauty of rhythm and melody enraptured her before rapturing her, as she played the harp. She had been only eleven when a more experienced performer encouraged her enthrallment. Emmy had been only eleven when her mother offered her to a pedophile cult leader. Then the inevitable happened. She had been only eleven. And then, she was alone.

Her mother had been well intentioned. Aren't all mothers? She had saved a bad man from bleeding to death and wanted to get right with God. She had been honorable. He had not. Wasn't that the bottom line? What did that say about God?

When they were children, she knew this man's sons. One of them still lived nearby. He had a temper. Pulling him into a fight would be easy. She remembered her school days. If someone laughed about anything, the boy thought they were making fun of him. He danced around, captivated by the other's regard, as in a Narcissi's mirror. Then, blaming bubble-gum disputes on his nearest brother or classmate, he said things like, "It's his fault. He started it. He did it on purpose." Later, his knee-jerk reactions made him the object of taunts. He was sometimes mistreated; he responded by putting rubber bands around the testicles of his father's dog. Then, like his old man, if you went by the rumors, he became an affiliated member of the Ku Klux Klan. At least he hadn't become the god of his own twisted church.

Emmy poised over her letter, pondering, "did my mother know about that? What planet had she lived on while Harper was alive? Did she wonder about his children; about what would happen to them?" Cutting out letters from old newspapers gave her a lot of time to think. Would time be enough to allow her to make sense of it all? Would putting two and two together end up tangled in a snarl, like a child's hair, in a bubble gum knot?

Being sure as death and taxes, or having unexpected fears, can lead to nasty stuff. People say you're paranoid when you begin to try to understand your own sorry luck. Do you think like a snake?

These critters will strike again, and again, until the threat is removed, if by any means this behavior is the result of thought. Hadn't bad luck happened enough in her family? But Jeremy's gig was different. He didn't just fall into a devils' bowl of indulgence. These dishes, empty of consistence, might be harder to manage than a *crème brulé;* the chef listening for the magical moment the sizzle slows down to let the caramel catch up with the sugar. But Jeremy couldn't crawl out. It was like he drank Mad Honey every day. Her mother wasn't that kind of alcoholic. Even if she drank too much whiskey, and understood too late what she thought of as her own bad luck; she did get out, if only to get locked up. What about Skizzum? Was it too soon to tell where fate would take her?

"Hmmff," said Mamere, as if someone pulled her string. "Sometimes, people get mixed up with a punch of their own makin'. Then, they pour in the spirits and serve it to others, before throwin' it all up all over themselves and each other. And life ain't all about balance. Syrup and biscuits never come out even."

"Like the choir at church, his girls, the *Angels,*" said Emmy. "Like me?" Hadn't she been served Harper's brew? Hadn't she offered it to others? Hadn't it, at last, caused terrible indigestion amongst them all? She didn't know how to explain it, but Jeremy's drink was different; he was part of the punch.

"Jeremy, is made of a toxic infusion", continued Mamere; her breath rustling the letters that Emmy tried to hold on to. "Hey!" she exclaimed, again annoyed at Mamere for sticking her wind into her business.

"He's thick with the fruit of some kind of forever rumba. Like his father, he holds his head high, and with blinders moves forward, then, side-to-side; ramrod straight in his four-count beliefs. Purity. Family. God. Country." Each word gained weight and moved sideways in step as it fell off her grandmother's tongue.

That illness was an ugly one. Emmy knew that. Hatred of others is always a part of it. Distilled and concentrated; it reveals a contagious poison closer to the heart. It was a solid block. *Onetruecertitudeforbothmen*. Harper's talent had been to convince others to force it down in one diluted gulp or another. He eased it in like Providence. His doctrine was God's will. Jeremy moved about, all his life, drunk on his father's swill. There wasn't much left to hazard. Early on, he became a gifted mixologist and added new, personal ingredients. Motioning to include the heavens as only spirits can see it, the opposite of a dismissal, Mamere said, "he has become one with his drink, one with his father, one with his beliefs."

"He ain't that fixated," argued Emmy. Even if she felt compelled to argue with her grandmother, she wasn't so sure. Jeremy's paranoia was a contagious one. It was again endemic in the area. He not only gathered up conspiracies of all sorts, he was a carrier since early childhood. Was there any cure? As a defense, to escape what seemed like a personal destiny, Emmy had begun thinking in hypothesis. If this, then, or if that, well...Of late, she was making fewer conclusions about life. In fact, she had long ago become wary of life's terms, which ended sometimes before the sentences did.

Rationalizations

By nineteen seventy-seven, Ferriday's citizens had heard that a conspiracy was behind the plot to kill President Kennedy. This news excited convenience. Potluck suppers, hair salons, and local bars were live with known agitators, sharing their cup. Sometimes, pride, or favor, leave behind desperate and angry drinkers who keep venom in their mouths, and spit out the toxic mix on the first person that comes along. Was it the talk or the reality? "Oswald could not have done it alone, I'll tell you,"one man said, holding his plate as he served himself another helping of mashed potatoes. "Yeah," the others agreed as they helped themselves from around the table featuring home-cooking for the Presbyterian Church's Family Night Supper. "We all know that. We all know that for sure now," he said, passing up the dish of steamed broccoli. "But where's the proof?" whispered another, as he filled his with candied yams.

They had already put it together. In Ferriday, citizens were still talking about it, only in other terms. They were so close to the truth. They weren't making it up. Carlos Marcello, lived just down the levee and across the bridge. This racketeer from New Orleans was behind the assassination of the president. He had to be. Marcello hated the Kennedys for trying to put he and his mafia family, behind bars...for good reason.

They also knew everything about the Watergate conspiracy that there was to know, and wanted to turn the page ever since the televised hearings. Start over. *Tabula rasa*. Change parties. "Yeah, except we'll keep the governor. He cracks me up. Democrat though he is." "Me too," said another from across the bar. "I guess he showed off his opponent; telling him he was so slow it took him an hour and a half to watch *60 minutes*." They all laughed, remembering the speech.

A lot of people in Louisiana thought they were smart like that, good at figuring things out. They knew before everyone else; and, as the Kennedy case started to open up, well, for some reason, mouths clammed shut. Some moved across the river, all the way to Mississippi. They wanted to be out of earshot. They didn't want to know. As the House Select Committee got closer to the truth, beginning to recognize the relation of Oswald and Ruby to the mob; some people in Ferriday started to run from it, especially the sheriff's deputies who had for years been watchdogs over Marcello's operations Up-the-River. Some scratched their heads. They thought they knew. Some left for Texas. Maybe they knew too much.

The famous sheriff of Concordia Parish, back from prison, would now only leave one way; two feet in front. And no one was sure that, even then, he would be gone. Instead of contributing further to build hard evidence, he looked for proof in similarities between the Lincoln and Kennedy assassinations. Hadn't they learned about proof by numbers at school? If you added your age to the date of the year you were born, wouldn't you wind up with the year of date? Wasn't this true for every single person on the planet on this very date? Weren't the similar dates of these presidents' elections, both to Congress and to the Presidency, significant? Wasn't Lincoln advised by a Kennedy not to attend the theatre, and Kennedy, counseled by a Lincoln not to go to Dallas? These coinciding facts could not be coincident. The proof by dictionary was out of the question. Many preferred magic to method. It wasn't easy to tell what was real from what was spun by gossip and lies, or from their own sheriff's conniving and doodling. Now he talked about new conspiracies. And so, they were back again, from across the river; yelling and drinking, fighting about the local police and sheriff departments; about who would go down now for discriminatory practices like the Supreme Court had decided they should, about what happened to Jimmy Hoffa, and all the rest. Some of them had information. They all listened. Ferriday had grounded its reputation again, all the way down to the heel of the swamp's boot. It was the wildest town in all the state.

After a time, Harper's son, who stayed tuned in with the news as much as he could, developed new rationalizations. These were often directed at the woes of governance: "They force us into submission. They own the banks. They own the newspapers. They own the industries. They are coming for us with the full force of the government," he would whisper, or say aloud, to a coworker, or to anyone who listened. As long as this harangue was along nationalistic lines, he would find sympathy. It was easy to hate someone who had no name, no consistency other than that of being part of a collection of televised effigies or shadows, like in T.S. Eliot's, poem, "The Hollow Men." They might as well be bullets or bowling pins, depending what side of the range they were situated. But now he knew who they were. His friend in Baton Rouge had told him. Was Jeremy one of these shapeless men, who filled out the vase he was poured into or was made from? Was he a violent soul, or only one of the stuffed men?

In his free time, Jeremy went with his pals to the *Twin Theaters*, watched *Star Wars* or *Saturday Night Fever*. Afterwards, they grabbed a beer in a nearby lounge, talked about Darth Vader and the Empire; pretended they had better moves than Tony Manero; and continued to hate *them*. Some of his friends were sons of the paper mill workers. Others were kids he had met at the private Christian Junior High School he had attended in New Orleans, after the murder of his father.

The new *Grand Wizard* of the Knights of the KKK was one of these. He had explained to Jeremy who *they* were, when Ducal came over to check the barbecue. "*They*'re *Jews*," the Wizard snorted, beer in hand, almost sorry he had to use three words to explain, even if one was contracted. "Didn't you know, Jeremy?"

Jeremy didn't know. "Ain't it enough to be White?" he asked, afraid of being excluded at some point from *The Bible* of belonging. "I thought it was okay to be rich?" He pondered. No, there was something that set the Jews apart, but the rich ones were worse, Ducal said. This was something beyond Jeremy's comprehension, even with his readiness to include another group of people into his personal catalogue of cloudy otherness. "They ain't Black, all the same," he said, his unease beginning to seep through his shirt. He had to change enemies or include new ones. For Jeremy, this should not have been complicated, as long as this other was identifiable as a threat to his way of life and as long as he had time to shift gears. He resumed his difficulty without realizing it, in his question to himself, "Do I know any Jews?" What he realized in that instant he had not realized in thirty years while his family and friends had hated Black people. He was unable to identify the people he was supposed to hate, so why would he waste energy hating them. He continued to listen as his friend raged, and used the n-word, as if it was clear, between the two, there was some sort of understanding.

"Hitler got that right," Ducal continued within the smaller circle of men who had gathered to listen as he talked at the Homochitto Hideaway Park. Jeremy took another bite of his hamburger and thought, "Wasn't Hitler the man their fathers fought in World War II? Wasn't he the head of the Nazis?" Outside the *New Testament*, he had never thought about the people from the *Old Testament*. He had enough of a problem trying to realize that anyone from that time had survived long enough to be a part of the war. "Weren't they gassed in Poland or some place?" He asked, stricken by his awareness that his friend had been making fun of him. Ducal laughed, "That never happened my friend! It's a hoax, don't you see! Don't you all see?" He punctuated his remarks with his fist directed at no one, in the air. He had seen Jeremy's twelve-year- old son staring from the back of the crowd.

Ducal was practicing on the recruitment of younger members who had never heard of Jim Crow, Civil Rights, of concentration camps, or of Jews, outside Sunday school. He wanted to run for a political office. Maybe President of the United States. There was only so much you could teach in a classroom. These topics were placed behind the subject of battles won in the wars, whether the Civil War, or one of the World Wars. It was the school policy to teach all about individual and state's rights as well as war heroes. Weren't those the lessons history wanted to pass on? America was the best place on earth. Wasn't that the most important lesson? All that was needed was to choose the right teachers, the right books. The rest needed to be banned, according to Ducal.

The adolescent had tears in his eyes, slouching with his hands deep in his pockets as he walked towards the principal's office the following week. He wasn't going to let girls interfere with his education. "No siree, not when Jews killed Jesus. Didn't you know?" he asked the principal with a cynical smirk that held back the tears and asked for a slap rather than a response to his question. Jeremy's son heard an echo in his mind that day from the Homochitto picnic where he had listened to Ducal. Seventh grader though he was, he had his own ideas, he thought, while smiling at the principal. He remembered an older boy, shooting the bird in all the class photos and thought he must be like the man who had spoken in front of them all at the fish fry. "Ducal is right. There's gonna be a revolution," he thought. The principal didn't have the electric paddle as was rumored. He didn't use his hands or other instrument. He expelled the boy for proselytism, a word his father couldn't explain any more than he could explain why the Klan had shifted their focus toward the Jews. Desegregation was well underway so the Klan had to modernize.

"By the time I got to less palatable topics," the teacher explained to the principal, when they spoke of the incident; "the kids, all hormonal, were busy throwing spitballs and passing notes. I couldn't tell them why one person could not choose for all; why events were recorded by many historians who studied archives and not just one who said whatever suited him; and why it was important to keep it that way. I couldn't explain why the majority of facts had shown that the concentration camps had existed, that the Nazis had killed millions of Jews. I couldn't find the words. It was all I could do to keep them quiet. Today's kids don't respect their parents. Too many of them read that Dr. Spock book and don't discipline their children. I sent the kid to the office for talking politics. He just kept asking---What if the majority thought the facts were wrong? And what if those who decided weren't the *real* majority? Enough was enough."

The worst had been avoided, but still there had been drops of disinformation that bore like cottonwood beetles into the brains of the children who had heard one of their friends, or at least one of their companions, speak in a defiant manner to the teacher. He seemed to be certain of what he was saying. "He belittled me," said the teacher.

"But is rebellion truth because it denounces the alleged wrongs of the authorities, calling them all liars? Do parents still read Spock's book in the seventies? Do people in Mississippi read more about parenting than people in Louisiana?" The teacher was ready to accept any reason for not being able to handle the class. Emmy puzzled over these questions, when she overheard her talking about the classroom incident in the line at the cash register at Nettles.

"Why are some people in such a hurry to hate?" she wondered, while she paid for her cigarettes and coffee. Emmy wasn't a regular smoker, but she liked to light up once in a while and this pleasure gave her an excuse to hear people talk in convenience stores and at car washes.

Fish Fry

The fire burned *Hickory-dickory* hot. The men at the Fish Fry were talking about prolonging the strike. "There are about two hundred of us ready to walk off again when the clock strikes one, tomorrow. When we tried to talk to management about it, they wanted two hundred reasons. There ain't that many. It's all very simple. Those of us that have a high school diploma don't git more than twenty cents more than the wage they give to the floor sweepers. That's twenty cents a week. And we're professionals. Our jobs are dangerous." The yeahs were loud, and they continued to get louder. "They want to squeeze us on our rest time. Hell, they ain't enough of us workin' and we put ourselves in danger. Our lives are complicated. Very complicated. They 'spect us to be on call all the time. We need more time off, not less. Hell, I spend more time with you guys than with my wife! I don't even get to spend half my nights with her. Y'all's a bunch of fine fellows, but, I cain't remember if any of y'all gives tail." The men laughed in grumbled agreement. "We want to have a walk-out, but the union wants us to respect the agreements that are for equal pay for the same job. Like they's got up north. That's bullshit. Changin' the union's name don't make no difference. Gaetano Franelli has been puttin' a large part of our dues in his pockets for years. Take my word for it. The bosses ain't gonna listen to us as long as they got him in their pockets. If more of us don't go on strike, for the ones that do; we'll get fired jest to fill his belly," said Sam Broderick, speaking loudly from his truck-bed at the Lismore property.

Could anyone say there was a conspiracy at the Natchez mill, a plot to destroy the workers? To reduce them to machines? To sell out? To destroy the mill itself? Was there a need to unionize more workers? To build a new union? Was the NAACP at it again with their demands? They were all paid decent, even good salaries. Although there were dangers at the paper mill, there weren't many accidents. But was anyone there a true friend?

Here is where the lines get as blurred as in painted smoke. In Lismore, it was hot, hickory-hot; and fuzzy, as in the burning Parliament of a Turner painting. "Sometimes all that a fire needs, is a tiny spark to ignite. I had a deep sense that this fire was a good way to be rid of unbearable laws and speeches," said one nineteenth-century reporter, who was glad to see the destruction of the Tally, and wondering if the fire had had nefarious beginnings outside Westminster. "Now that would make a believable narrative," he may have thought if he were Dickens. But Emmy was not Charles Dickens. She knew nothing of unions, nor of their fires. Her skill lay elsewhere. Her incendiary plot was being crafted somewhere in the vicinity, and all the way to Natchez, the sulfur filled the air.

Chris Buhler yelled, holding up the cooking tongs for emphasis; "someone call me a scab because I got six kids and had to go back to work. At least I was with you guys, part of da time. I wanna know who sent dese bullets flying through my house? Dey could've killed one of my kids!" "Yeah," yelled out someone else, agreeing with the speaker on the flatbed pulpit and not biding by the scab's denials.

Jeremy turned towards his sons who had settled on the steps of the house to drink their green Kool-Aid, while Buhler fried the fish in a deep cast-iron pot over a half-drum double pit that had been welded to an elongated wheelbarrow, and propped up on cinder blocks. It could be moved around to the shed with a riding mover when the party was over. For the moment, it was consigned to the side-yard, while the women were confined to the house, grating carrots and cabbage for the coleslaw. The cornbread was ready to go. They gutted the fish and removed their heads. They scraped the flinty scales with spoons; flattened flecks flicking onto floors and faces. Then, placing the fish in a paper bag, they covered them with a mixture of cornmeal, flour, salt, and pepper; then shook.

The fish, mostly bream, but a few perch, were caught in the same lake where the Klan had thrown in more than one man of color and watched him sink with their leaded work-boots. For some of these men at the fish fry; there were no limits; no boundaries about what they could do or what they could say. As long as they were White, this was America. What law could stop them from feeding off the waters where they submerged the bodies themselves? Once the fish were cooked, fries were added to the boiling oil; "to refresh the grease," explained Buhler to Jeremy.

"Around two thousand employees work around the clock at da paper mill," Jeremy said, distant from the man with the megaphone voice. "It's Natchez's largest industry and where ya wanna work when you grow up. Got good people. Decent salaries. And if you work hard, you can become a foreman." Two thumbs gripped a new leather belt, as he spread his legs; strutting his one hundred thirty pounds outwards, through his chest; puffing up his feathered muscles as if he were a rooster about to crow. He had just gotten a raise and was resizing himself upwards. He had every reason to be proud. He wanted his boys to know it. But he was worried. There was recent trouble at the mill, and if he went on strike this time with his friends, it might cost him his job. One of the wives came out and dumped some leftovers mixed with fish guts into a large bowl for three grumbling hounds. They nudged each other out of the way, chomping and slobbering, drooling from their chops. *Blop-blop-blop-blop-blop-chomp-chomp, pththth.*

"Yeah, well I'm telling ya," said Buhler, this time talking to him in a loud voice, taking a sip of his beer, leaning with one hand on Jeremy's shoulder. He looked down at the Harper boys, keeping an eye on another batch of frying fish. "Not a day go by dat I don't worry about putting dem niggas on da machines. Dey is paid 'bout good as us now. Too good fur 'em. If I had my way, we'd use 'em as logs instead of da cords of wood. Whittle dem down in da chipper. Turn 'em into black pepper. But I wouldn't stop there. No siree. I like my pepper the way it is. I'd roll 'em out real flat." He flattened his two hands together, sliding one out, arm-length, into the air. "Dat's what we should've done wit' dat Edouard fella." Jeremy shrugged his shoulder and inched away . He thought, "Buhler gettin' too personal, and openin' up where he should keep it shut. Makin' me look like a queer, too, in front of my kids, in front of everybody. He bent on revealin' Klan secrets to anyone who listens. Bet he's an informer. Gotta be with a tongue you can see waggin' the dog a mile off."

"Only... no one would buy da paper dat come out." Bulher continued, "Whatcha gonna do wit' black paper? Huh? Buy white pens?" He slapped his hand on Jeremy's shoulder, admiring his own jokes, shaking with forced denial. He didn't want anyone to remember that he crossed the picket lines so he focused on racism. They all laughed; even Jeremy's youngest boy of eight, who didn't understand anything other than that he was making cruel jokes about grinding up Black people. "Well, whatcha think we got dat bleach fo?" Buhler guffawed, removing the fish from their Crisco bath; issuing repeated racist maxims. "Dat's why we's got so many of dem high yellers 'round here. Couldn't get all de black out if we tried. An' we tried. An' we keeps on tryin'." He laughed, a peg-tooth horse-laugh, then yelled at his wife, "Hey, Stacy, we need some more fish out here ready to go!"

Jeremy snickered, but he didn't like it. Not that he had other fish to fry. Not that he was sure he believed in equal rights. He never had before the war anyway. He thought he still believed in White supremacy. Weren't Whites smarter? Didn't they have better jobs. Why should they just give Black people the same jobs if they weren't qualified to do the work? He taught as much to his children, but not like that. "I cain't have him jokin' around with my kids; meddlin' with my affaires," he thought. "He gotta learn to hold his tongue. Dem kids liable to go to school and talk about this shit again. That'll lead to more trouble. This ain't fairytale shit. This is real."

Jeremy agreed with the others, they had to do something about what was happening at work, but he was engulfed by his emotions. There was the sarcasm; Buhler's joke that he wanted to laugh about, but not sure it was funny. Was it the fear of being involved in a crime, the longing to find a father figure, to belong to a movement bigger than himself, and the feeling that his people were now under threat? Why was he worried about the kids? The anger that this man would involve them in something they needn't be troubled with? Was he more worried that they could not keep a secret? Was the NAACP about to unleash its dogs? There was too much to think about. Jeremy couldn't get it figured. He felt like he was being lied to, again. First his father, who told him that everyone else had been lying to them, and now this man. He couldn't tell what side he was on. When satire paints such a clear picture of truth; it is hard to know how to react. His emotions conglomerated with those still unnamed. These pulled back like the ocean, and came back with a tidal slap.

"Well, at least I ain't no scab," he heard himself bark, scowling. Then he widened his eyes and shrunk his mouth to keep more words from getting out of their place. Buhler's forehead crumpled and his thick eyebrows lurched. The corners of his mouth dropped. He shook his head and looked away, tussling the hair of one of the boys. Then, letting his hand fall to his side, he looked at Jeremy, his mouth opened as if to say something, then, shaking his head, and the corn-flour covered-fish; he closed it, this time with regret.

In a moment of desperation, Buhler would have liked to act like the cold coming up from the ground was one of nature's tricks; like anger that comes out of the wind. If that anger exploded into rage, that wouldn't make a pile of beans to him. "Don't call me no scab," he threatened, suppressing a growl.

The skin on Jeremy's Adam's apple turned red and hung like a combative lizard's dewlap as he bent over to tie his anger and his worries with his shoes. He puffed out his neck again. He was worried about his oldest son having problems in school. "It's harder and harder to have authority over that boy," he thought. He was remembering his own dismissal from school and how his mother was obliged to at last send him to a private school to keep him enrolled at all, after his father was killed. He sometimes wished he had listened to his teachers and graduated from high school. Now, there was the strike brewing at the paper mill. There was talk about the big boss of the United Paper Workers Union filling his pockets with government money as an incentive to appease the strikers. There was talk about the local union bosses lining theirs with members' dues. Jimmy Hoffa, having disappeared from the *Machus Red Fox* restaurant, was about to start all over, but this time with a reduced local mob.

Jeremy had received an anonymous letter a few days before, mentioning the tensions between Blacks and Whites at work. "Buhler' right about one thing, if he was bein' sincere. The Blacks hold janitorial jobs, not technical ones. It's the way things are, the way things were before. It should stay that way. They ain't good for nothin' else. These problems come up before. The NAACP had to learn a lesson or two. So why the letters? Why now? Why me?" wondered Jeremy. He had thought it was easy for him to remain poised over the same place he had been, to accept the ways of life he had acquired from his father without questioning these. When he was younger, sometimes, there was a question. Then he had met Ducal in school and fell back into the ease of living without doubts.

The letter was the second bill of its kind. In his old man's day, there had been lynchings; like the ones still hushed about in Ferriday, like the ones his father had boasted about, like the one Buhler was hinting at in front of his boys. All at once, Jeremy thought he had too many enemies. There *had* been stories of Blacks being roasted in the furnaces at the mill, about them falling into the boiler vats or slipping into chlorinated gas clouds. He didn't think these could be true. The mill never shut down. Accidents would have been recorded. If there had been police inquiries, he would have heard about them.

True, there had been the crews of Klan members that set out to threaten and destroy Black men and their businesses. As an adolescent, he had been privy to a few of these, and had kept quiet. Harper made sure that his sons would keep the fear of their father in their innards at all times. In absence of their father, this fear still circulated between the brothers; like the stink around a cadaver. They handled it best by staying away from each other; leaving nothing but fumes and mistrust for any eye-rolling buzzards ready to pick them apart instead.

Jeremy's suspicions turned its talons on his brothers and his friends. These folded under the vultures' feathered bellies and circled overhead with fresh meat dandling from their beaks, before flying back to their starting point where his enemies had remained, openmouthed, unsure how to answer the fly-by-night attacks that up until that moment had been their protected game. Of late, the first list, that of his friends, was growing shorter, while the second, those of his enemies, grew longer. He straightened and looked at Buhler then smiled, but only on the outside. If the man had looked closer, his Adam's apple, the now-discolored flap on his neck, would have provided him with the rundown of the story. It was like a red flag of distress. While desperate to belong to the group, he couldn't help but exclude them all. He didn't know why. He wasn't sure why he suspected them or of what, but it didn't look good. Jeremy's plight was that of a man who didn't know himself.

"Is he for real? Does he really got an accent like that?" Jeremy continued to talk himself back up onto a strongman's podium. "He bound to be a Yankee faker and a fag." He took a sip of his whiskey, trying to swallow his anger with his worry and now, fear. He could hear another voice. Was it his father's voice in his head he was hearing, or someone else's he heard behind his back?

He was no longer sure. Pearls of sweat formed a chain at the base of his neck. He was putting it all together. "This man drinkin' our liquor, fryin' our fish, 's become an informant for the FBI, the NAACP, or for some other no-count-lettered cop shop or club-of-spades that wants to replace us. He gotta be. It happened before. The FBI done got to a few Klan members and heard part of the story. Only a few of the Wizards know the whole story. But we knows who's goin' to get lynched; before they got it."

Little by little, Jeremy was slipping deeper into a mortal lock that he would have a hard time removing. He was pumping himself up like a tire, using the abject language he had learned in childhood, but had avoided since his father's death. They weren't supposed to use that language anymore. He thought that all of the men he had ever known were liars, except his father. Wasn't that what he had always taught them. They could not trust other people. Other people were liars and would lead them to Hell. "If my dad were here, we wouldn't have these problems, he thought. "At least there would be one person to guide us, one person telling the truth. Buhler here, gotta be a foe, pretendin' to be a friend, tryin' to get me to talk truth 'bout somethin' I don't know much 'bout. Tricks, a bunch of tricks. I do know for a fact that he the one who pointed his own goddamn gun out his own goddam window to make believe in a drive-by. Pschaw. Ain't nobody gonna do that here in this part of the country. Nobody that stupid. Not even the Ace of Spades. Everybody know that. Gotta be him who done wrote them letters, too. Just like his fake insurance claims, always tryin' to accuse someone else, tryin' to get attention. Well, I ain't the claims agent and sure the Hell ain't no Black and no watcher to his show." Buhler nodded as if he heard Jeremy's thoughts, and started removing a new batch of fish from the hot oil without saying a word. It occurred to him just then, that the oil in the cooker could kill a man if dumped on him.

What might have been questions in another's mind were becoming hard certitudes in Jeremy's. He was building a case against one, that would soon spread its net across Concordia Parish from Lismore to Ferriday, from Vidalia to Clayton, and on up to Waterproof, following back down, past the lakes, making a full circle; before crossing the Mississippi river, and going all the way to Adams,

Franklin, and Jefferson Counties, catching fish, both large and small, on the way. It might then flop back and grab a few curs in Catahoula Parish. "Who's bringin' down the country? Who's causin' the trouble at work? Who's attackin' my family? These letters have to be from someone on the inside," he thought, "and it's all connected to the rest of this mess." What was belief for some was evidence enough for another. "It's the communists fault!"

Woodville Worries

The sheer number of possible culprits at the mill should have discouraged Jeremy. Many were sworn members of the Klan. Some had been approached by the FBI in the past. How this became linked to communists was anyone's guess. The bosses wanted names of union members who supported the strike. Were they on the left, or were they on the right? His work buddies said, "Niggers are all communists." Anything to turn hate against them. Jeremy should have known that no one could tie him to the scene of the Waller shooting, but just then, he thought he was beginning to understand. He was seeing inklings of truth *they*, this time, the Klan, had kept from him. "I wadn't there. I didn't kill Waller. That was a long time ago, back in the sixties when we was either kids, or off in Vietnam. Even Hiram, from Chocolate Quarters, fought in my division against the Vietcong. He wadn't no communist! And Buhler! Buhler admitted he, himself, was at the shooting in Dolorosa and got away with it. The cops ain't comin' after nobody so long after. Ain't nothin' gonna happen to us," he thought, the afternoon's discussion was coming back to him. He turned over and over in his bed. The alarm would go off any minute and he had not slept.

It wasn't guilt that fit the pieces together for Jeremy; at least not the kind that would sign a perpetrator's crime. It was again suspicion, an old ghost dragging a heavy chain. Disembodied, relentless, yet imprisoned souls, circled around him. Visions of his father came back to haunt him from something he did to his father's dog. He regretted hurting the dog, but not his cruel vengeance on his father. From culpability, grew mistrust. He worked nights on the dot-connecting crew; connecting the dots from one dog to another, to the dog owners, the ones that drove the same model of cars or trucks owned by these dog lovers; to the vehicles owned by some of his coworkers, and who might, or just might not, be connected to the Klan crimes, who might possess silver dollars, and then be connected to him. "There must be somethin' goin' on at the paper mill besides the strike. All the whisperin' that goes on. I know Buhler ain't the only enemy I got there. I better keep an eye open so I can see what is goin' on."

Here again, in his simmering distrustfulness, was a short cut; not like Poor House Road to State Highway 563 from US 61 near Dolorosa Hill, but one that put Jeremy in direct connection with the Klan activity of the sixties.

The alarm rang. He threw the clock against the wall for the second time in a week. "Jeeereemmyyy," his wife called. He threw his legs over the edge of the bed, sat up massaging his neck, and looked around at the drab room. He shuffled to the bathroom and sat down on the commode. "Goddamn it! Why isn't there any toilet paper?" he yelled, knocking jars of make-up to the floor.

Shelley opened the door and stuck in her arm, holding out a roll of paper. "I only put one in there at a time because the boys run off with it to do Lawd knows what." Taking the paper, he banged the door closed with a sideway fist. The dual faucet handles of the sink glared at him from across the room. Water splattered in a continuous drip of iron disgust, leaving a rust-colored blotch in the sink around the drain. One corner of the porcelain was broken from where, in a rage, he had hit it with a wrench.

"Your breakfast is ready," she yelled from the kitchen.

"I can't even take a shit," he yelled back. Through the peeled underlayment of the vinyl floorcovering, he could see the plywood, stained, like the fixtures, and grinning where it had cracked under the weight of time, water, and of the two men who brought in the new hot water heater. He rolled his eyes towards the ceiling as he thought of the repairs the shotgun house with add-ons, still needed. He didn't seem to get anything right.

"Someone's tryin' to frame me," he told his wife, closing his belt when he came into the kitchen to eat his meal. He sat down on one side of the table. His plate was full and in front of him. Grabbing the fork, he took a bite, then pushed the grits around with his biscuit. It all tasted so, bland. "Ma put cheese or somethin' in her grits. These don't taste like nothin'," he said, pushing his plate away with a scowl. "Why would they give me a raise if they were going to fire me?" Jeremy wondered if he had become some kind of marionette for his managers. They'd given him a raise, but it had come with strings attached. They wanted names. He didn't know any.

The family sat around the rectangular table, pushed against a dented chest freezer. Shelley, squeezing in on one side of her husband, opened its door and took out two packages. "Field peas and venison," she announced. "Is that okay for supper, with cornbread?" The boys were trying to kick at each other from under the table. Jeremy was still looking at his plate, moving his mouth as if he was chewing his words. He didn't answer. One of the boys threw a piece of biscuit at his sister. "Stooppp," she cried. His father glared at him from the end of the table. "She's a retard," explained the boy. The girl started to cry. "Retard, retard," sang the other boy, his face lighting up. Jeremy slapped him on the back of the head. The lights dimmed.

"You better hurry, you'll be late." Shelley was picking up the plates. She wanted the kids out of there. The two boys jumped up at once, and hurried out the kitchen door. The paper mill was only about twenty miles away with almost no traffic, but his wife was telling him again it was time to leave. Jeremy expected her to continue to harp on this line, but she shifted, saying, "Why don't you call your, Mom?"

"Grandma!" smiled the little girl.

Shelley didn't like his mother. "Why did she go on about it, bringing her up every time he..." The phone rang and she hurried into the living room to answer.

Jeremy put his face in his hands. He could not go back and fix the past; he could only try to prevent the future. He wouldn't torture any more dogs. Or drown his girl's kittens. He avoided the drive- by family pastimes of his childhood. That was all finished now. Law enforcement wasn't the same. He'd grown up and the Klan was busy with other things. They were thinking of long-term operations, of revolution. They were trying to reorganize, to reestablish segregation. They had leadership now. He was a friend of their new wizard. They were becoming a militia. He was teaching them to shoot with military style weapons. Jeremy dreamed of greater things, a real role in the white robe community. Why not try for a red robe like he'd seen Slaughter wear over his deputy uniform at the King Hotel wake? Weren't they called a Cyclops something? The vision of a corpse wearing the same crimson robe as the group of men came back to him. The body had a silver dollar on its chest, under a green wreath. The envious boy that he was pocketed it, at the last minute. The man in the coffin looked like a Christmas tree even without the added decoration.

No one ever knew. Or had they? He tried to remember if he had ever shown it to anyone outside the family. Jeremy took the coin out of his pocket. He held it in the palm of his hand, turning it over. It was dated 1929; the year the dead man was born. He remembered that this piece of change, the one he had taken from the body as it lay out in the coffin, had been his father's. The man in the coffin had a wig to cover up the missing forehead and skull plate. It was an honor, one man told him, for the man to lie in the hotel, surrounded by the group of cloaked men. They were to be his pallbearers instead of his sons.

The honored man looked like an overstuffed scarecrow with a waxy made-up face, and fake hair. Not even that. It wasn't a real face. It wasn't a real body. It was more like an inflated red caterpillar with human clothes, arms and legs pumped up and tied in place, onto which, someone had pasted a magazine image for appearances. Why did they make him look like Toho's *Mothra*? Would he rise up to fight *Godzilla*? Jeremy had seen the Japanese film as part of the Saturday double-feature show at The Arcade when he was a kid. He thought it was corny for science fiction; the idea that a moth, even a giant one, could beat a monster, or that a woman could beat a man. What was so scary about a monster stuffing his face with Toyotas? Now if they had been American cars...Could his real father be dead? The only metamorphosis that this caterpillar, however giant or made-up, would undergo was to transform into a rotted goo. Jeremy covered his mouth and moved his jaw from side-to-side, trying to loosen words that would not fall out. He wanted to yell. He wanted to scream his confusion and his grief. "Why-had-they-let-me-take-it?" The words came out with the rhythm of a beating. He hit the table once with his fist, making his daughter jump. He seemed to pull within himself, wondering if he would been cursed for having stolen from the dead? Stolen from his father. Had he thought that this was his father's fare for transitioning into another world, his fear could not have been worse. It was a malediction. His face hardened, and he put the dollar away when both of his sons came back inside and started to speak. He could hear his wife from the living room, answering the phone. "The wig wasn't even the right color," he said under his breath, with aversion. His daughter stared at him, holding her spoon in her mouth; puzzled by the distraught look on her father's face, as much as by his words. The boys looked around the room to see whom their father had been talking to.

Jeremy shuddered, "I don't care about Black people, one way or another," he thought, his head now in his hands, denying his racism, without knowing it, in a way similar to Adolf Eichmann's public denial of his hate and anti-Semitism at the nineteen-sixty- two Jerusalem trial. His organization and operation of the Nazi machine they called *the final solution*, was another dimension of hatred.

It was one of horrific, incomparable proportions. Yet at the base of this Nazi-machination was the same kind of scourge, the same kind of contagious disease, that generated Jeremy's petty, *almost* inherited prejudice that only his fears made him question. Now, these fears of the other kept him awake at night and gnawed at some final sense of humanity. "Am I just a robot?" He wondered.

"No, I won't let you talk to him. He's got graveyards and needs his rest," Shelley answered.

In a croaking, ghostly voice, the only voice she had left, Emmy uttered a sentence she felt would have impact, disturbing the family, at least for one day. "You shot me. Now I'm comin' for you. You thought you was clear, but you jest one more silver dolla. I heard the boys yell out yore name before I died."

Jeremy's wife didn't sound scared. She was used to kid's prank calls and she knew little about the Klan. She answered without skipping a beat, "Is that so?" And waited.

Adult now, Emmy didn't expect that. She might have expected that Southern women will have that sort of overprotective reaction. She had to invent something fast so she said, "Watch over your kids. You have to pay for the crimes." Then, she hung up, her heart at once pounding Dave Brubeck's "Blue Rondo à la Turk," jumping roof to roof, and racing down the stairs. "Did I really say that?" She wouldn't hurt his kids. Never in a thousand years would she hurt any kid. She had to run. Get away from the guilty telephone. She felt like a criminal about to get caught. Her heart took a leap. She had to slow down. It was just a phone call. She hadn't robbed a bank, or killed anyone. There were no police, nor anyone else, after her.

"Jeereeemmyy," Shelley yelled. "Some woman calling for you. Said a bunch a crap about you shootin' somebody. Did you shoot somebody? He said he was a ghost and threatened our kids. He said you were just one more silver dollar. What does that mean?" Jeremy hurried into the living room and grabbed the wailing device from her, listening to the tonality. "Fuck!" He spat out the word. He threw the receiver against the wall and it rebounded a few times with the recoil of a yoyo. He watched her hurry towards the kitchen and followed.

"Why didn't you let me talk to him? Or her? You said a woman, then you said he? Can't you get yore mind straight?" He yanked her ponytail.

"OOwwww," she cried. "I think it was a man, but he had a strange croaky voice, like a woman who smoked too much. But not a woman. Almost like a ghost. He said he was comin' for you," she continued, giving over to the idea that, that if he was scared, maybe he would leave, or at least leave her alone. She shirked away, into the living room and watched from the couch, as her disabled daughter struggled out of her chair.

"Dumb fuck. Stupid bitch, can't tell who called. Worthless as a cap gun. Just a bunch of noise. How can I protect our kids if you can't remember a goddam thing?" He mumbled. "Where's my cigarettes?" he yelled.

He slammed the screen door, calling from outside. "I'll teach ya how to use the phone when I git back." The boys forgot their question. The girl followed her father.

Shelley was sorry her daughter had problems. Sometimes she felt ashamed as an idea of life without her came to her mind. Her husband, with all his anger, seemed to accept her pouty face, her slip-slide walk, drag-across the-floor foot, her drool, her fingers in her mouth, her nighttime diapers, her slurred speech, her lack of words, her threats to burn the house... "She's cute, but she'll never be a cheerleader. What will she become? Am I going to have to take care of this shit for the rest of my life?" It was all too much, too much for a mother such as herself. Afterall, she had been a cheerleader and a runner-up Miss-Lou beauty queen. "I could've had my pick of men," she flipped her pony-tail. If she had found a better husband, none of this would have happened to her. Not the leaky faucet, not the house on the side of the highway, not the boys' insults, not the handicapped daughter. The list of the smaller and greater deficiencies went through her mind. She opened the cabinet and found the small bottle of rum and took a gulp. Serving herself two more biscuits with oleo and cane syrup, she sat down at the table to swallow more of her ruminations. The margarine melted and pooled in hog-slop swirls with the brown molasses. It formed two kaleidoscope eyes that were staring back at her. It was all too much. She had put on thirty maybe forty pounds since the twin's birth. What the fuck? Who cared anyway? "Fuck him and let him eat fish heads. I'm not gonna run after Valerie every time. Jeremy can take care of her just once."

Emmy watched from Nettles' Truck Stop the stirring at the house on the Woodville corner. Shaking, she left the phone booth and went inside to buy a package of cigarettes only to see Jeremy; ten, maybe fifteen minutes later, coming out of the house, kicking toys off the step, all over the yard, with his daughter, behind him. She heard him yell the word, *cigarettes*. His face was a scowl and he was swearing. Emmy could see the girl, step-dragging her foot in the dirt. Looking both ways before he crossed, he walked across the road to Nettles. The young girl was just behind him, but he didn't seem to notice or to care.

Emmy ducked behind her truck, pretending to look at a tire. Had he seen her? "Had he crossed the highway?" Although she recognized a few, she didn't know the Klan members, and as far as she knew, other than Jeremy, and his father, she had never known them or their kids. She had not thought that there might be one sitting at a booth at Nettles, watching, creating a film in his mind from what he observed in the parking lot scene. "I'm too near the door," she thought. "They're gonna think I'm mad if they notice me."

Emmy should have listened to the buried-slave chorus. She should have left well enough alone. Didn't she suspect that there was a price for being a self-appointed henchman? She didn't want to think of death, or an afterlife. She knew that the dispatches sent to Jeremy were like maggots in a wound. The messages would fester, and then turn green. It was the one time she hoped for a disease; for a pandemic even. "Being hated for something is better than ..." She couldn't think of what, but she felt that she was getting a new lease on life that hope hadn't granted, and didn't want to get caught just when she was beginning understand what that meant. Excitement coursed through her veins.

Jeremy's father had had his imagined conspiracies. His dithyramb was made of scraps of overheard conversations and other bits of gossip from reality's table instead of a hymn you might want to sing at church. These went so far as to have him considered as unreliable by the chiefs of the Klan, but he still held on when he wasn't begging a free meal off a member of his congregation or sending a faithful church-member's body to Tulane Medical School in exchange for a small compensation. And the Klan remembered him for his devotion, at his death.

When Emmy thought about how her family's secrets affected her, pushing her to the brink of her own grave, she realized how her dicking around (if a woman could say such as that) clocked in with Jeremy's delusions, and might push him over the edge, into oblivion or into the same kind of dung-slung soup that his father's mind had lived in. "What will make him lose his mind?" she wondered, worried what the loss of mind might mean, remembering her visit to the psychiatric ward; worried about what would be in its place.

"These men are like the Nazis my parents fought," said Emmy. "None of them will be nice company for the other patients; but without evidence to send them to prison, what else can be done? I don't want to kill anyone." Tampering with their memories enough to send them reeling over the Jackson, Mississippi Whitfield house for the insane or to make them wish they were dead, was within her reach, she felt. "If a preacher can do it, why can't I? Deviling Jeremy will make it an easier job, one that looks like it was managed from the inside; one that will almost be fun."

She opened her truck door and saw to her astonishment, Jeremy's young daughter, sitting on the passenger side of the truck, surprised to see Emmy. "Daddy's truck," she said. Green truck." For a second, confusion passed through Emmy. Neither was moving. Emmy realized that the girl had mistaken her truck for her father's. Had they both bought one of the U.S. Department of Wildlife's trucks when these had been auctioned? "Shoo" was all she could say with her raspy voice, adding a sweeping gesture along with her words." The girl looked angry and wouldn't move. Emmy didn't want Jeremy to find her or his daughter in her truck. "Oh, no, no, no, no. Not now," she screamed in her mind, moving her lips. Thinking of nothing better to do, if such quick movements could be considered as the result of a thought, she got in her truck and started the motor. Not for once did she think of looking for Jeremy. Not once did she consider taking the girl by the hand and leading her into the store. Whether she was too absorbed in her own project to think of the consequences of driving away with a disabled child, or whether she did not consider the child's safety a priority, was anyone's guess; anyone that might see them, of course. Emmy's mind was empty on all accounts. Fear had overridden all. But fear of what? Having created a monster in her mind, she now had to escape it. She peeled away towards Natchez with Valerie clutching her seat.

Emmy looked over to her right. The girl was still there, looking angry, ready to defend her father's truck. Emmy wondered what was wrong with her. It was clear, she had some sort of disability. What worried her now was that she was making her good on her words before she was ready, as if she had had ever wanted to kidnap one of Jeremy's kids, and in front of at least a dozen witnesses. Someone must have seen her. She continued to drive, trying to think what to do. The girl got on her knees and was looking behind the seat at Mamere, seated in the tool space.

"I swear you have one hard head. You can almost reason yourself into giving yourself reason about anything you want," warned Mamere.

Emmy glared at her in her rearview mirror, annoyed. "Can you watch her?" she mumbled. She wanted to give her grandmother a task. Emmy needed to assemble her thoughts. She had to drive, to get rid of the girl. But her grandmother had vanished again. She would never stay in place long enough to be of much service. Revenants never do.

The girl climbed over the seat and was fooling around with who knows what. Emmy was trying to remember what she had back there. "Maybe my gun and ammunition!" Inside sirens were wailing. Valerie, still confused about the ownership of the truck asked, "where's Teddy?" Emmy didn't know what to do with her, but knew she was in deep trouble now. She had threatened to kidnap a kid, and now she had. "How had this happened?"

She was also thinking, about her grandmother's warnings, and about her conversations with her. Emmy knew she was gone, but sometimes she thought that maybe that her grandmother didn't know it yet. For some reason, she just kept coming over, sitting there with skin that looked like softened sawdust, and talking like she always had, giving Emmy instructions now instead of her mother.

Before the murder, Emmy had never been a lonely child. Before she was old enough to have friends, her parents and grandparents were there. Each of them was from a different background, but all were recognized as Cajuns. They all shared crawfish *étouffé* or gumbo, laughed about stories of the world's creation, Boudreaux's cremation or his coffee and ice-cream-filled thermos. They had played circus music, jazz or Zydeco. Now all that was gone. She wondered if Mamere was there because she knew that her granddaughter was lonely, or if the dead have their own reasons for moving on to whatever they do. "It depends on where they end up," she speculated. "Some probably don't want to go." As much of a trouble maker as her grandmother was to her, Emmy couldn't imagine her ending up in a bad place.

On a street she remembered from some far inside cove in her mind, she stopped the truck. She could see the Natchez *Paramount*, but no one was there. For an instant, she thought she saw Harper taking Valerie by the hand and leading her to the ticket booth. The *Paramount*, later the *Ritz*, had been closed for at least ten years, but seeing it gave her an idea. She drove to Junkin Drive where the new theater had opened. The movie was announced in black letters on a panel so high you could read it from the next hill top, had it not been for the trees. *Star Wars* was still playing. Turning to offer money to the girl, she saw that she was no longer there. "How did she get out?" Emmy couldn't understand where the child had gone, how she managed to hop out of the truck without her seeing. Had her thoughts turned like a curve-ball? Was she so unaware of her surroundings, of what she had done with the girl, that she had escaped? Had she left her in front of the *Ritz* after all?

Emmy looked across the parking-lot. Under the Edward Hooper- lights, she saw Tom the ticket man, or thought she saw him in the booth. Seeing him, she thought she remembered him from another time. He was staring right at her. Other people were walking by and didn't notice her. She thought she saw the girl ask him for a ticket, but couldn't hear what was said. How had she known Tom? "What does he know about me? Why was he there now, on the pavement, outside his booth?"

Tom was a tall, slim man with salt and pepper hair and a beard cropped short. Ageless, she thought he must be ten, fifteen years older than herself. Perhaps she had met him with Harper when he had taken her to see the *Sound of Music*, at the *Paramount-Ritz*. Children remember things adults seem to forget. Every note of that film, every image, was engraved in her mind. It had been a special day. She had started off wearing a fluffy white, crinoline ballerina skirt that she had wound up loaning to Bee. She had been happy about it, even if her friend's homemade blue skirt was not as nice. Harper was proud of her and had taken her to a restaurant and then to the movie. At least that is the memory she preferred.

Would Tom remember? Would he remember her? Was he only a ticket taker, taking thousands, maybe millions of dollars a year to pay for seats to the cinema? Had he known Harper because they were both musicians? It was a small world, but being a musician didn't make one a good person. She had found that out the hard way. Perhaps he was angry at her for causing Harper's death? Or, was the penetrating gaze of this man an acknowledgement of sorts, one between musicians? *DidiT- DidiT - DidiT - DidiT; DidiT - DidiT - DidiT - DidiT.* She thought she remembered having seen Tom play drums, with a backbeat and swing that could only mean jazz on a band stand at some outdoor festival. She had not been to many. Had he been a teacher at Mrs. Maizy's school for the blind where she had tried to get hired as a piano teacher? Her lack of voice put an end to that. The children already faced one sensory problem. Why give them a teacher they could not hear speak? Emmy thought he recognized her, but couldn't figure out why. Giving him a role; friend, perpetrator, or other, creating a sketch about him, was the manner she evaluated each person with whom she became in contact. It was better than living in a faceless nightmare where anxiety comes when it is impossible to see or hear the thing that is after you like in a bad dream. She gave her enemies a visage; friends too, so that they would not become enemies.

Then she thought she saw the girl point, not at the truck, but in some vague way. Was she missing Emmy in the picture because of her lack of ability to point? Would she be able to identify Emmy in a police line-up? It was becoming clear to her that standing in a place reserved for heroes was becoming something else altogether. But was that really Valerie? Was Tom's stare that of a man who has understood that the child was not hers and that she had committed a crime? Valerie was holding two tickets, as if she thought Emmy would join her. "Where did she get the money to pay for them?" Emmy wouldn't wait around to watch the film with her. She looked at her hands. These were the hands of a musician, not a kidnapper.

Management

Jeremy came out of the store, and lit a cigarette. He looked around, and walked across the highway. He had not missed his daughter because he had not seen her following him at a distance. He went inside and grabbed his cap. "Where's Valerie," his wife asked, because after finishing her biscuits and syrup, and a cigarette, she had thought of her daughter. The boys were outside fooling around with their bikes and she had noticed the child gone. Jeremy looked confused. "She followed you," blinked Shelley. "Did you leave her over there? She said with a tone of accusation only the guilty bear. "Oh my God, she crossed alone and might come back alone and get hit! I told you we should move." Jeremy was already out the door. He ran across the highway. He loved his daughter, and was frightened by his unconsciousness, afraid of what might happen.

Inside Nettles, he looked around the store, then the diner. In a frenzy, he ran to the bathrooms, calling her name. He asked the cashier if he had seen her. "No man," said the young guy who must have been a hippy with his hair up under a cap. "How could he have noticed anything?" Jeremy jerked around, nervous and distraught, thoughts crashing in on him, remembering in an instant the hippies having their heads shaved alongside his own, as they prepared for bootcamp and Vietnam. He ran out the door again and looked around the parking lot. There were at least twelve cars and five or six big trucks. Running between them, he was recalling the telephone threat in his wife's words: "Watch out for your kids!"

He ran back to the house and grabbed his cap and gun off the rack. He headed out the door; armed to face the kidnappers, his father's enemies, or worse, his phantom. He kicked water guns and plastic trucks out of the way . "Fuck," he yelled again, clinching his weapon. "Call the police," he yelled to Shelley.

Emmy watched as the girl went inside the theater and hoped that she would forget how she got there. There wasn't much else to do. She bolted from her parking place, hoping that Tom, under the milky lights, had not identified her as a kidnapper or anyone he had ever known. She thought she heard a whimper, a mew, behind the seat, but didn't dare look. "Has she come back?" she remembered asking herself when she neared the strip between Vidalia and Ferriday. But she did not stop to look; not in this barren area of KKK-friendly bars.

Jeremy had passed her on the highway without noticing her truck or its resemblance. In Ferriday, he pulled up in front of a house, and examined the weapon, used for killing large, dangerous game. He turned his eyes towards the door where the Klan member stood. "Where is she?" he yelled, getting out of the truck and pointing the weapon at the man. "Where is she?" he yelled, determined.

"Now hold on, son," said the man, holding his up hands as if to surrender. "Let's not do anything we'll regret."

"Where is she?" Jeremy commanded.

"Who the Hell are you talkin' 'bout?"

Jeremy let out a long sigh and tears came to his eyes. He was realizing his error, realizing his daughter might be lost forever, but still behaving like he might shoot the man. He wanted it to end there, wanted to kill this man, resolve his problem, and get reparation for the deed. He wanted Valerie. He missed her crooked smile, the way she laughed at the faces he made, his childish jokes. He liked trying to teach her letters of the alphabet. But this man knew nothing and he didn't want to waste time with him. He turned to get back in his truck. By then the other man yelled. "Stop right there. Let's call our friend the sheriff and get this straightened out." Jeremy had put his gun on the seat and this man was pointing a pistol at him.

Still, he pleaded, as if the man would by now be his friend. "My daughter. Someone has kidnapped her. We had a threat, but Shelley didn't take it for real. I went over to Nettle's and she followed me."

"Don't you worry about that right now son. Whatever happened, we're gonna get to the bottom of this." Thinking this was some kind of ruse, he didn't believe Jeremy. He directed him with his gun and they walked over to the front steps of the house. Buhler's hound was lying on the ground and Jeremy stepped on his tail. The dog jerked up and yelped. Jeremy kicked at it. "Hey!" yelled Buhler, "watch it! Go on inside." He called the sheriff's office. "Slaughter, come on out here. I got Harper's kid here who is accusin' me of kidnappin' his daughter. I donknow nuttin' 'bout it. Yeah. He's armed alright, but I got things under control. You need to get out here and talk some sense in him."

He hung up the phone. The two men sat there, eyeing each other, one on the couch and the other in a chair. Buhler kept his pistol trained on Jeremy. "Now, we're gonna wait for Slaughter to get out here so you might as well calm down." But Jeremy couldn't calm down. He was worried sick. His mind was racing like a greyhound behind a dummy-hare.

"What are they doin'? What are they goin' to do to her?" Jeremy imagined the Klan had his daughter and were going to hurt her; payback for something he had done wrong, perhaps something he had said. "What did I do?" he pleaded with Buhler, who was still holding the gun. Buhler only shook his head, thinking Jeremy was a hot head like his old man. "He should be excluded from the Klan once he shoots that low-down son-of-a-bitch who been writin' them fuckin' letters." He thought, then said, "We'll just sit here calmly and wait for Slaughter."

The next day, *The Natchez Advocate* read, "Local Man Arrested for threatening a Ferriday resident." The article continued. "A Woodville man, armed with a shotgun, showed up at the house of one of his coworkers on Thursday evening. The sheriff's office was called on the scene at 6:15 P.M. when the caller was sitting down for his supper. He said the younger man appeared to be under the influence of alcohol and accused his coworker of making threats to his family, of kidnapping his daughter. Both are workers at the paper rayon pulp mill in Natchez. Charges of disorderly conduct were filed. The accusation of kidnapping is being investigated. One man's best hunting dog was kicked. Details forthcoming."

There was a blurred photo of Jeremy, handcuffed and pushed into a squad car. Ferriday's authorities were used to brawls between men. Sometimes they took them home to sleep it off. Sometimes they took them to a shared-cell for drunks. Sometimes, they took them to a small room out of sight from other cellmates.

Slaughter said, "I'm takin' the kid home, if nobody sees any objection. We'll see what the Natchez cops have come up with." Nobody did, although, Woodville was in another state. The town was the very birthplace of the President Jefferson Davis; and for some of the deputies of Concordia Parish, the Confederacy still carried all the weight that Jeremy was missing, and more. It seems like flags and monuments hold on to stories that aren't banished by scorched earth.

As it turned out, the girl turned up in the shopping center with a bag of popcorn. No one knew how she got it. When interrogated, she seemed to say her father had taken her to the movies and bought her some popcorn. She didn't seem hurt or frightened. Slaughter wondered if Jeremy was missing a screw. He didn't admit to having taken his daughter to a movie and seemed as confused as the rest of them. Jeremy didn't press the point. He was happy to find Valerie when he got home. "Little Daddy," she said, when she saw him. In spite of her disability, she understood he had been worried and wanted to comfort him. Jeremy picked her up and hugged her, then hugged his wife. "I'm sorry for sayin' what I said. I got a lot of worries. These calls and letters are makin' me go nuts." Shelley lowered her head. She was relieved her daughter had been found. The feeling of shame was that of an exhausted mother who remembered an easier life, a life before their daughter's disabilities began to shape their world into something harder and harder to bare. "It ain't her fault," she admitted to herself, her feelings of confusion tugging at her womb and making her lose her balance. They all three sat down on the couch and turned on the television. It was early evening. They watched the weather report. Their lives were anything, but simple.

Chips

Jeremy was proud. He was proud to be an American, proud to be from the South, and proud to be promoted to the position of shift- foreman in charge of the digester and blow tanks at the Paper Pulp Mill. The engineer in charge of safety and hygiene for the company began to show the new foremen the ropes. He had been teaching men from all parts of the country how the machinery worked. If he understood how the use of simple memory constructs could help a man recall the different steps of the process; he understood less how men of the South processed information coming from a northerner, although he tried to use a language as close to theirs as he could. "The chipped wood is sent to the digester, where it is cooked under pressure with a solution of lye and a sulfide to make a *white liquor*; but it isn't anything you would want to serve up right away. As Cajuns say; first you make a *roux*. And this roux, more than a *sauce béchamel*, has to cook, under pressure; for about six hours." Jeremy wasn't being apprenticed to a famous chef, he was learning to work a machine, listening to the plant's engineer, and taking notes on a clipboard, with the seriousness of a court reporter, tinged with mistrust. "As far as I'm concerned, Cajuns is colored people and no better than the Spades or the Jews," he thought, as he spit on the ground. He wanted to work with people like himself. "The bosses at the paper mill ain't got it figured out. I ain't no traitor. I got nothin' to say to the bosses," he thought.

"This action dissolves about anything, or anybody, that cooks in the sauce, and leaves behind the cellulose fibers or pulp; a thick brown gravy. From the *blow tank*, this brown stock is then separated in the *pulp washers*. We then call it *black liquor*. The diluted black liquor comes from the washers and is still not fit for landfill, or for drink. What Buhler had said to his kids kept coming back to Jeremy, "Had they really made black paper from black bodies?" He was still fuming about the kidnapping of his daughter. It was like a threat; wielding their power with a poor girl. He felt like Buhler and his buddies had pulled it off. He had had such a fright. He was wondering if it was all worth it.

"After concentration by removal of water in an evaporator of sorts, it is further concentrated, *like with industrial fruit juice*, it becomes compacted," the engineer continued. "Then it goes to a mix tank where the *salt cake* is mixed with the liquor to make up for the chemical losses in the system." Jeremy wasn't sure if the idea behind this remix was to save money or if there were new environmental laws that required chemical recovery and disposal. It made sense that there would be some of both concerns. The engineer explained it all, but Jeremy was beginning to be concerned with the smell; wondering if inhaling the fumes could be harmful. They would all die and no one would care. No one.

"The heavy black liquor with its salt cake is still not fit for happy hour and is heated to lower its *viscosity*, or slime." Jeremy knew about slime. It was not only another work hazard that figured in with the noxious smells, but regularly coated the side of his house and his driveway. Even his so-called friends were slime, when you got right down to it. "When will we get that new protective gear?" he called out. "Why was I offered this job?" he mumbled under his breath. No one heard. He began to think that his bosses were making an example of him and the other foremen; sending southern White men to the pits to make them suffer what was still thought of as the sins of the Confederacy by people in the north. On one hand he was in denial of that wrongdoing, and on the other, he was embracing it, thinking that it had led him down the road to Hell, even in the present, even for his children. He was not a man of little philosophical concerns. "It's all black and white, as plain as day," he thought, "it's gotta be."

"The black liquor is thus pumped to the *recovery furnace* where it is sprayed on the walls for dehydration prior to final combustion of the dried char on the hearth."

"The man said *char*." Jeremy thought. "Could that happen to us? Buhler feedin' my kids more bullshit. There's no way the flesh of a person could come out of this process any other color than black. They would dissolve, dry out, and become particles of dust. Sodium-sulfate dust in the boiler gases. Yellow dust in the wind. No wonder it smells of Lake Charles here."

"This is finally removed by an *electrostatic precipitator*," said the man. Jeremy was trying to concentrate. He wanted his digester license, but it was hard for him to keep his mind on the explanations and out of his digestion. Getting over the false alert for his daughter's kidnapping was easier said than done. He was beginning to feel sick. "What if they do get her? What if they had molested her and she couldn't say so?" He, too, was writing the script for a movie where the perpetrators had faces like his father and other members of the Klan.

"Then, intense heat in the furnace fuses what is left of the black liquor to form what is known as *smelt*. The smelt is tapped from the furnace and runs into a dissolving tank where it is mixed with water to form this time a nasty *green liquor*. Carbon and other impurities found in the green liquor are settled out in a clarifier, filtered, and, not to soon, sent to landfill. Any questions?" No one had any. They all looked at the Babcock and Wilcock Co. Builder pressure gage as if it were a clock telling them it was lunchtime.

"The clarified green liquor gets a new treatment with *hot lime* (not limes or any other citrus)," the engineer chuckled. "In a lime *slaker* (not a shaker) the lime is converted back into *lye*; not rye. The insoluble *lime-mud* produced is settled out and reused, but not as an antacid, and not for mojitos, although nothing is wasted here." He laughed again, but Jeremy didn't get the joke. This was too much. He was beginning to think the man was making fun of them. He was overwhelmed with emotion and tears came to his eyes. He wiped them away with the back of his hand. "The resulting sodium, now called *white liquor*, is used again as a new cooking liquor for the wood chips in the digester."

The man summarized the process, "the bleaching of brown pulp to white pulp is usually accomplished with chlorine, followed by extraction with lye, which chemically is called, sodium hydroxide; then calcium or sodium hypochlorite, relatives of limestone; and finally, a chlorine dioxide treatment, better known as bleach." All of this sounded too clean to Jeremy . He thought he finally understood why the plant smelled so often of dead rats all the way to Ferriday because of the sulfur dust.

"The white, green and black liquors all tend to be *corrosive* and may contain several different *toxic* or hazardous ingredients," said the engineer-hygiene official explaining the various dangers of the papermaking process. "Hazardous chemicals can be found in storage tanks, process piping, process equipment, waste handling systems, and environmental control systems. Some processes may emit gases, vapors, or dusts that may be hazardous. There are potential emissions, leaks, and residues. There are potential exposures to caustic substances and asbestos."

Jeremy thought about the asbestos. He had thought it was good. Didn't they use it in housing? Trying to jerk himself back into the brawl, he raised his hand, "I thought they sprayed asbestos on pajamas for kids? Are you saying it's dangerous?" The teacher guffawed and glared at him. "Mr. Harper, if you'll permit, we need to keep moving. We've still got a lot of ground to cover. You know the size of this plant." Jeremy looked at his shoes, hiding his red face. He mumbled, agreeing; "yeah, yeah." His face flushed. By then he was thinking about what it would be like to put this man in the digester.

"What about the noise," another young foreman yelled. The machines were turning, making a sound like a new garbage truck chewing refuse; and the engineer turned to continue the tour.

"Air emissions associated with recovery boilers contain sulfur dioxide, sodium sulfate particulate, and slat cake.

Basically, a dusty nuisance. Duct systems require appropriate precautions during repairs. Potential exposures to quick lime and calcium hydroxide dusts can be a problem, particularly during cleanups. Every step must be logged in one of these red logbooks. Everyday. Every hour." The engineer held up a thick red volume like a preacher holding up a *Bible*. "If someone ain't right, we want to be able to set him straight," Jeremy thought he heard him say.

"Was it a *Bible* or a book of recipes?" The other apprentice foreman asked Jeremy. Jeremy surveyed the room. He was standing in the back where he heard the machines over the engineer, from the workshop behind him. "Why would you want it in your kitchen anyway?" he responded to his colleague, almost yelling, wondering what he would say in the logbook about the workers who screwed up. "I'm not rat," he mumbled.

It was Jeremy's new job to keep as much of an eye on the pressure building within the men on his shift, as it was on the water pressure. Paper Pulp Mills require so much water that corrosion is a constant problem. Leaks are as perpetual as prison terms, and with the leaks, loss of pressure. The workers worked often like plumbers, changing huge nuts and bolts as big as bullfrogs that bit down on the metal flange-lips holding these in a tight kiss. Too loose, and boiling water dripped from the overhead pipes. Too tight, and boiling water steamed out from below. Split flanges had to be replaced. Although dealing with these headaches was easier than to replace split lips, it took more time. This meant downtime. Time when the mill could not fully function. Jeremy knew. Before becoming foreman, he had been one of these plumbers. He knew about the burns one could have when the pressure was released too fast. The pressure built up on one side, and steam blew out on the other. It was best to stay out of the way. He knew about a Black man who hadn't.

"Let me put it like this. This is what you need to know to do the job," said the retiring foreman to Jeremy during their lunch break on the first day. "This little 'splanation will help you remember somethin' important. Did you notice how the digester and blow tank look like vertical or tilted steel igloos; one longer, one larger?" Jeremy nodded that he did.

"These are equipped with a centrifuge, a sort of inside merry-go- round. Now, you know them husky dogs that the Eskimos got?" Jeremy nodded that he did. "Grey slate huskies run through the door at the top or on the side of the igloo, and leave only a blur of snow-white dust behind them when they're done with their ride. Some days, the humidity; or God help us, the cold, grips the baskets so hard that the dogs cain't escape. Debris gets stuck. Mud oozes out through the cracks. The dogs scratch and howl like wolves when that starts and keep howlin' 'til someone goes in and, with a shovel, empties the sludge into the washers like it was supposed to do in the first place. Who then, lets the dogs out?" beamed the old man, his two front teeth missing, content with his story and his riddle. Jeremy looked at him, frowning. "We do," the man answered, giving Jeremy a slight nudge with his fist. "They ain't real dogs, of course. It's kinda like a Boudreaux joke." Jeremy smiled back. He was happy to have the job explained to him in a way that made sense even if he didn't have much of a sense of humor and didn't care a hill of beans for Boudreaux.

A sign posted on the outside said; *Confined Space. Enter by permit only.* When Jeremy saw the sign, he felt his privileges returning. He was qualified enough to enter a section where only a few had the right of way. Wasn't his promotion the proof that he was a man? He felt his selection for this task was decided upon because his knowledge of the machines was superior to that of other men on his shift. He had taken welding classes at a vocational high school and understood that precautions were necessary. "Now get with it, mud-dogs," yelled the engineer, ready to see how the new foremen would perform.

Once he began his new job, and for a time, Jeremy stood like a nightclub bouncer, guarding the door of one of the digesters. "Whatcha' standin there all de time for, Jeremy? 'fraid somebody gonna steal yo' belly why yo out to lunch?" Bulher said, as he and his buddy, James Lloyd walked by, sneering. James Lloyd said, "never trust them digester guys. Their brains 're too close to their assholes." Buhler slapped him on the back and they went away snorting and laughing, proud of their mockery.

After a while, Jeremy began to consider that someone else might like the opportunity of keeping an eye on the dogs. He knew now what he had suspected. There was some discomfort associated in dealing with toxic gases in small places, no matter what kind of security material his bosses provided, and even if the man had compared the smell to dog farts. It was worse than that. Much worse.

He decided huskies weren't like normal dogs. They smelled worse on account of regular indigestion. Entering the igloos was not only subject to authorization, but also to size. Jeremy decided these machines were more like space capsules than igloos, but without the glory or fame of having traveled with NASA. As emotional as being held captive by the pretend *Star Trek Enterprise* had been in the farm equipment junkyard of his childhood, just above the graves where *real* Black people had been buried, it did not come close to what he was feeling now. He felt low and no count. No matter what people said, he felt he was not like his father. Confusion was bubbling up like vented papermill gases. He fingered the silver dollar in his pocket. Now, he had doubts about a lot of things. Nevertheless, he wasn't ready, or able, to stop himself from using his father's words to explain what he was feeling. "Words," he thought, without realizing he had thought it, "aren't they part of what make you think?"

The foremen were among the smallest men at the IP Pulp Plant. Jeremy's sizing up had in fact, been a sizing down. No one envied his position. "Not even a Black wants to do this job. *They* all want to poison us with them fumes," he concluded. He saw a doctor and asked for some pills to help him sleep. He tried to get Buhler and Lloyd, and his father, out of his mind, while he thought he was beginning to go out of his own. He wondered if the pills the doctor gave him were okay. He kept thinking someone was telling secrets behind his back and was worried they were plotting to kidnap his daughter again or do something worse to her.

A bad reputation

Jurors, as much as the Sheriff's office, had been complicit to Klan crimes, and the children of the Klan members, at least most of them, did not want to know the truth. "Don't you see?" One woman said wrinkling her nose. "They give Ferriday a bad reputation." She had taken the place of Missy Dey Dean, perpetual busybody, at the head of the local Ladies' Community Service Group. Missy Dey Dean, died, and now busied the bodies in the Natchez Cemetery where she had become a full-fledged member. Hebert Miller couldn't hear the end of it. He passed away before finishing paying her annuities and she had to sell her family home again to yet another family so she could continue to live in it until the day she died. When that day did come, the house was beginning to fall into disrepair like its predecessor. Herbert could not make enough amends.

"Good people aren't as good as moths when it comes to seeking light," rasped Emmy to no one; "they flutter away from its brightness instead of embracing its torch. They worry about what is said more than what is being done for real. Who's worried about a town's reputation when people are burned alive or children are raped? How can people move on, if, crimes like these go unpunished, or no one believes they happened at all? They believe prayer is enough." Emmy tried to break loose from her confusion and her censorship. She held fast to the rail and still couldn't find the footing. She felt divided about her allegiances. Had she been able to step outside her body with the part of her that had compassion for the people she had grown up with and look upon the *Fury* that remained; she would not have been less surprised by the acerbity that was brewing inside her. Had her parents joined Harper's church to appease the forgotten memory of Ferriday's souls? Both were from South Louisiana, not this little up-the-river town. Why had they stayed when they realized Harper was off the rails and taking over their lives and property? Didn't they understand the dangers? Prayer had not saved them. "Yet," she thought, "there's something in the words of prayer that might have had an effect on their actions."

Then, rage took ahold of her body again. She realized that she couldn't live with a loose-leaf history like some people did. Like her parents had. She had another kind of notebook; one, where torn out pages show up with their glyphs coming to life as visions dancing among the *ignus fatus* ghosts of the swamp. She stopped her car and got out. She had to breath. The smell of earth after a rain. "I like that," she smiled and had wanted to say thinking about the earth's aromatic breath. Had it rained? Coming home, she had not noticed it. Listening to Dvorak, *The Nouveau Monde*, the humus came to life. Earthworms, *Lumbricus* her mother had told her, were burrowing through the soil, releasing the metallic- musk perfumes. Or was she smelling what she was hearing in her head? For the moment, she couldn't tell if it was the music she imagined or the fragrance. She inhaled the gardenias in her yard. No scent of rain there. Once inside, again, the odor of mold. "Will it ever go away?" She opened the guest room door and looked around. It was suitable. Nothing that a kid could hurt himself with, not even Valerie. She picked up her typewriter, closed the door and brought it back to her bedroom. She stretched out on her bed. Emmy was so tired. She couldn't think. She didn't remember the last time she had had something to eat. "Is the girl still asleep in the truck? When she comes in, will I have to lock her in the bedroom, at least until I could figure out what to do with her?" Was she resigning herself to a life of crime? Before long, Emmy fell asleep and began to dream.

In her nightmare, Harper was driving a car to the Black part of town. He was going up and down the doodled streets in search of an adolescent to frighten with the headlights, or worse. "There's one," Harper pointed, but his son was slow, and undetermined. He couldn't get the hose out of the window before the kid, a light brown boy of about fifteen, spotted the mischief and reeled away. Harper drove out of what he called nigger-town and stopped the car. He reached over Emmy, grabbed his son by the ear, and twisted it until the boy was crying from pain and humiliation.

"You better mind me boy! We gotta do our part to take care of these niggers or we won't have any country left! Don't make me have to tell ya again."

He released the ear and, at the same time, pushed his head onto Emmy's lap. She was frightened by the outbreak of violence and didn't know what to think. "Get in the back and let your brother get up here and show you how it's done."

"You!" The boys were playing around, slapping each other in some kind of hand game, and not listening. "You, hear me? Get up here and do what your no count wimp of a brother can't handle." His eyes reached into the overhead rearview mirror. "Dickless cunt," he murmured.

He didn't seem to know his sons' name. Harper's oldest boy got out and opened the door for Johnny. "Get out, Johnny," he said. "You'll be alright. Girls ain't 'spected to do a man's work." He was grinning with pride for some kind of privilege that he alone, among Harper's boys, thought he had earned. And, in a twisted way, this was true. Jeremy had been selected by his father to do his bidding, and all of his life, she imagined, he would be a pawn for others' devilry.

"Well, we should leave him here and let him walk home. Whatcha' think, boys?" said Harper, his eyes squinting mean. "Don't look at me like dat." Johnny was terrified and looked as if he might cry.

When he got into the back of the car, Harper reached around, trying to grab him by the shirt. "Doncha' move away when I try to get ahold of ya. I'm gonna get out and take the strap to ya, ya little bastard. Harper got out, pulled Johnny out the car by his shirt, and knocked him hard against the head, making him fall down, then grabbed him with both hands, pulling him up, and pushed him against the car. "Now lean over on the trunk. And get dem pants down. Let everyone watch dat fine white ass turn red." There was no one there, but a carload of kids. Johnny lowered his head with humiliation as he lowered his jeans. He knew it would be worse if he resisted. "Now, put them hands on the hood of the trunk and bend over." Harper waited, taking off his leather belt, folding it in two, holding both ends together with fisted hands. He pushed the ends together, and then all at once, bullied them apart, clacking the circular band that was formed, several times. The boys in the car were recounting the scene to their older brother as they watched.

"He hit him yet?"

"No. Not yet. Nah. He's just clacking 'is belt. Don't ya wanna watch Emmy?" Emmy sat there petrified.

Skin against skin. "Don't you yell boy! If you yell, it'll be the last time."

"One-Two-Three-Four-Five-Six-Seven-Eight-Nine-Ten-Eleven." The little boys in the back seat counted, heckling. Jeremy passed his coke to Emmy, as if he was sharing popcorn in a movie theater. Her mouth was dry and she took a sip. Burning liquid bumped in her throat and burned her nostrils. She turned her head away; putting her hand over her mouth as if she was afraid that she might throw up.

"Next time you pull such a stunt I'll leave you wit' da niggers. Dat's where you belong. Any boy dat act like that gotta be half nigger and it ain't my half. I done tol y'all yore ma's a whore," he said, glancing around the streets to see if anyone was around, then back to the carload of kids. "Jest wait to we git back at the house." Harper hissed. He then shrugged, and bent his head to one side and to the other, as if to put his hatred back into what he felt was its rightful place, put his belt back on, and got into the car. Johnny got back in, trying not to cry.

"I don't wanna hear another peep out of ya," barked Harper. "Fuckin' pussy." He started the car again, circling back through town and driving back towards Vidalia again in the Black part of town, mumbling to himself.

The acceleration eased. Harper's older son got the canister ready, held the hose out the window, and yelled, "Ac..ciiiddddd,» slow and deep, while spraying a poor Black youth with the contents.

Emmy woke up in a sweat, scratching both her hands. Like the boy who was dosed with the chemical residues, she didn't know if the contents of the fire extinguisher were toxic or if the contents burned their skin. Hers felt like it needed peeling; a prisoner inside her skin wanted out of its small cell. Harper's beast had been hungry for fear, and he was fed.

She never forgot the terrified eyes of their victims. As Harper's boys, including the one with the twisted red ear, bruised face, and sore buttocks, cackled about the white foam or the blue powder covering the horrified Black child; she had felt unshed tears wobbling on her eyelids. She had swallowed these, willing them to not trickle down her cheeks. With Harper's boys, not understanding the ultimate use of the extinguishers, she had helped steal these, one by one, from the Baptist Church, the Elementary and High Schools, and the Concordia Parish Hospital. They had told her that they were just borrowing these to make sure they worked.

She would do anything Harper asked; everyone knew that. Now, she was afraid to show compassion. She felt guilty. She was afraid to be afraid. Harper sneered, looking at each one of them. Emmy couldn't believe she had been in that car. Now, as then, her tears gasped for air in her belly, like a hundred netted fish dumped onto the bottom of a boat. And fear had gloated on disbelief. The beast delighted in this delicacy. She had to face it, and chase it away. She thought she felt Harper's hand, squeezing her thigh, and saw him smiling with approval. He had done it again. Forgetting all about the events from the day or the week before, she hurried out of bed to the shower; her heart still back beating as in a rock and roll song.

Empty pockets

After her grandmother's property and houseboat near Breaux Bridge on Bayou Teche had been sold, Emmy was able to take out a small loan and have the remaining broken trailers pulled off her mother's land in Ferriday and taken to a junkyard. She had forgotten about the silly flag her grandparents had brought with them from Houma; whose inscription, a Cajun motto, *AUSSI INEBRANLABLE QUE L'ÉCREVISSE* (as steadfast as the crawfish) was all, but readable by then. Sometimes, it appeared to say: *EN CREVÉ*, or usually used as in, *tu peux en crevé* or just *creve*. Either way it was no good. Translated into English, and to put it bluntly, this might mean, *you can die from it*, or *JUST DIE*. She let it fly. It's a good thing that the people of Ferriday, people with memories of the trailer park neighborhood's habitants, did not, for the most part, speak French. The occasional Cajun visitor, noticing the remaining letters on the flag, wouldn't read the sign as she had. They would see random letters and imagine a fortuitous past. This symbol of days gone by harbored no threat to Emmy. No one would take her for one of the radical communists opposing the incumbent politicians. If there were any red candidates, she never saw their electoral campaigns. Even if the whole town had heard a lot about them and might have benefitted from some of their policies; Louisiana people are proud and thought of welfare like a handout. No one would take her for a murderer either, not with a flag that sported a crawfish with a human hand pinching itself when the wind was unchained, and became wicked. Emmy wondered why her parents had not embroidered the hands over the crawfish or made a new flag. Either way, it wouldn't have changed the undoing of their motto, or her family.

She had the burned church knocked down, scavenged the wood she could, had a pier built, and a boat ramp installed out on the point. People without frontal property needed lake access for their fishing and ski outfits. She charged a small sum for use of the docks and was able to afford groceries, buy typewriter ribbons and paper, and still live at the house across the Lake Road. By that time, she had written two novels, but neither had been accepted for publication. She supposed that she was writing them for herself, the quiet girl with many writable voices, but none that could be heard. What use would her silent protest be?

"How you doin, sista?" called out a Black man from his boat. She had seen him fishing next to her property. Emmy waved. Did he know what had happened to her family? Of course, he did. Everyone knew, but no one talked to her about it. His hook was caught in a swamp willow and he was holding the line taut, looking at the branch overhead like a boy caught in a candy shop with empty pockets. "You mind if I pull my boat close to the ramp and unhook my fishin line from the hangin leaves?" Emmy nodded her head, "okay". "The bass ain't bitin today. There's a big catfish I've been after for some time. I hooked him at least twice in the past month, but he always gets loose. I bet your pilings full of hooks. He likes to take my cornbread chitlins for a spin right under there, and I have to cut the line every time," he pointed.

Emmy looked down. She could see the yellowish minnows schooling close to the surface near the green patch of duckweed. They darted away as the armor of a bigger fish surfaced not far, with an early morning splash of its tail.

"Do you remember me? My name is Hiram. I live right over yonder," indicating the direction with his head. We played together sometimes when we were kids, right after your parents bought the place. Then I had to stop comin' over." He hesitated. "I reckon I messed up my line all by myself this time," he grinned, while watching for her reaction. I should find another job." Emmy went on sitting on her pier, her cork bobbing once, then twice, before she pulled out the bream, reaching for the orange and turquoise bandit. She had had her own dealings with sneaky aquatic creatures, as much as terrestrial ones. She didn't want to reveal much about herself.

Hiram kept glancing in her direction, until he said, "You ain't much of a talker, are you?" Emmy looked at him. "That's some fine fish you got there," he remarked as she added the bream to her stringer. He unhooked his line and started to reel it in. Although he was a little older, she thought she recognized Hiram. He didn't know she knew about him and she couldn't tell him what she knew. He was the father of Skizzum's baby; the one they had taken to the Fortune-teller to find adoptive parents. They had been too young and their differences made it impossible for them to raise a child in Ferriday at the time. He was a full-grown man now, filled out like an athlete, about thirty years old, maybe a little older. He had survived Vietnam. Of course, there were children of various shades in the town, but in spite of the *Civil Rights' Act*, most of these were born to Black mothers and were not the fruit of a wanted union.

Both, Emmy and Skizzum, were Cajun; they were considered White, by most folk. Although she had Redbone-Creole mixed parents; Emmy was a *whiter shade of pale*, even among Whites. Everyone in their community thought that her grandmother had been the fruit of one of these unwanted unions, and that, that *unluck,* that *malchance,* had been passed on to Emmy along with the color of her skin and her eyes. Mamere had said as much, "It's just like what happened with my mother. At least you were too young to get pregnant," as if that was a consolation. And if you thought of it, in a way, it was. It was kind of like the day she and Mamere had been fishing and a fourteen-foot alligator poked his head up near the boat, eying her as much as the fish she brought out of the water. Mamere conked it on the head with her paddle and said, "now that was lucky. At least you didn't go and fall in! You'd have served as his dinner. Now we get to keep all our fish and he has swum off to bother someone else." Mamere was like that, weighing outcomes with luck. Like a lot of people in Ferriday, they considered themselves lucky to be White, or almost White and almost lucky.

Hiram had two other children now, and they would sometimes fish with him. They ventured onto the pier and sat with Emmy on those occasions when she was fishing alone and no one else appeared to be in sight. She let them touch her hair or braid it. "Can you hear," they asked, waving their hands in front of her to get her attention. They thought her dumbness was due to deafness, or some other speech impediment. Hiram had supposed as much. The children were the only ones she allowed to touch her. They fussed about her as if she was a new kitten or puppy. She didn't mind, and welcomed their giggles when one day, they tried attaching a live lizard into her hair. At first it bit the strands of hair in defense, but soon abandoned that idea and leapt into the water, preferring to swim.

One day, while the children were preparing another style, she realized she had been holding her left hand with folded fingers over her heart while she caressed it with her right hand, as if it were a baby rabbit or kitten. Other than her parents, her grandparents, Skizzum, her old friend, Bee, or these children, whose lives she did not know; no one had ever touched her with affection. Not wanting the children to notice, she put her purring hand to rest on her lap. That day, her loneliness was too much to bear.

The Whites, who used the boat ramp, accepted her lack of speech. If they knew what had happened to her, they would raise their beer in acknowledgement of her recovery . Sometimes, these would be tainted with undertones of a less soothing melody. Emmy ignored these. Instead, she punctured their tires before they came back to the ramp. She used all sharp instruments, leaving these in place so the tire would empty itself on its own time.

A little more than ten years before, when she was fifteen, Emmy had come back to Ferriday for a visit. She had tried to fit in. Skizzum had taught her to drive. She bought a truck, got a license, and visited her old home. She went a few times to a local church. Sometimes, she noticed some of the men looking at her and overheard their conversations. "*The Bible* tells us that a girl that tempts a man is a girl that has been improper with her attitude. Men are weak. We try to keep them on the straight and narrow path to God, but we are sinners. We must beg for forgiveness, both men and girls alike. The attitude of some girls doesn't change with the intervention of God. Some men act as God's instrument in teaching a wayward girl a lesson. It's God's way of preventing her from detouring other devout men from their wives and families." The preacher looked at her as he talked. "Is he confusing me with someone else?" Emmy, becoming more and more uncomfortable with what he was saying as much as with his pointed glares at her while saying it, didn't rightly know. He seemed to encourage some sort of fantasy about what kind of girls get raped; using the crime against her to build on more than one of his unhappy sermons. He never spoke of full-grown women. One day, she was followed to her property and attacked by a man she had recognized from the congregation. Lying face down in the dirt while he grunted, claiming she liked what she was getting; she vowed to herself that she would not let this happen again.

When the roses didn't come for two months in a row, Emmy tried using Mamere's concoction of *Carachipita, yerba de la perdiz, and oregano*. When that didn't work, she took a clothes hanger, straightened it on one end, wiped it down with alcohol, and squatted over the studio's makeup mirror with its lights turned on bright. She had never peered inside her body like this before. It reminded her of a flower or some sort of loose-leaf pink lettuce heart. With the handle of a wooden spoon between her teeth, she stuck the point deep inside. The hanger twisted past the tight, bottleneck opening, drawing itself into her warm womb. Her body felt like a war-zone. Alone and feeling like she had no choice, like the boys who were drafted to fight in a war they opposed, she sobbed and winced with shame, as much as with the quick pain. It was too much to ask of her. Raising a child on her own was beyond her capacity and she didn't want to bring this child into this world to remind her of this man who had inflicted upon her, his violence and his fascination with power. Her uterus was her battleground. She felt she was a prisoner of a war, foreign to her.

She thought of the millions of women in the millions of years before her who, faced with silence to the point of denial, had exposed their babies to the elements for a certain, and sometimes unpleasant, death. Mythology was full of it, so were stories from the Middle Ages, and even *The Bible* had prescriptions for unbaptized children. Beings without souls from birth. "The evil eye," Mamere said, "had fallen upon them." Emmy never understood if *it* were the babies who had the evil eye themselves, if their mothers were witches, or if the evil came from Hell. Nobody talked about these undesired infants, and that was just it and why, they never became *real* babies, because no one talked about them to say that they were unwanted. Hell must be the place where words go to die before they are born, she decided.

Two days later, with the infection, pus oozed out with nineteen- sixty-eight casualties. She felt the waters trickle down her legs. Blood, sweat, and tears flowed. A tiny, featherless baby-bird-like fetus slipped out, its closed translucent eyelids bulging, its fledgling wings folded, and lifeless. She forced herself to look at it. "Didn't Skizzum say goodbye to her little girl before the nurse took it away?" Tucking a clean handkerchief around it, she put it in a watch-box. Thinking this made a better coffin than her grandmother had had, she couldn't make herself spread the legs to see if it was a boy or a girl. Perhaps it was too early. Naked, she crouched in the bathtub, shaking with fever and holding onto the sides. She doubled over, into a position of the baby who would never be born; the girl, who could not become this child's mother. Without waiting, she forced down a treatment she had prepared with the same medication applied to those who lost their limbs in the Civil War. The result was the similar. Her uterus was amputated for all practical purposes. She could never have children, not this one, blessed with her *unluck,* or another. Her tears were not enough. Her family's saga would end with her. She wondered if they had endured all that they had endured, of immigration and deportation, of hunger, hurricanes and floods, of fire and prison, all for nothing. The foreign monarchy monster that had pursued the Cajuns from Acadia had caught up with them after all, and quenched his thirst with her blood. End of story. But not. This ogre was marching upstream now, from the mouth of the Mississippi, and from another time, still hungry, searching for the souls who had survived.

Emmy slept in the cold tub, trembling, until her fever subsided late the next day. Putting the little coffin in her refrigerator until she could bury it, she thought about death. She wanted to die. It was horrible to think of, the little being lying there in the cold. She lay in bed for almost a week without food. She could not distinguish her grief from the anger or the guilt. Her landlady, a ballet teacher who had been kind enough to let her play the piano for her classes and pay her a small salary, wouldn't put up with a naked girl lying in bed and not feeding herself. She pulled Emmy's arms and told her to get up or get out.

"What would she say if she knew about the hanger?" Emmy asked herself as her face contorted and she scrubbed the bathtub with bleach, and more tears.

Arranging the little watch-box like a piece of precious jewelry, or fragile glassware, she packed up her few belongings in boxes, put these in her truck, and drove without stopping to the family plot in Evergreen, off highway 29 near Bunkie. Beside her father's headstone, she buried the tiny coffin under the lavender dusk and prayed. "Lord, please welcome this child into your world; this one is too cruel for any one of us." She kissed her two forefingers and touched her father's headstone. He would understand and would have recomforted her, had he been there. He had witnessed burials of children of twisted fate. He would understand why she did what she did and why she had cried. As much as she hated the man who had hurt her, she had mixed feelings about the undeveloped being that had been with her for weeks. She could not have kept it. She had raised so many strays and tried to save so many runts. But in truth, many had not survived their *unluck*. The world was not a nice place for those abandoned by their parents or by fate. It had to be done. She was confused by nature's trick of granting her a conscious, yet obliging her to be of a nature she did not choose to be. It was finality of death that pegged these meanings, and the one that estranged her from her faith, to her soul. It had to be done, and she had to tell herself this.

What choice did she have? She was forced to move back to her mother's abandoned home in Ferriday and started carrying a gun tucked into her jeans. It wasn't just for show. Shooting her dick off was not a possibility; she didn't have one. But she might obliterate the fly of the man who had raped her if he ever showed it around these parts again. If a man stared at her long, under her t-shirt he would see the quiet bulge; and his own would deflate. "I'm not a woman to mess with anymore." Mostly, she counted on her mother's reputation. She didn't have any brothers. Nevertheless, the time would come, as it had been coming since she was a little girl. Her glances over her shoulder were not idle. She knew she was prodding a predator.

A life, lucky or not, isn't it still a life? A ruby-throated hummingbird flitted in front of her, hesitating an instant, before flitting back to its partner in the tree. It wanted to taste the nectar of the orange trumpet vine she had planted near the porch when she arrived. Would it risk its life to suckle? Saying she was unlucky; wasn't that statement also a kind of prison? "Does fear make you unlucky?" she murmured to the colorful winged-speck. She sometimes wondered if she was locked up in a pointless prison of her own making; a dungeon with more than one set of bars. "If there is a God, that hangs the stars and planets in the sky, the course they take around their stars, the seasons, and all these things in the heavens and on earth, how can luck or fortune dominate his world?" Her friend Bee would have changed the subject, turning it over to a question of sexism. "Why," she would ask, "is God a he? Can you tell me that?" Bee looked at the practical side, not the spiritual one, thought

Emmy. Did she wonder if things could have been otherwise?

Abundance

The road was covered with thousands of crawfish, and hundreds of snakes. It was 1973. There had been another flood, and after more than thirty days, the water was receding. Homes were still covered to the eaves. Businesses were flooded out, and so was Emmy. Where her family's camp had been across the Lake Road, the overflowed river slurred into the lake and swallowed trailers like drugstore lozenges. When the rains had started and the news came that the river would soon crest, Emmy jacked up her trailers and tied them to the trees. It helped, but not enough. It would be years before she would be ready for guests.

Every able-bodied young person had been to the levee to sandbag. They had worked all night, for several nights. The levee held, but there was still a lot of water inland, and a lot of homes and businesses were under water. There were also the people, the ones who could not afford dry land, who lived beyond the levee. The Atchafalaya Flood Basin took a lot of the water, but the endeavors of the US Army Corps of Engineers never seemed to prevent all disasters. Weather was somewhat foreseeable, but was foresight ever enough? All they could do now was to wait until the water lost ground.

One of her childhood friends, Mooch they ironically called him, was having a party at his house out near Clayton to celebrate the end of the rain. They were going to have a crawfish boil and a goat roast. Emmy was not intending to go. She didn't like crowds, but as her truck slid almost off the road, her lights showing the thousands, perhaps millions of crawfish crossing; she thought of the party, of Louisiana's favorite food, and how she might make a little easy money. Their shiny shields shimmered under her headlights and she thought there might be as many crawfish as stars overhead. That was to say that there were more than she had ever seen, or caught in gunnysacks and for sale in a store. Emmy had been carrying shovels, and containers in her truck for over a month just in case. This had been happening all over the flooded parts of the state and she wanted to be ready. She parked and got her flashlight out of the glove box. Under the clear night sky, was one of the Louisiana flood's rare gifts.

She tried using the shovel to scoop up several at a time and put them in containers, but decided that it might injure them and didn't want to deliver dead crawfish. She started picking them up, holding each one by the thorax so they would not pinch, and pitching them into the truck bed. There were so many. Sometimes one would grab her by the sleeve as she picked up one of his companions. Sometimes a crawfish would manage to pinch her and she would be cut. "If a picture had been taken, it would look like our worn-out flag," she thought. The real problem came from the water moccasins. Emmy did not fear snakes. She had handled water moccasins in Harper's weird service. As long as she didn't surprise them in any way, she had nothing to fear. She continued picking up the crawfish, shining her flashlight around to find the largest ones, until her bags were full. She was thinking she had about four hundred pounds and was about ready to call it a night, was about to close her tailgate, when she stepped on a large snake that had slid from underneath the truck. It bit her ankle. Had she stopped a second, she would have recognized its odd watermelon-skunk hybrid scent, its musk heavy in the night.

The fangs of the animal ripped through her skin. She opened her mouth to cry, but no sound issued forth. She took a cord from the truck's bed, made it to the driver's seat, and she thought about making a tourniquet with a stick, but decided against it. Emmy knew how poisonous these snakes were. She had to decide fast if she wanted to get to a hospital or try to go it alone, like she did with most things. Cajuns are independent people.

Mooch didn't live far from the Clayton Highway. She drove as fast as she could, honked her horn and waited for him to come out. Mooch, shy from his dealings with the police in a drug bust for only a few planted seeds in his Volkswagen van, peered out through the window into the dark. She could see his long scraggly blond hair peaking beyond his moon-pie face. He slipped out the front door, his old bell-bottom jeans slinking down without a belt, and walked over to her truck with his flashlight. "What the Hell?" Emmy opened her door and turned her leg towards him. "What the fuck!" But he knew. "Hold on," he said. Mooch had been a medic in Vietnam. In his home, he kept supplies. He carried her inside to the couch. With his poor teeth, he wouldn't risk sucking on the wound. It was already dark and swollen. He poured hydrogen peroxide on the cut, made an incision with a flame- sterilized blade like a cross, and used a suction device he had made from a child's rubber bicycle horn and a hose; forced the poison out of her wound, at least that was his intention. He wasn't sure it was enough. He didn't have an antidote to the poison and felt that he should do something. Anyway, doing something kept him from being anxious. He was certain that the toxic substance was winding its way to her heart. "I'm takin you to the hospital."

Emmy shook her head. By now she was feeling light-headed and her ankle hurt. It scared her more to look at the black blisters now forming where the snake had torn her flesh and her swelling leg. But she didn't want to go. She motioned for paper and a pen. She wrote: "Crawfish in back of truck. How much for them? There are about four hundred pounds." Mooch was stunned. He knew that they didn't have much time to lose. He said; "I'll take 'em." Then Emmy passed out.

She woke up in the emergency room in the Concordia Parish Hospital. It wasn't the first time she had been there. When she was about nine, she had had a scare with tetanus. One night, she couldn't get to sleep. She kept smiling. Then her nose started to wrinkle. "Mama, Papa," she cried, "I can't stop smiling and wrinkling my nose." They said, knowing that she didn't much like going to sleep, "go back to bed." She did, but soon, her jaw shifted way over on one side and it hurt. She began to cry. She got up again and went to her parents. Both were alarmed. They had both heard stories about tetanus and since they worked around horses where the bacteria liked to live, they were careful about getting their vaccinations. Their daughter had had hers. What went wrong? They hurried to the car, carrying Emmy who was in her pajamas.

Once in the emergency room, she was given a muscle relaxer. The nurse asked questions. "Had Emmy been injured? Did she have a small cut?" They began to pour over her, checking her fingers and toes. The medication began to kick in and it appeared that Emmy was going to be okay. The doctor had arrived and asked more questions. No, she hadn't been without her shoes (a lie.) No, she hadn't tried to open a coke with her teeth (another lie.) No, she hadn't blistered her skin on horseback (again a lie.) No, she hadn't handled any snakes (another lie.) The questions all seemed like moral uselessness when she didn't have tetanus and was afraid to answer. That much was clear. When the doctor got around about asking if she had taken any medication, her parents were confused. Emmy had almost always taken herbal cures. These cures had never been shown to have adverse effects with their daughter. Emmy remembered. "Bee gave me some stomach medicine when I ate some green persimmons. She told me not to, told me that you had to wait after a frost, but they looked good, so I ate them anyway." The doctor smiled. He thought he knew. Emmy had had an adverse reaction to a medication called *Reglan*, usually given for nausea. If she ever took it again, she should be careful. This might be an allergy. And so it was. Her jaw relaxed and her parents with it. This allergy warning had accompanied her to the children's psychiatric ward and the doctors were reluctant to give her medication.

Emmy remembered the incident as one of those unavoidable incidents that kids go through: bicycle accidents, skinned knees, stitched chin. Irritated, she wanted to go home. Trying to step down on the floor, she lurched forward. She couldn't put any her weight on her foot, but wanted to leave. Concerned about the crawfish, she worried that once paid, she could not afford the bill for the emergency room. Leaving was against the doctor's orders, but the nurses couldn't stop her. They brought her a pair of crutches along with a release form. She hobbled to the waiting room where Mooch was waiting for news. He took her back to his house and made her a bed on the couch. Emmy thought it was strange how this snakebite had brought her closer to other people and wondered about the meaning of the snake in *The Bible* once again. Sometimes, poison took a strange, convoluted path. Was kindness enough to change its course?

Harper had been shot and left for dead. Her mother had saved him, before killing him for good, and for a good reason.

"Maybe instead of a crawfish, I'm like a snail." Emmy glimpsed the idea and started to develop it. "Perhaps, not just any slow crawling slimy snail. This snail ate an *Amanita muscaria*, the kind you see in children's books. This cute mushroom will kill you if you decide to eat it. However, if you are a snail, or an elf, I suppose, you can tolerate the mushroom toxins. Now suppose, I had a little red polka-dot snack. Its poison circulated in my system, and did something to me. Would it also wait to envenom the creature either unaware, or who forgot to purge me of these contents..." She thought of the word contents as in being contained and with its meaning of being the opposite of discontent. "Could I be purged of my discontents?" She wondered, thinking of the literal meaning of words.

Thousands of years of living have taught humans a certain amount of wariness about foods they have never eaten. Children harbor a certain mistrust as they look at mustard greens or collards on their plates and wonder, and question, "what on earth is my Mama giving me today?" People don't go around eating poisonous mushrooms or snails. They are cynical enough to avoid swallowing rubbish. They learn through love, observation, and advice.

Emmy didn't know how to purge poisonous propaganda. Her parents didn't know how either. They had all been in a cult where confusing words had ended up scrambling their minds. "Then...do I...Have I...?" Her thinking evaporated like three points on a page. Emmy did not know the answer because she didn't know how to ask herself the rest of the question. A fleeting sensation warmed her from the inside and caused her to forget for a moment her endeavor to overcome hostility by pitting one force against the other, and caused her to forget what in an instant before she had envisioned. She might just become like the snail and become one with her venom. As for snakebites and secondary mushroom consummation, you never know what the outcome will be.

The 1977 drive-by

The blood striped the inside of the window-shield of the Sheriff's car like an American Flag decal. Coming from Clayton, a driver saw the warning lights of a police car stopped in the middle of the road. "What was the patrol car doing there?" Another driver sat in his truck, near the corner of the town's main intersection, US 84 and US 65. Jeremy sat waiting in the parking lot, close to the Delta Bank for the last hour. It was about the same place Frank Norris had had his shoe repair shop, but the Ku Klux Klan attack was far from his mind. Now, there was a fast-food joint going up; but when things were going to come down about the murder tonight, and traffic got heavy; he would be ready.

Jeremy left home at about nine-thirty to begin his nightshift at ten. They called it the graveyard shift. His wife didn't know that he had called in sick. Jeremy had been nervous for the last few weeks. He carried his shotgun in his truck. He waited now, as he had waited before. He was good at waiting when he needed to wait. He had sat low with the brim of his cap tipped down over his short forehead. Earlier that evening, when he saw the 1977 new Catalina Pontiac pass by on its rounds, he had called Buhler from the corner payphone and told him that it was Crowder's shift. Buhler joined him a half hour later on foot, walking down the alley behind the Arcade Theater. They would do this together. Buhler knew the ropes. Jeremy started his truck and they waited. Now he was alone again, waiting for the ruckus to clear before turning left, and continuing to Woodville.

He knew who the informant was. He had always known. He had been on the ski boat on Lake Concordia when the man had cried real tears, telling Ross that the FBI was threatening him in order to get information about the Orville Lounge. "What a liar! What a fake!" Jeremy thought. His own father, as Crowder's minister, was there too. The man helped him put on his skis. Helped him out of the water. That was a long time ago. "Who else would be sending us letters? Who else would have had the gall to kidnap my daughter and take her to a movie, only to set her out in front of the house a few hours later?" They all knew Crowder had been the one to sell out Slaughter, and Ross, too. If he had given up secrets about the payments so easily, why wouldn't he talk about the rest? "A rat." He murmured. "A god-damn muskrat." He had told the Klan at the next meeting. Someone had to pay. He and Buhler were assigned to the task, to help them make up after their differences. Jeremy had not forgotten that he had suspected Buhler of sending the letters, that he had pointed a gun at him and almost killed him for taking his daughter.

They had come to stop another man, before the man carried out his threats again and kidnapped someone's kids or before he killed a whole family. It was a preventative strike. "I cain't wait no more. It's my only chance." Now as he saw Crowder catfish by, fiftyish, graying hair, full cheeks, he thought, "I'll put a hole between dem cheeks to match the one on the other end." Jeremy turned right. But just then, when they had approached the Country Club on the end of town, the man slowed to a stop in the road and did an abrupt U-turn. The deputy recognized them and pulled his car alongside Jeremy's truck. Jeremy had his window rolled down, but the deputy, in the new squad car, had the push button variety that he hadn't figured out yet in the new car. The time it took him to fumble around, Buhler had Jeremy's weapon in hand, propped on Jeremy's left elbow just below the truck's windowsill. Jeremy looked at him, surprised. Buhler was looking straight ahead, watching for cars.

"How ya doin' boys?" asked Crowder, his window sliding down. They were still stopped in the middle of the highway. The deputy was lonely for conversation. "Y'all lookin' for some action?" Jeremy, on the driver's side, didn't know how to answer. His foot was jittering on the floorboard. He was trying to keep his arm still. "Y'all know, there ain't no girls at the King Hotel no more," the deputy said, looking in front of him. There were no other cars. "That place is little more than a shady bar with rooms for transients now. The Sandwich Bar is closed. Now you can get you a good pool game if y'all go to the Pastime Lounge. Mona will make you a sammich if ya want. Otherwise, nothin' else open." He checked his rearview. "You remember where that is, Jeremy, don't ya?" he said, turning his eyes towards the barrel of the gun; seeing what he had not looked for, had not suspected tonight. He had always known it would come from a friend. His mouth rounded like a fried onion-ring.

Buhler pulled the trigger before the sound came out, sending bits of brain and bone all over the new seat covers, and blood all over the patrol car's windshield. "Go," he ordered. Jeremy's tires squealed as they hightailed it towards Clayton. Buhler put the gun under the seat.

Before Jeremy could make it back to Natchez, taking the road east through the Helena pecan grove, Slaughter was on the scene and on his radio. He announced that the Deputy Crowder had been receiving threats from anonymous letters before the attack. The Sheriff's department sent cars from Ferriday to Clayton and then moving towards Natchez, to Ridgecrest and Vidalia. They drove all the way to the Black River Bridge near Jonesville. They watched for drunk drivers and other vehicles deemed suspicious with Black drivers or out of state plates. Jeremy was furious. "I was gonna do it. Why didn't you let me have the gun?"

Bulher lit a cigarette and turned to Jeremy. "For missions like these, we have an opportunity. One opportunity most of the time. It ain't a question of revenge. It had to be done. I put the gun out there for ya to grab it, and ya didn't. You weren't gonna do it. He's a cop. I knew he was gonna see it, so I pulled the trigger before it was too late. One informer less. Rid of the anonymous letters. Now why don't you drop me off as planned over near Mallard Landing where my car is parked? Then follow the plan." He took a drag from his cigarette. Jeremy kept shaking. "It's easier to wish a man dead than to see it happen," he thought. "It wasn't like in Vietnam." Seeing how the man was happy to comply and to seize the opportunity, he now had doubts again about Buhler.

After leaving him, Jeremy arrived from the Lake Road and sat low, near the gin, near the old trailer park. He opened his pickup's door and lost his dinner all over the grass-covered tire tracks. Other than the ejections, the ground was dry. Emmy saw the headlights come up beside the gin, where now there was not a trace of the watchman who was once there. She turned off her light and watched from her office window in the trailer beside her house where she was cutting letters from newspapers. He waited there until no more cars drove by on the Lake Road. Using his flashlight, he got out of the pickup and took his shotgun towards the agricultural junkyard; where another work force, all slaves, lay buried beneath cotton-pickers and tractors. He thought he heard their union-member voices and shivered, but still hid his weapon and the cartridges under the body of a John Deere two-row picker; the same one they pretended was a spaceship with the other neighborhood kids. Emmy noticed the spacewalker nearing *The Enterprise*. "A Klingon," she thought. She gathered her letters with purpose, as she might have grabbed a nineteen-sixties' *Star Trek* laser-gun. For a minute, she thought once more of the girl. "Did I lock her in the guest bedroom?"

Then Jeremy returned to his truck, turned right on Lake Road, and drove over the railroad tracks to First Street, then to the alley behind the Main Street shops, where he backed into the empty parking lot and waited. "I sure could use a beer," he thought. "The Pastime is just a block away." He hesitated, but decided that if he wanted to avoid suspicions, it would be best if he were not seen in town. He waited until he saw the Sheriff's cars coming back from Vidalia, and eased out into the night.

The following day, *The Concordia Post* read: "Concordia Sheriff's Deputy Mike Crowder was shot and killed in a drive-by attack near the Ferriday Country Club, while doing his rounds on US Hwy 84 North last night. It was said that he had been receiving threats and anonymous mail in preceding weeks. Police Chief Hickson said that they were taking over the ongoing investigation from the sheriff's department. A copy of the following anonymous letter, written in pasted type, was forwarded to the *Post*:

"To the deputy of Concordia Parish whose wife is astoundingly garish. He stepped out to fight, on one rainy night, now someone is going to perish.

Both the Concordia Parish Sheriff's office and Ferriday's Police Department are taking this lead seriously. They request that the public remain calm and call about any information that might lead to an arrest. Deputy Crowder was a long-standing member of the force. Hired by Sheriff Ross in the mid-fifties, he continued to work with the department throughout its darkest days. He is survived by his wife, his two sons, three granddaughters, and four dogs. Plans for his funeral will be forthcoming."

Waltzing in Central Louisiana

Considering the *darkest days*, there were all kinds of whodunit theories. The most viable one, according to Mr. Civic's report, which read almost the same way, like his name, from left to right, and from right to left; was that the deputy's wife, who wore lavish clothes and jewelry, was being insulted and referred to as a prostitute, by someone at her place of work at the tire company. The Strong Tire Company was just the place where another man, who was known to be a fanatic on the race issue, held court. In earlier weeks, he too, said he had received anonymous mail. It was rumored that he was on the warpath. According to an independent source, a letter accused this same tire company's worker. There was a plethora of outside sources, but no viable witnesses would come forth. Nevertheless, he was accused of lying about his own accusation of a Black man, for assault. When the sheriff's deputy showed up after work in the parking lot of the supposed delinquent, a tiff heated up between he and the cocky braggart, who worked with the deputy's wife. They squared off like a lamppost and a gas-lighter. Once they were both sweaty with bruised faces, both men went home.

The deputy's wife, outraged at the journal, confusing the printing of the article with the writing of the anonymous note; felt that enough was enough. They had called her a whore. She phoned several times Mr. Civic to complain about the letter appearing in the newspaper after the death of her husband. "I don't wear garish clothes! Where did you get that? You would make up anything, and insult me just to fill in the blank part of your newspaper. Why I never!" Then she hung up, only to call back ten minutes later and shout the same reprimand. Mr. Civic, who was trying to remain civil and get the story straight, started to formulate condolences. He finally gave the phone to his secretary and left the office for the day.

After the sheriff's deputy's death, the tire company's worker (Emmy thought of the redhead as Rover, like the dog in the schoolyard game) was arrested. Several weeks of detective and forensic work ensued. A Christian Association, according to the local newspaper, paid the suspect's bail and he was released. All charges were dropped for insufficient evidence. The sheriff's deputy had been a long-time acquaintance of the accused man, and at one time they had been both members of the same chapter of the Klan. They could also count on the reputation of the Sheriff of Concordia Parish. His arm was long, though he was dead; no one would mess with him. No one would mess with the Klan either, not even with a governor who never played the race card, but who didn't meddle for fear of interference with donations received from other sources. "What people will not do for money!" said Emmy's grandmother, from her armchair.

"No one will call out Red Rover," said Emmy. "On the river, I overheard that his name was becoming one of controversy within the Klan, and without. They think he may be the author of the letters or might be talking to the FBI." She hesitated; "his name is kinda spelled out in that very word; cont-rover-sy." Mamere shook her head. "A man's life isn't something to joke about; and a mean man...even less."

Little did she know that one newspaper man tripped over the incident himself when he typed: cunt-rover-sial, while referring to the witness. He then reset the linotype, the letters then used to print newspapers; and, having cast the *run down* ETAOIN SHRDLU to make a bad slug and deal with his error, wrote the two lines, in less than one minute: "All Charges Dropped Against Vidalia Man, victim of drive-by witness." As his colleague dropped the cast line in error, as well as its almost secret-word signalization into the molten lead, he concluded that drive-by errors were not harder to correct than that. Had he given it much thought, he would have realized that this was a cynical idea, and one without any more morals than a regular printing press. Thinking in letters was bound to lead to new acronyms, and that, was a road straight to Hell for anyone of decent literary tastes.

The City Council had voted to close the Sandwich Bar, after the drive-in restaurant had had too many drive-by fights. After the drive-by shooting, would readers soon expect to get their news from posters and drive-by journals? Concerned citizens wanted to know. It took some fancy footwork, as well as forensic fortitude, to side step the real issue. Soon they were *Dancing with their darlin's*, waltzing all over a nameless Central Louisiana dance floor. What was the motif of the anonymous letters? Why had the deputy been killed? What was his name anyway? The Klan members were asking themselves the same thing.

Rover was a shiny, red-faced man with long ears who'd been seen passing silver dollars to some of Harper's closest friends. It was rumored that he had fired bullets into a home full of children near Black River, and tried, with an accomplice, to kidnap the children's father, a man named James White, who Rover believed to be a Muslim communist. For some, having one adjective wasn't enough to stir hearts and put the other in the enemy camp; there needed to be one or two more *descriptives* to create alliances.

As usual, it was impossible to know if any of these stories were true. Private affiliations aren't public privilege. Ross had been seen on the man's property the next day, along with Hogden and Slaughter, who walked all over the scene, and destroyed the evidence, in a way similar to the linotype operator. Some of the stories had to be true. When writers are the perpetrators and publishers destroy the proof, what is left is a fictional account. But isn't that what readers want? Only victims seek truth. They want to know why they hadn't seen it coming. Was that the source of their disbelief? Was the absence of foresight the source of their trauma? Was Jeremy's paranoia an attempt to control his environment and to disallow whatever had escaped his preview? Emmy did not know.

In the barbershop, she had heard that Rover was also behind the Natchez car bombings where Black NAACP, or the National Association for the Advancement of Colored People, activists were victims. Even if he hadn't been guilty of all of the crimes, even if he hadn't himself installed the bombs; Emmy was about to drop one on him. She felt that it was her duty to call him out, to discover the truth. "Red Rover, Red Rover, why don't you come over?" she heard herself say. In some ways, her prose was stacked, made of layers built up and written to cover the secret agony she had uncovered by pieces within her soul when she tried to understand these crimes that had been committed during her childhood, some right under the dignities', and the dignitaries, noses of the community. One of these layers was a fanfaron of courage. She thought she had learned this from Skizzum. Whether it was true courage or if it nourished itself through acts of bravery was another question, and perhaps it led to another piece of armor protecting her heart. Whatever was the case, a false bravado would not protect her from danger.

To the tire worker at Tire-Strong, whose chum chimes like a ding-dong. He stepped out of line, and will soon serve time, as the new wife of an old King Kong.

Emmy knew that she was pushing it. These were dangerous men. According to a conversation she overheard from one of the boats near her property , the Federal Bureau of Investigation was following Rover. When he read the note, which he found in the bottom of his tackle box, Rover's head turned, kind of like that of the linotype operator's chair, or else, that of a demon from a horror film. He traded murder accusations like baseball cards, but this, this, well, this put him outside of himself, and his head, on a new axis. His fishing buddy, sitting in the boat with Rover, holding a can of beer, slapped the frog tattoo on his own exposed beer-belly five times in succession, as if applauding the performance.

The cathedral

Emmy got out of her truck. High above the crows were looping with the wind, executing elaborate acrobatics. *Oo-oo-rauck- aurck-aurck-aurck, oo-oo-rauck-aurck-aurck-aurck, oorauck- aurck-aurck-aurck.* This raucous sound was almost the only natural sound she could still make. She gurgled and spit as she made the bird sounds. *Oo-oo-rauck-aurck-aurck-aurck, oo-oo- rauck-aurck-aurck-aurck, oorauck-aurck-aurck-aurck.* She could now call the crows without coughing, but the cawing made her throat feel harsh and dry. A few circled lower, clapping their coal-colored wings against the air currents. A long call from them meant that they were coming. *Oo-oo-rauck-aurck-aurck-aurck, oo- oo-rauck-aurck-aurck-aurck, oorauck-aurck-aurck-aurck.* They called back to her, and she to them. Cawing and ooaurcking in a strange melody, she rounded her mouth, but could feel the song clawing her throat as it struggled to escape. "How do they do this without coughing?" she wondered. "Are they like Bee, as she does her comedy routines; when she pretended to be Charlie Chaplin, Buster Keaton, and at least two of the Marx brothers, without laughing? Everyone else laughed."

After a few minutes of this brass off-key improvisation, one of the crows flew down and stood on the ground near her. She recognized him. Instead of a sleek combed back hair fifties hair- job, he had a feather that stuck up like Alfalfa's hair spike in *Our Gang*. "Must be his rebellious nature," she thought. "Hungry?" she whispered. "Sure, you are. Hold on a minute." Talking to the birds wasn't a problem because she did not have to speak in a loud voice. "As long as I bring treats, they'd put up with any voice," she thought. She got the boudin sausage she had cooked for them out of the knapsack, cut it, and spread the pieces out on a board. She didn't want to make them human-dependent, but hoped to discourage their search of baby birds in the area long enough for these to fly away. It was nesting season for many birds.

The crow turned his head to eye her, pretended to be interested in an insect, pulling up a piece of grass, scratched under his wing with his right foot, hopped a little, then started up behind his ear like a dog with his left. Like a mechanical toy, ticking in the *Giant Steps* of a forward pitching metronome, he *long-legged* over to eat. His congeners, sitting on the branches, overhead, were more reluctant. Some made short calls as if alarmed.

"If you don't come, John Coltrane is going to eat it all," she croaked to them. "Miles, you know how he likes boudin as much as music." She had named them all after jazz musicians, male and female; not because of their voices, although they could imitate many; but because she loved jazz. Wasn't she part of the Crow nation and part jazz herself? Her father was from the Houma tribe, and if you looked back far enough, on her mother's side, she figured that they must have common relatives from somewhere farther north. At least she could lean that way in her fantasies until her genealogical gaps were otherwise filled. In doing so she could contain the otherwise fleeting feelings of floating out of her own name, her signature or her tag. Aimer the Crow, restored her a name. She was Crow and she was *Aimée*; the sound and meanings close enough to Emmy to satisfy her longing for a father, a tribe, and a voice. She wanted to honor her family and her favorite players in a world where it didn't seem they got enough respect, especially now that disco started taking over the airwaves. She was sensitive to musicians' conversations and baseless rejections of all types. Now that she listened to Weather Report, she decided she could include in her Birdland, modern instrumentals and be sure not to offend her friends. "Hey Jaco," she squawked to the newest arrival, "You and Peter Erskin better come down."

Another great crow, still sitting on a branch, she called Wayne Shorter. He pulled his beak from under his wing as if uncloaking a blackened horn from under an inky cape, and turned to the other members of his band, hesitating. Was he consulting the others about what arrangement to play? He glared at Emmy, unsure as how to judge the human solo. His eyes were the color of the blackest night-ink. "So, Coltrane wants a dense sound complex for his *Ascension*. Shorter ain't convinced. He don't believe independent melodies will fuse into total sound. What do you say about that," she said as she turned to the one, she called Elvin. "Yeah, I know, you ain't happy about it either, but you'll see. It's gonna be great!" She made up stories about how the band she played in as a child organized their gigs, explaining her fantasy as she had done with her dolls before Harper had come into their lives. Some of the birds recognized her utility, if not her capacity for crow-song. She found tiny pieces of glass or shiny metal scraps they brought as presents for her appreciation. She collected them and set them on a shelf in her home. Some days, John Coltrane would let her touch his rebellious plume before hopping out of reach. He would lean over, his throat filling with air: *Bubba, bubba, bubba*, he would say, turning his head to the side. "What do you mean, bubba! I'm no bubba and there is no one else here but us," she assured each time. One day she had seen Elvin extending a wing like a matador, facing off with a bull snake. He raised one wing and turned around as the small snake raised its head, ready to strike. He folded it back, and lifted the other, then turned around in a dance until the snake this time was hypnotized and missed as he struck out against the air. Elvin did not miss, and speared the snake through the head. As it turned out the bull was not a bull snake at all but a canebrake rattler, one of the most toxic varieties in Louisiana. Elvin, on the other hand, was an experienced snake fighter and seemed to delight in these contests. It was not difficult to predict his future if he continued these performances. Facing the fate of many bull-fighters, he would end up, face down in the corrida arena. She thought he should stick to music. "Don't you know that playing music is an easier way to impress the ladies?" she croaked. "Although," she thought, but didn't say, "unless they're rich, or you are more successful than most, it won't help you to feed yourself." One way or the other, his future didn't look bright.

Emmy looked at the trees. Her mother used to come to this place, a forest where solemn oaks and fiery cypresses beheld each other, debating the interest of rising waters and eroding levees. The frustrated alligators, trying to pitch their point of view, considered they were stuck between the two, not caring for the roughness of the Mississippi beyond. Like brothers, the trees understood each other without words because they had the same concerns. When the water was high, they stared down with disapproval at the alligators. Now, these giants winked at her between their branches.

Emmy didn't know if her mother talked to the birds. She thought she remembered her doing so. She could fool mockingbirds, and cause blue jays to flee with her birdsong. Emmy had overheard her talking to her horses and other domestic animals. Like her grandmother, her mother had known so many things about the natural world, both wild and domestic; which herbs you could eat, or use as cures, and the ones best left alone. Mamere had taught her daughter some of this; but having seen her mother's catalogue, Emmy realized now that she had an encyclopedia of knowledge about Louisiana wildlife and medicinal treatments. Emmy learned almost none of this when she was younger. She had wasted her time listening to Harper whip up crowds, instead of crows. "It's a pity that one letter can cause so much trouble!" said Mamere, intruding again.

"Where had she come from?" asked Emmy to no one.

She walked among the trees, keeping an eye out for snakes, as well as for poison ivy. This custodian wasn't as watchful here as in higher places because the spring floods had always been the more vigilant. The crows kept cawing. She wondered about why each of their flocks was called a *murder*. These just sat around and watched, waiting to be fed, or to snatch up an eyeball that no one needed anymore anyway. Emmy sighed, "I suppose it's better than being called a *court*." John Coltrane glared at her, and got away with the murder.

The Treehouse

One day, as she was walking towards her mother's old treehouse, Emmy found a few crows staring in a clearing at the body of a fallen brother. It was the one from an older generation. She had named him, Hoagy Carmichael. The birds, stricken with grief, leaned in and appeared to compare notes about the fate of one of their own squads. They looked like *Dick Tracy* homicide detectives, wearing black trench coats and hats instead of the yellow, funny paper ones Chester Gould favored.

Broken-hearted about the bird, Emmy wished Ella Fitzgerald had been there to sing "Heart and Soul" for him, and for her, as a tribute. That song was one of the first she had learned to play on the piano. She felt alone and worried about what her aloneness was doing to her. She thought of her parents' families; her father's brothers near Houma, her mother's, on the Island of Parrioc, in St. Martinville or in Thibodeaux. Both families, or what was left of them, had returned to Southern Louisiana, or had never left; yet she had all but lost her trust in other people, even her own blood. She backed off without a sound into the woods to the tree she called *Ezperanza*, after her grandmother. The old oak's limbs bent towards the ground. Emmy stepped upon its branch and, balancing herself with the upper limb, walked up towards the trunk. The bark smiled with phellogen lips while the wind in the nearby hickories crooned soft whispers of content. Their leafy shadows mingled with those of the oak leaves, casting curved figures with tiny keyholes just out of reach. Love could not open their locks. For Emmy, love went the way of luck. Her heart sagged like the treehouse. Most of the boards had fallen and swirled away with the wind and the Mississippi floods. If she wanted to use this camp, she would have to bring it back from neglect. She needed new materials.

As she began to pull away the remaining rotted boards, a proudly dressed, black and orange rat snake slid off one of the boards onto her arm, and then sprang to the ground. The reptile caught Emmy off guard, and she gasped, but didn't fall; she still wasn't afraid of snakes. They had been present all her life. She respected the ones she found in their natural environments. Although this one was nearly six feet long, flashing through the air, its rust-orange tartan posed no danger to her. It was a nonpoisonous friend. "I need rope, boards, and nails, just to get started", she rasped. She put her hand on a nest where she felt the warm silky skin of three tiny birds without feathers. *Cheep-cheep-cheep.* "Hey, you callin' me cheap? Brother *Ventrambulons* left without dinner. He'll be back, with or without the boards. So, all ya got is me." She tucked the nest into the pocket of her shirt to keep them warm. The mother, a tufted titmouse she heard calling, *peter-peter-peter,* on a branch above her, was nervous. "Oh brother. Now what?" asked Emmy. She had to choose. A moment of mother's grief grazed her breast; but she couldn't just abandon the babies to the serpent, although this was nature's way. The mother could not help these tiny featherless birds. Emmy didn't want to leave them to be devoured, even by a creature as beautiful as the snake. "You're lucky I came along when I did," she whispered as she offered condolences, with survival. She was only half Crow, the half that did not eat baby birds. Again, she was thinking about the girl. Emmy couldn't remember if she had given her something to eat and wondered why she didn't hear her call out. Had she become voiceless like herself? She looked at the snake, still not far, not wanting to give up an easy meal.

She was reminded of the Houma tale of the creation of the world. There was a snake in the story, like in *Genesis*, in *The Bible*. And again, the snake knew it all. "Mamere," she said, "here is a story for you. Papa told it to me.

God created man and woman, alike, from the earth. He held them in his hands and blew into each one the breath of life. He then picked up a snake, and broke it in half. He took the half with the tail and presenting injured end of the snake faced outward; stuck it on the man. He took the half with the head, and stuck it deep inside the woman, all the way to the head; where it could peer out of her eye sockets. Each one of God's creations went on with his part of God's work to make his way in the world and to unite with the other. The woman seeing; the man blind, vibrating his seeing- eye cane; trying to find the woman who could show him the light."

"Ha," said Mamere. "There is somethin' I don't get. Why would the woman who had eyes to see, want to find the man; unless it is just a story about a snake lookin' to make itself whole? *Pschaw.*

That ain't creation. That's fixation, or no, that is reparation. Oh, you know what I mean," she added with frustration. "Anyway, if a cicada can talk a Cajun into eatin' a crawfish, in exchange for a song, why can't a snake talk God into using something else for a...?" Her voice petered out. Mamere had been married for forty years and had raised four children. "I prefer *Genesis*," she said all of the sudden without finishing her sentence. She had thought of saying *pecker*, but then thought that the mere mention of sex or contributing to *Bible* variations, might get her into trouble. "Now I'm gonna have to serve more time here in Emmy's trees." She sighed. This time she couldn't just fade away.

"But Mamere," Emmy insisted, "maybe the woman couldn't see without the snake's eyes? Isn't that about the knowledge that God didn't want them to have in *The Bible*. Here it is like he wants her to see." Her father had not been clear on this point when they had talked about the story, and Emmy did not know the answer.

"It's just a story. If you cain't respect the content, you might as well make up one that has apples with ribs." Mamere said, fading into the turquoise with her guitar.

Emmy walked back to her truck and went home. She decided that early the next day, once the crow funeral was finished, she would return. She might bring the girl, if she was awake. Emmy couldn't remember if she had given her something to eat. "Did I say something about it in my last letter to Jeremy?" She decided to rebuild her mother's treehouse and found her father's old tool bag.

She remembered watching him cut and measure boards, using a carpenter's pencil, a metal triangle, and a measuring tape. The memory did not bring sadness. Repeating these gestures was a way for her to feel closer to him and to appease some of the feelings of loss she had never been able to quiet. She loaded her truck with the boards she had stacked, with shims of wood between each one to let the air circulate so they would not rot.

A wasp had built its nest on the underside of one of the boards and she had not seen it. They rushed out in a sudden flight to punish the culprit who had upset them. Backing off without an argument, feeling lucky to have avoided a sting, she thought to herself, "these boards are gonna have to wait until later when those angry critters answer present to a roll call. I've got a can of liquid *Death* and I might just invite all those present to end their future then and there." But for the time being, they had managed to alter her projects and make her think of her mother's way of speaking. "You can't always get what you want", she decided. "But if you try sometime..." she continued, imitating Mick Jagger, trying to chase the thought of her mother's rotting away in prison.

She surprised one of the wasps, catching it in the air by the wings. She blew on it and set it down on the board. It wiped its antennas with its feet, before flying back to the nest. The sun shone through its cellophane-like wings and cast a colored shadow with tiny lines. Wasp whispering was a trick she had learned watching her father. "If you can murmur secrets like that to them all, you wouldn't need the bug killer," he said.

Some of the boards were already pulled away from the pile. Measuring the longest boards and the two-by-fours scavenged from her camp, and a few she had managed to gather from a dump site, Emmy began to work, using her father's sawhorses. First, she cut the two-by-fours for the frame, removing any burned or insect or parts damaged by fungi. Although she thought she could figure out how to use a circular saw, she didn't have the money to buy one. "Besides, its scream cain't be a part of any musical arrangement worth playin'." Large circles of sweat formed under her arms as the sun rose high overhead. She cut the boards to length then, one by one, and carried them to her truck. Mamere was standing there, ready to direct the whole operation. "Why didn't you cut them on a tree stump when you got to the forest? You got a sunburn now." Emmy looked at her arms. At least she had her Sportsman Paradise baseball cap. "It wasn't that hot when I started," she explained. She hadn't yet realized that it does no good to rationalize your behavior when you are wrong.

Emmy sighed. She began to load the cut boards onto the truck bed. "Are you going to bother me all day?" she turned to ask her grandmother, but she had gone off on another mission.

Later that day, just at sundown, once the wasps lay all in a heap at the end of the stream of insecticide, Emmy loaded the remaining boards. She decided she would cut these as required, as she progressed on the treehouse. She gathered her tools and the rest of the things she needed.

Early in the morning, before returning to the forest, she rummaged in her kitchen cupboard to find a bag of peanuts to share with the crows. They weren't always around, or didn't want to come, but now that the baby birds had left the nest, she could share these little tidbits with them, and that would be enough.

The grass was slick with the morning dew and so was the canvas army tarp over the boards in her truck. It was already hot. By the time she got to the treehouse, both would be dry, but she thought a thundershower might be headed her way by the looks of sky. She found some small pieces of rope to tie the tarp to the tree. She would make a sort of tent over the branches, as much to keep herself dry as the boards. If there was lightening, she would get back to her truck.

As she turned onto the Lake Road away from Ferriday and towards her plot of land near the Mississippi, she noticed a car with one of the men she thought she had seen in the barbershop, parked in the John Deere parking lot. She turned her eyes away as soon as she recognized him, hoping he had not recognized her.

When she arrived at the site for the treehouse, Emmy unloaded the boards, one by one, and attached the tarp over a limb. She sat down on the soft earth against the old oak. The birds weren't around. She tried calling them, but there was no answer. While she rested, she ate the peanuts for lunch, and leaning against the tree, began to sing and hum a Hoagy Carmichael song, changing the words where the lyrics spoke of love.

Up a lazy river by the old possum run

...

Dream a dream with me.
...

Blue skies up above, I'm not in love
...

Under the trees, her voice almost wore the same pastel shades her grandmother had carried when she would say her songs with just a few notes to hold the melody.

Carmichael's voice didn't do much more for the harmony other than to carry something in his voice that Emmy thought was lost in her own. His was the warm tonality shared by musicians as they tune their instruments or joke between sessions. But it was also the way friends spoke over a shared meal, as well as the timbre used by kind adults when they meet a child for the first time. Gone. All gone. Most of the time, she thought she sounded like a radio without a station; she frizzled and sputtered when she tried to talk. Perhaps the nervousness from social pressure was what kept her now from talking. Emmy didn't know. She thought her voice had frightened the girl and that is why she never called out. She still hadn't figured out what to do. "How many days had gone by since they girl got into my truck?"

She didn't know either that her mother had once thought of ending her life there, using the branches of this very tree. Mérite- Lajoie had taken a rope, pleaded for mercy, and swore she was against the death penalty; before turning herself in to meet the judgment of men. Under the cathedral oak, the peat moss, a layered graveyard of millions of fallen creatures was as thick as her mother's agony. White mycelium arms reached through the top layer of leaves; waiting. To the humus, one more body would not have made a difference. It didn't care what people did, or why they did, if their deaths were timely, fair, or horrific. "Animals could mourn their dead," thought Emmy. "But eternal life exists only for people because only people can imagine it. Maybe only imagination is eternal, whatever eternity mean; our imaginations float about like heavenly bodies in the universe, bumping into one another, requesting *pardon* for our wanderings and our misdeeds."

The Hog's Den

Had she not been a child of the river, had she not heard the fallen Fs and tell-tale Ks with accents so thick you could cut them with a knife; squatting under the bushes, she might have taken these men for foreigners. Their liquored voices and the whir of their trucks were set at odds against the snoring Mississippi. It wasn't April, yet the river was backing up like a cesspool in August. Still, there was the undertow. With the debris, eddies flushed the smells of the sludge. Churning waters were something she knew how to negotiate; at least better than she knew how to deal with the men in the trucks. "Well, I've got 'n idea about who done it. Fuck 'im. He's boss of da dollas. I'm done wit' waitin' on s'planations. He's 'bout ready for his last 'prise. I say, let's fuckin' string 'im up. Rover gone too far. Lit' Jeremy is right. Ross, will you cover for us?"

"You know he got us all by da balls. We all touched dem explosivesss at the Fish Fry," replied a slithery voice. "You can say yore prayersss to Rossss, but he ain't here to hep usss no more."

She eased the boat out into the night. She had heard them, but she would get away this time. *Tshtke-Ehhhhh-ou. Tshtke-Ehhhhh-ou. T shtke-Ehhhhh-ou. Crzzzzzzzzhh Crzzzzzzzzhh Chrzzzzzaahhh.* The forest edged in with the moon litigation. The insects rubbed each other's backs like politicians. *Crzzzzzzzzhh Crzzzzzzzzhh Chrzzzzzaahhh Aaahhh Aaahhh Aaahhh.* The sleepy bank grumbled with its tangle of kudzu hair, bending overhead for a nighttime wash. Along the shoreline, Emmy let her boat drift towards the mouth of Saint Catherine Creek. *Sui sisi sui isi sui sisi.* She could hear the tree frogs calling out to their friends. When an intruder approached, their silence was a judge of character on all sides. There wasn't a whistleblower among them.

She had escaped the men with their pumped-up trucks, as their party of six, talked about Rover and Harper's kid. "Oh yeah! His name is Jeremy!" She remembered now, exclaiming to herself. "Once I get home..." She glided along the bank. "Toc-a-toc-a-toca- ta. Toc-a-toc-a-toc-a-toc, diiing," went the typewriter without the instrument. She had two or three hours to compose a Requiem in her mind. She wondered what side of Hell they would wake up on.

Emmy let her boat glide on the Mississippi, avoiding as much as she could the clacking of her paddle on the surface, or on the trees. News travels fast over water. Cypress trees extend their arms low and rake their red nails against the bodies of all who pass too close to the bank. Like tall, cramped adolescents with peeling, sunburned skin, their wooden knees bump against the aluminum sides and bottoms of fragile boats; stirring emotions along with the algae.

She cast her eyes ahead, listening to the rest of Bach's *Sonata Solo number 1 in G Minor*, with memory's ear. The *adagio* began with the sound of metal on metal, warning her from a distance. The bow of the interpreter, transcending obstacles, delivered the rest.

Near the protected landing, a tugboat parked its barges. Two men got to shore on a skiff, headed in someone's car to Miss Milly's bordello. Why else would they stop there?

While the last notes of the *presto* raced through her mind, Emmy waited; her heart beating with each stroke, standing in the shadowed water, pulling her boat close against the shore. When they were gone, she got back into her boat and paddled to the landing. She would hide it there and come back for it in a few days.

Bach had again improvised a song in her heart, appeasing her strife. Would he play *King Porter's Stomp* in a jazz arrangement if he were alive today? His music washed the remaining metallic echoes from her mind with a clarinet's swing. Then she remembered that in a way, Bach had entered the twentieth century top-ten in a more recent manner with his *Suite Number 3, BWV 1068* and his organ melody, *BWV 40*, « Choral du Veilleur ». Procol Harum had gotten it right. So had Percy Sledge. Admitting this inspiration had not hurt his sales one bit. People seemed to cherish links shared with others from the past. It gave them foundation; firm ground to stand on. She pulled her boat out of the water and, pulling some weeds over it, tied it to a cypress tree so a ruffle in the river would not sweep it back into its stream.

About a week later, back in Ferriday, she heard a slimy voice; one she had heard in Natchez, Under-the-Hill, and that had made her forget why she had put her boat into the water. She put a face to Bill Hogden, who was smoking and talking with a stranger in Bubba's Barber Shop. She was on her way in. He was on his way out. Twice a week, she cleaned the ladies' area of the shop, on the days the barber's wife did her business elsewhere. The men were used to seeing her gaunt frame. Emmy couldn't talk, but she still had an acute musician's ear. About the same time her mother was put in prison, she remembered hearing her grandmother speak of the kidnapping of Joseph Edouard. "The whole area is a Godforsaken. Why did you come back?" asked Mamere from the shampoo station where Emmy washed the basins. "You're bound to have questions. What I can tell you is that *The Concordia Post* had some speculations about them civil rights' workers in Mississippi back in nineteen sixty-four, I think it was. They disappeared. All three of 'em. In the paper, they said they was safe in a hideout somewhere in *their communist Cuba. Mon Dieu!* People say whatever suits 'em. They didn't know or didn't care. Else they knew and didn't want it to be known." Barbershop rumor had it that there was a connection between that case and the Edouard's disappearance.

"Hogden, you know's as well as I, dat locals believe drug addicts and radicals got dem boys workin for the NAACP in Mississippi. All ya gotta do is keep yore head low when it comes to talkin' 'bout Edouard. It's been over ten years." Hogden indicated the direction of the back of the shop with his head. "Nah," said the barber, looking out over his glasses towards Emmy, as he held up a row of black hair with a comb. "She's deaf and dumb. Helps out with the wife's business. Cleanin' and dat sort of shit."

It is a common idea that hair styling businesses are a place of female prattle pride; but, just like every other old adage about a woman's place, gossip ignores the boundaries of gender, but not the boundaries of truth. She remembered her childhood confusion about many overheard conversations. "But this time, maybe it was true?" she thought.

"Yeah, well he had it comin' to him," said Hogden. "He was messin' around wit' some of our women folk and we couldn't let dat get out of hand. It'd be an assault on our reputation, ya understand." It was an answer more than a question. "Evolution'd gone backwardsss if we'd let it happen." Now, Emmy wondered if the man had a misunderstanding about science, or if he just wanted to protect himself from the truth, the one she would mention in her next letter.

Joseph Edouard was a Black man who had lived in Clayton with his family. She and Bee had seen him a couple of times visiting Jim, the former Cotton Gin guardian, when they were girls. He had a wide smile. According to Bee's mother, Edouard joked around with the nurses at the hospital while he was being treated for flash-burns he got at work. She told us to steer clear of him, but not because he might harm us. She was trying to keep him out of trouble.

Bill Hogden, a sheriff's deputy, the same who botched evidence in the White case, and one to throw his weight around (along with his s's), was not the kind to appreciate colored friendliness towards White women. He was like the gluttonous troll under the bridge who wanted the turf all for himself, and would fight anyone to secure it. Bee's mother knew what these men could do to any of them if they had heard of Skizzum's talking to a Black boy.

The men in the shop began to talk about World War II as she swept. Hogden continued, this time berating imagined supporters of Israel, rewriting history with denial. "Y'all know da Polish prison thing was all a hoax.

The Germans didn't gas dem Jews. *Psshaw.* Ducal said we's all foolish to believe dat bullshit. He's right. Deys all been kilt by de communists before the Krauts got there. The problem is, it seem like he brought us the FBI the last time he came and it don't seem like they's leavin' real soon." Hogden didn't seem to like anyone. Emmy wondered who the Ducal fellow was.

Once home, Emmy crushed a caterpillar with her fingers, adding a drop of water, and fed the goo to the little birds on a Popsicle stick she had splintered. One of the babies had died the first night, from dehydration, she presumed. The other two would live, and now had downy feathers, a week after she found their nest. They looked at her with their scraggly crowns, their old-men frowns, and their long, nosy beaks, until she got close with the feeder. Then their *Commedia dell'arte* masks lifted, as if part of the act, opening wide to peep out funny *lazzi* in exchange for a meal. They struggled to get on top of one another to be first. "You must be kiddin', Horace? I only fed you fifteen minutes ago. Give Isabelle a chance! *Hmmff.* There you go," she whispered, smiling as if they could understand. She fed each one until the dead insect's metamorphosis was complete. Now it was no longer a bug, but part of a bird. The tiny titmice were thriving.

Washing and drying her hands she sighed and sat down at the piano. She had wanted to have it tuned, but the water from the flood had warped the soundboard, and the man, the piano tuner from the Association of Blind Piano Tuners, said it was useless. Many of the notes came out flat, or without sound, like her voice. Emmy played more of Bach, this time using the wood of her ruined instrument. She was afraid of losing her hand, along with her voice. On her grandmother's side, there had been many circus musicians who had to play with precision to the dangerous step of the high-wire walkers. A false note could mean a fatal step. Mamere had sold her treasured harp to get them through the hard times after the flood. Where Emmy had once plucked both classical and Cajun tunes from the brass strings, she then tapped on the wooden rails of the houseboat. Music rang out in her ears and in her soul. In the Atchafalaya Basin, she had memorized a *Concerto* in the key of D minor; if you could talk about a key, when these were only etched on with a pencil and had to be redrawn every day. Other than her private internal concerts, nowadays, her only other music came from a radio in her office. Most of the time, she could get two stations, the one in Ferriday, and the other in Monroe. On good days, she got Natchez and Alexandria as well. The frequencies didn't seem affected by distance, but to float on wind; just like trouble.

Fire

"Most poisons are bitter. Is it the same with poison pen letters, even when these are not written by hand?" Emmy pondered as she cut out the words and letters from her magazines. It was easy enough to find words like *hog* or *flag, color,* or even, *wife,* from her mother's old almanacs. But most words she had to spell out, and glue, letter by letter. She didn't want to use her typewriter and be reminded of her interference every time she started to write a page of her novel. Her epistle would take time.

When she finished, she read:

To the Hog den mother fucker, who flags down drivers and truckers. He sucked Technicolor, from an alley bowl bucker. His wife now stares with a pucker.

The letter was vague, with notions about something that happened near the bowling alley. She didn't know much about what really happened, but she knew the lack of clarity in her poem would send him into a more than imaginary rage at any rate. At midnight, she had finished. She thought about how she would get it to Hogden. The Post-Office was the easiest solution. A mailbox was safer. But she wanted Hogden's friends to read it first for a full effect. Seeing the citation, their sacrosanct homophobic feathers would ruffle and their racist tongues would flap. Hogden's would coil back and strike. No one could call him a queer. He would never be ready to accept that alliance, deep within himself where lovers were bound to fantasy, and by a pact of silence. "You boys know I hate the sodomites as much as I hate them niggers," he said. Then, the bowling alley reference

146

would start its short-legged race around the track. By the end of a week, perhaps two, he would find his target. She hoped it would be Rover, but she didn't know the name of the man she had seen talking to Hogden and the barber. This wasn't a game she was playing. She knew that; but sometimes she felt lost in whatever it was she was doing. Setting the future in motion, as Skizzum did, did not mean she could predict the outcome. However, some things are foreseeable.

Emmy went into her shed and found her father's old bike. He had taken to riding it after his first heart attack and it had hung from the shed's ceiling for more than a decade. She changed the tires months ago and now, set out to deliver her letter. "Crossing the tracks near the old train station is too risky. There might be someone at the grain elevator. I'll go the long way." Glad that the neighbor's old toothless wonder-dog was no longer of this world, she rode down Iowa Street to the tracks. Pushing the bike over the tracks, far from the station, she continued to walk it behind the swimming pool and the trade school where Bee's grandfather had taught welding to Harper's son. All that was closed. The welders went forth with their torches to light up the world or to dim it down. It looked like Ferriday's citizens turned to other resources now. They didn't want to swim with Blacks and didn't want to teach them trades either. When she got to the Public Library, she brought her bike out to the street. From there she maneuvered it towards Virginia Avenue on Third Street, where she crossed the Clayton Highway, or Fourth Street, checking out her next hideout. There were almost no cars. She continued down Fifth, until she got to the armpit of the King Hotel.

Her skin raged like burnt glass as she hid with her bike behind a neighboring trash bin when the hotel's bouncer took out the night's trash. There weren't many trees in that part of the alley for cover. When the passageway was again quiet, she removed the envelope and latex gloves from her knapsack, and wearing these, she ran to the door and taped the open letter. She then grabbed her bike and was off down the block, away from the highway, away from the Hog's den.

As with her boat, she could not take her bike home right away. Biking, or walking alone at night in Ferriday was a free ticket for places like Orville's Lounge, where a young woman could be held a long time against her free will. Emmy hoped to keep her clothes and to travel unheard and unseen. One of her childhood schoolmates had an empty water cistern next to his mother's house that, as a child, they used as a fort. It stood there, on rust-colored stilts, but she had to take a chance. She would be safe there for the night. Old Mrs. Johnson wouldn't know she had been in her yard. It was easy for her to let herself in and out of the back gate, climb on to the edge of the roof from the pink mimosa, before scooting over to the cistern's cover. She pried loose the gunk fallen from the surrounding pecan trees, and slid back the metal cover.

Now a grown woman, tall like her mother, it was easier for her to lower herself inside. She didn't need the crate that was there for the kids. There was also a mattress, and blankets, and pillows in a plastic bag. There was even a Monopoly game board. Emmy opened the box and flattened the game-board. She looked at the pawns, as well as the regrets, arranged in the slots like dollar bills. The next generation of children must come here to share their secrets and play. *"Mon Dieu*! Good grief, Emmy," complained Mamere sitting on the bench in the corner of her mind's eye. "When will you leave well enough alone? Haven't you figured out that no Dufrene or Robichaux could ever own Boardwalk property? No Cajun could. You're becomin' more and more like your mother. She wanted to have a casino on the lake. You know where that got her." She thought again about Jeremy and the games his father had taught him. Did her grandmother never question these? She remembered her watching everything and doing nothing until the day of the flood. Then she did save their lives and a few of their belongings, only to continue unmaking her soul, at least, according to her. "Why do I keep undoing myself?" she would ask, as if she thought she could unravel like a piece of cloth.

In the early morning hours, Emmy drifted off to sleep. She dreamed she woke up on a mattress at the shopping mall in Natchez. She had been talking to a dark man the day before, and the next thing she knew, she was waking up on the floor with the stores opening. Feeling embarrassed to be sleeping on the floor in the mall; she thought she recognized the man, hurrying away. She wasn't sure where she had seen him before. Realizing that her clothes were strewn all around, her first thought was that she had been drugged and raped. She began to toss and turn, whimpering in her sleep, trying to shake off the imagined drugs and run away. Then she sat up and noticed that her purse was gone. There was something in a small paper bag on the floor next to the makeshift bed that looked like a school lunch. It was heavy, as if there was a treasure inside instead of a po'boy, but she did not open the bag. Had she been robbed, and the man had he left her loose change? She was puzzled, and looked around frantically for answers. The shoppers were indifferent; as if she wasn't there. Then she looked inside the bag and found many keys. Now awake, she stirred.

It was mid-day when, like a motherless baby bird watching out for predators, she poked her head out of her nest. No one was stirring, above, or below. Her grandmother had gone back to her resting place. The dream-maker had followed. Emmy faced the empty lot where a house had burned the same year as the Frank Norris shoe shop fire. One was an accident. A little boy, the age of one of Bee's brothers at the time, got up at night and played with old birthday candles, returning them once more to life on the stove's pilot light. Its charred hull had been hauled off and renovated near Horseshoe Lake. No one had been hurt, not even the caged parakeet. The father had been able to return inside to retrieve the bird while one of his little girls, old enough to realize the danger, teared up outside. She stood with her family, all in their underwear, in front of the whole town, terrorized and shameful. The other fire, two or three blocks south, was ignited by the dealings with the Devil. The Ku Klux Klan. A man had been forced back inside to die from its flames, and a bulldozer took care of the remaining hull. No witness came forward. Ferriday wanted to forget. Frank, in his four-day ordeal of suffering, refused to reveal the name of his assailants to any of his friends, to the medical core, to his preacher, to the police officers, and to the FBI. A White deputy stood guard.

Emmy had known Frank. He took their shoes, putting his nose to the toe before rotating each one, his eye close, examining it for injury, from front to back, and from back to front. From repairing belts and bags, to sewing new soles on soulful boots, Frank understood both human and animal hides, except when his philosophy failed to drive his gaze deeper than the surface. Even when nothing was left of his shop, but the crisp match that started it; even when his own skin bubbled, flaked, and peeled; even when the bones in his hand came forth to point at no one; he told his best friend on his death-bed, "I just can't believe it."

Emmy was learning, piece-by-piece, where her disbelief had taken her. What had Frank not believed? The Lord Jesus Sensational Star-lights sang every week, "Everywhere I Go" and the Bradley Singers sang, "He'll Roll Back Those Dark Clouds," on the gospel show Frank had hosted on the local radio. Was it his faith in God that had forged his disbelief in the evil doings of man?

Hypnotized that day by the flames dancing a Lindy hop between the eighty-eight black and white piano keys, Emmy reflected back on the church that had burned around her until an unknown hand had forced her outside. For many years, she focused on that surreal memory; until Skizzum queried, "who pulled you from the fire?" She remembered then; someone had saved her. That fire too, had been evil in the making. The death dealing with that blaze ended with Harper's dog. She remembered him barking, then a garbled yelp. "Someone had stopped him, and for good. Was I chosen over the dog?" Emmy's beliefs had started crumbling with the events leading up to the fire, or had they? "Why didn't

Frank believe? Why would anyone local want such a kind man dead? What kind of hatred, what kind of greed, would inflict destruction upon a shoe repair shop? Had someone wanted that property for themselves?" Ferriday was a small town, not a big city where would-be landlords struggled to outbid one another. Had Frank wondered when he would awaken from his nightmare? When would they all wake up? "Frank Norris surely understood what it meant to be Black in Ferriday, Louisiana in 1964. Why hadn't someone saved him? What had he missed?" She thought about the keys from her dream. Keys to unlock doors. Doors to unlock dreams. Dreams to unlock souls.

Before she had had the burned-out church removed from her property, she had walked on the ten-inch soot and broken glass. Even after the flood, even after the years of neglect and waterlog, even after mice, raccoons, and mold had run amuck, the odor of burnt wood, and more; the acrid smell of the giant melted plastic Jesus and the charred bones of the piano had invaded her nostrils as she had gained entry and stood on the hellish pomace. Was her tormenter leaving a final clue as to his inner core? She was trying to unravel beliefs along with early sixties crimes. Was there some connection between the three fires? Was there some intrinsic evil lurking in the area? Are people just mean? Although in the late seventies, when the hate crimes against Black people seemed to be in the past; most of the perpetuators had never been punished. Yet they had all left clues as to the layer of corrupted pulp that lay beneath their skins.

Too much hot air

"There he was, sprawled out on the asphalt, on Highway 65, with two sheriff's deputies holding him down, attaching handcuffs, as if he was a criminal. 'We got him,' they said, pulling him up. They pushed him into the white Oldsmobile with the red flashing light on the dashboard, and he was never seen again." The young employee of the Dixie Lane Bowling Alley served Emmy a coke and looked both ways to see if his manager was around, before continuing. "I wasn't there, but this is what my boss said when he heard that Joseph Edouard went missing. He said that Edouard had been talking to Sonny Boyton, a Klan member's son that hangs out here. Can you believe it?" There it was again, the shard of disbelief. Emmy flicked her cigarette. It was mostly a prop. Her lack of voice gave others the sentiment of trustworthiness, and, encouraged them to share their secrets. But she still needed to contain her nerves and alone, sometimes used her fingers to wave air for that purpose.

"How much did Sonny know of his father's dealings at the time," she wondered. "Had he been given a silver dollar like the others of the Silver Dollar Group? Harper and the old man hung out with Rover at the Four-leaf Hotel where Edouard had worked. That's where the Silver Dollar Group had its infamous beginnings. This branch of the Klan would have attacked her family, had they known of their racial mix. Interracial marriage scared the Dickens out of them, and some of the Shakespeare, too; if they had either. Still, there had been other rumors. Joseph Edouard had not only flirted with nurses; he had said a young receptionist at the hotel where he worked was smitten with him. As with similar slippery-soap-tales between Whites, how much of this was true was hard to say. His relationship with a White woman discovered, she would never be the one to take the heat. This wasn't, *As the World Turns*. Other than sports, Hogden and his hangmen didn't care about television anyway. They would kill a Black man if he sneezed in the wrong place. "Mr. Edouard's friends warned him to stay away from White women. He bragged about spinnin' in a Ferris wheel, *kissin' a Missis*. He didn't know stickin' his lip out would send him on a twirl with a rope," said Sonny Boyton.

As she walked out of the bowling alley, turning her head, she could see the road where a white-over-green Buick four-door sedan had been parked by his kidnappers more than a decade ago. Had he heard the bowling balls as these were dropped down to the alleys, rolled along the smooth parquet, and knocked into the pins as they forced him into their car? Once you have heard these, you never forget their, *k-klunk k-klunk k-klunk....roc-roc-roc rocollollrollollolloll*, sometimes speeding into an all-at-once boom of a strike, applauding pins clattering away; the opposite of a musical venue. Did Joseph Edouard know he was going to be hit? How acute the senses become when the body knows, before the mind; that it is about to be martyrized. She thought of the body of Ben Whitney, another KKK victim, an old man, riddled with bullets and his shotgun blown-apart-head. Emmy wondered if that had been Edouard's fate, or if his had been worse, as this bowling alley braggadocio explained, that he had been caught, hung upside down and skinned, like a squirrel; his body thrown into a lake, and his skin, on a Hogden's wall.

The hot-air artist, wiping down the counter only a half hour ago, following bowling balls with his eyes, jutting his head in and out as he waited on a customer, pretended he knew. But did he? Emmy needed to be sure, sure enough of the details of the crimes to make the Klan wonder more than ten years later, if they had been exposed by one of their own members. Some men could be led to confession by lies or rumor, if these resembled the truth. The barman's interpretations were the workings of ordinary men, and did not always lean towards horror. Emmy wondered what pleasure could there be in repeating such tales when the stories did fall on the side of terror. Was their ornamentation of hideousness a way to deal with disbelief?

The leather strap

More specific details had to go into her letters. Emmy was thinking about Hogden. He was by now getting antsy and you could see him peacocking around town, rolling his shoulders, twisting his neck, acting like a strongman when he and his friends were afraid of the pieces of paper that might be slipped into the ballot box. Ross was dead and could no longer protect them. Hogden wanted out with a pension. The little birds were crying for their breakfast. They were almost ready to fly. They competed for life in a way that the Silver Dollar Group never would. "Not a single one of these men ever got a death penalty. They believe in it for others. Oh yeah. They did not get life in prison. They continue to foment their belief in White supremacy, and they kill. The deaths were all official. The others get classed as disappearances. And there were a lot of Black men who never found their way back home in the sixties," she concluded.

Emmy prepared her letter with the thoughtfulness of a woman in love.

We know what ya did with dat leather strap to dem Black boys in the jail. You thought if you handed Harris over to yore partner, you'd get off da hook. We took care of Ross and now we're comin' for ya.

Hogden read the letter. He started to tear it up, but on second thought, put it in his pocket and headed over to King Hotel. "Where'sss Farlow," he asked the barman. The younger man shrugged. Although the Klan still held informal meetings there, the generation had changed.

"You can't count on nobody no more," he lamented. He started over to one of the rooms. "Hey, you can't go in there; you know the rules. No one in or out during a card game. Strict orders from the boss."

"Well he ain't bosssin' me. Not today, not any day," Hodgen boasted, kicking the door open.

"Hey," said someone in the room. The men all looked towards the door. "I gotta to talk to Farlow," Hogden replied, fixing his prey. "You little bitch. After all thesse yearsss, you done talk to the FBI?" The sentence had the tonality of a question, but the answer was already tingling in Hogden's mind.

He took Farlow by the neck and shook him like a hound with a squirrel. He looked at Rowen, who had participated in the beating too. "You wasss there too. What'cha gotta say about it?"

Hogden pulled Farlow up by the collar. "What the fuck is you talkin' about? We gotta card game goin' on here. We're all friends, as ya can see. Sit down and have a drink with us," said a man they called Blackie, a common nickname for anyone with black hair, as much a vaudevillian as a villain, and absentee voter-card collector.

"I know all about your card games. I was in thisss businesss well before you. Now shut the fuck up."

Farlow was a nervous, medium-built fellow with light brown hair, sporting a thick mustache. He was glancing around the room, thinking about shaking loose and rushing towards the door. His mind flashed back to when he worked for the Sheriff's office. When he wasn't filling out ballots with the sheriff and Blackie Cain, he and four other police officers had whipped Black prisoners into confession. "You talkin' 'bout them three niggers? Them boys who stole them undershirts and got 'bout seven years in Angola State Prison? "For the last one", he remembered, "threats of death were enough to make his black skin shiver. He got only three years." Three years in one of America's worst prisons. They were all promised that the next time, they would leave the courthouse two feet in front. "Hell Hogden, everybody knows we beat dem niggers. Nobody gonna talk. You know there was more than dat. 'Specially when Slaughter had 'em in da Ferriday jail."

Emmy had heard details about the beatings from Hiram's mother. In those days the older woman had been the Concordia Courthouse cleaning lady and had heard many things. Emmy also remembered what the Presbyterian preacher's son had told her at school. He said a man they called the Butcher told his father, "People in this town don't want no niggers votin'."

"Yeah, well I already heard some shit from Jeremy, come in from da paper mill, talkin' about the Edouard thing. I've about had enough of you assholesss blabbin' off thingsss you don't know about. Somebody talkin' to the FBI. You know it ain't Slaughter, he jest got out of jail. They caught him with thumb cuffsss, strap, and prod. But he didn't talk. Ain't Rosss either. He'sss dead. Both served time and didn't tell no one nutin'. Y'all turned communist or what! It's dat damn governor. He got y'all all by da ballsss." Hogden was yelling, slathering out the s's, trying to hold on to Farlow who was kicking and pulling away. Blackie Cain stood up and said to Farlow, as part of his usual act, "A fish never git caught if it keeps its damn mouth shut."

"It's dat Boyton kid I tell ya. Got nutin' to do wit' us," Farlow pleaded.

"Yeah," said Rowen. "He talks about Edouard to anybody who will listen, even niggers."

Rowen got up to help Farlow. Farlow tried to grab Hogden's gun, while Cain and another man got up and grabbed Hogden by both arms. He shook them off with his fury. Hogden pulled his gun and, with Farlow's hand on the barrel, Hogden shot him straight through the neck. He fell to the floor. Before wide-open, bloodshot eyes, new roses bloomed on new carpet. Hogden was as surprised as any of them.

Emmy read: "Brawl in local bar leaves carpet ruined and one man, dead." The article followed: "Sheriff Deputy Stan Hogden kills a local man in a struggle at King Hotel. It was reported that the man, Ferriday resident, George Farlow, barged into a private meeting at the hotel on Friday, and, shouting incomprehensible phrases, argued with Deputy Hogden, who tried to escort him outside. In an inebriated state, he then reached for the officer's gun and was accidentally shot. After a short investigation, it was determined that Hogden was trying to recover the weapon from a drunk and threatening Farlow, who was bothering guest, David Ducal. King Hotel manager, Doug Knight, who was not a witness, says the carpet had just been replaced." Emmy suspected that the reported incident got only the names and carpet stains right. The rest of the article was like a Ross re-election; composed of two versions of voters, either coerced or dead. Of course, the news story kicked off a new round of debate for chatter and local lip service, both in and out of the hotel.

A diabolical fug of foul

Fresh spring briars were tickling the small windows of the trailer, and the rank of the black mold soured her mouth and nose with a diabolical fug of foul. If criminal rot would not deter her query, why would the inevitable toll of nature's putrefaction? She was a soldier of her own misery. She thought that as a child of Louisiana, she could rise above the decay the way a phoenix could rise from its ashes. "Why can't you leave death buried?" asked her grandmother, peeking out from the trailer's living room. Emmy waved thoughts of her away.

She chuckled over her last letter, pulling her make-shift scarf close, thinking of Hogden's friends, and then, of the culprit himself. As she read the old copies of the local newspapers, Emmy's bravery and mirth changed to horror and then to outrage as she faced the truth inscribed there. Tears ran down her cheeks as she read of Frank Norris' last moments, of his scorched flesh, his skin, burned white, and peeling off in shreds as he somehow made his way alone into the emergency room of the Concordia Parish Hospital, leaving bloody footprints on the pavement. The cruelty of the world hit harder than fear of the men who committed the Devil's acts. From compassion, there was strength. From the ferocity of the men who had murdered him, she would learn to be careful, and cunning. Emmy folded the papers and put them on top of the old fridge. She had had enough of it all for one day.

In the middle of the night, Emmy sat in her bed, shaking, not as wretched as Joseph Edouard had been when the white Oldsmobile had pulled him over, and nothing like poor Frank Norris, but still, she panicked. Her words caught in her throat that squeezed shut and snared her scream. She panicked, as she thought she caught glimpse of Harper in the corner. Outside, a lovesick cat moaned. The noise sounded like a police car siren. The weapon of local fertility control screamed as it whirred past her window, but there was no light flashing on the animal's head.

On such mornings when trauma sloshed in, filling her stomach instead of breakfast, she feared she had brought about the death of someone who had not deserved it; someone she had not wished it upon. But wishes could not kill. Her hand could not deal this card. Nevertheless, death's hand was never enough full, and how numbers were drawn was not random. She had spoken to a Louisiana State University student about the Klan. She considered it was a mistake and didn't want to think of it again. "It's hard to know who to trust," she thought. And who would find the right path to take to protect people from the Klan," she mumbled to herself.

Pierre was Skizzum's and Bee's younger brother. Emmy had seen him on a few occasions in Ferriday with his wife and had visited them in Baton Rouge. Did they understand better than she why Frank would not talk? Had he been thinking that the truth could hurt someone else? Or was there a loophole in the contract between truth and belief? Her own fright poised over her like a bird of prey using its shadow to oust a field mouse. She thought of being outside, naked and shameful, having just escaped with one's life. Perhaps there was some secret passage between trauma and humiliation. Why hadn't Frank, or even herself, taken that way out, if it existed? Neither could believe what happened really did happen; not before, not during, and especially not after it had come about. The fire, the injury, was more than real. It was unreal. It was belief undone, by any account.

It was several minutes at least, before she could make herself run to the bathroom, hop into the shower, and force some breakfast down. The lump of milk and cereal shuddered in her throat as it descended to her stomach. She could have counted each ring of her esophagus, had she been so inclined. The process was painful. But today, she wanted to focus outwards, on something else besides body functions. She was trying to shake off her fears and work up the nerve to drive to Baton Rouge to see her friends again. Mistrust? Judgment? She had to make sure that they would keep the information under their hats. And she could not call them to ask for an invitation. She opened the bedroom closet. Anxiety again invaded her nostrils with the smell of mildew, old sweat, and mothballs.

There were her mother's clothes still staring back at her. She could not bring herself to send these to a church or someplace where old clothing was collected. Her grandmother had always been on her ass for wearing her mother's clothes, unless she had better things to tend to. "Wear that and you will get in trouble". She had many superstitions. Now she was gone and Emmy was alone. No one would scold her now, she was thinking. Why had she thought about it in the first place? Was Mamere right? Did she have trouble burying the past?

Her pitiful body peered back at her from the mirror, holding her mother's last pair of jeans with a badly sewn seam in front of her to mask what she had become. Gone was her baby-like skin and angelic beauty. Her distinctive long, thick, shiny black hair had thinned and dulled. The smoldering fire within her now had burned the sheen away, at least two or three times. "Ashes now," she murmured. The spark still flickered in her northern eyes. She had to go through with her plans. She felt she didn't have any choice. Clothing was only part of the problem. Anything was better, but for now; just getting dressed weighed on her. The fabric scraped her skin. The coals kept on churning. She felt them burning in her eyes, under her skin; burning her soul with the desire of revenge, but more than that now; the desire to set things right.

Emmy did have some qualms about what she had been doing, about what she hoped to accomplish. She wanted to do right, right in the scheme of larger things, and not just seek vengeance for her abuse. Although it was awful to remember, it wasn't like she had been through what the people of color in Concordia Parish, and elsewhere, had suffered, although Cajuns *had* suffered and were now a recognized ethnic group, with the same protection as anybody else (if anyone had ever been protected by laws written on books.) Yet, neither she, herself, in her own body, nor her parents or grandparents, nor any of her kin, had been rolled down a levee, run over by a car, hung, shot, skinned, or burned alive because of their skin. Those were horrific things. Torture. Fear. Words weren't enough to say just how horrendous this torture had been. In spite of the fact that two or three hundred years ago, Cajuns had been abused and deported, they had been chained up and forced to fight, Emmy didn't equate her troubles with those of the Black people of

Ferriday and didn't want to be remembered as a victim. She could still get angry and fight back; fight something, even the men who had harmed her. "Don't corner somethin' meaner than you," warned her grandmother. But she had been the cornered one. Was she going to become the meaner? Was this injustice? Something else? She thought about words. Words that make you act in retaliation, or not. Words of appeasement for which she reached, but couldn't find. These were either not in their places, or she had forgotten, or had never learned them. Her body knew, if her mind did not, that peace was absent from her repertoire. She sometimes slept open-eyed. When she followed her ophthalmologist's advice, taping them shut, she had nightmares, night terrors she could not describe. She had been there. They took away her memory, but not her hellish dreams.

Emmy's mother had wanted her to go to the Children's Ward of the Psychiatric Hospital in Pineville as soon as Sheriff Ross had suggested it. She remembered now, as she put on the jeans. Why had she signed those papers? Was she trying to shelter her in an uncommon way? Did she believe the sheriff was her friend because he was not Slaughter, and did not torture her? Did she not know about his absence of scruples when crimes against Blacks were committed by one of his deputies? Was she still bent under the influence of some sort of blinding shame? A crutch, another thought retrieving device popped up in her mind, about how one could become more understanding of the other's predicaments, and of their ensuing actions. For a long time, she figured if she could wear her mother's clothes, she could understand why she did what she did; understand why she had allowed a predator to get so close; and why she had killed him, too late. Her reasoning wasn't based on a superstition, but a belief. If she lived in her parent's house, wore their life's garments, then she would understand how her mother became the person she had become; why she had ditched her careful plans, and reacted as if someone had pulled an invisible trigger in her mind. Emmy would then understand why she did not try to hide her act; understand why she shot the minister of their church in front of a hundred people; understand why she confessed to a corrupt and racist sheriff who wanted her out of the way. Emmy had been only eleven, but she still thought that somehow, if she could walk in her mother's shoes, or wear her clothes, or live in her house, then she would understand why her mother had abandoned her. She would understand why she refused to allow her to visit at the Louisiana State Penitentiary for Women, from where, after the country modified the death penalty conviction, and her mother had been sentenced to spend the rest of her life; she did not write a single letter in almost fourteen years. If she could understand these things, she could understand why her mother had accepted to have her hospitalized; why, before her condemnation, she had signed the permission that granted the doctors to give her child electroshock treatments. If she could understand; then she'd be a better daughter. She would not have to seek revenge. She would have another voice. She wouldn't have to feed her guilt like a dog does a tick and has to scratch at it until its skin bleeds. But just now, as she held on to the jeans, she couldn't help wishing she would have had another mother; one who had another outfit; one who had not listened to the sheriff, and had questioned his motives.

"Fuck it", she thought. "A good pair of jeans is a good pair of jeans. I might never understand her." But just then she thought of the girl in the crinoline skirt. "No, that couldn't be right, she had changed with Bee. The girl was wearing pants." Emmy felt confused. She couldn't remember who was wearing what that day when she went to the movie with Harper. She wasn't sure she had been there. "Wasn't it then I was kept home, punished for getting the ball-point tattoo?" Everything seemed to float and slop together like colored paints or like Boudreaux's coffee melted ice- cream.

"Mamere said she wore a size ten. These are the right length, but really! They're like prison pajamas!" exclaimed Emmy , in a whispered breath. Now, her mother was attired like that. She would never wear jeans again. Why was it so strange that the only part of her mother's life that Emmy could now imagine was her clothing? Aren't garments our most intimate objects? Once we get to that age where we can walk, when we no longer must be, want to be, every second in our mother's arms, doesn't their vestiture become, above all else, the thing we don't want to take into account, along with their bodies and its functions? Noticing the stretched seams, Emmy took the pants back off, grabbed a stitch with her teeth and pulled it back tight on each side. She slid the jeans over her hips. "A stitch in time saves nine," she muttered, thinking how odd it was that she was only just now realizing that the stitch in the saying was a stitch done *on time*, and not some sort of heroic repair of Time itself. It wasn't that Time needed repairing; it was how people used it. It was how Time used them, and was now, using her. But then why was that one little stitch so important? Why was its inattention so unforgiveable?

167

Why did she feel like she needed to prop herself up on these prophetic sayings? Why did she now feel the need to envelop herself in her mother's attire, and use the expressions handed down to her for generations?

One day, Bee learned from her grand-father when he took her back to school after lunch, that at the same time Kennedy was assassinated, Emmy's mother had been condemned to die in the electric chair. At that same moment, Emmy was dead. She had stopped breathing for a minute, perhaps more. What is a minute in the mind of someone who believes forgetting is a cure? The therapy was emitted from a machine that looked almost like a nineteen-sixties record player, except there were knobs instead of a place to put a record, and no music other than a click and a buzz. Male nurses held her down as they shaved part of her head, placed the electrodes on her temples and placed what seemed to be a horse bit, covered with rubber, in her mouth. Instead of galloping into a wave, violent seizures had overtaken her small body on an electroshock table.

The goal was to make her forget her preceding traumatic experiences with Harper, her mother's sentencing, and her talking tooth. She did forget for a while. The night in the church was forgotten along with the Mardi Gras picnic before she got to the hospital. Listening to her tooth, she could hear herself breathing, or was that a wave? She had blocked out all the rest. Before the treatments, a part of her had gone missing. She forgot what the tooth said about her sisters. She forgot her parents. She forgot her friends, and her love for people and animals. She forgot what Harper had done. She wanted to remember. Needed to remember. Why did everyone want her to forget? The treatment had not only caused more memories to go missing, but also a part of her, a piece of self, her self. Gone forever was her *bel canto* singing voice. Gone forever was what had made her Emmy.

The nurses told her she had had a seizure and that she might have others, but soon she would be well. She had to take her medication. She could not talk. She struggled every day to remember. Where was she? Why was she there? Where were her parents? When could she go home? She could not read a book because beyond ten or so pages, she couldn't remember what she had read. After her grandmother picked her up and took her to her houseboat, she did not return to school. Her grandmother used a lot of sayings to illustrate things that happened in their lives, like, a bird in hand is like two in a bush; or if you don't have a head, you'd better have legs; you are like a rabbit, you lose your memory as you run. Some of these, she didn't understand, but she remembered them and they created a bridge, like in the past, when she had created a tune out of a few notes, disassembling them, and reassembling them.

At first, the memories came back to her with a nonsensical narrative, but little by little, she could put them back in order. She rejoiced when she thought about her grandmother saying: *if his brains were leather, there wouldn't be enough to saddle a June-bug*. It was so funny that at first, she thought it was another phrase that had waltzed off in a crooked two-step. She pondered, "June-bug saddle rides on a brain? No. Brainy June-bug rides a leather saddle? No. There is something to do with a man." And then she caught it, saddle, brains, June-bug, man and all, even if the one Mamere had talked about didn't have much of these. And with the sentence, the saying came back with images she wished she could forget.

She felt lucky she remembered her music, but she could no longer sing. Losing her voice was almost as terrifying as...she didn't remember. But in the months that followed, her grandmother told her of the fire, and told her that her mother was in prison. She started remembering more on her own. Then one day, all of her memory seemed to come back; but her voice never did. Just now, she was trying hard, but somehow, there was a girl somewhere she could not remember, but whom, she could not forget. She was supposed to take care of her. It was part of the plan. The girl seemed somehow linked to Harper, but then with fright and anger, she thought the girl must be herself and she spooled away from the thought with the energy of a whirlwind.

The Abattoir

Frank Slaughter had gotten out of a federal prison where he had spent several years for charges of violence and corruption along with Ross. Emmy had seen him at the church fire. Before becoming a sheriff's deputy , before becoming a Ferriday policeman, he had been a fireman, and that day, he was there to help. Most of the time, at least from the Ferriday jail, he was there to kill. Slaughter wore his name well. With a silver dollar bearing his birthdate in his pocket, given to him by the Grand Dragon of the Mississippi Chapter, he had had his own little mafia. He extorted goods and services, orchestrated kidnappings and killings, and ended the life of more than one Black citizen of Ferriday. The town council rehired him once out of prison, in spite of his record. And they rehired him with the approval of a Black alderman, who was trying his best to find his place in a town still burning with racial *realism*. Had the alderman believed these stories to be of the fictional variety? Was it enough to be elected in a town where the majority of Black votes still did not count to believe that racial injustice had ended? To believe the violence there had ended or pretend it had never happened? Instead of a reckoning, it was as if the Black people of Ferriday wanted nothing but reconciliation. But with such a past, could such a thing be granted? Would there one day be justice?

Slaughter had learned from Cain, his own armed bandit and booze boss, that he should keep his mouth shut. And he did. To Emmy, and to a lot of others, he was a *pig* from the *Hog's den* and Emmy wanted to make him squeal, along with the others, but she did not know how to make that cry literal. Most of Ferriday's old Klan members still worried about his power, or wondered if he was somehow in touch with Ross beyond the grave. Their doubts could be funded by the Orville lounge. If he had the slightest suspicion about their loyalty, they knew they could count on his retaliation. It would be fiery hot, and savage. It is enough to say that most worried about what would happen if...

Everybody knows that fire ants are creatures to be avoided, so when the four men dragged Sam Broderick, a long-time Klan member, over to an ant bed, which stretched under the earth for miles, he screamed bloody murder. Four stakes were already in place when Slaughter, Jeremy, Cain, and Barker attached ropes to his hands and feet, removing the handcuffs and ripping off his sheet. Broderick was an average sized red-faced man. The tops of his small ears drooped liked those of a fox terrier's, and his lower lip was so low it exposed the base of his gums when he talked. They had told him that they were going to scare a Black man outside Natchez and rode with him, in his car, stopping in a small lot where there was a *point of view*. Slaughter had followed with the equipment, and Broderick thought, a Black man by the name of White.

"We know ya flapped your lips to the FBI about Norris. It had to be you. Ya might as well admit it and get a bullet instead of being food for those little devils. Ya already told me and Cain enough back then, so we knows you's a little shit." Slaughter nodded to the other men. Broderick kicked and yelled. His semi-pricked ears quivered. "Last chance. I'm gonna put a rag in yo stinkin' mouth and those ants gonna eat your eyes right out their sockets, but not before you done swell up like a tick."

Seeing for the last time his life pass before his eyes, before seeing the ants on the ground, Broderick remembered steering a ship during a World War II battle. How had he become involved again with these people? At the Paper Company, he had worked with Jeremy Harper, and wondered if that is how all this came about. He was having some last-minute regrets. He had talked with him about the kid's father and had joked about it all, but nothing like telling the Klan's secrets. Being *Exalted Cyclops* did not allow him to foresee that he would end up like a dead roach, eaten inside out by others like him. He hated insects. Roaches and ants. One way or another, they prey on you; first they eat the food in your plate, then the food in your belly.

He had ordered Slaughter and Cain to hand over some money from the Orville Lounge, and they hadn't much liked it. The Klan had to get their finances from somewhere, but Ross and his deputies had a double agenda. He could see that they were uncooperative, but hadn't expected that they would lie about him having revealed the Klan's secrets. He'd seen it before. Forced to step down, lower, and lower, until now stepping back up, but to this; this anthill, teaming with union workers all steamed up and ready to turn against anyone who crossed their lines; bosses or scabs. Why didn't he have a white flag?

There had been Frank Norris. Had he mentioned the nigger's name to Jeremy? Had he bragged about it? There had been so many. There was the gin's watchman, Jim Taylor, who everyone in Ferriday believed had moved away from the town after his interrogation about that Cajun girl's rape and the church fire. He had to be the guilty one. The sheriff wouldn't have let him get away. Taylor had the girl's skirt in his bathroom. And Harper wouldn't shit on a little girl. Would he? Sam might have mentioned it to Jeremy, in attempt to defend the boy's father. Sure, there had been some talk about Harper's fooling around with his choir of *Angels*, all young girls. But would he have been that kind of blackened soul? There was no longer honor in being an old Klansman. Sam Broderick had never surrendered before, and now, wouldn't use his sheet as an emblem of defeat; not with Slaughter. Not with that old hound dog, Cain. Not with any of them. He said nothing.

"So yo sayin' you was the one who wrote dem letters? We got 'em right here. Sho looks like to me dat you wanna get roasted like a weenie by Hell's little critters." Slaughter was smiling through his red sheet. They had given it back to him after he got out of prison. Slaughter was a big man, weighing over two hundred-fifty pounds, with a full head of gray curly hair. The blood-red creases of his robe undulated in the furry moonlight.

He was hiding more than one kind of skullduggery. Slaughter had been convicted, but not for the horrendous murders he committed against Blacks. He was sent to prison on charges of prostitution and for beating a White man. Five years later, he was at it again. Cain said, "looks like ya got da hook in yore mouth, Broderick. Ya should've kept it shut."

Sam figured he would be dead fast enough. They had taken his money; now they were taking his luck. At least he had his pride. Better die with paralyzing ant stings instead of in his own piss at the old folks' home. He had

174

his legacy to think about. "I didn't send no fuckin' letters!" He heard his voice pitch higher than usual. His fright was overcoming his desire for remembrance. Maybe a bullet in the head wouldn't be so bad. Knees on the grass, tears rolled over his eyelids.

"These little ladies likes salt water. So, cry, you little shit." They stuck a rag in his mouth as soon as he started to scream. The dice were loaded. The crap game was rigged. He could no longer decide for himself. He was faced down in the ant bed. Their fiery tongues were licking his balls and his neck. Not his idea of a good whore. His eyelids and lips were soon swollen from kissing their nest. He tried not to yell for fear they would enter his mouth. He thought of the girl at the Orville lounge who spit out his seed along with his shaft. The pain was unbearable. But the shot didn't come. His luck was that allergic syndromes work faster than ants.

"Let's go," said Cain.

"Shshshshsh. What was that noise?"

Slaughter looked at the trees on the edge of the woods. Barker and Cain had heard the cracking branch and began to run towards the trees. Cain, who looked, and sounded, more like a jewelry box than a gambler, jingled as he ran on his short legs. Jeremy looked at Slaughter, and at Broderick's body. It was humping the ground with seizures. "What'cha waitin't for?" demanded Slaughter. Jeremy ran after the two other Klansmen.

Slaughter directed the beam of his flashlight over at Broderick. He looked at Ross, still wavering in the

175

moonlight like Spanish moss, and gloating about the Orville Lounge money holdings. "They ain't never gonna find my stash. Not now I'm gone and Sam is out of da picture. Why did you want him dead after all this time? Ya gonna have to wait awhile why them critters clean him up. The FBI'll find that rope ya know. It might have prints or somethin' on it. Them little gals ain't gonna eat it."

"Shut up Ross. I can't be talkin' to you with the guys around. Jest let me think." They had been in the federal prison together, but Ross had since died. He took off his hood. Ross had kept him company in the years before. If someone overheard him talking, Slaughter denied seeing or hearing anyone. He said he just kept on murmuring their conversations after the Sheriff was gone. But he knew Ross was there all right, with his witty jokes and his sly smile. He knew he was dead too, and figured one day, he would tell him where he kept the money because he couldn't spend it there where he was. He just had kept him interested. "Nosy ol' rat," Slaughter thought. "Figures the Devil wants his part too."

He went back to the car, folded his robe and hood and put them in a small suitcase. He then got his gaiters out of the trunk. His large body was slow after spending time in the pen. He put his foot on the scuff plate, took off his shoe and put on one boot, then the other. Then he sprayed the boots with mosquito repellant. "That oughta keep ya little bitches off me while I cuts the ropes."

He looked in the trunk and brought out a pair of shears and a broom. "I should've kept one of the men for this." He lumbered over to Broderick, breathing heavily. "He's gotta be unconscious by now." He cut the rope holding the left foot. Broderick didn't move. Wondering if he was still alive, he prodded him with a stick, sending the ants running in all directions for an instant. A couple of them were already on his arm, stinging him. "Shit," he puffed, annoyed. Slaughter couldn't afford to waste time with the ants. He brushed them off. The guys would be back any minute with the idiot they had heard, and he needed to have the place tidied up and ready for the new customer, once they caught him. He crouched down on one knee and slipped the blade between Broderick's ankle and the rope, slashing it and pulling it away with the shears. He stepped back to wipe the ants off the tool in the grass, already covered with dew. Two more times, he bent down and worked the blade under the rope, sawing and cutting it until it gave. He pulled out the stakes. He watched the soldier ants tearing through Broderick's skin around his hairline. "Ha! They gonna scalp him and carry off his goddam crew-cut like a trophy if I let 'em!" Slaughter wondered at the ferocity of the tiny creatures. Pulling him away from the ant bed, he sighed before removing the epidermic needle from his pocket and giving Broderick an injection. "This wasn't supposed to have gone this far," Slaughter said. Pulling him further over to the side, he brushed the ants away with the broom. They had crawled at least ten feet from the hill, looking for their tormentors.

Slaughter walked back to the car, brushing off the ants from his boots, and his sleeves. He put the pieces of rope and stakes in his toolbox along with the shears. He put the broom back in his trunk. He had to remember to get rid of it all or give it to Jeremy to burn in the furnace at work before sunlight. Taking a bottle of whiskey from under the seat, he took a swig, and said to Ross, "it's done now. Would you have me leave him there until there was nothin' left, but bones?"

"They'd still know who he was." Ross spit in the direction of Broderick. "If he don't die, they'll listen to him when he comes to and talks. How do you know they won't trace it back to ya? I told ya to let thangs alone. This is Adams County. The cops here ain't yore friends. If ya leave him to the ants, they'd call the FBI once they figure out who he was with his teeth. My arm is long, but it don't reach beyond de grave to no dentist office anymore." Struggling to remain tough in the memory of his friend, it was the first time he'd ever lied to Ross. The plan was to let enough ants bite him to provoke an anaphylactic shock, pull him off the pile, treat him. He considered opening a hole in his trachea. That would be for the hospital team, if he lasted that long. Slaughter was bending in Ross's direction.

"Well," said Slaughter, walking over with his light to watch the carnage. "Some still think you can still control people beyond the grave. And the sheriff's son owes me a favor or two on account of dem drug charges I got taken off." As calm as he had been about torturing Broderick, and then treating his allergy so that he would die in the hospital instead of on the ant-pillory, he was wondering what had happened to his men. The *Exalted Cyclops* was now one- eyed like his brothers, but that couldn't help him see into the future or into the past. The other eye was looking at him from the pile of ants, jiggling with the muscle still attached. "This was all part of the plan to make him talk. Tight lipped son-of-a-bitch.

I should'a kept that kid here to help me. Breath ass-hole!"
He kicked Broderick's foot. Ants fell out of his shoe.

Rover stopped his car on the side of the road. Slaughter
looked up and recognizing Rover's car, he waved.
Slaughter thought he would have come sooner to
participate in Broderick's interrogation. Rover walked
over with his cigar and stood beside him a minute, shook
his head with something like regrets, then, walked back
to his car, cigar still in his mouth. Torture reminded him
of the power purges of the sixties. "Other than the
Louisiana Rifle Association, what other organizations
and establishments were considered by the IRS as pure
fronts for the Klan?" He wondered as he drove off.

Slaughter went back to Broderick and checked his pulse.
Still alive, but still unconscious. He now thought Ross
was right. He should drop him off at the hospital. *A
concerned ex-fireman with experience in saving lives, I found
this fellow when I stopped my car to relieve myself. He was
covered with ants, trying to get to his car. Looks like he lost an
eye.* They would believe him. Maybe. Unless someone
knew him, but they would keep quiet, seeing what was
going down. Grabbing Broderick's ankles, he pulled him
towards his car, opened the back seat door, put him half
inside, climbed over him, pulled in the rest, and drove
towards the Natchez hospital. The others would have to
wait for his return. "Damn you, Broderick," he muttered,
brushing another ant off his arm. "You brought a bunch
of ants into my vehicle! Little bitches are fuckin' hard to
get rid of and sting like Hell!"

Emmy in the woods

The cricket chorus was silent, but the mosquitoes were buzzing away. An owl turned its head and blinked its golden eyes. It unfolded its great wings and lifted itself like perfume on a summer breeze. Concordia Parish sweat reeked out above the grass with the night flowering Devil's trumpets. The wind gave away the scent of the southern White boys. She had followed it to the forest's edge and stepped closer to listen, and to see what they were doing in the dark.

The light was dim, just enough to see across the field to the tree line. The moon was the kind that shines through the night, after you have spent the day, weeding and watering your vegetable garden. Leaning against your hoe, one foot on the blade, you look out at your watermelons and decide these are ripe for picking. After your bowl of jambalaya or gumbo, you go to bed on the porch, under the quarter moon, pondering about that hot Louisiana sun with its humid cape that won't let up; thinking about how you will have to rise early to pick the fruit of your labors and to be on the roadside by morning. Your dreams are watermelon sweet. You've already figured out that you might be able to make a down payment for a new used truck.

The next morning, you stumble out of bed, and after your coffee, you mosey on over to your garden, the fog still fingering the foliage like a guitar, and you find that every watermelon, every single head of cabbage, and every onion have disappeared during the night. You wanna run for your shotgun to scare the varmints away, but they have long since loaded their vehicles and left the premises. You might find them a few hours later on the side of the road, selling your goods from their trucks, certain that, if you do recognize these as your own, there is nothing you can do about it.

Emmy called the grifter's moon, a testimonial. She watched from the wavering shadows of the trees; the way Bee had watched a crime unfold all those years before, on Mardi Gras. Although adult, Emmy didn't know what to do. There was nothing about a man's torture or death that she wanted to be party to. She was not a voyeur. But there she was; witnessing a crime that the moon didn't commit, but didn't hide its face from either. Neither would she. These ants were almost as terrifying as fire.

Hypnotized by the horrendous show she watched, in a state of archaic empathy or corrosive joy, and unable to turn away, Emmy surprised herself by stepping on a branch, dead, but not rotten. Lichens and fungi covered branches before they touched the ground in the Saint Catherine Creek Forest. The limb cracked, nevertheless. Now she had to run. She had parked her pickup with its trailer on a logging road near the Carthage Point Road, but she couldn't make it back now. Her boat was closer, hidden in the trees on the Mississippi where she had planned to retrieve it with the ramp. She ran through the mossy oaks and scraggly dogwoods. She ran while cat-claw briars hunched their backs, spit, and scratched her arms and legs. Voices cried out behind her. She ran faster. Her body was weak, but other than Jeremy, who got a late start and didn't know what they were to do; the men were at least fifty years old, out of shape, and had to stop to catch their breaths.

She slid down the bank on the kudzu vines and unhitched the bowline from the piling. Wading into the water, she lunged onto the seat of her skiff, launching it into the water. The men were barking at each other from the embankment and calling out to her. She had a cap on with her hair tucked in. She was a mere stick- figure in ample clothes. They could not recognize her unless they were close. There were a couple of other boats on the bank, but she had not had time to push these into the water, away from their use. The men were moving fast. She recognized Jeremy's voice, crying out to the men from the distance. He was trying to find them in the woods. "Dumb fuck," she thought she heard Cain and Barker say in unison. "Kid don't know how to keep his trap shut either."

Barker, a lean man with small intense eyes, and a ruthless chin, pushed the boat with Cain into the Mississippi and jumped in it. They both started to paddle.

Emmy in the water

The boat came up fast and heavy behind her.

In the stolen light between the cypresses, aluminum jarred against aluminum, screaming with her absent voice, rupturing the absolute silence of the watchful frogs. She knew the men would catch her sooner or later. She felt remorse at the man's murder, but no guilt for watching. She didn't feel sorry for her letters either. He had it coming for what he had done to Frank. "I didn't kill anyone," she thought. She paddled faster. Her speed gave her strength. She felt stronger now as they rammed against her boat, her internal trumpet still blaring, boasting that she had seen them and exulting to no one, like a warrior in an opera she had never seen. But she knew, she wasn't finished. Could they do worse to her than men had already done? She knew that they could. They were stronger and faster. They had a different agenda and she was a woman. Her recourse was the river. She knew it would be. It had more wisdom than she did. Grabbing the starboard, one of the men jumped over and lassoed her before she could bail. The boat rocked. The eyes rolled. Whites gleamed, and teeth flashed. They pulled her into their boat and pushed her down into the filthy bilge.

As she fell, she saw the wispy veil that cloaked the rust-colored barges. She watched her little boat, floating away. If it made it to shore, someone would find it, and think she had drowned. She wanted to live. All she had done was to retake a life, her life. But that was a lot.

Tall white letters covered the red kidney bean hulls of the barge with premonitory fading: C-R-A-W. What was the rest of the word? She could see its vestiges from the smaller boat. Flotsam collected around the stern, rattling with *senza sordino*; t-thump, t- thump, t-thump, frrrrrrrr. Other men were parked near the boat landing at the mouth near the river island. The water carried their voices from the bank where they talked in murmurs, to the small craft where she lay. She knew she had to get away before they got to shore, or where ever they were taking her. "Boss says to lock her in one-o-four. He's gonna' have some fun with her before he cuts her up to feed her to the fish," the man said, leering down at her. The other laughed with disgust, prodding her thigh with his foot, "she is so skinny, there ain't much for 'em."

Feet joined, lying on her side and from the bottom of the boat, she kicked hard the man's standing leg. Arms flailing, foot grabbing, thud falling portside. Weight shifting, boat wavering, flipping starboard. All three fell into the murky water. Emmy's arms were still bound by her side. She felt chips of wood hurled against her skin, pricking her like pinecones in the dark water. The undertow whirled and tugged. Rotten eggs never smelled so good. A hand reached out and grabbed her foot. The man pulled himself alongside her, not to free her, but to hoist his body upward, using her body as a ladder. He put one foot on the rope, then on her shoulder; pushing her deeper into the blackness, twirling himself into an eddy. In Baton Rouge, the Father-of-Rivers, with its snakes and humpbacks, sometimes coughs up bodies from upstream; before it vomits the I's and hurls its name like a banshee; *M-i-s-s-i-s-s-i-p-p-i-i-i-i*.

She thought she could make out the dancing image of her great-grandmother, a dark-haired flamenco in the form of Persephone's catfish. Mustached, with full lips, both feminine and masculine, it whispered the letters painted on the barge, completing the word in a comic strip bubble: *Crawfish*. "What did it mean?" she thought.

Emmy's head bobbed up. Gasping for air, she thought she could hear the river sobbing regrets for swallowing indigestible savors. The other man put a hand out to grab her, pulling at the rope. It had inched toward her elbows, and she was wriggling an arm free. He was suddenly yanked under with gurgling sounds of voices from the Styx, calling for amoral flesh; "we've been waiting for you." The overturned boat crashed, clanging into the barge, before it turned and bumped, crumpling against the side. She rolled on the river, just like in the song.

Emmy flattened her body with log-like determination, then bent herself towards her feet, arched back like the familiar crustacean, and propelled herself away from the man, away from caustic laughter emanating from the holes opened in the water. In these parts, Hell had not been emptied for long. "Devils don't like water," her calm breathed. "They can't swim."

She arched her back and pushed again, jackknifing with her legs. Propelled with the force, she began to move her hips, and her freed arm, crawfishing and scissoring through the black water. She could not hear the men on the shore. She didn't know if they could see her. Her biggest problem now was the undertow. It had taken her away from the men, but now, she had to get back to shore. She had only her dead ancestors, peering at her through Hades' curtain, to count on.

The moon shone through the moving water, slicing it into a thousand fish swimming together in a school. She again began to bend and kick, forcing her head up when she needed to breath, feeling at last the tangle of bottom weeds against her knees, until she reached those of a familiar friend. She bumped her head against one of its knobby wood projections as it extended towards the surface. It knocked her breath out, and Emmy came up for the fight. She exhaled, gasping; "Ouch! What did you do that for?" The old cypress reached out its arms for her protection, and she smiled. At its base was the only congregation whose secrets she did not fear.

Barbara Bonneau

Trauma

Most people, having witnessed a horrific murder, most people, having escaped from a murderer's desire to reduce them to a pile of bloated torn flesh and shattered bones; most people, having fallen from a boat in rough waters far from the safety of solid ground; most people, having survived the onslaught of two men, both full of hate and drowning in the said twisting waters; most people having been set to the torrent without arms to fight or swim; most people, if they have survived this long, and having these said experiences might believe they were dreaming and follow their aggressors with the Mississippi nightmare as it wound through the night, on out to sea. But that was just it; Emmy had survived, and survived what had happened yet before.

What had not killed by sheer force would try to kill in intention. Hatred is a powerful motive. The drama of survivors of accident or of crime, is to repeat *ad nauseum* the vision, the gestures, the actions and the words in dreams and wake--if they remember at all, over and over and over and over--as if they could go back and avoid the confrontation; as if they could go back to a before time, and change the outcome from the past. Is this the stuff of crimes not yet committed? Are all murders beleaguered shots to set things right? If the person emerges from the water, from the fire, from crash, shootout, or attempted murder, there comes a time where there is an absence in one's archeology; a whole string of events in a drama that swirls away in an eddy like a loosened fish- line. Before it gets away, the haunted must hook the memory and reel it in, then recount it. Like a frightening big-fish story, that grows and transforms, until like a chimera (unless others live through it as well), it succumbs to myth.

Emmy couldn't remember who had saved her from the fire. For a time, she couldn't remember that she had been saved. Flames surrounded her and then she found herself outside. She couldn't remember the fire. She couldn't remember what had happened in the church or how she got there. She remembered the early evening, playing music for the Mardi Gras celebration. She remembered the feeling of floating on music and love, almost like when she had been just a little girl, maybe of two or three, and she had fallen asleep on the floor as her parents tuned their instruments and practiced for a gig. Fighting sleep, she felt her father lift her up from the blanket and enfold her into his arms. As he carried her to bed, she felt the warmth of his strong body, while he rubbed her back with his gentle hands. The delicious feeling of love, happiness, and security, whatever that could mean for a small child, overcame her once again with sleep, before she was tucked into her bed, and the music continued to play as she dreamed and danced with her family.

From disbelief, to missing pieces, survival isn't enough. People who have not been through a life-threatening experience do not understand. "Why can't you get past this?" Pierre asked. "You are so lucky to be alive." If they understand survivor's guilt, why it is hurtful to recall those that have instead died? Well-meaning friends don't grasp the need to return to the place, to share with other survivors, to recreate the memories, to seize something of the love that was before, and to understand that your companions had suffered and were no longer all there to talk about it. Some people don't understand that when their loved one falls into alcohol or drugs; it is not to forget. They want to remember the love that has been lost, to recreate that instant of pure joy, of before, of what could have been, before they can realize, what will never be. Never again. Emmy found it hard to resuscitate that love that had been hers before her father had died, and so held fast to the scrap of maligned and malignant love that was Harper's. She would not have killed anyone, unless he had instructed her to do so. Although the love towards Harper had found its place of rest, what persisted was its passion. *Tantoene animis coelestibus iroe.*

Hatred is a powerful motive. It leaves survivors feeling like they have no reason to live. They stand accused, the object of wrath, so why go on with life? Hatred is a powerful motive for a crime, but also for a victim's self-abandon, and sometimes, his or her restoration. On one hand; there is the overwhelming sentiment of annihilation; a feeling that your life is not worthy and you should die because it was so willed, because it was written on a misread banner, because your head cannot pull itself far enough into its shoulders or you can't drop your hands to your sides low enough, because the weight of the accusation squashes the part of the survivor that held any pride. On the other hand (thank goodness for two, and that makes all the difference), there is this new feeling that is an inkling of survival, of grief for oneself and, if only a drop of thirst-quenching choice; the rage, the fleshless, disembodied desire for revenge. "And yet," wrote Emmy much later, "that heinous desire, after pulling you out of deep river waters, can drive you to madness and to a foreseeable death." But just then, at the moment she made her way out of the water, she thought, the way the condemned somehow think; that somehow, she, more than the next person, had, and would, somehow be able to negotiate an ultimate time, and not fall victim of her hate or crimes. That gave her the promise of a clear sky, then a feeling of ascendancy. And in a way, she had won. Her triumph was once again that of good over evil, but it was an illusion, nevertheless. In finality, if evil is death, death is patient. Beyond the child-like fantasy of flying and overcoming one's enemies, there is, but one predictable outcome. "But isn't evil something beyond death itself?" She asked herself more than once.

Did her need for vengeance start with hatred or from some place beyond death that she could not grasp? Different from the need for which her mother had been convicted; her need came from a loss deep within herself, a *desideratum* greater, at least for the time being, than death's soulless outreach.

The reserve

Feeling her way through the water to avoid tripping over the exposed roots and keeping an eye out for water moccasins, she realized, she did not know where she was. Five miles down the river from Saint Catherine's Creek? Ten? All the way to the Homochitto River? Her bondage had been short-lived, but she still had to get out of the rope. Like her t-shirt and jeans, it was torn, in part. She couldn't untie the wet knot so she rubbed against one of the taller cypress knees until the threads started to crackle and pop, with soft sounds, more like a crumble and a poof. The hemp tie loosened and fell away, following its aquatic brothers. She was glad she still had her work shoes, although they had hindered her swimming. No respectful whirlpool would turn down a fight.

As she allowed herself to float away with the undertow, she had heard the cries of defeat of the men who had chosen to contest their will. They were now spiraling naked, with their dicks dangling down as fish bait, decaying pieces of carcass for underwater creatures of lightless worlds. Cain and Barker were gone. Once she got to dry ground, she would try to keep walking east, until she found a path or a road.

Although it was called the Father of Rivers, the Mississippi was more like a woman, its body curving both inwards and outwards. If you came away from its bank on the Mississippi side, you might think you were headed east, and find yourself traveling north or south. Her father had taught her from the earliest age to look to the sky for direction. She found June's bright oriental star and made her way through the forest.

She was used to walking at night through her familiar woods without a flashlight. Here, she had to keep an eye out for snakes, logs or roots that might grab her foot, or even the men who might come after her. She was safe from them for now. Other than an occasional hunter, no man had come this deep in these sticks for over a hundred years. While the paper mill loggers cut down hundreds of acres every year, it remained hidden by a sort of ironic curtain.

Emmy did not cry from exhaustion or from defeat. Her disposition was unyielding. With resolute determination she continued onwards in her wet clothes. Tiny bloodsucking behemoths landed on her arms. She swatted them, and picked herself up when she tripped or slipped on the ground still wet from the spring floods.

Her stomach, wrought up with hunger, growled for food. She remembered throwing away yesterday's breakfast; two yellow eggs sunny-side up on a diner's plate. Remembering her bout of anorexia when she was fifteen, and her operation to separate her inner and outer envelopes, never again, she thought, would she let a couple of oocytes stare her down. She continued on through the dark trees until she came to a body of water, she thought she recognized, and continued east. It was the Homochitto River. It led to Highway 61, just north of Doloroso; a town named after distress. As she got closer to it, the fog lifted like a side-to-side-two-steps-and-a-kick fandango, following the trail of cricket castanets. It was there, thick and low hanging; it spun around, then, it was gone. This was not neutral territory and now, she was in full view of headlights that dissected the landscape, looking for roadkill. In spite of the danger, she decided to hitchhike, south, to Baton Rouge where her friends now lived. Before stopping herself, she began to wonder what had happened to Broderick. It would do no good to make an anonymous phone call to the police. She could not call them. She had no voice and would not have been able to explain her presence in the woods.

Motorcycle Madness

Emmy hitchhiked, following US Highway 61. As she walked along the road, her heart began to panic and take off running. When she saw a pickup, she dove, down behind a tree or in a ditch. Her fear of encountering one of the men was illogical. It was not based on a calculation of probabilities. "What are the chances, after all, that either Jeremy or Slaughter, recognized me? Had they recovered enough sense to follow me and know where I went? Would they be in a pickup truck?" she wondered. Other than direct encounters with predators, aren't these fears more imagined than real? Still, Emmy hoped to avoid an encounter of the unwanted kind by avoiding pickup trucks. This apprehension of what *could happen* was a sense that Black people of the area were forced to develop.

A man in a 1970 television-series style Ford Falcon picked her up just south of Dolorosa and drove her all the way to Baton Rouge. The driver, a young man who looked like Freddy Mercury, but with Elton John sunglasses, wearing a T-shirt and jeans, let her off at Greenwell Springs Road. She walked the rest of the way. When she arrived at her friends' house, on Camellia Avenue, she felt exhausted from her journey, exhausted from the need to tell someone, but unable to talk. She got out of her car and started to walk for the door.

"Over here, I'm on the ground," called out Sandy, trying to wipe the tears from her face with the back of her hand. Pierre was laughing at her, too. They were always laughing. Apparently, she had said or done something funny, again. Emmy couldn't laugh like that. She didn't know why. She had no voice, but it wasn't that. For years, other than her own rare personal jokes, she had not found much to laugh about. She walked around the motorcycles. The exhaust pipes were gleaming, but not smiling back at her. She could see a crooked image of herself, bent like a Z, staring out into nowhere, blurring in from another life. She should have commanded a straighter face. Like a motorcycle when it starts, she tried to assemble her words. Her thoughts sped ahead of her lips and her tongue. Crackling like the old school speaker, but without meaning, she coughed and spit out a semblance of a sentence.

Instead of talking, most of the time, she carried a *Magic Slate* with her to write what she wanted to say, but she had left it in her truck before following the death squad. She remembered one of their choir members using one when he had lost his song. Wondering what happened to birds that could not sing, she thought of her crow friends, imagining them writing messages, giving up for lack of ink, or instead, wringing out their feathers, dipping their quills into a fallen brother's blood. That would explain their constant cawing. Those Agatha-Christie crows had murder on their minds. Someone was bound to squawk.

The couple's jokes kept knocking at her chest, gargling for a giggle. Emmy smiled, at her mind's eye-image of crows with writer's block as they scratched out their tales, and not about her friends' jokes. She waited for them to finish working. Sandy cackled on, running back and forth, responding tit for tat, tasking about nothing, and not thinking because of that. "Have you seen Skizzum?" she asked. "We hear she is playing with Bonnie Raitt. Playing the piano. You wouldn't think she could stand to play ""Angel from Montgomery" after what happened, would you?"

The couple didn't seem to understand how important her visit was. Whatever Sandy knew to be true; Emmy didn't care for other people's interpretations about what happened. Bonnie Raitt's story wasn't Skizzum's, wasn't hers. Had she forgotten that songs were how people could connect? Once her mind was focused, it would not grin. Was the trauma, that was so hard to believe and that would be harder to share, the cause of her silence, beyond the loss of her voice? Pierre brought her the page size chalk board they used most of the time, for writing grocery lists.

Writing in small block letters, she turned their focus towards her preoccupations. "I think I found out something important, something I was not supposed to hear." She added a few more words. Pierre peered at her from behind the Harley's handlebars. "My God! That's frightening," he said and he believed it, but had other things on his mind, other things besides laughing and Emmy's discoveries. Pierre rebuilt motorcycles with his wife while working on his law degree at LSU. Parts were strewn about their workplace, like the carapaces of broken insects.

The couple had often spent hours working under fluorescent lights in the garage. Taking pieces from different machines, mostly Harleys, polishing them, piecing them back together, hoping to give them a new life. They knew that some of the bikes had been stolen, but looked the other way in order to operate their own *tchouflangue*, Cajun for small cheap businesses. Sandy watched without batting an eye as Pierre discussed prices for the crates of motorcycle parts before the gang's negotiator disappeared with their cash. Once the bike finished, they would pawn it off to some other biker. There wasn't much leeway in this line of business. They both felt that the good fight had to sometimes use dirty means. But did either really understand what that meant? Wasn't what they called the good fight just their own attempt to make a living? Without boundaries how could anyone know what was right? This was a world where people killed each other because of whom they were. Emmy's mother had not killed because of someone's color, or anything that identified him, but because of what he had done, and that; that was bad enough.

Another husk of a black insect appeared in the driveway, blaring and riffing like thunder. This time, Pierre got into his car and followed the man. Could she tell Sandy about her plans? She decided to tell her about the articles and see if she put together the information.

She wrote, "David Ducal is now after Jews. He has captured the interest of the KKK, pretending that with the Civil Rights Law, to continue adhesion, they need turn their interest in what he is calling another plague."

"I know," said Sandy, "we saw him in front of the Student Union."

"Did you know that he is stirring up the Silver Dollar group of the Klan in Concordia Parish?" Emmy wrote, asking Sandy.

"What's the Silver Dollar Group?" asked Sandy.

"They are the most violent group of the Ku Klux Klan in existence, and they started in Central Louisiana. Jeremy's father was a member."

Sandy shook her head in dismay. She was Jewish, assimilated, not practicing any particular rules, but Jewish all the same. She had grown up with the Holocaust as part of her culture. Pierre had told her about Harper, and Harper's family. Tim, the former LSU president years before, had been to the same synagogue as she, although she didn't make light of this to Pierre. It just never came up and she had been private about some things. "I knew Tim from a small neighborhood south of the LSU campus, where I lived for a while, in what must have been at some time, a group of slave shacks. It wasn't a commune or anything. Just cheap living. We had no running water or electricity. We thought we could live off the land. I didn't last six months before I moved back to a shared apartment off campus, but Tim still lives there. He, and his girlfriend, are of tougher stuff," she said.

When Pierre came back, two hours later, slamming the front door, Pierre had a six-pack of beer under his arm. Sandy was sitting spread eagle on the floor, tolling over a newspaper. Emmy could only point to an article she found, and take notes. Pierre had made a deal, but wanted his wife to be out of the way, for her own safety. With some of the motorcyclists, you didn't know what their affiliations might be and he didn't want to take any chances. The guy knew where he could find him, nevertheless.

Emmy called Pierre, T-Pierre, meaning, *petit* or little Pierre, but even when he acquired the name, as a small child, he had a loud mouth. Now gloom deformed his usual jaunty tone as he strode over towards the women. He looked at the charts they were making of newspaper article evidence. One was for the perpetrators, one for the victims, and the last one was for the witnesses. They also had a chart with David Ducal's name, and the title of the article from the LSU student newspaper, about his speech at the campus Free Speech Alley. Sandy had put a few articles from the *Chronicle*, in a three-ringed notebook, with dividers, like in school, only with names like NAACP, David Ducal, LSU, Joseph Edouard, Andy Goodman, Gerry Mitchell, names of the reporter with the victims.

On the LSU campus, they had heard the crowd hoot before the student union like Cajuns at a football game. Holding hands, Pierre and Sandy had glanced at each other in disbelief, not wanting to believe that this part of Louisiana culture could have any part of what was going on that day at the Free Speech Alley. David Ducal was talking about the new target of the Klan: Jewish people. Emmy had brought news of his connection with their neighborhood child-thug, Jeremy Harper.

Pierre wanted no part of whatever they were doing. Drawing back, he explained, "you both saw the man I sold the parts to earlier? I know he looks shady enough, but he's got the Klan on his back now for some reason. It's an odd coincidence that he shows up and tells me this at the same time you are going over these articles. Maybe they're after him because he betrayed their confidence. Maybe he's Jewish. I don't know." It was Tim on the motorcycle, but Sandy had not recognized him with his helmet, in spite of his long, stringy brown hair and his distinctive hippy look. She would have invited him for coffee and they might have shared a few laughs about former times. But these had changed. And Emmy was there. Coincidence is kind of like luck. Does anyone believe there is any reason behind it? Yet, believe it or not, when it happens, we run with it like it was destiny, and like there was no choice.

Repeating what they already knew, he continued. "He used to be a student body president and was present the day we saw Ducal on campus, ranting about the Jews. One day, I recognized one of these guys throwing something at his motorcycle in front of the Seven-Eleven near campus, like a neighborhood bully. Anyway, I got the feeling that they knew whose bike it was. I don't like them and I'm worried about getting deep in this shit can. Paying for Law School is how I got into this mess. If I get barred before I finish my exams, there is no use to any of this for me. David Ducal is not only a student at LSU; he is the founder of the Knights of the Ku Klux Klan, a new group. He doesn't even try to keep his anti-Semitism or his association with the Klan secret. This guy wants to run for Congress maybe one day President. He believes a lot of other people are as deranged as he is. Now that I know about his dealings with the motorcycle gang I deal with, I'm wondering if and what he knows about me. There are men who are members of both the Klan and the gang. This mix might rat out Tim, the ex-LSU student-body president, who comes here for parts, and he might talk about us, if forced to do so. I don't want anything over our heads. I don't want to push his luck, or mine. You know what I mean? If what you say is true, Jeremy hangs out with that White supremacist asshole, when he comes to Natchez?" He was asking what he already knew, not as any kind of trap, but to acknowledge to himself that his relationship with the motorcycle gang was becoming more complex, more distasteful, than what he had intended. Was he realizing that talking about it unraveled the essential?

Emmy wrote, "You know about the upcoming elections. In Ferriday, they talk about *Constitutional Sheriffs*, self-appointed election fixers that fill out absentee voter forms like Ross and his deputies did before, but only now, with support on the state level. I'm not sure who is behind it. Maybe Ducal does their bidding, as well as that of the Klan. Ducal plays craps at the King Hotel in Ferriday with Cain and the others? How do you think people from the sticks rise to position of power?"

"I don't wanna be mixed up with any of these people," winced Pierre. "It seems like what they mean by states' rights is that thugs rule when there is no government."

Emmy looked at him, wondering if he would back down. She shook her head as if to shake off the thought.

Pierre continued, trying to alter his mood with another idea. Emmy let him go. She knew she could not force people to handle subjects they didn't want to deal with. Pierre was thinking that Emmy's ideas could be relevant; her hypothesis could even be correct, but he also knew that his sister's friend had a past history of trauma and mental illness and he didn't want to upset her by his refusal to get involved. People understand so little of others. Her research was not much different than that of a journalist, in spite of her mental health. It was so easy to discount thoughts of people whose minds work in a different way than yours.

Pierre Leblanc was of average build with dark hair and Mediterranean eyes. He had had a summer job with the Paper Company before going to LSU. He knew the Klan had a group there, almost like a union. He tried shifting the subject back in time, talking about what happened a while back, at the paper mill. "Do you remember what I told you about his name? People at the mill called him Chuck, because he chucked the wood and they got him mixed up with the former chucker who was named Chuck, for real. He didn't much care for that. Buhler was the first because he said Jeremy chucked lies. Buhler's a real asshole and a mean guy. Jeremy was probably just trying to make friends."

Emmy, picking up on the subject, but this time, not on his attempt to move away wrote: "Maybe we should use code names when we talk or write about him? Call him Chuck instead of Jeremy? Would anyone guess now?" Because if Emmy's mind could lead down a dark alley, it would be straight and narrow. She stayed on her path and Pierre, diverted to his.

"Jeremy tried to fit in with the other paper mill union guys and be regular with everyone, just to catch snippets of conversation from somewhere. I feel kind of bad now. If we had been nicer to him, maybe he wouldn't have fallen in with the Klan. Maybe his loyalties would have been different. We teased him, because he was an easy target, and dismissed him as if we felt that he and his old man were one and the same. We didn't give him a chance. One day, seeing him chewing his nails, I said to him, 'Jeremy, why are you biting your nails?' I paused just enough to make sure I had his attention and said, 'if you like nails, try biting mine.' I laughed, but he didn't think it was funny. Before I said more, he yelled, "I ain't no god damn queer. I don't put nobody's fuckin' fingers in my mouth!'" Pierre laughed. «But I don't think he ever chewed his fingernails again and figured I should get my method patented before one of the other guys beat me to it." Sandy laughed at her husband.

Emmy listened and smiled. She no longer had her sultry contralto song, or even a voice like Sandy's; as slow as Louisiana molasses as it is poured onto rice cakes. You have to give it time. When Emmy could talk at all, she croaked, but what could she say? Without motivation, without a goal, she would not be able to withstand the world, or the wind. Gravity alone wasn't enough, not even that of the earth's attraction. She knew a lot about Jeremy and his loyalties. She needed her friend's help, but she wouldn't let him talk her down by pretending Jeremy was different than his father, weaker somehow. She was in for a lot with her letters to him and the Klan. She had kidnapped his daughter, although she had not intended to do so. It was as if her heart, swelling with bile and black blood, felt it would explode. She had become impatient. All her fire and fury, all her passion, had to be laid out line by line so it could penetrate the purpose of someone else. She had sent an article in an envelope to the newspaper about the possible burial of Klan victims in the levee to that poor girl, Mary Straboni, who had a summer job with the newspaper. Now she wondered if the girl understood the risk she would be taking if she meddled with the Klan. She worried that she had given information to people who would lead these criminals back to her. Worried, but not worried enough because hadn't she kept writing the letters? Hadn't she taken the kid home? Or had she? She never could remember and didn't want to look in the room. There was a festering smell coming from there. The odor of something dead. She didn't want to admit to Pierre that she had authored the anonymous letters, and felt the desperate need to continue. She wanted to laugh, but she had to keep pushing forward, she hugged them and told them she wanted to shower and went to the room they offered to her for the night.

Ignoring his warnings and his fears, and emboldened by her earlier escape, she began again to cut and paste.

Don't you see me? I's got blood on me. I'm comin' fo' ya. You dun run me down with the Olsmobile. If I can't get to ya now, I'll be comin' fo' ya in da grave.

It was her third missive to Hogden. This would stir him up again. Now she now knew that there had been a lot of car tracks on the levee that night. She didn't know if Edouard had died like the man in the bowling alley had said, or was run over by a car. But she was sure that there was something there that would tick Hogden off his rocker.

Later that evening, she wrote to Pierre and handed him the board, "I need you to take me back to my truck near Natchez tomorrow. Can you do that? Also, I need to go to the post office."

When she went back to the bedroom, Pierre flipped off the TV screen, turning to his wife, he said, "Emmy left her truck near Natchez because she was being followed and hitched a ride here. She needs me to take her home tomorrow." Sandy flared, her dark eyes flashing. She cursed. She had had other plans and, although she had helped her to organize, wanted to limit her involvement with Emmy and her projects.

"Let's talk about this." She reached out to touch him. "Pierre, you are so trusting. Emmy has been through so much; she is my friend, too. But she is becoming invasive, coming over here, involving us like this in I don't know what. It is too much. It's almost like since she can't talk, we allow her come over, invade out privacy whenever she feels like it, and interfere in our lives. But she sees and hears. She knows about things that could get us all into trouble. She knows about your business."

Pierre sighed. "Oh, she doesn't care about that. I know that spending so much time with my sister's half-crazed childhood friend is not what you had in mind this weekend, or the other times she has shown up. But she's scared and needs help. How much time did you help her with that chart and that notebook? It isn't just for her. I don't know what it means to help those dead Black people or to prepare for something that might happen later. I'm worried that stirring things up like this might end up getting someone else killed. I don't think we have to worry so much about us. Still, she has found a cause, for herself, and to help others. That is important. I feel part of something too. Don't you?"

"Well yeah, kinda. But I'm not sure what she says is real. I mean, it seems like the Klan stopped when it lost its handle fifteen years or so ago? Ok there is Ducal stirring up shit. But that doesn't mean it will go anywhere. That doesn't mean the old Klan's people will do his bidding. Anyway, I will look for articles for her in the library when I have time, but we have to set boundaries. I also picked up a form for a good student loan so you won't have to accept stolen parts." She picked up the papers she had left on the table as proof. "But can't she ride the bus?"

At the same time, he tried to convince Sandy, Pierre was wondering if Emmy had learned how to use Harper's tricks and was trying to use these now to influence them. Skizzum had tried when they were young, with her preaching and silly, and not so silly, prayer corners. It was a way of isolating them, getting them to admit wrongdoings or trivial injustices. In this way, Harper could sink in his clutches through the snares of guilt and lift them into his fold like a hawk as it swoops down on its prey. As children, they had resisted, making fun of their sister. Was Emmy doing the same thing now with her own projects? It was hard to compare her to a bird of prey, but he had learned something about manipulation in law school. Reading defense law with one of his professors, they had studied a case about a junior college dormitory counselor, who had been accused of raping a student. The student, along with three other boys, had tried to burn the dormitory down during spring break.

These students were caught, and tried to get off the hook by accusing the defendant of rape. They said was that they wanted revenge for what their friend had suffered.

They all acted as witnesses, saying they had all four been to the counselor's office, after lights were extinguished, and drank beer while watching pornographic films. The beer and pornography in the college was considered reprehensible by law, but that was beside the point the professor was at present making. Three of the boys were eighteen when they were arrested, and the other, seventeen. When the firm's client was arrested and taken to trial, arguments were made to keep the crime at that level of exposure and not to resort to indictments of corruption of a minor or worse. The defendant got off with a warning and did not have to enter a guilty plea. He was encouraged to resign or he would be fired from the school.

However, the story with the lawyers didn't stop there. The former defendant had sent them a letter thanking them, promising to "return the elevator" to them for their service, offering in fact, to go beyond the payment of their fees. He had found a new job as a watchman in a building in New Orleans, where not only a competing law firm was located and had an apartment used on occasion by their visitors, but also a strip club. The law professor was leading up to a *quid pro quo* situation, where the lawyer found himself accused of accepting gifts from a possible criminal in exchange for his services. In fact, this former client had provided the free use of the competing firm's apartment to his former defense attorney, as he had promised, one night when the lawyer had had too much to drink, as well as the visit of a prostitute working for the club that was a cover for prostitution. When the police raided the club and investigated, they found the embarrassed lawyer in the room where he should not have been, with his pants down. The professor warned the students to avoid getting involved too deeply with their clients. But could Pierre consider Emmy as a client?

He also wondered what had happened to Emmy that night. She hadn't explained why she was in muddied clothes with matted hair or why her skin was scrapped and her face bruised. Where he thought she would spill out an upsetting story , she never explained how she got into such a mess. Yet she was so passionate about Jeremy and Ducal. Sometimes, he supposed she had acquired her mother's addiction and had had too much to drink, and had fallen, or worse. Sometimes he wondered if the marks on her body could be self-inflicted. Didn't she have purple round scars like cigarette burns or something on her hands? Pierre knew nothing of the anonymous letters. He had never considered such things. He would have warned her, like her grandmother and the voices from the tomb had done, against stirring up ant beds. "I will talk to her, Sandy. I'll tell her she has to give us notice before coming, but I have to take her home. Her truck is parked in the country somewhere, and as I understand, she needs help with her boat trailer or something. A bus won't work. She has no one. No one else except Skizzum and I, and Skizzum, well. She is unreliable and, in Tennessee, right now."

When Emmy got back home, her grandmother was in her room with her guitar. "Why are you in my room playing the guitar?" she asked. "Don't you know I need to go to sleep?" Mamere sighed and started to play the *adagio* of the "Concerto de Aranjeuz".

Amor mío,
En el agua de las fuentes
Amor mío,
Donde el viento los lleva,
Amor mío,
Cuando cae la tarde
Se ven flotar pétalos de rosas.
Amor mío,
Seres resquebrajan las paredes con el sol, El viento, con el
aguacero,
El paso de los años,
Desde esa mañana de mayo,
Cuando llegaron,
Y cuando, cantando,
De repente escribieron en las paredes
A la punta de fusil,
Cosas muy raras
Esas cosas son rosas,
Amor mío.[1]

---

[1] Joaquin Rodrigo Vidre, author's translation and adaptation from French, both in Spanish and in English: "My Love. In the water of the fountains, My Love, Where the wind takes them My Love, The evening come, we see the petals of roses floating. My Love, and the walls are chapped, My Love, by the sun, the wind, the rainfall, and by the years that come and go since that morning of May, when they came and while singing, Suddenly from the point of their rifles they wrote on the walls very strange things, These are roses, My Love."

She hummed, and then strumming her guitar, in the way of unknown ancestors, *talked the song*, in Flamenco Spanish. Emmy didn't know where she had learned these things. Near midnight, she fell into a deep sleep. She dreamed of roses blooming and petals floating in a fountain where lovers met. Strange marks spattered the wall. That was all that remained as witness to their love, through all kinds of weather, and for the years to come. These were the roses of Aranjuez.

Emmy awoke, terrified for her friends. It was not a logical fear. There was no wolf waiting outside their door. No alligator swimming alongside them. There wasn't even a wasp. Playing with her life was one thing, and that was bad enough, but including her friends, or even strangers, was something else altogether. She thought again of the little girl and her anger as she reproached Emmy for getting into what she had thought was her father's truck.

The responding officer (Hogden)

Cathy Broderick pushed on the front door. "Is anybody here?" She tried pulling on the handle. "Hey, is anybody in there? What the Hell is going on? I'm going to call the police ..." she called out, pounding this time with the base of her fist, her painted nails outward, overriding the ham. She had already called the sheriff's office, and had not yet gotten past the front desk. It was her usual preoccupation, to worry about people, her husband, in particular, whose goings-on she knew little about. These were supposed to be kept secret, he had told her. Her worries tended to be unfounded; prompting law officers to believe she cried, *WOLF*, for no reason. One day, it was about a child that didn't come home before his usual five P.M. curfew, the next, a grandmother who lost a shoe in the driveway. She was convinced that there had been a kidnapping. Someone had disappeared. Sounding the alert was an imperative, wasn't it? The police, the sheriff's department, and now, the local newspaper, were all wary of her false alarms. Still, determined, she turned around and started for the back door. "I hope that door is open or I'm going to have to get help. There is always someone, always!" She was muttering to herself, imagining the news crew gone missing, as if they had been swept up by a flight of extraterrestrials in a mission to turn humans into laboratory rats. No concerned citizen took mind to her worries much anymore. *The Concordia Post* locked the front door so that the journalists could do their early morning work in a relative calm.

Coming in from the back door, the sheriff's deputy stumbled over the piles of newspapers on the hall floor. The whole office smelled of politics. As he was having his breakfast on the road, he had been called to the scene by an informant, and the only information he had was Klan related. Sam Broderick had gone missing, and he was to report to *The Concordia Post*. While he figured this call was related to the anonymous messages, he thought that nothing would come of it. Waiting for his colleagues, he wanted to talk to witnesses, but if this was the crime scene, if there was indeed one to be found; it was already walked over with heavy boots, as well as by the feet of the early news room workers, unaware that anyone had disappeared over the weekend. Trampling crime scenes, when these involved murders of Black people, was the usual operating manner. But here, in this office, were only the records of past crimes, and the news about new ones. The impression of foul play came from another deputy, unable to clarify much of anything in front of his new colleague. This time, the caller, Cathy Broderick, had called in with the facts. In truth, without Mrs. Broderick, they would have been oblivious to many of the banal, *unnewsworthy* movements of their fellow citizens. Nevertheless, the sheriff's deputy had to make good on his pledge to members of the community, and members who shared his secret oath. And Sam Broderick was an important member of both.

"Hello there, were you looking for me?" The mayor called out, opening his car door, and noticing Mrs. Broderick. "Used to, she stirred up more than one hill of ants," he thought, looking her up and down. "Soon the place would be crawling, clumping together like bits of flour, in what Cajuns call, a roux. Still, she looks hot for her age." Cathy blushed, as if she could hear his thoughts, turning about-face, stumbling on the edge of the parking lot in disrepair. He held out a sycophant hand to shake hers, as he did everyone's, in a politician's way, with a crocodile-smile. He'd been in office for over twenty years and now had bottled-dark-sixties-cream-slicked hair, and wore thick nineteen-eighties glasses. Smiling was his most important activity. There was a chance that you might vote for him in the next election, and getting out and about was no challenge for a man who had been a former Ferriday High School basketball and football player. This was his favorite part of the job.

"I'm sorry to frighten you. I was looking for someone myself," he said, smiling.

"This is a place of work. Where is everybody?" Cathy asked.

She didn't know the employees were in the back office going over the days' newspaper, a little later than usual. Deputy Hogden came out of the office and shook the mayor's hand. The mayor had come to try to put a lid on the story the journalists were busy printing. There had been too many negative stories. Deaths, anonymous letters, and now, disappearances. No one would want to move to Ferriday if this got out, and that, well, that would limit the city's revenues, along with his chances of reelection.

In the parking lot, Cathy answered Hogden's questions as best she could, concluding that her husband, Sam, had gone missing for almost seventy-two hours. He had not been at home in two days. Cathy thought her neighbor had suspicious behavior. Knowing these details did not make the investigation easier. In the eyes of the deputy, Emmy was not a suspect.

"I keep an eye on that woman. A few days before her disappearance, I saw her in her truck, crossing the Lake Road, headed towards her campground office. After that, she pulled out onto the Lake Road going south, at half past seven that morning, with her boat trailer attached. This, in itself, is nothing unusual," she reported. "That woman takes her fishin' boat out of Lake Concordia and heads off to who knows where any time she gets a hair. But just like Sam, she's been gone all weekend. Only she came back and Sam didn't. I wonder if she knows somethin'? Honestly, Deputy, you should ask her. She just goes off anywhere at any time. Day or night. I swear, she is like that mother of hers. Liable to shoot someone any day now. I just don't trust her, you understand? Keepin' to herself like that."

Hogden had out his notebook. He jotted down her words, but didn't try to make sense of it all. "She keeps to herself," said Cathy Broderick, trying to dictate his notes, believing now that she was starring in *Colombo*. "We almost never see her out and about, then all of the sudden; she's gone. And he is too! These crimes could be linked, don't you think?" She added.

Hogden and the mayor gave each other a bewildered look. Emmy had been all but excluded from the local White community long before and wouldn't have been tied to the disappearances without someone, other than Cathy Broderick, having seen her in her boat on the Mississippi. Her insistence had an inverse effect. Emmy's research question: how many Black bodies were covered up or taken back into the folds of the earth by the Mississippi, or by its levees; aided in this endeavor by its human overseers; was thus far unknown to the deputy, and unknown to the mayor, as was the loss of Emmy's boat. Mrs. Broderick added material to the confusion.

In the post-*Jim Crow* era, conservatives were still talking about states' rights, turning their focus to other ways of keeping down people of color. They were appealing to the Dixiecrats, still talking about leaving the segregation laws to the states. Some were furious about the *Roe vs. Wade* Supreme Court decision about abortion rights. "It's another way *they* controls us. We gotta do somethin' 'bout it. They's killin' little babies. It ain't right. It should be God's decision. He the only one who knows. States should be the ones decidin'." As if states cared. These preoccupations about states deciding about women's bodies confronted those about the rising costs of gasoline. It was all discussed and decided at the *Pastime* Lounge.

"It's Carter's fault. He makes us drive at fifty miles an hour so the DC fat cats can get cheap gas," said one.

"That's bullshit!" said another.

"Just plain, old, stinkin' bull..S..H..I..T, and I'm not goin' to swallow any of it!" added still another.

"And I'm voting for Reagan! You'll see. Dem Iranians gonna be so scairt that he'll have dem hostages back home in a week once he's elected! Mind my words," the first one repeated, like a parrot, from what he had heard on a television news report about the GOP campaign.

"Yeah, yeah," said another player, adding to his former bullshit remark. "As if you knew what went on behind closed doors." Soon they were back to throwing verbal punches, drinking beer, and finding each other in a pile on the floor. No one was sure how they got there.

Cathy didn't hang out in bars, but she was afraid that someone at *The Concordia Post* might be keeping the truth from her. This fear collided with those of journalists everywhere: fear of a truth too inconsonant to reveal, too tough to bear. They could be guilty of falling back on general concerns. Revealing information to the wrong person, at the wrong time, put their own lives at risk, as well as that of their informants. If any of these journalists knew what had happened to any of the Klan members, they were keeping it under cover for now. And Cathy's concerns were not theirs; or at least, the way they would frame the disappearance of her husband, was different.

Cathy leaned over, squinting her eyes at the deputy's notes. "Deputy Hogden," she said, moving her head back in recoil. My husband is a hard worker. That's why I can't understand why he didn't come home from the paper mill Friday. He's tired after work. We ain't no spring chickens. He hasn't been home all weekend. Something's wrong. Why are you here, anyway? Does it have somethin' to do with him? Has somethin' happened to him?" Her face flushed this time with concern. "I've been tryin' to call the sheriff's office or the police, but they just repeat the same thing; yes, Mrs. Broderick... as if I'm some kind of idiot just callin' them to attract attention to myself! I'm just lookin' for my husband who didn't come home. Isn't that normal." And it was. No one had thought to call the Natchez hospital.

In the past, the Natchez police had cooperated with the FBI to help uncover the truth about Klan crimes, but Concordia Parish's law enforcement had been covering these up just as fast, and for a long time. Noel Ross had done what the law had required with his prisoners. He put them in jail. He was kind to the witnesses in so far as they gave him information, or kickbacks. He let the White prisoners, who had rendered him favor, go home without much questioning, as long as they didn't admit guilt or participate in crimes against other Whites. Sheriff Ross and Deputy Slaughter had both served time for involvement with mob-operated prostitution and gambling. But Hogden was still untethered, as were other law officers, members of the KKK. And the mayor wanted to keep his job until it was time to retire.

Nevertheless, he had questions. He pulled Hogden aside. "Do you think Broderick's disappearance has anything to do with Cain's or Barker's?"

Hogden spit between his teeth. The spittle, not escaping the crocodile's eyes, fell in a flowerbed. "It's too early to tell. We don't know if the victims who were found in the water, drowned from accident or from foul play. The investigation's still ongoing," replied Hogden. "Men were gettin' killed," he thought, grinding his teeth. "And there was Harper's girl who was kidnapped."

"I got called out for a hate-related crime. I don't know if this is someone's idea of a joke or not. It seems like there is some relationship to dem letters. These people were White, Mr. Mayor. All of them. It's not like 'em to just fall off their boats, lose their heads, or run-off without notice.

They all have families. And what about that girl over in Natchez?"

The mayor shook his head. Other than trying to keep the journalists at bay, he wanted no part of it, no part of the whole lot. The hand-shake proved nothing. The girl was the problem for the Natchez police. He was disgusted with them all. He was going home and would wash his hands and not think about the murders of Frank Norris and all the rest until he got close to reckoning day.

Hogden, by contrast, chomped and gnashed on his ideas about the Klan members' disappearances and deaths. He was missing something; a twig, a licorice stick, something to bite on in place of the donuts he was trying to give up. "Did the Wizards suspect these men to be informants," he wondered. "Had they done something to detain or to hurt my friend, Broderick? Was one of them behind the kidnapping of Harper's daughter?" Hogden could not make his mind bend enough to imagine anything but a wreck at the end of the tunnel. Sinister. Was history on a left- handed loop like the universe? Who's turn was it to die? Was there any way to tell?

There seemed no way out. "In spite of changes in the law, Mr. Mayor, somethin' is goin' around and around, repeatin' itself all over, again and again." The mayor shook his head, trying to remove the haunting memories, and as well as the one that clung to his shoe. Scraping it on the flowerbed's wall, the possibility that someone had plotted revenge for all the sixties' crimes came to his mind as it had to Hogden's. "I didn't do it," he thought, like a condemned man. He wasn't guilty; unless guilt comes also from sitting by and doing nothing. It was all too much for the small town elected official. An odor of truth emanated from the now- open door of the newspaper office. One day it would all come out.

Although Cathy Broderick had no real information, she knew something was wrong and as a concerned wife, went about making things worse. If doing nothing when you suspect a crime is abject, what does it mean to reveal your suspicions to one of the suspected criminals? She never worried about her personal danger. No one would harm a middle-aged busybody for blabbing, unless she stumbled onto a party that didn't know that she wasn't privy to any secret. But didn't she defeat her own purpose by these revelations? She wasn't aware of her moral dilemma as she blurted out her worries to the guilty party. Or at least someone guilty and belonging to that party; if not party to the crime, then party to the purpose.

Hogden thought he was putting things together without the mayor's questions. Cain, Broderick, and Barker had all disappeared over one weekend. Barker's wife had called the sheriff's office too. Harper's son and Slaughter seemed evasive. He was wondering if they were keeping secrets. He wondered about Rover's involvement. Rover didn't seem himself. They used to cover these things, or cover them up, walk all over the evidence, together, but now he was beginning to have doubts about Rover's silence. Knowing that Cathy Broderick was jealous and that she imagined her husband was having an affair with the Cajun girl, he cast aside her ideas about potential female perpetrators and nearby neighbors. He said, "has anyone thought to call the hospitals?" Cathy Broderick looked at him. This time, she was the one who was bewildered. She had put together a plot for a TV series and had forgotten that there could be different ways to pitch a story.

And that was also part of it. Emmy had not gone missing; she had taken a detour. She had been to see her friends in Baton Rouge. Once Pierre let her off near the riverbank, on her way back from collecting her truck and boat-trailer, Emmy saw five buzzards, their beaks unsheathed, standing around a fallen possum. Was this the *Ok Corral* all over again? June instead of October, but the hot sun was beating down on Mississippi instead of Arizona. Five justiciars, closing in for their own good. Emmy knew what might be going down, except the possum lay on the ground, disarmed, not playing. Dolorosa, a place of pain, of death. You could smell it coming from Hell to tomorrow.

Pulling off the road, she got an old towel she kept for checking her oil from the back of her truck. Then she grabbed her pistol out of the glove compartment and walked over to the buzzards, trying to frighten them away. Shooting her gun in the air was an option, if they didn't move away from their prey. Killing them was not. Buzzards are useful creatures, she knew that. With their sharp beaks and their powerful talons, they keep nature clean. Like grim reapers, they meet with death often; but she didn't want them to consider she had passed her weapon to the other side just yet. Some people had ideas of ridding the earth of ugly and would shoot animals they found displeasing. Emmy didn't make a stop in Dolorosa for that. Neither would death.

Possums are pretty homely themselves, with their jagged teeth and their mangy-looking gray robes. To appreciate the diminutive, mostly in jest, *Possum*, or even *Radbwah*, (*Rat au bois* or woodrat) as the Cajuns called them, one must understand the part they play in nature's design. Sitting like bareback riders taking a stroll through swampy plains and forests, they rid other mammals of superflux. Hundreds of ticks and other parasites, are pilfered every day, right off the hoof, so to speak. Is a free ride ever just a free ride? People need to ask themselves such questions before they grimace, and before they nickname their children because this can catch up with them in school. Don't you know how kids are? Arachnids attaching themselves to terrestrial vertebrates, sucking life's essence from deer and dogs, marsupial magnets stuffing their faces with eight-legged bon-bons; such is the way of the brave in the land of the free. At school it wasn't a question of simply forgetting the O, in opossum, the nickname became, *Tick-licker*; earlier version of the better-known *Dick-licker*, Skizzum had been so proud of repeating with the Junior High school yarn. *Sigh...* Children.

Emmy raised her arms and lunged to frighten the bug-eyed birds, growling as best as she could. Not afraid, but cautious, they bounded a few yards away. The odor of death penetrated her nostrils. Was it coming from the black-feathered cloaks or the furry belly? Examining the bloated possum, she saw what she had come to see. Its innards were dancing with life.

Was this a womb full of maggots waiting to release its putrid bloom? Anyone not familiar with these odd animals might conclude that these movements of the womb were due to parasites, or that this was a female still alive enough to do a hoochy-coochy dance, or to give birth. Emmy didn't hesitate. Her mother had taught her enough about these creatures to know that their pockets are full of surprises. This one had nine. One after the other, until the pouch was empty, she counted. Nine little joeys. Two were dead from the impact of a car, or from suffocation. One was baring its milk-teeth and hissing at her. Two tried to climb back inside. Picking them up and wrapping them in a towel, she looked around to make sure there were no others jolted outside their mother's pouch from the car's impact. "If there were, the buzzards got them," she sighed. Emmy tucked her gun into her waistband and, holding the smelly babies, she lunged once more, this time towards her truck, making them sniff at each other and in the other direction for an instant. "No use to get huffy about it," thought Emmy. On the passenger-side floor-board, she lay the bundle, and regained her place behind the wheel. Peering down at the little joeys she whispered, "y'all aren't startin' off with the best of luck. I'll do what I can, but I can't promise you, you'll all make it."

Putting her truck in gear, she drove away, feeling down-trodden and sad for the possum mother and her babies. She knew what it was like to grow up without a mother's care. For an instant, she thought of her mother being alone.

Rover

Emmy wasn't sure what pronoun to use as she prepared her letter. On one hand, it was getting harder and harder for her to use the first-person singular pronoun. She wasn't going to chop anyone to bits. This wasn't the first time she had asked herself this question. On the other hand, using the first-person plural, we, would associate her somehow with the Klan. She decided for the first-person plural pronoun because it was vague as to the number of people associated. "This isn't my first lie," she thought, as she dropped it off in a Natchez mailbox.

Red Rover, Red Rover, why don't you come over
We'll cut off your head and your dick"
We'll do you in double, Yore lookin' for trouble
For fryin' up Sam Broderick.

Now Rover thought he knew that this note had to come from Slaughter. "Who else know what I done to the Japs? Who else knows what happened with dem fire ants? "Cain is dead. Barker is dead. Now Broderick is, too. Only Jeremy, knows, but him? He ain't got the smarts to write like dat."

Rover stood there holding the old paper. He noticed that his hand was shaking. What had gotten into him? "Am I losin' it thinkin' that fat ass Slaughter done back-flipped and turned into a nigger- loving-communist? Or is Hogden in on this too?" He began thinking about George Metarie again. "Has that nigger started up again? He still green or somethin', runnin' after White girls, if he can stand. He ain't happy about where he got with his

223

NAACP? It's his own damn fault if his nigger friend, Wally Jackson died with that bomb instead of him. FBI WALBOM his fault too. And that other nigger; what was his name, that we tried to fix up with Harvey Lee? I wonder what he is up to now? His birds are all gone. There ain't no smoke without a fire. No sir-eee."

Rover was thinking how Ross and Slaughter got investigated when the FBI came to Ferriday about the Jackson case. They had brought in a bunch of agents and had named the investigation after the bombing and the name of the victim. The agents talked to a lot of people and had informants at the Strong Tire Plant. Ross and Slaughter got investigated at the same time and that was how they ended up in prison, although, not for the bomb. Was this their revenge? Were they jealous about the Silver Dollar Group? Slaughter and Ross had been stupid to admit that they were Klan members. It was their own damn fault if they got put in jail for their racketering and prostitution. "But Cain? He was the owner of the Orville Lounge. He would have never opened his mouth and he stayed out of prison. I learned my lesson when that informant talked to us about Waller. I should've never talked to that little shit," he grumbled, sitting in his car. "I told Cain and Barker they should take care of Broderick and how to do it. They shouldn't have involved Slaughter. Now he's tryin' to turn suspicions on me 'bout that, and 'bout that other fella."

He began to think about making a car bomb to get rid of Slaughter and Hogden, anyone that could connect him to his past. It was easy enough for him to find the blasting powder and C-4 explosives. He had done it before. He had taught them all how to do it at Lee's fish fry in

Lismore. He was wondering if he could teach Jeremy. They needed young blood. He knew that Jeremy was a friend of that new leader, David Ducal. They were all in an itch about the Jews now. "The Jews ain't communists," he remembered arguing to Slaughter. But Ducal was right about one thing; they were causing trouble on other fronts. "They want to replace good White Christian folks and control the world. That's worse than desegregation, I'm tellin' ya. Besides that, by blood, we Whites are superior. Niggers ain't evolved, but that don't stop 'em from becomin' Muslim radicals, just like that El-Shabbaz fellow, used to be called Malcom-X. And Jews are degenerates. I learned all about genetics, about aberrations in prison. And Harper was right. Jews are full of genes. That's their problem. Too many genes cause degeneration when the body tries to adjust itself. That's where the word comes from," Slaughter had replied, holding his girth as high as he could manage for a sixty-year-old man who had spent the last seven years in prison, without much activity.

Rover wasn't convinced about anything Slaughter, or Harper, had said. He seemed like he didn't have much wits about him since he got free. Rover didn't care if anyone thought he himself was paranoiac. His disposition had kept him alive and out of prison thus far. He didn't know about Jeremy's involvement with Slaughter or with the ants. "Just rumors," he murmured to himself. When I got there, Slaughter was alone with Broderick on the ground. What am I supposed to do with this note? Is Broderick dead." He shook his head. "There ain't no need to get my bowels in an uproar before I get all the facts," he said to himself, as he took out his lighter and he lit a cigar. Then holding the lighter to the letter, he watched it as the edges flamed and the cinders crumbled to the ground.

A child is dead

A child was dead. With no warning the little boy lay on the parking lot outside the Winn-Dixie. Emmy didn't know him. She ran over and kneeled down beside him, touching him, like another child might do. There was a young man standing next to them, eyes opened wide, looking about with terrified eyes.

Two other men were there with their motorcycles. They took off their helmets. They both moved closer to the child. One was a doctor, the other, a priest. They both looked like Jesus. The doctor bent down, touched Emmy on the shoulder so that she would move away, and started a cardiac massage.

She watched as a breath, soft as a dandelion's feathered seeds, lifted above the bruises of the South. For an instant, the scars of Ole Dixie smoothed over as people gathered and united on the asphalt battleground. The child did not come back from whereever he had gone. Had he had enough of life and was ready to move on? There was no visible mark on his head or body. Emmy stood. The ambulance was on its way. She could hear a faint siren bleating. Ten, perhaps twenty-minutes, had passed. Time moving as death. The massage continued. The paramedic intervened. Nothing could be done.

The doctor was in shock. No number of adult deaths had prepared him for the sudden death of a child. The child's mother came out of the store. She seemed to take the child's passing better than anyone else, saying he was better off where he now was. Comer's Funeral Services were called.

The priest gave a small flask of holy water to the mother who put her groceries in the car, then sprinkled the water on the child as she kissed her son. The child could not have been older than ten or eleven. Emmy didn't know. His peaceful face seemed to cast a soft light upon them all. The little boy was loaded into a hearse. An ambulance could do nothing more for him. The doctor cried in the arms of the priest. He thought he could save the child. The priest said some prayers. He could do nothing more.

Nothing and nothing more. Wasn't more than nothing already something? Emmy didn't know. She wasn't sure she still believed in God after all that had happened to her, all that happened to everyone she knew. She believed in the order of the universe, believed that faith in that order was sort of like the coarse lignin supporting soft cellulose layers of a tree so that it could stand against the wind. Yet, somehow, with the death of this child; she felt there was something that had come apart, some instant storm or disruption that could fall even a forest.

It was the suddenness of death. This was not in the order of things; dying when one was so full of life; untouched by disease or crime. Was the universe a chaotic place after all? Had they, for just an instant, been thrown out of the cosmos and with a sudden jolt, come back to earth? It was the bizarreness of the parking lot; the grocery bag split open, the bread and jam spread around as if to share. It was traumatic, yet somehow peaceful, like a child's picnic, in a setting, odd for adults, but not for a child who might play in a parking lot as well as in a forest or near a stream. Aren't such questions for the living? Do the dead care where they have died? What notion of his or her own death does a child have?

There was speculation that the boy had been hit by one of the motorcyclists. The strangeness of the sudden death was unreal. Emmy's senses seemed to fold together like an accordion. At last, she pondered on what seemed like a moment of infinite, yet infinitesimal change in the universe; that moment when sound stopped, space contracted, people and objects moved in slow motion. She wondered if that sensation of a shift in the balance, the movement before the creation of a new equilibrium is what makes us human. She had never felt it open her chest and climb into her like a thorned and flowering kudzu the instant life had left the child. She wondered if or how it could affect people across the world or if it changed anything at all other than the loss of a child to a family, and the ripple felt among the group of onlookers and assistants.

Police were asking questions. Out of the corner of her eye, she saw one of the deputies who had been talking with Jeremy. The deputy had a small notebook and was asking questions to the men on the motorcycles. Rumors buzzed, but she could not focus on what she was hearing. Emmy went over and sat on the curb in front of the diner. The door was open, but she was away from the crowd. Stunned, the accordion continued to bellow, but she didn't hear the music; she could not find her keys, her words, or even remember to look for them.

There was the anger, the impotence, the realization that this was a public place, the lack of being able to respond, of not knowing how to respond, of responding and of not being able to perform, of performing and not saving. "If my mother had been here, she would have known what to do. If I had pushed in front of him, he would not have been out the door so fast. If I would have been closer, I could have pulled him back, pulled him back from death," or, as some believe; from a better place. Stay with that, Emmy thought. "But why does the mind think these things when it knows good and well that it is impossible to go back to that before place," thought Emmy, still sitting on the curb; watching the priest and the doctor as they stood, heads down, arms hanging out beside their sides, their helmets rolling on the ground.

Little by little there were the should haves and the could haves rising like odors of burned food above the patrons, ordering grits with eggs sunny-side-up or paying for their coffee and pancakes. People talked as though they could somehow repair the past; arrange life to be like it was before the child died, before the grits coagulated in the pans (or in stomachs), before the syrup ran out. There were those who were quick to pass judgment: "The mother should have prevented him from running to the car." Or, not knowing the cause of death; "Motorcycles should not be allowed to drive through parking lots." Or, "Where was the child's father?" "The mother, was she seeing someone else?" People had different opinions on how to make things right. But all of these were backwards. You could not fix the future by recreating the past. Reality would have nothing of it. There was that void again. Even if Mamere, and Papere before her, seemed to hang around, holding on to life or not being allowed to leave it; there was nothing to be done about death itself. A child is dead. That was the phrase that was hard to put in the past.

A man, with a Stetson hat, came out to see if she needed help. She stared at him, almost as if she did not understand his question. Was she so far from reality that she could no longer respond to kindness? The strangeness of social codes, of simple manners hit her as she was there, trying to figure out if she had anything physically wrong with herself; almost as if the death of the child, had also affected her in some way that prevented her to stand, to put one foot in front of the other, to move forward, and to her truck. Was it possible that you die a little bit yourself when you witness the death of a child? Was the universe moved by the instance of this disappearance?

Emmy didn't know. She felt something different. A yet to be named wave of emotion submerged her. The faces around the child had worn expressions of worry, of caring, of failure, of devastation. Life seemed to be suspended for an instant. Instead of moving on with its fuss and bother, its need to hurry off to the next task; its thrust lingered there, not thrusting at all; like an interval of silence, a soundless score of musical rest notes; a shared sentiment of irreparable loss. What made it different from other states of disrepair and loss was that others shared it. For the first time in many years, Emmy realized that she was not alone. Her aloneness was not the fact that there was an absence. It was the emptiness that came from pushing away others with whom you could share feelings. Since she had begun her crusade against Jeremy, against the Klan, she had not realized the rippling effect of her activity. She thought that she had contributed during the past year to the violence between the members of the Klan, had feared for her life on a couple of occasions, but she caught only a glimpse of how her plan contributed to her personal isolation. Had she thought about the implications of her toxic concoctions, perhaps she would have changed these. She put the groceries for her lonely Christmas dinner in her refrigerator. No more thought was given to these questions than there was to ideas about possible harm to herself.

Death

Emmy opened the bedroom door and gazed at the little possums, piled up on each other. There were only four left. "One is in the corner of the box. It doesn't move. It must've given up on life." Picking up the hardened body, flattened and shriveled, she muttered under her breath, thinking of the weight lifters she saw on TV, "It isn't with life that you will be getting any muscles. You won't ever hang by your tail or climb a tree." She didn't notice the flies or the maggots. Sighing, she took the dead possum outside into her side yard; there where her family once had horses, and dug a hole. She placed the animal inside, recovered it with the soft dirt and said, "please take care of this precious soul," knowing full well that the Church held that animals didn't have one.

Wondering if she hadn't drowned the little possum when she had last fed them with the dropper, the milk plume curving like a fairy-finger of death into the lungs, she returned to the bedroom and removed the mealy worms from the jar she had bought at the bait store to try them on the remaining young animals. "Perhaps instinct could teach them to catch the worms," she thought, closing the door behind her. "Why are they dying? The others grew up and are now playing near the treehouse. I wish Mama was here, or Bee, to help me with them." It was as if her distress was so great that she had not realized that the remaining possums were all dead, and had been dead for some time. She needed them so she would find hope to dream of her mother's release and hope for the return of her friend, Bee.

"How long has it been?" she tried to remember the date. But the date had gone the way of the possums; time had died with the child in the parking lot. Emmy could not remember how long her mother had been in prison. How long had she been promised life; to have it taken and put away, like the mealy-worms, in a jar-like room, with the forever-top screwed down tight? That was what life in prison had to mean for that beautiful, freedom-loving woman who cared for people and animals, but had cared for her daughter, even more.

Emmy was standing in the middle of her living room. These thoughts filled her mind and she forgot about her dinner. The narrative didn't fit the script. She sat down at the piano and scratched a few notes of music on a piece of paper. In the past, she had written entire songs, but now, she forgot where she scribbled her thoughts. These were penned on pieces of paper along with bits of future novels and poems for lyrics, losing their meaning a few days later. Withered oak leaves coming loose like bats, blinking wings on air beneath the burdened moon. Death. Life turned upside down like the creatures, hanging themselves inside caves and hollows, careful to swing back up to avoid their own excrements. Death knew how to perform. Like the living, it could wear a disguise.

Emmy sat there. Had she fallen asleep? She wrote a few more lines, then walked to her couch where she lay down and soon fell asleep again.

During the night, she woke with a start. *Dung hill. Fertilizer for farms and gardens. Flowers, indecent, with their genital organs staring outwards.* Her mother had catalogued them all. *Cats, licking their crotch. Dogs, that smell each other's ass. Double-dicked creatures.* "All of them. All of them as bad as Harper. As bad as that other man. It's logical; the drive, the instinct, like reality. Inescapable." What had she dreamed to come up with such ideas? It was all so confusing. "Didn't he want to find love? Didn't he want to go on with God's plan." Emmy walked over to the piano. She was finding it harder and harder to chase these ideas of some sort of universal perversion, harder and harder to address these concerns to herself without resorting to something like mathematics, but not mathematics because she didn't know any math. Harder and harder to address herself as herself, or even as belonging to a vague *we*.

"Harper and Harper go to school. They are identical twins. One sits in the front. The other in the back. The first one says, *the first person is me*. The second says, *the second person is you*. Who is the third person? *Us*. The teacher says, *that is incorrect. Anyone else?* These students are bonkers. Their teacher isn't fair. Being twins can't be easy. But easy, isn't that hard? The first Harper leaves the class. The second one moves up to the front. When the first one comes back from the bathroom, his pants still unzipped, he says, *hey, he took my place!* The teacher says, *go sit down!* The first Harper curses his brother under his breath, *Dick*, he whispers, as he moves to the back. The second Harper says, with a grin, *dat bird's gonna fly if you don't zip dem pants*. Now the second Harper is first." Emmy was trying to figure something out.

Like a riddle, it was all so muddled. The first Harper was the second and if the bird flew, maybe she was one of them. But she knew she was an only child and couldn't be a twin. She knew she was not a Harper. She was a Robichaux. A Dufrene-Robichaux. Redbone, and Cajun. Cajun and Redbone. She looked at her bare arm, then her hands. She thought she was too White to be a Redbone. Porcelain hands, her grandmother had said, when she took her to the red-water basin and clay oozed through her fingers like thickening blood. Like *Red blood and Bone. Redbone.* And she was reborn; reborn a Houma Indian, like her father. The ceramic- like hands did not remain folded in a cemetery pose or painted on a flag. These cut and pasted, in a fury, like a ripper's scalpel, cutting through tender flesh.

Cigars

Red Rover, Red Rover your cigars are all over,
You've lit your last... Little Prick.
Your fire is burned out,
No more than a pout,
't'll be shoved up your ass like your dick.

Emmy kept preparing her poisoned pen letters. She enjoyed this part of her mission. It gave her a sense of purpose.

Jones, ol' crone, bag of bones,
Of colors blue, Black, and Norris

Your face is a rag,
You look like a hag.
Your dick is all out of service.

"Even you buckshot, pock-faced incapacitated guys deserve to be tormented for what you did to Norris," she said to herself. She gave herself an excuse for her own form of cruelty, as she slashed through the journals and cut the tiny print *i*'s as if these were the eyes of the Klansmen, as well as their dicks. "This ain't nothin' compared to what you deserve. You hadn't been in a wheel chair the day you struck that match. If your face got shot, it was because you tried to kill yet another man." She addressed the absent men as she prepared the letters. Emmy was pretty sure of how things had happened, after what she had heard at the barbershop. Rover deserved the same treatment as Broderick or worse.

She put the letters in an envelope made from the newspapers and put it in the pile between the December fourteenth nineteen sixty-four edition, the day Martin Luther King won the Nobel Peace Prize, and the following newspaper, with Frank's obituary.

She opened her refrigerator and got out her TV dinner. It was the first time she had bought one and thought it might make her holiday special. As she sat down at the table to eat, her first forkful proved her wrong. She settled with the apple pie with a scoop of ice cream. Her little birds had long gone and she wondered about getting a cat or dog to keep her company on such nights. Most of the possums had survived and she had set them on their way in the woods near her treehouse. Was this melancholy a feeling of nostalgia for past Christmases when they would all gather around with their instruments and sing? Or was her weariness that of the aloneness, and of missing of herself as she had been?

She sat down at her keyboard and played around with some chromatic changes from C major to E flat. It was the bitter sweetness of the Rachmaninoff Piano Concerto Number 2 she was looking for, trying to remember the second movement. Why did "Three Blind Mice" keep coming up in her mind instead? Either would express her sadness, as much as some Christmas songs. She didn't want to go there. But there it was. As plain as the absence of Mistletoe, the Yuletide Carols, and the Santa whose eyes twinkled brown and not blue. Nat King Cole's « Christmas Song » made you feel whatever you were supposed to feel once a year. And she could feel the thoughts of the song more now that she was alone. She wondered why she couldn't go on with her music even without her voice. She could listen to others sing, or play an instrument whenever she wanted. What part of the tale was preventing the coziness that could come with the nostalgia? Was it the chord change, which occurred when she picked up a knife, scattering the mice hither and thither, causing them to run here and there? It was true; a chord change could do that, take one from feeling sadness and pity to feeling angry and murderous. She had seen it before. Where was Mamere when she needed her? Had a chord change modified the course of her life?

She wondered about Jeremy. Did his family celebrate Christmas? Were they joyful? Were his kids as awful as Harper's had been? She had assumed they were, without thinking of how a different life could have given them less miserable prospects, even happier constitutions. Could Harper's own kids have been different if Harper had left sooner? She wondered what had happened to the others. Were parental frustrations enough to make them lose their minds a generation later? The key change brought her emotions to the surface, like a drop of water brings a fish. But it was the story she was thinking that made her feel whatever and wherever these were. She thought about how the child's death brought about modifications in the universe, but she wasn't sure yet what it had changed for her. Bee would have been more scientific about it. Thinking about her friend brought Emmy back to the modulations of the chromatic voices in her head. She thought if she could just stand with her feet flat on the ground, engaging her body with the earth, she could capture some of the strength that she remembered had been there, and sing again. "But then there was the little girl. Was she still in the guest room? Should I give her a TV dinner? A Christmas present? What should I do with her?"

She was about to write something on a slip of paper so that she would remember to do it, when she heard a knock at her front door. Petrified, she sat there in front of the piano, staring at her lifeless hands. She wondered if the men had seen her from the riverbank. Would Jeremy be her executioner after all? Maybe she should keep her gun in her pants, even in her house. She wondered how long she had been sitting there.

"Emmy," a voice cried. "Emmy, open up. I saw you through the window and know you're there." Emmy didn't move. An ache between her shoulders made itself known. Seated at the piano was a shadow of herself. She had been curved over the piano longer than she had realized.

"Could it really be Skizzum?" A sprinkle of warmth radiated her body, like when the sun first comes out from behind a cloud on a winter's day, only from the inside. She lifted her head a little.

"Emmy, hey, open up. It's me!" Skizzum started looking around the front steps. "Is there a spare key?" she muttered, looking under the potted plants. "Emmy, don't shoot me. I found a key and I'm coming in."

Skizzum turned the key with caution and opened the door. The smell of boxwood, dirty clothes, or worse, was overpowering and she put her hand over her mouth and nose. She saw Emmy, slumped over the piano. She discharged the two grocery bags she was holding on the couch and ran over to her friend, throwing her arms around her, and trying not to show her distaste. The redolent emanations coming from this girl she had known since she was a small child reminded her of the homeless men and women, standing with her in a soup line when she had been down and out like them, in Los Angeles. They could only clean themselves when they could manage an entry into a public restroom and that was discouraged in many places. But Emmy? "Maybe it's worse because I'm clean?"

"Emmy, dear Emmy! I'm so glad to see you," she exclaimed, hugging her tight in spite of it all. She wanted to say, "How long have you been like this? Let me take care of you," but she knew that her friend could not hear that just now.

Emmy didn't move. "Is that Skizzum," she wondered, trying to bring her mind out of some dark place she had been visiting for her novel, or from the song she had been playing on the piano. Her brow knitted and she turned her head to look at her friend with worried, almost frightened eyes. She let Skizzum take her by the shoulders and lead her to the couch.

"I brought some Christmas things," Skizzum said, as if their meal together had been planned and everything was normal. But everything was not normal. She thought, "Oh my God! Emmy must weigh less than ninety, eighty pounds? She looks awful. And the smell. The house smells of urine and cabbage and, death."

"I see you've been practicing the piano," continued Skizzum.

Emmy sat there, immobile, her arm still lifted where it had come off of Skizzum's shoulder. Skizzum put it down on the couch and patted her friend's leathery hand. She noticed how the skin bunched where she had touched her and took just a second to regain its form. "Dehydration?" She wondered. Her hands had little round, purplish scars, and places that looked as if she had been scratched. Familiar with the states that Emmy could get into, she had never seen her so far gone. True, she had not seen her in a year, maybe two. Skizzum had vowed never to come back to Ferriday. But now that her grandfather was dead, and all the others moved away; her mother, T-Beaux, T-Pierre, were in South Louisiana, and her sister, Bee was on the other side of the planet, doctoring someone else; she felt she could come. "Where was a family doctor when you needed one?" she mused with irony. She caressed Emmy's hand and looked around the room before announcing, "I'm going to look in your kitchen and see what you have for Christmas dinner." She thought she saw Emmy's face twitch a little.

A doctor in Natchez said that Emmy had suffered multiple traumas, but he didn't think she was anorexic. "He should see her now," thought Skizzum, not knowing if the state of deep-freeze was part of an anorexic syndrome or something worse. She thought it must be something else. She wondered if the girl she had come to love was still in there. In the past, she had helped Emmy get through some of these states she had later called, *white noise.* She had fed her and washed her. Put her to bed. Just now, she didn't know what the best route would be. Should she take her to the hospital? Knowing how hard the hospital had been on her as a child, she talked, filling up the uncomfortable empty space between them.

"Did you hear that John Lennon died?" Skizzum asked, not wanting to say the word, *assassinated*.

"Of course, I heard about Elvis dying. Although I'm a little younger, and not with the music scene, I felt the ripple as one of music's greats went out like a damp fire. It had been months since he had died, but John Lennon?" Emmy stirred, but couldn't say what she was thinking.

Emmy sometimes listened to the radio. It wasn't on now, but she did have one. Sometimes she heard the news. She had heard about a cult in the forests of Guyana and wondered about the hundreds of men, women, and children who swallowed Cyanide-laced Kool-Aid. "Did they drink it of their own free will or to the beat of a machine gun. Nine hundred and nine dead. Nine hundred and nine. Why had they done it? When had they done it? Was it before they left Indiana? Or when they arrived in Guyana?" She wondered if Harper would have made them drink poison had her mother not killed him. "Weren't they already drinking it before he died?" Feeling depressed that she had not been able to help the Black community with anything other than anonymous letters, she wondered now if she could do something to help an unbalanced sky. "What amends could be made for the *revolutionary suicide* squad from the Peoples Temple, and all the other wrongful, hateful, insensitive deaths that we could feel somehow linked to ?" her mind was wandering off on one of its many tangents, again, and this time, forgetting who she was. Now, as Skizzum talked, she winnowed the information she was hearing.

"What had happened to this wonderful musician? It seems like only yesterday, we sat with a hundred other girls, in the seats of the Arcade theater during a showing of *A Hard Day's Night*, while Bee, forever and always Bee, marveled at us, instead of the show." They had loved the *Rubber Soul*, *Sergeant Pepper*, and the *White Album*. Emmy loved them all.

Skizzum looked at her friend, and thought she saw a glimmer of life. Immobile eerie eyes shifted once, twice— watching from deep within a body of stone. One of the *Fates*--Lachesis perhaps, had taken flesh anew.

Wishing she knew how much her friend had kept up with the world since the last time she had seen her, Skizzum went over to the radio and turned it on. Static. Turning the nob, she found a station, probably Natchez or Alexandria. At this time of evening in Ferriday, on Christmas, she wasn't sure anyone was there. She found Chuck Reynolds on KEZP for Alexandria and Bunkie, announcing new releases and Christmas music for the *nineteen-eighties*. "Jingle Bells" by the Carpenters, she thought, not sure Emmy had caught on to the news about John Lennon. Afterwards, she turned her attention back to the room. Perplexed by her friend's time warp, which the odor of rotting food and an unwashed body's effluvium revealed, she looked around the room. "Where is the smell of death coming from?" she wondered, almost saying it out loud.

The kitchen was in the same disarray and filthy condition as the living room. There weren't many dishes, but some crusted over partially eaten TV dinners that looked like they could be as much as a year old. Some kind of blue and white glue looked like it had spread on to a piece of what could have been a pie. Overflowing garbage bags sat on the floor. Under the kitchen sink, she found a new bag and tossed the dinners. "I'm taking out the garbage," she called. She opened a window.

Skizzum remembered when Mérite-Lajoie and Deux Ours were alive. The house had been warm and friendly, with family photos and decorations at Christmas. Sometimes, the overstock of stuffed or ceramic Santas and Angels had been disquieting. Mérite-Lajoie's watercolors: landscapes, animals, especially horses, so many horses, outnumbered the empty places on the wall. She also framed and hung Emmy's drawings before Harper took over their lives, which he had begun to do early on, before they moved to Ferriday. Different from the Christmas decorations, the paintings made with powders extracted from earth, vegetal dyes, and cochineals, had a professional quality, but Mérite-Lajoie had that naïve, childish nature that delighted children. Her decorative schemes seemed garish to many adults. Not one photo or painting was left on the walls now. Skizzum wondered what Emmy had done with it all.

When she came back inside, Emmy was standing in the middle of the living room, swaying from side to side. Skizzum ran over to steady her, afraid that her friend could not stand. She appeared to be staring at the open window. Skizzum led her to a chair in the breakfast nook, next to the kitchen and put some water on to boil. "I'll make us some tea," she said, but she felt it was urgent to get some food into Emmy. "How 'bout an orange-Julius instead?" she asked, putting one of the raw eggs she had brought for the Christmas dessert in a bowl and beating it before putting it into a glass with some orange juice.

She pulled a chair close to Emmy. "Now I want you to do something. Can you open your mouth and let me feed you, like a baby bird?" Emmy opened her mouth and Skizzum put in a spoonful.

Emmy swallowed. Hard. Her throat was scratchy and dry. She thought she had eaten a TV dinner, but could tell now that she had not eaten anything in days. She couldn't remember if she had remembered to drink. She must have; her pants were wet. She couldn't remember what she forgot to remember, what she should have known, without remembering. As ordered, she opened her mouth again.

Skizzum repeated the gest until Emmy had swallowed five spoonfuls. "Success!" she thought to herself. "Kinda." It would take more than one session of feeding before Emmy could feed herself. She opened the refrigerator. There wasn't much in it. That was a blessing, seeing the rest of the place. There were some half-full jars of jam, and an open can of ravioli. She threw the can away. The jam looked alright. Skizzum wiped the shelves with a clean wash cloth and put the groceries in it. She couldn't imagine cooking anything for either of them just now and opened a beer for herself. After taking a few sips, she asked Emmy if she could use the bathroom. Emmy stared at her. Her brow was wrinkled, deep in thought; and her pupils looked like tiny black vessels floating on a deep northern sea. Glacial. Distant.

Skizzum wandered down the hall and found a bathroom in the same foul state as the kitchen. She cleaned hurriedly, dumping bleach she found under the sink into the bathtub and toilet, scrubbing, and rinsing. The sink was in the same state with a grayish gunk, the mirror covered with a film of dust. Returning to the kitchen she found Emmy tottering in the middle of the room again, focalizing, she thought, on the open window. She closed it and wrapped her arm around her friend's waist and led her to the bathroom.

"Emmy," she said. "You need a bath." Emmy inclined her head like a nod. Skizzum didn't think Emmy could sit in the hard bathtub. She thought, "It's like before. She hasn't got any ass and sitting in the tub would hurt. She doesn't look like she could hold herself up and might crumple and drown if I leave her." But Emmy needed a bath. "Maybe if I just sit by her and scrub her back?" But Emmy just stood there. Skizzum sighed. She unbuttoned her friend's jeans and pulled them down with her underwear. "Now step out," she ordered, as if Emmy was a three-year-old instead of a young woman close to her own age. She turned her head away as to not notice Emmy's soiled clothing and tossed these into the hall. Pushing her shoulder so that she would sit on the toilet, she began to fill the tub with warm water. Opening a cabinet, she found a forgotten bathroom floormat, and put it in the bottom of the tub. "Emmy," she instructed. "Don't move. I'll be right back." Skizzum sprinted to the kitchen and grabbed one of the gifts she had bought for her friend; potpourri that she had found in Nashville. "Better in the bath than in a drawer," she thought.

When she came back, Emmy was standing again, but otherwise immobile, still staring at the window through the venetian blinds. Leaning over the bathtub, Skizzum pulled the strings to close the slats. "Have a look," she said, "this is for you." Emmy turned her head to the side as if she didn't want to see. "Well at least we are getting somewhere," Skizzum said, as she opened the gift and extracted the cloth package. She untied the ribbon and sprinkled some of the tiny flowers in the running water and put the rest on the counter. She checked the water, then continued to undress her friend. Sharp angles and loose skin were there where had once been, had once been... a slim, yet curved shape, and rosy, opalescent skin, as blemish-and-freckle-free as in the Vermeer painting of the *Young Woman with the Pearl Necklace*. Skizzum's stomach, not yet turned sour by the acrid smell of her friend's body, turned over. At least it felt like it had. She thought she might vomit and made a compassionate retch, herself hurting as saw Emmy's backside in the mirror. She helped her into the bathtub. Emmy , herself more liquid than solid, sloped and began to collapse and slip under the water, taking the form of the bathtub, in spite of the mat.

"Oh no you don't," said Skizzum, pulling her back up. "Mind if I get in with you? Asked Skizzum. She was already undressing. She didn't need a bath and didn't much want to get into the bathtub, already turning brown, but she felt like it was the only way. Her friend couldn't bathe, and could not sit up in the hard tub, even with the mat. "What's a half an hour of putrid body odor when you love someone?" she thought to herself, looking away, trying not to gag. She pulled the plug and left the water running while she got in the tub behind Emmy.

They had had a degree of friendship, a degree of intimacy after what they had both gone through. For an instant, she was like a pocket to a child's treasure, a nest to a small bird.... On this point, Harper was right. They were like sisters. More than sisters, she was now more like a mother with a small child.

.

Skizzum took a wash cloth and soaped Emmy's back. Then she washed under her arms, avoiding scrubbing more than necessary. The brownish water, clearing with the fresh running water was clouding up with the soap. The potpourri flowers were frivolous. She reached around and put the plug into place. The tub filled again with clean water while she washed the rest of her friend's body, pulling her legs apart, and noting the eschars. "Mosquito bites rubbed with shit? Jesus," She whispered in her mind wishing she had not dared to think of it. "Lean back Emmy, far enough so I can wash your hair." Legs scrunched up in front of her, the young woman let her body fall into Skizzum's arms forcing her to the back and the side of the tub.

Feeling lucky that she was not as tall, Skizzum thought she was perhaps as much as six inches shorter than her friend, and no one ever thought of her as petite. She felt luckier that Emmy had not been in contact with anyone and didn't have lice. But what is luck if not a comparison, a deduction that somehow, you've got it better, or not so much better, than someone else?

Once her friend was clean, Skizzum placed both of Emmy's hands on the side of the bathtub, and putting her own hands, on top, as she had learned to do when she trained to be a life-guard for the Ferriday swimming pool, so-many-years-ago-before-Harper, she lifted herself out. Although Skizzum was not heavy, Emmy winced a little under her friend's weight.

"She must be a crumple of pain," thought Skizzum. Then she bent over and pulled Emmy out. It wasn't easy, but after pushing an upright piano around Nashville on more than one occasion, Skizzum had acquired some heft and muscle and knew how lift a weight almost as heavy as herself. With a soft towel, clean except for the dust, she patted her friend dry. She had forgotten to bring a change of clothes into the bathroom. Putting her arm around Emmy again, she led her to the bedroom and sat her on the side of the bed. She was thankful that in Louisiana, the weather had not yet grown cold. Emmy slumped, but did not fall. Her spine bent, her vertebrae cracking as they settled like a fallen *chateau des cartes*. She looked like a woman much older than her years.

The sheets were just as filthy as the rest of the house. These were gray and Skizzum wondered when the last time they had been washed or slept in. "Stay here," she ordered. "I'm going to get clean sheets. She looked around until she found some in the armoire of the master bedroom. When she returned to the room, she found Emmy standing again. "What's with the standing in the middle of the room?" she asked, but Emmy only blinked.

Skizzum led Emmy to the chair near her desk. She noticed a lot of paper scraps, but didn't take the time to examine these and didn't comment. While Emmy was in the chair, she stripped the bed, put on clean sheets, and pulled back the covers. "I guess I better look in here for your pajamas?" It was a question without being one, and without asking for permission either. Skizzum was already fumbling in Emmy's chest where she found a large T-shirt. Again, she dressed Emmy, as she had undressed her, more like a doll than a child, without the ability to lift her arms or to bend them. She then picked up a large toothed-comb on the chest and began to tug at the snarls. It was like fighting with briars, and the thorns were winning. "Emmy," said Skizzum, "We are going to have to cut your hair. It's falling out anyway. Unless you want me to fix it with little pigtails, like Popeye's Olive? You could play her role in a film!" Emmy sat there, passive, neither encouraging nor refusing the care that Skizzum was offering. "She didn't laugh about Olive Oyl. Has she become indifferent to losing her hair or teasing?" she pondered. Skizzum picked up the scissors from the desk.

Again, she was intrigued by the scraps of paper and what appeared to be letters that had been cut from magazines or newspapers, but didn't say anything. "Emmy, I'm going to have to cut it pretty short so it will get thick again." Emmy still didn't react. Skizzum sighed remembering Emmy's once thick, beautiful hair, as black and as shiny as an obsidian rock. Holding up a handful, she noticed how some of it pulled away from the scalp as she combed. Wincing in silence for Emmy, and suffering to see how poor her friend's overall health had become, she cut until there was only a couple of inches left. She wished she could glue the fallen hair now on the floor, onto the bare parts of Emmy's scalp. Emmy might not ever recover her health.

She brought Emmy to the bed and laid her down, then covered her. "I'll be right back," she said. Still naked, she carried the sheets to the washing machine and stuffed them in. She looked around for some soap and not finding any, settled with a prewash and some more bleach. Anything to get rid of the overall house-stench.

She found her bag, put on a T-shirt with a silkscreen of John Lennon and the word, *Imagine,* and clean panties. She returned to find Emmy standing again in the room. Leading her back to bed, Skizzum climbed over her and turned off the light. The smell of death's rot still permeated the house. She was too tired to investigate further.

Putting her arm around the fragile body, snuggling close and feeling the sharpness of the bones with the sadness of their friendship. She said, "I love you, Emmy," pulling her closer so that Emmy's head was in the crux of her arm.

Sometime in the middle of the night, maybe two or three, she became aware that Emmy was absent. She got up, calling, "Emmy, where are you?" She began to worry, wondering what her friend had been up to all this time.

She walked around the house and found that the young woman was nowhere in sight. From the kitchen window, she could see that there was a light coming from the old trailer office. She put on her shoes, and slipping out the sliding door, she walked over to the trailer and knocked. Emmy did not answer. She turned the handle and pushed the door. There, Emmy was standing with a terrified look on her face, and pointing a pistol at her friend.

"Whoa!" she said. "It's only me." Rattled, she pushed the barrel towards the floor then took the gun out of Emmy's hand, placing it first on the desk, then in the drawer. "What's going on?" she asked. She could see more scraps of paper on Mérite-Lajoie's old desk, some of them glued to a sheet of paper. Emmy still wore a frightened expression. "It's just me." Skizzum said again, hugging her close and rubbing her back. The trailer not only had a smell of old, unwashed bodies, but of mold and mildew, and she suggested, "Why don't we go inside and talk about it. There is no one in the yard. We can get some tea and maybe nibble on something. It was late, and she realized that she was hungry now, missing the Christmas dinner she had wanted for both of them. Missing a holiday moment, the effect from the beers she had had, was worn off. Skizzum led a stiffened Emmy back inside and locked the glass-door behind them. Behind the house, she eyed the old graveyard with the machine-cemetery on top, and wondered if Emmy had been spooked. There weren't many machines now, and the tombstones were all gone, but at night, there was still something creepy about the place. Fog groped toward abandoned bodies, emanating a spectral light. Hunched bramble-hellhounds, growled and prepared to lunge at each other's throats over rusting machine corpses. Although some effort had been made to clean up the area, the people who were buried there could not find repose. On some nights, with any wind at all, with any imagination at all, the air whistled through the gin siding and the metal junkyard agitated in protest. Clanking chains rattled, awakening iron bars to life as if they were hungry zombies. Yet Skizzum could not help but wonder what else could be troubling Emmy. She would not have needed a gun to protect herself from a ghost.

A sea of trouble

Emmy had heard something. She was worried for Skizzum who seemed unaware, who did not know about the risks. "She doesn't know that Jeremy, or some other member of the Klan might be here, just outside the door. I saw him myself, in the graveyard beyond the house hiding something, a weapon, under the machine we called our spaceship. He had put his arm up into the airlock transfer place where we had made him sit, and wait for expulsion for doing what he did to that dog. Where's Mamere? I need to ask her something." But her grandmother wasn't there. Skizzum was there, at her place, sitting at her table and talking. She could hardly believe it. She realized that she was not opening her mouth to talk and felt all at once ashamed. She hung her head.

Skizzum put a pan on the stove to boil water. The smell of death was so invasive now that she was awake that she had to explore. "Sit tight," she said, while she walked down the hall. She was about to open the guest-room when Emmy came up behind her and blocked her from entering.

"No," almost growling. Skizzum was surprised, but not frightened by Emmy. It was the first word she had said.

"What is it? Don't you want me to get rid of the smell?" Emmy looked terrified.

"She's in there," thought Emmy. "I forgot to feed her and now she is dead. What will Skizzum say?"

"It's okay," said Skizzum. "Whatever the problem is, I can help you solve it."

But Emmy didn't move. Barring the door with outstretched arms, she lowered and shook her head at the same time. Both frightened and ashamed, she was not ready to allow anyone, albeit Skizzum, to enter the room with the dead girl.

"Can we talk about this," Skizzum said. "You can't stay like this. Your house can't stay with whatever is in there."

She led Emmy back to the kitchen table and sat down beside her. Emmy sat there. Skizzum tried to get her to drink more tea, but this time Emmy turned her head. Skizzum took another beer for herself. She sat near Emmy and held her hand on the table. Not knowing if she should ask questions, play some sort of guessing game or what, she just sat there. Time passed. She had another beer, and another. "I need to go back to the PicQuick soon for more beer, do you want to come? I want you to come." Emmy looked at her and motioned for the *Magic Slate*.

"It's Christmas," she wrote. "It'll be closed." Skizzum started looking around the room to see if Emmy had anything stronger, maybe something left over from when Mérite-Lajoie was there.

Not seeing anything, she thought, "I'd better go easy on my last beers." She asked Emmy if she still had a guitar. Emmy nodded, but then looked horrified. "The guitar is in the guestroom," she thought. Mamere couldn't walk around the house with it."

"Come on, Emmy. We've been through a lot together. We need to help each other. I need a beer or a guitar. You need to get your life back together. No secrets. No more secrets. We've lived through that enough."

Emmy looked at her, pleading with her eyes like a dog that understands and does not want to go the vet's office. She held the stylus and began to write. "There is a girl in there. Jeremy's girl. I forgot."

Confused, Skizzum shook her head. "I don't understand. Can I peek ?"

Emmy was reluctant, and thought a minute before writing. "She's dead. I kidnapped her. I didn't mean to, but she got into my truck."

Now she was worried. "Could Emmy do such a thing," she wondered, shaking her head without realizing it. "Look," she said, "I think I should help you figure this out. Like I said, you aren't alone and whatever it is, I will help you." Skizzum was trying to picture this girl, Emmy, who at present could not walk for fifty feet, doing something as rash as her mother had done. "How old was the girl anyway? Wouldn't she be at least six? Seven?" Emmy nodded. "Do you want to look together?" Emmy shook her head. Skizzum realized that she had spoken of the girl in a past tense.

Skizzum got up and walked down the hall. She turned the knob and poked her head in enough to see what the problem was. In the corner of a room filled with paintings and photos, was a large refrigerator box. Peering inside, as if a she was looking in a coffin, she saw the remaining mummified possum cadavers, still giving off stink. Most of the flies were dead on the windowsills. The maggots had almost all taken flight and died. Pulling her head like a turtle inside her sweatshirt, she picked up the box and carried it out the back door. "I'll deal with that in the morning," she offered, not knowing if Emmy listened. "She didn't remember she had little possums," she thought, "but remembered the girl. What happened to her? Where is she now?" She could only guess. Guessing was not like playing a riddle where there is a clear answer. Trying to understand what happened was more like a game of poker and figuring out what was behind the opponent and not the cards, trying to see gambler's pitfalls, and steering everyone away from it. This was something she could play with Emmy, but it would take time. At some point, she would have to get back to Nashville, where she made her living, where she had gigs with several bands.

Skizzum brought Emmy a cup of tea and added a little cool water. She brought her a straw. "Emmy," she said. "Remember when Bee was little and didn't want to wear her glasses?" Emmy smiled. "Remember that time we were in the car with my grandfather and we drove up to your house and Bee squealed, *look how cute, those kittens you have on your steps!* We all almost rolled over laughing saying, *Bee, those are some old shoes!* Well, Emmy, in that box out there, there are some dead baby possums. Three of them, as flat as pancakes and almost empty of maggots. On the windowsill in the bedroom, there are about a hundred dead flies, if not more." She felt like laughing from relief. But Emmy looked distraught. Skizzum put her arm around her. "Don't worry. You did what you could. Possum babies have a hard time living without their moms. Listen. We'll talk about Jeremy's girl later. She isn't in there. Wherever she is, you're in the clear."

"Now I'm going to make us some food, said Skizzum. "How would you like some pumpkin pie?"

Her friend was asking her something about pumpkin pie and ice-cream. Out the sliding glass door, Emmy thought she saw a shadow pass and she ducked.

Skizzum saw her movement. Her eyes shot towards the door, but there was nothing there. She got up and closed the curtain. Emmy looked worried. "There is nothing there," she told her friend. "The little possums are gone." She didn't understand what her friend was afraid of this time.

Even though she had known she could not bring answers to her friend or lighten her suffering by exposing her to the reality of the dead possums, she tripped on the snake in the grass. It was almost as if she told Emmy that the girl had somehow escaped, or worse, that the kidnapping was not real, before making light of it. "Why didn't I keep my mouth shut and not try to reassure her about the dead possums? Why did I make jokes about Bee not seeing? I'm the one who didn't see! Other than the funk, the possums weren't the problem," she thought. "Emmy thinks she has let Jeremy's daughter die, a prisoner in the guest bedroom."

Emmy began to rock herself. Her face was tense. She wanted to explain, but just then couldn't remember what she had wanted to say a second before. Her voice was in its forever deadlock. "Why wouldn't it give way just this once. I've been too long without food again. How long?" she wondered. She had promised herself she would eat, but since she came back from the river, since that awful woman had come over to see if her husband was there, in her house, as if she would have allowed such; she had been afraid. Afraid that her neighbor suspected her. Afraid she had let Valerie die of hunger because she was afraid of what she had done. Afraid that one of them would come for her. Afraid of the police. Afraid for her mother. She was afraid. Whirlpools of thoughts were spinning through her head, like many hands grabbing at her body, bringing her down into a Hell of nonsensical word-song, blurry faces, and mush in her mouth. Trying to force herself to stay in the world of the living, she started shaking again. Only the living can fear. "Here," said Skizzum, "sip your tea. It's still warm."

Skizzum served herself a plate of what looked like turkey and dressing. She also had cranberry sauce, and candied yams. Emmy knew these weren't homemade. A small plate sat in front of her too, with a spoonful of each dish, at least each dish that could be swallowed without chewing. There was a spoon on the side of her plate, but it was as if the different dishes and the face she had seen in the shadows outside had become one and was looking at her with a cranberry sneer, one mash-potato eye, browned with gravy, and the other, a yellowed yam--a broken face staring back at her.

Skizzum didn't think Emmy could or would chew, as in the past when she had had bouts of whatever she had. "Now I want you to try to eat something," said Skizzum. Emmy lifted her head and studied Skizzum's face. Skizzum took a drink of her beer, and ate her turkey.

"How long have you been here, Emmy?" meaning how long have you been like this. Emmy looked at her; her eyes unblinking. Skizzum sighed and moved closer. She picked up Emmy's spoon. "Open your mouth." Emmy hesitated, but didn't want to disappoint her friend. She closed her eyes and did her best to force the invisible strings in her jaw to loosen and her teeth to part. Skizzum fed her a small spoon of the cranberry sauce. Emmy glanced at the plate. The smile withered. She swallowed. Skizzum managed to coax her into tasting a little of each dish.

When they were done, Skizzum cleared the table. She took Emmy to the living room and they both sat on the couch. Skizzum noticed the old piano again and walked over to it. "If I can get to her with music, she might have a chance," she thought. She touched a key, "Hey, there's no sound!" Then she pressed another, and realized that it was off-key. She touched all eighty-eight keys. She looked at Emmy who shrugged. "So, you are playing anyway?" Skizzum asked, wanting to believe that Emmy still held onto something. Emmy nodded, or at least Skizzum thought the slight movement of the head was a nod. "Come here," she said. Skizzum noticed that with maturity, and the lack of mass, Emmy looked more like her father. She had inherited his high cheek bones. Skizzum thought she could have been a striking magazine model. But her skeletal frame, her malnourished skin, her blading scalp, and her scratched raw hands, left her once exotic beauty in a place of celestial springtime.

The two women sat in front of the mute piano as if they could get it to speak with a sound-disabled language. They both placed their hands in front of them. Skizzum began playing the lower octave and looked at Emmy to her right. She stopped and lifted her friend's hands, placing them on the keys and began to play again. Emmy pressed one finger, then another. They began to play a duet, moving their hands over the keys. At first, they played "Silent Night", "White Christmas," and other familiar Christmas-time favorites. The rich aroma of sassafras came to her mind. "Did Skizzum smell the lime-blossom tea?" she wondered.

Then, they played Greensleeves with Skizzum making up words along the lines of Shakespeare and *The Merry Wives of Windsor* where Falstaff exclaims, "Let the sky rain potatoes, let it thunder to the tune of Greensleeves". She laughed and she thought she saw Emmy's lips widen when she went on about the potato rain which transformed into the reign of potatoes and potato chips. The rain of potatoes might have seemed like a Godsend back in the day, but now it just seemed funny.

Little by little, the smattering of Christmas songs and silly, took on the beat of Alfred Newman's music from the film, *How the West Was Won*. Skizzum tapped on the piano like a drum. Emmy inhaled the sweat and the leather. *Ra-ta-ta-ta-ta-ta-tat.* "Come they told me, par-rum-pa-pum-pum." *Rum, a Caribbean drink. Pa, a name, I call my Dad. Pomme, an apple said in French...* "I'm so tired,

I haven't... No that isn't the song," thought Emmy, changing the song in her mind, as it bellied up to a Beatles' album, while she played on. *Me a name, I call myself.* M-E. Emmy.

While an outside observer could see the movement of hands over the piano, hear a rare *la, do,* or *mi-flat,* and the gracing of Skizzum's make-believe drumstick-fingers; inside, their smiles were growing wider and wider, until they could remember a smile as wide as the Mississippi, too wide for the cowboys to cross, at least in their minds. "Cowboys would just stay on their side, or go around, if they didn't want to cross on a barge and wind up way up north anyway," thought Emmy. She liked cowboys in old westerns because they liked horses. She thought about how her mother had come to mind, galloping on a horse in the wind, riding like a frothy wave, lashing the shoreline, before the setting sun. But they were in Central Louisiana, and the cowboys could venture forth on horseback, if they liked. Her association of ideas was rampant, darting from one side to the other, following the words and their sounds, while her fingers kept up with Skizzum, ambidextrous in both body and brain.

Skizzum enlaced Emmy once again. Then, she led her back to the couch and sat down beside her. She made some hot chocolate and brought it over with two little marshmallows floating inside. "I know, you don't have to say it. These are a poor substitute for Mamere's famous marshmallows, but this late in the day, this is all I could come up with. Emmy smiled a little more, remembering one of her grandmother's specialties. If she could just slow down and remember without crossing over to Mardi gras again.

Skizzum noticed the *Magic Slate* on an end table and asked Emmy to use it. Emmy nodded. "Tomorrow, let us do some catching up," she said, her deep Louisiana accent, loose like a ripe plum, giddy, but with fewer grammatical errors than before. She was keeping the conversation light, wanting to avoid communicating her pressing desire to know what had provoked Emmy's fear, her belief that she had kidnapped Jeremy's child, and her weight loss, hoping to avoid pressuring her friend, if she didn't want to go there. These weren't easy topics to get into. As much as she was used to blurting out whatever came to her mind, she realized that her friend was harboring a deep sea of troubles.

She held the cup of hot chocolate for Emmy, although after seeing her play, she realized that she must still have some reserves. She didn't understand how that could be. With all her problems, she had never been there; although she had at least heard of LSD, and what hallucinations might be like.

Emmy was grateful that Skizzum had come. Not knowing how to tell her or to get in touch with her. Unable to telephone and not knowing Skizzum's latest address, she had been unable to write, not daring to hope that she would ever see her again. She leaned her head toward Skizzum, and Skizzum, did likewise. The two sat there with their heads touching for what seemed like a long time. Then, Skizzum reached over to her bag, and took out another present for Emmy. It was a piece of sheet music scrolled up and tied with a ribbon. Chopin's *Nocturne Opus 9, Number 2*. Tears came into Emmy's eyes as she read the music. She got up and walked over to the piano. Placing her hands over the keys, she slowly lifted them and played. Skizzum could hear the gentle, lonely notes that sang to them both without sound. Emmy remembered playing the harp and could smell the perfume of heaven, or at least a breath of night blooming jasmine.

Morning

Emmy awoke to the scent of burnt butter and cooked pastry, of pancakes on a griddle. It had been so long since that aroma had been in her home. She walked to the kitchen. Some strange shaped batter was on the flat-iron skillet. Skizzum said, "it is zee map of France," with a fake accent. "Zit down and let me just take care of yoou some more. I will take yoou to Paris, yes?" she said.

Obeying, a slight curve in her lips, Emmy noticed the curtain was open. Outside there was a breeze making the brown leaves of the Louisiana autumn *shake, rattle, and roll*, and *the sky was gray*. "Do you want to go to Mass," she asked. Emmy started and jerked her head towards Skizzum. Skizzum was joking, of course. Plenty of times she said she didn't believe in God any more. "What? I would go, if you wanted to?" Emmy made a short quick movement of her head to indicate that she would not like to go. Although she still believed in God, she felt she just could not go. Too much had happened to her and to her family. If God was with her, he understood why she did not see the church as his house. Her church was the forest, and it had been thus since she got out of the hospital. After all, hadn't he taken her to the treehouse? Hadn't she saved the baby birds? That was enough. But Skizzum knew nothing about the little peeps, nor the squawks and slithers. Emmy wasn't sure how much she could tell her about that, or all the rest.

After breakfast, Skizzum did some more cleaning. Noting that Emmy took two bites, with only molasses and no butter, she felt encouraged. "That's a start." If she could just get her to eat for a few more days, maybe she would snap out of it. Not wanting to be impolite to her friend by noticing how insalubrious her home had become, she was careful not to stare at the mess, or at Emmy, or whir around with a mop and brush. She would buy some cleaning products tomorrow. Between chores, she sat with Emmy, who seemed troubled in spite of Skizzum's efforts. "You can't just bring softness and love into someone's tortured life and expect all to heal," she thought as she sipped another beer.

Emmy noticed that Skizzum seemed to drink a lot of beer. At ten in the morning, she had already finished one, and had untwisted the top of another. She readjusted herself on the couch. Skizzum came and sat down beside her, taking her hand. "Emmy, can you try to tell me what is going on? I can tell you're stressed out, and more than that."

Emmy looked at her knees. Skizzum had helped her to dress and had chosen a pair of her father's khaki pants and a T-shirt. She liked the big pockets, but the pants were much too big. She didn't have any clean clothes, she figured. "Emmy," said Skizzum. Her voice sounded far away or like it was under water. Wanting to hear her, seeing her struggle through the depths of thick, black-gumbo waters, she looked at her friend, her concern showing through her eyes. "What are those news clippings and cut-out letters I saw last night in the office? Do they have anything to do with why you are so afraid?"

Emmy thought she understood what her friend wanted. Last night, the darkness had moved over a little and allowed Skizzum in with the music, but just now, she was struggling. She had been pulled under with the men she had let drown and had to breach the surface before she could be with Skizzum again. Her finger lifted a little towards her slate. Skizzum handed it to her. Trembling, she wrote, "Jeremy." Skizzum's eyes opened wide. "Are you saying he has been around here? Has he threatened you?"

"No," she shook her head and wrote. "KKK."

Skizzum's eyes were wider still. "He's a member of the KKK and he has bothered you? Have you been to the police?" She affirmed rather than questioned.

Emmy shook her head and wrote, "I can't. Mama. And the cops, some are part of the Klan."

Emmy's mother had escaped the death sentence following changes in the law, which converted her sentence into a life-time behind bars, but gave her hope to be released, someday, as with keeping with the laws of the time. The Supreme Court decided one way, then with the Nixon court, even though Nixon had been forced to resign, they decided another. Now Mérite-Lajoie had no hope of ever coming home except in a coffin.

Emmy knew about these changes. For a child to believe that she is at fault for the death of a beloved man, for the arrest of her mother, then for her impending execution, then to have hope that she would come home, only for that hope to be crushed, is more trauma than a child should ever face. How can a child still believe in truth or compassion between humans? The effects of changes in the law, as well as pronounced death sentences, or life in prison, are cruel and unusual punishments for the condemned inmate's children. The Supreme Court never considered, not any more than these were considered by the proponents of such laws, what might happen to the children. They let the States decide ; they were guilty too. And as Mérite-Lajoie was of an ethnic group no one cared about, then as with other people of color, because theirs were the sentences that had been considered in these rulings, a life-sentence meant no escape. Emmy was purging her pain, as was her mother. But she herself had almost no compassion for her mother now, nor for Jeremy, "the boy, who," she thought "grew up to be like his old man. The old man who loved and hurt me. The woman who abandoned me for her pride. The law and the words of the law. The words and their lies..." How does anyone sift through their beliefs to find the nuggets of truth?

"Can you show me why you cut out the letters?" Skizzum asked.

Emmy looked hard at her friend, trying to decide if she could share this secret, her deepest secret now, with Skizzum. Skizzum had brought her back to life, again, but she was afraid that if her friend knew too much, that she might be pulled into a grave as well. Covering her brow with one hand, she imagined Skizzum running from Jeremy or another one of Slaughter's henchmen. She imagined her see the flesh of a man, torn away by the fire ants. Her eyes pleaded with Skizzum, "Please don't ask. Please don't make me tell you."

"Emmy, you have to tell me. I need to know. I'm here to help. If you don't tell me, I can't leave. I want to take you back to Nashville with me. Anyway, I'm not going to leave you here if you are in danger."

Emmy covered her face with both hands now. She didn't want Skizzum to guess how abject she had become, a blot on the Cajun's escutcheon, although a praying embroidered crawfish on her family flag could hardly be considered a coat of arms. "More like a coat of harms," she thought, "a stain of shame." Yet why was she feeling that? She had been proud of her Civil Rights' work. She was thinking now that she had gone too far, that having caused death, she could only reflect regrets, and from these pricklings of conscience, only hide away with a flea in her ear. Like a family dog that had just gulped down a whole birthday cake, candles and all, she crouched and hung her head with remorse. But that was just it, she had had the cake. She had eaten it. Wasn't that something to be proud of? Emmy could not answer. If only her voice would come out with birthday whistles and toot with its long-colored unfolding tongues, instead of following the dead to their watery and terrible graves.

She contemplated Skizzum, looking deep into her soft brown eyes. "Doesn't Skizzum deserve to know? Can't I have faith in her? Could she be in danger as well, now that she has come back, now that she knows something about it? After all, she had been one of Harper's Angels. Jeremy had been jealous and mean to her, too. Did Harper make her ride in his truck into the Black part of town, as well?" Emmy decided to show her the last letters she had written. The ones she had not sent because she was almost too weak to stand, let alone drive. She took Skizzum by the hand, and walked to the sliding door. Skizzum opened it for them both, and they went out into the cool Christmas morning, their bare feet getting wet with the dew.

She opened the door to the trailer and made her way to the desk. Skizzum looked around. Other than the quick trip the night before, she had not been there since she had hurried in with a fawn in her arms to find Mérite-Lajoie. She must have been about twelve then. Still such a child. Bellowing, the fawn had had the skin of its neck ripped by a dog's angry fangs. Skizzum had heard, then seen the animal try to run on its still wobbly legs. As the dogs brought it down, she ran up on them with a stick, yelling to frighten them away. "It was their pack instinct," Mérite-Lajoie had said. "They're not at fault. Dogs shouldn't be allowed to roam loose, even in the country. One day they will attack a calf, or a foal, and the farmer or average guy will be just so sorry, so sorry, that he let his dogs out. And when he finds himself paying two hundred dollars or so, then he will get twisted-out-of-shape-two-hundred-dollars-short-sorry."

She took the fawn and wrapped it in a blanket, explaining to Skizzum that the mother deer was not far. They left their babies on front steps and in drive-ways sometimes while they were grazing in the distance. "Baby deer are inodorous. Most of the time, predators don't find them because they can't smell them. This one was out of luck. Her Mama left it on the steps of a dog's house." And true enough, Skizzum thought of the two-legged dogs who lived in that house with the four-legged variety. She knew that wasn't nice to think. To tell the truth, she liked their dogs, and almost all dogs, but she didn't like what they had done. Mérite-Lajoie disinfected the cut while Skizzum held the fawn with its spindlelegs. Mérite-Lajoie held a rag with some stinky chemical on it, just a second over the fawn's nose, then she shaved a bit of its fur, before sewing the long tear. She explained to the shaken girl that the fawn was lucky enough to not have its arteries torn. She put a bandage on it, and told Skizzum that the bandage was to keep the dirt out for a few days, but it would fall off on its own.

They put the fawn, already waking and struggling, in the side yard with the horses. One of the mares licked the baby. Mérite-Lajoie had some hope that the mother would show up in time to claim her baby girl and that, her horses would keep an eye on it, protecting it from the dogs. Skizzum never knew for sure what happened. The next day the fawn was gone. Because there was luck to go around, but sometimes, just not enough of it. She hoped the fawn had been saved. She wasn't sure that dogs knew about luck either, or if they knew enough. The day before, when she had chased them away with the stick, they had seen things in a different light.

Now Skizzum watched Emmy, as she pulled out a folded piece of old newspaper. Inside were sheets of yellowed paper with cut-out letters pasted on them. As Emmy positioned the unsigned letters on the desk, Skizzum's eyes widened. With all the terror she had the day she saw the dogs attack the fawn, her stomach, this time, was bellowing like the baby animal. It wasn't what the letters said that frightened her. It was the implication that Emmy was intending to send them. Perhaps she had already done so. Bursts of rumors, reports like guns, came to her mind as she remembered the mention in *Concordia Post* of some anonymous letters years ago. At that time, there was a lot of gossip about Mérite-Lajoie and the Cajuns who had left with the flood, but there hadn't been much to it. They all thought it was Missy Dey Deed again, being her crusty old dabbling self, stirring up gossip like dust and dead leaves.

Skizzum wasn't sure, but she came about it fast enough to ask, "Are these for the Klan?" Emmy nodded. Skizzum understood all too fast for her own sense of stability and held onto the back of the chair. She asked anyway, trying to avoid sounding like the Zola's, *J'accuse*. "Have you been sending letters like this?" Emmy was on the right side of history, but just not on the right side of the law. It was like being in the sixties all over again with firm faces and fists raised, teeth gnashed and posters blazed. Now Skizzum, who had no idea of the breadth and depth of Emmy's crusade, and with the suddenness of a whirlwind, was frightened for her friend.

"Emmy," she said. "I'm taking you back with me."

Emmy bowed her head, shaking it and covering her face. "What didn't Skizzum understand? What didn't any of them understand?" Having never told on Harper, or Jeremy, for what they had done to those boys on the street, she had to do this. She had to keep going, cutting, pasting, composing, mailing these letters to these men who had gotten away with their crimes for too long. She deprived herself of sleep and food to get it done. If she didn't do it, who would? No one would listen to her. No one ever had. As much as she had tried to tell people around her that something was amiss, every time it was amiss; no one listened. No one cared about the Black people in Ferriday. There were signs that they suspected. Oh, they suspected alright. Some more than others. A man would flinch in the chair as he was getting a shave when he heard the barber throw the N-word like a pie. A woman, a kind, church-going woman, would hurry her children away from a sheriff-deputy harassing a Black man. They knew alright, but they did nothing. How did parents sleep at night without explaining why they had cringed, why they had backed out, why they had swept their children away on the street? Perhaps sometimes one of them knew more than he or she let on, but did that change anything? No. Emmy felt sick with what she had discovered. They would never stop. The Blacks, the Jews, no one was safe. How could running away keep anyone safe?

"Oh Emmy," Skizzum said, hugging her. "You can't do this alone. Someone has to help you, or you've gotta let it go."

At the same time Skizzum was fomenting a plan to help Emmy expose the wrong-doings of these men, she was having doubts. Here they were, just days before nineteen-eighty-two. The Civil Rights' Movement was over, wasn't it? Who cared about a few fools prancing around a picnic table yelling at each other about freedom of speech and equal rights for White men?

"Do the men who receive these letters even care? Don't they just throw them in the garbage without bothering to destroy them? There was no proof, why let these letters become such," Skizzum demanded.

Emmy croaked, "four dead."

Skizzum's eyes widened again. She thought about the Ohio, Kent State shootings of students, about the Neil Young song. It was how Emmy had said it. With so few words, how could one know? People interpreted and drew their response faster than John Wayne's pistol. If the gun was loaded, the person in front, would be dead. Yet in those few words, there was a blast; the force of the struggles of youth in the sixties, fed up with the war in Vietnam, sick of police violence and the attacks on the Civil Rights of colored peoples, angered by unbridled capitalism, as they came out from under an American anesthesia as shown in Haskell Wexler's 1969, *Medium Cool.* "Four dead in Ohio." Those four words framed the loss of America's belief in its innocence and stirred Skizzum's soul as Emmy pronounced them.

"Is Emmy living in the past? Or is she talking about something going on at present with the Klan? Are we on the same page? Had the KKK killed again? In Ferriday? In Natchez?" She thought about Emmy's gun and wondered if she resolved her problems like her mother had.

Was she scraping her distraught friend out of slovenliness and slop, only to find herself committing to something she had not thought about? She said, "Let me get a beer and I'll think on it." Skizzum had participated in the Chicago protests after Martin Luther King's assassination. She had heard about the one at Kent State two years later.

Now, this, this was a Christmas to remember, but she could think of nothing, just then, that she wanted more to forget. She left and went back into the house, to the refrigerator, thinking, "It would be better to write on the inside of a fish belly than to send these letters out, no matter how anonymous, to these men."

Skizzum was considering how to handle this subject with Emmy, who, when she came back inside, sat down on the piano bench. It was her place. She placed her hands over the keys like she was about to play something. Skizzum watched her from the kitchen table. She sighed. She walked over and put her arm around Emmy. "Come back to the table. You need to eat a little more of your breakfast." Emmy obeyed. Sitting down, she picked up her fork, and looking at Skizzum, put a small bite into her mouth. Chewing was as hard as swallowing, but she did manage.

After breakfast, Skizzum asked, "Can you take me to the woods, to the treehouse you've told me about, but I've never visited?" Emmy looked at her, trying to decipher what was behind her friend's request. Skizzum thought she had to spend more time with Emmy in order to regain her trust. "Should I help her with the letters, but then encourage her to wait before sending them?" she asked herself. She thought that if she imitated Emmy, but then stopped short of sending the letters, she would best be able to help her. She didn't know why. Afterall, as long as these were not sent, the letters could do no harm.

"She doesn't know about Mrs. Broderick's suspicions," thought Emmy. "Her husband must have been buried now for months." Emmy had not seen Broderick. She didn't know that he was still alive when he arrived at the hospital. She had seen the family or friends drive up with their multiple cars and carrying their large casserole dishes, and her neighbor glaring at her through her distinctive curtains, when she went outside.

Outside, Skizzum stopped to look at the flowerbeds. Hummingbirds had caught her attention. These flew from dahlia to dahlia, pollinating as they tasted the nectar. One appeared to be resting on the U formed by a petal. It lay on its back, its beak turned upwards, itself like a U, its feet curved into a deflated ball. When it saw Skizzum, it jerked them up, flipped over, and flew, in a thousand two-hundred fifty motions, into the redbud tree; its tiny cellophane wrapper-wings forming diaphanous shadows as it crossed the path, its tiny heart no doubt ticking at one thousand two-hundred fifty or more beats a minute. It was an ordinary day for a hummingbird. Suckle, rest, and tremble. Tremble to fly. *Teh-teh-teh-teh-teh-teh-teh-teh-the-teh-teh-teh-teh-teh-teh-teh-teh-teh...* Emmy could hear the little bird's wings. "Ah," she whispered, nodding with a childlike delighted smile, the mocha taste of the tuberous roots of the dahlia came to her tongue. "That was a nice sound," she thought.

When they arrived at the clearing near the treehouse, Emmy climbed out of the passenger side and began to walk towards the woods. She was surprised not to see the wood she thought she had left to rebuild, and more surprised to find the job done, and done well. Had she forgotten she had finished? Was her memory playing tricks on her thirty-some-odd-year-old mind? Skizzum was surprised that there was no ladder, until Emmy pulled a rope draped over a low limb, behind the tree, and a hand- knotted-rope ladder fell from the treehouse, as if by some miracle, she had known a secret entry to a pirate's den.

"Did I finish that?" she wondered, fingering the knots, trying to tie her memory to the making. Her father had taught her to make knots and nets like his brothers used for fishing. She was wondering if it was the lack of nourishment or the now far-off shock treatments that were causing her to doubt her memory. She knew she wasn't strong enough to go up, so she sat on the low limb under Ezperanza's arms. She wondered where her grandmother was. She had not seen her for days. Skizzum hadn't thought about Emmy's weakness here, and went up the swinging ladder to have a look. As she stood near the railing, she could see the Mississippi in the distance. It wasn't that far. She remembered springs when water would come up to the trees' ankles and they would have to hurry home before the river encircled their knees as fast as the snow melted in the North. Emmy had rebuilt her mother's treehouse, but had never furnished it. Skizzum thought helping her with this project might be something they could do together, if Emmy didn't want to leave with her to Nashville, right away.

Emmy looked overhead. She could see and hear the crows cawing, circling. They knew she wasn't alone and she did not try to call them. She wondered, "who's flying in your thriller-wing-writers' club today? Look up in the sky...How many are playing *Mack the Knife*? A thief, a murderer, an arsonist...A cement bag, on a tugboat? Frankie, Ella, Louis, Bobby? Anyone? *Dig man*, there he goes... Did our boy do something rash, dear? *Scarlet billows*... Oh, Macky's...back in town. The line's formin', on the right, dear...Oh, Macky's...back in town." She could hear *The Threepenny Opera* above, bringing the old highwayman song back to life with its usual jazz interpretations. Humming the song like a breath, she started to laugh with piccolo squeaks. The way she understood it, the crows incited this upbeat call to murder. Metallic cloud sounds. Scarlet billows, with sulfurous linings, indeed. She wondered if they had talked to her mother. These thoughts made her forget her problems with Jeremy and the Klan.

Skizzum had seen the birds. She didn't think of them as bad omens, just not good ones for Emmy right now. "Emmy, I wish you could come up. It's amazing up here. And that tree!" But she was coming down, as she spoke. "I think we'd better get going. We need to make our plans."

The two women walked hand-in-hand, out of the forest and got into the truck. Skizzum wanted a beer. She didn't want to think of how Emmy once was, before Harper, before her health problems. She had started to realize that she wanted a beer, more and more often, and one more, and one more, and just one more, but she stopped herself. "Isn't that negative thinking? Won't thinking like that make me feel more ashamed and drive me to drink even more?" Skizzum knew that she was becoming like an alcoholic, rationalizing away her need, to get what she wanted. Calling herself Bobby McGee hadn't changed that. Why couldn't she see that she was like other people who at one point in their lives, would slip into beer, wear it like whiskey, and take their spirits with them to their graves? But that was just it. She wanted to. Sometimes she admitted to wanting nothing else. "If having insight causes pain, why go on with it? With all the progress the country made in the sixties, not even my family accepts that I was born queer and will die queer. Whether or not

I once loved a man, whether or not I find someone else to love, or whether I kill myself or live, is irrelevant to my family. They still think of it as a mental illness."

They went to the PicQuick. Mrs. Gosset, still looking as old as ever, looked at Skizzum with piercing eyes beyond her glasses. "I know you, don't I? Aren't you that Leblanc girl I caught stealing those *Riverdale* comic books about twenty years ago." Skizzum put a six-pack on the counter. "Not me," she smiled, remembering how she had liked the cartoon's Veronica, a girl with sass and spunk, whose face made her think of Emmy's. But they both knew it was Skizzum who had stolen at least ten editions. Shoplifting and other forms of trouble are not forgotten in small towns, even when these are committed by brazen children and their parents make them pay the shopkeeper for the stolen goods. Just how many were stolen by her, and not some other neighborhood child, was the only mysterious element in the conversation. Mrs. Gosset looked her up and down and shook her head. Skizzum didn't like numbers, other than in bawdy songs that said things like *there must be fifty ways to do your lover*, parodying Paul Simon's song of ending a relationship. She smiled again at this idea, as Mrs. Gosset put her six-pack in a bag.

"In fact, if you think about it," resumed Skizzum, still considering all accounts, when she reached the truck, "there is a song about almost everything. We need to work on some new ones when we get rested."

Alone, Emmy didn't think much about feeding herself or resting. She spent all of her time thinking. Sometimes she thought of song writing. It's amazing how much one can get done without even picking up a pen.

As they drove around the bend on the Lake Road, Emmy ducked, as if she saw someone, she knew, in a car parked on the side of the road. Skizzum wondered if Emmy hallucinated. Although she loved her, and remembered how everyone, including her straight sister Bee, had felt attracted to the beautiful, almost mystical, child she had been, her feelings towards Emmy now were those of concern from one human to another, as well as a bond of sisterhood and friendship. If someone saw them in the truck together, her holding Emmy's hand or hugging her, she was not concerned about their interpretations and didn't think Emmy would be either. Mérite-Lajoie had raised her daughter to accept differences, and not just those of color or culture. And that was also why she had been so easy to love, and so vulnerable to Harper. Skizzum thought that she had never learned skepticism. In the past, to Emmy, everyone was good, and this idea was not church-whipped or Pinocchio-piped. "So," Skizzum wondered, "what is going on in her mind about Jeremy? Has so much happened to her that she has lost her way? Yeah, I drink a few beers, but isn't it better than whatever has eaten her up? Maybe I'm more lucid about people than I thought, and less than I want to be."

She pulled into Emmy's driveway. Helping a still weak Emmy, out of the truck, she saw the monkey on the curtain across the street, as it swayed on its vine, trying to pull the designer-tiger's tail. "This place is a jungle. Hell! The world's a jungle!" she thought as she led Emmy into the house.

Percussive as a drum

"Hey, you wanna go to the Under-the-Hill Saloon in Natchez?" asked Skizzum. "We can play some pool. Listen to a little music."

Emmy stared at her in disbelief, and shook her head. "Oh, come on, Emmy, it'll do you good. You've been cooped up for too long." Skizzum became enthusiastic about her project. Whether her ardor was stemmed by addiction or from a desire for her friend's recovery, would be hard to say. Would it be wrong that her fervency could be provoked by both? What was a little alcohol when measured against a friend's recovery? Why couldn't Emmy go into a bar and feel normal again? Why did she, herself, have to go just to feel normal? Emmy didn't have to drink. She could just watch people if she didn't want to play pool. They both needed to see other people. Both needed to talk. But, if silence and alcohol were ways of dealing with reality, one turned the noise into a haze; the other, tuned it out.

The Under-the-Hill Saloon was a two-story brick building with wooden floors and furnishings, founded in the early eighteen hundreds for men who, like Mark Twain, worked on the river. The bar had a partially covered brick patio with plants and high-walls for privacy. Ceiling fans turned overhead in every room. In the main room with the bar, posters and photos covered one wall. In the other room, a mirror reflected these, when the room was empty (which it rarely was). Live music was featured on weekends. Once a haven for prostitutes, thieves, and cutthroats, you could now sit on a bench on the front porch and watch the Mississippi

River as it descended lazily towards one of its bridges, without losing your money, unless you wanted to.

"Emmy, the Under-the-Hill bar is not like it used to be. Young people go there now, I'm told. There isn't much happening around here. Haney's Big House is gone. Burned up like Frank's. The days of great music in this town are probably forever gone with Muddy Waters. We could never have gotten in anyway, so why not try Under-the-Hill?" She could kick herself for reminding her of the shoe shop's owner. She had seen what an impression the Klan crimes had made on Emmy. At least no one had been killed at Haney's. Muddy Waters, and the other blues legends, had no doubt heard about the KKK and had stopped coming to Ferriday long before the fires. In spite of the mayor's desire, the town had a reputation, and not a good one. In spite of themselves, Ferriday's residents, past and present, kept talking about it, as if local color gave them reputation instead of responsibility, and a good one at that. Trauma will do that to a person.

"Come on, Emmy," she tried to be persuasive. "We don't have to stay long."

Emmy knew Skizzum was tired of babysitting for her. But wasn't the bar full of men spilling over from the town and spilling their beers on each other, after that? Didn't Skizzum realize that these people could be dangerous, both sober or drunk? Did she know that Jeremy might be there?

Skizzum said, "Look Emmy, if you are worried about Jeremy, maybe you should think that if we have him in our eyesights, he can't do anything. Everybody will see him. He won't try anything, and besides, I *need* to see him to try to understand what is going on with him. I could ask him about his family, about his little girl. Don't look so horrified. We need to get to the bottom of this." She was forgetting her promise to herself that she would not talk about this with her friend.

"But what else can I do?" she asked herself, finding an excuse at the same time she had regrets about asking. "Emmy will forgive me. Emmy is a forgiving person." But did she realize how much the souls of the words themselves impacted her friend's mind? These did flips around the young woman's dreams, like little flames dancing and doing cartwheels around an open fire, glittering and sparking, igniting all at once an unfurling flare. A word was not just a word. It had guts. It had brains. In Emmy's ear, a syllable was as melodic as a musical note. A sentence as percussive as a drum. Every vowel had its fragrance, every consonant, its musk. A word is a living thing.

Emmy got up and started out the sliding door towards the trailer- office. She wanted to retrieve the pistol that Skizzum had left in the desk drawer. "She doesn't know these towns anymore," she thought.

Skizzum seemed to understand and rushed behind her. She slammed the drawer shut before Emmy could retrieve the weapon. "No," she said. "You won't need this. I promise you." But Emmy wasn't sure. She stood there, helpless. Too many times she had been caught short. She wondered that she had survived. She wanted to tell Skizzum about the ants. But these seemed to run about her mind. "She was *sick of ants. Sycophants. Rosicrucians.* She had read about those. Oh, she knew who they were. *Mystics, illuminati, roaches. Not crustaceans.* Not insects even." She laughed without sound. "No matter how you pronounced *si-ons,* or *shuns.* Not with their barks, yelps, howls, and grunts, under their sheets. *Weren't they all flatterers, impostors, usurpers?* Kick them all in the shins. Perhaps higher. Maybe that's why they were disguised. They didn't want you to see where there were no balls to kick."

Skizzum caught the half-smile, yet distressed look on Emmy's face. It was an ambivalent expression, hard to read. "Come here," she said, pulling her friend into her arms. Emmy let hers fall by her side. "Didn't Skizzum see that forcing arms to stay down and to not strike out was hard?" Emmy felt as if she were contouring a crowd, trying to find a better view, hovering overhead, her body its own obstacle. She wanted, she needed to *see* Skizzum holding her, so that her mind, and her body, would stop racing around the room. They stayed like that for at least a minute, swaying from side to side, rocking, like mother and child. She didn't remember why they came into the office, and allowed Skizzum to lead her back into the house. As they left the trailer, closing the door, her eye caught a flurry of the letters over the desk; their sharp edges winking at her, as if they knew. "Oh, they know, alright," she thought.

"But what could they know, the letters, cut out and wailing. They don't know yet what is intended. How much time has it been since the trip to Pierre's? One month? Two? There was still Hogden, Rover, Slaughter, and Jeremy. Have to go out. To find out what these men have been doing all this time and put a stop to it. Four dead and five to go. Nine men on the list. Like the possums. But those five won't get away." thought Emmy, or the woman she had become, and who was ever present in the room.

She picked up her *Magic Slate*. "Ok," she wrote. Skizzum wondered what had changed her mind and worried a little, but perhaps not enough.

Under-the-Hill

Skizzum said, "I usually save these clothes for performances, but you never know; there might be some women Under-the-Hill." She winked.

Emmy studied her friend as she brushed her long brown hair. They had known each other since childhood. Emmy had watched her pretend to be Tarzan to a Jane, a Romeo to a Juliet, a Clyde Barrow to a Bonnie Parker... Emmy was four years her junior and could not act the part of her partner, even if she had wanted to. Skizzum's best friend, a girl from Waterproof, volunteered for the roles; but when Skizzum joined Harper's Angels, Jane found someone else, and wound up marrying some old boy from Natchez.

For Skizzum, these weren't roles she was playing, but *The Real McCoy*, or almost. What went with the pair, didn't pair up to her feelings. She wasn't a man and didn't aspire to be one, but she wanted to be the partner of those beautiful screen actresses. Beyond being a tomboy while she grew into her body, she had no desire to wear a beard. She said she liked tits and didn't like *dicks*, and she meant it in every sense of the word. That did not mean that she didn't like men. Oh no. She had many male friends, including the owner of the bar, but had never felt desire for any of them. It wasn't as if she excluded the possibility of having sex with a man again, she just didn't seek it the way she did with women. When she had tried to talk to Bee, the doctor, her sister had shrugged it off saying, "Doesn't everyone love women's bodies?" And Skizzum agreed, because she thought this must be true. But it didn't help her figure out her feelings of being somehow left out of adolescence and not finding love, the physical kind.

Skizzum was heartbroken from so many things growing up as a teenager in Ferriday , but not resentful, beyond her initial outpourings of rage about Harper and her fears about the pregnancy. With time, she had come to understand her make- believe love stories were more real than fictive. Nevertheless, in Ferriday, as with much of the country at the time, love relationships between women were most often discounted as improbable, *de passage*, or foolish, in cordial terms. Lesbian couples were thought of by heterosexual men, if they were thought of at all, as playthings for voyeurs. *Can I watch*, she heard whispered, more than once, as she was walking arm-in-arm with a girlfriend. In literature, she knew that women who loved women, appeared as diabolical fornicators, (*witches, I tell you*), or a thing to be hurt.

In terms of identity, the only thing more complicated than being a homosexual woman, in those days, was to be a homosexual man. They didn't even have the witch option, which today, could raise a chuckle, or a glass. She thought Bee was as lost in limbo as she was, but didn't want to dwell on her sister's problems more than her own. There were big unanswered identity questions that she walked around with, carrying one in her pocket to pull out and use to confront a stranger. *What did they think of women who liked women? Had they ever tried same sex, sex? Did they fear this new illness everyone was talking about and calling AIDS? Did they believe it was a punishment from God?* She never thought that some people would feel uncomfortable, or that had never given much thought about her questions. These were hers, after all. Some lanced out with attacks on her, calling her names, and not pleasant ones.

As with most rumors and hate talk, Skizzum did not bother much about it, unless someone confronted her. Figuring out her feelings after Harper, after Hiram, and after the birth and abandonment of her baby, she left Ferriday for Woodstock, and the world. She had come back to help a friend, not to find a lover. "What's wrong with having a few laughs with a cute girl? And you never know," she added, looking at herself in the mirror one last time and flipping her hair before picking up the keys.

"We're taking my car," she said. She didn't think about what might happen with Emmy if she did meet someone, or if, she herself had too much to drink. The bar was twelve miles from Ferriday. As with the snake- woman tattoo she had drawn on Emmy's back so many years before, with her own complexities, she didn't think much in advance about consequences of her decisions for other people. As for Emmy, she thought Skizzum might need her, but she wasn't sure for what. As for possible misunderstandings or misinterpretations, there was room for plenty. Skizzum looked at Emmy, wearing dark jeans and a black sweater. "With any other color," she thought, "those clothes might have added a few extra pounds to her." She sighed. Does anyone ever comprehend the other's needs?

Already in stealth mode, and as with many times before, Emmy was carrying two unsent letters in her purse like a loaded gun. One for Rover, and one for Jones. One for the maker of bombs, and one for the bomber. One for the puppeteer, and one for the puppet. The Post-Office wasn't far from the bar, but these days, she never went out without protection. In fact, of late, she never went out at all. She was living in another decade, remembering what she had done a year or more before, acting on events that happened more than a decade earlier.

"These men should pay," she mumbled. She felt her determination growing, giving her strength; but whether her letters were composed as retributions for past crimes or whether these were harbingers of another, was anyone's guess. While Skizzum was getting ready, she had slipped out the sliding door and retrieved her gun from the office drawer. *Yé krik, Yé krak,* she heard the trees bend and rub their old spines together, cracking like the opening of a cemetery vault. "You aren't real," she whispered to the darkness. Yet, to say that was to also admit that these phantoms were unbridled figments of an imagination gone wild. "There aren't any vaults in your graveyard. Almost no stones either. Just a few grey, rotted teeth and old rusty farm equipment that no one needs since we switched from cotton to soybeans." *Ooot ooot ooot, tii tii tii, ooun ooun ooun. Yo-o-o-o-o. Ooot ooot ooot, tii tii tii, ooun ooun ooun. Yo-o- o-o-o.* Sound washed over the sunken graves and fallen tombstones. Shadows leapt from behind the Harvesters. "Just owls and frogs, and maybe some insects and blowing trees." she rasped. *Kou-te ti-moun yo. Koute timoun yo.* "Listen child. Listen child," she heard, and translated the wind echo, in the same way you might hear a birdsong or a washing machine sound, and attribute some kind of human expression to help pass the time. *Pa Fè sa. Pa Fè sa. Pa Fè sa.* (Don't do that. Don't do that. Don't do that). "You aren't real," she said again to the now familiar Creole chant, giving herself the courage that the letters lacked.

"Besides," she said, talking back to them, "this is only for defense." She patted her bag with its secret message. Unseen ghosts whispered warnings into existence. They gained consistency when Emmy listened. Would visibility transform them into enemies that could be dealt with? Invisible, they wore the colors of nightmares; she could not determine their strength or on whose side they were. If she had to call them out to have them all killed, then she would. Was she willing to become a martyr, like her mother had, almost twenty years ago?

When they pushed open the door to the bar, two young men were strutting around the pool table like they were doing a southern cakewalk on a Ramones', « Rocket to Russia ». Skizzum walked over, and looking them up and down, put her quarter on the table. « Rack 'em up, boys, » she said, as if she knew whom she had to deal with, and she already had had a couple of beers under her belt.

Looking far less dangerous than she was, Emmy just stood there a moment, arms hanging limp by her sides, her loaded bag swaying from her shoulder. Thinking she was a bit like the woman in the Emily Dickinson poem, standing in a corner, herself a loaded gun, she couldn't order drinks, or talk to anyone. Finding an empty table, she sat down and watched the room, her body tense, and ready.

Her eyes, half shaded, followed an itinerary around the room, noting the other customers, standing at the bar or sitting at tables. There was an older man, perhaps sixty, with puffy bags under his eyes, overdressed for the joint, and sipping a whiskey in the privacy of a corner. "Who is he?" Part of her was contemplating another incendiary report; the other, was fingering a revolving brass band inside her bag, ticking out its beat as it rotated its song and played near a short barrel with black ink and gunpowder. She remembered, thinking how she had weaponized her letters. These weren't the fine poetry books or fiction, banned and burned in the *Autodafés* of Germany and that were thought to be dangerous enough. Hers were sneaky, more like *Maxwell's Silver Hammer*. They were charged, and stood ready and would come down on someone's head from a neglected memory. They could kill. Could all memories? Now, she remembered, and felt she needed her gun to protect herself more than ever. Were all those days and nights spent sitting and preparing these letters, building up to a faceoff? She waited and watched the man, her eyes turning with his, from time to time towards the door.

A man came over with a Coke and put it in front of her. Her eyes flared and she almost pulled out the gun. "Lighten up, lady! Don't shoot me!" he said as he held up his hands in jest, not realizing how close he had come to the truth. "I'm just the bartender. The girl over there at the pool table told me to bring this to you. It ain't got no alcohol in it, if that's what you're worried 'bout." He backed off, shaking his head.

Emmy took a breath and sipped her Coke. She knew she needed to be calm if she was to deliver her messages. Through all the moments she had sat in fear, in the children's ward of the psychiatric hospital, holding her sides, rocking back and forth, developing, little by little, a pounding rage and roving indignation, she knew that she had to respond to something she felt was wrong in this community. "How can good people allow these things to endure? There is a mission and, by God, it will be followed, through and through, with or without help." Her tooth seemed to murmur again. "Was it the part that knew the answer? It had said what Harper was doing when he stuck his, stuck his, stuck his…. He said it was how the Angels were sisters. I believed him, but the tooth did not and seemed to say, *bite*. Didn't bite hard enough, but Harper got mad and grabbed his alligator belt and spanked hard. Butt and thighs, black and blue the next day. 'Black and blue. Black and blue,' said Mamere. Then he stuck it, stuck it, stuck it…"

"He left her crying on the floor to die when the church burned," she told the doctor. 'She's eleven years old, God dammit.' She said a lot of hard things for a church-going woman of her age. Skizzum just goes on playing pool as if nothin' never happened, as if her tooth never told her and she didn't know that it hurt, as if all these good people just stuck their heads in the black gumbo mud or up each other's ass and would allow a man, allow a man, allow a man…."

In her inner voice, Emmy switched back and forth from past to present, without realizing it, and without pronouncing a punishment for the people who allowed Harper to go free, but condemned her mother. "The tooth could forgive her mother for killing the man who, the man who, the man who…," but *just now, just now, just now*…the words could still not come out from under the dissonance resonating between her grinding teeth. "They didn't all agree. Some said it was her fault that Harper was dead. Some said it was her fault that her mother was in prison, some said it was her fault if the town was mad.

Some said, some said, some said.... But who was some?" the question rolled around in her head, but not all the way to her tongue. "And what did they do? And why didn't they do right? Now his son would pay. They would all pay."

Skizzum was directing the solid-colored balls into their sockets, one after the other. Her competitor took on a serious look as other men put up their quarters. Skizzum was giving them a run for their money, but knew that it would do no good to upset their egos. A couple of these men had been schoolmates, years before, and she wanted to keep things friendly. This is not to say that she would or could beat their pants off if she tried. The two, the six, the ten were still on the table, along with the eight. She kept the score tight, and they had to pay attention. But they were all practiced pool players here. One had even been to Las Vegas in a competition. There wasn't much else for the young from Ferriday to do, beside racing cars, or having sex in the back seats of their Fords. Wasn't that why the teenagers with pickup trucks, didn't find many dates?

The man in the corner got up and walked towards the bar. He paid his bill and lumbered over to the exit. With swindler eyes, he glanced at Emmy as he went out the door. "I know what you're about", she mumbled. "You can't fool me." Her mission was unraveling her, quilting unmatched pieces on the inside and the out of another's vest; dressing a network of ordinary men going about their ordinary lives, discovering themselves turncoats, if not outright harlequins. Whether these men harbored racist rhetoric or they were humble or shifty drinkers, to Emmy, just now, they looked like they might be members of a secret group, with secret plans to kill her friends and neighbors. "They have some sort of dirty glow about them, like a yellow bar-room light," her whispers now turned mean. Thoughts were bouncing about her mind, causing her to forget that they were in a bar, and the lights *were* yellow, and she was creating a *primum mobile* for old news articles, and adding status to random photos on the same page. *These were all solid proofs that unidentified killers were allowed to roam free. The FBI ignored the truth and someone had to let them know; someone had to gather the material, and somehow, had to make them stop.*

And in truth, there were at least twenty men in the area, law enforcement and ordinary citizens, who had frightened, tortured, and killed Black people, and who had never been condemned for their hate crimes and who never would. Now, there was a man allowed to go around and preach hatred towards the Jews. "Free speech," they tweeted, parrot-like, as the words of the speaker burned into the minds of the listeners waiting to be recognized for their purveyance and their fidelity to a man, then soon an idea, they thought they recognized. The FBI knew. They had informants, and the informants, like almost all the rest, never paid for their crimes. "It's all logical," she thought, building up her case against a man she had never seen, no longer realizing that there were reasons that people could not be tried and sent to prison. *Tous des menteurs à triple étage,* she concluded. "All of them, every last one, are three-story liars." Thereby, hangs a tale.

While Skizzum was occupied, Emmy left her Coke on the table and went towards the bathrooms. The alley-exit door was next to these, as in a lot of bars. She slipped out into the parking lot behind the saloon. Beyond the garbage bins, she could see the side alley, that went towards Silver Street. The LP's turned into the slurred light, sending out disjointed punk music intertwined with older rock whiplashes and country toe-kicks. Holding her bag against her so that it would not knock against the metal trash bins, she realized that somehow, she had forgotten that the streets curved around and that there was no quick route to the next street. While she peaked around the corner and looked up and down the street, she watched a raccoon as it slipped out a piece of pumpkin- rind, scraped from pie-makings. The animal made a low clicking growl as she passed close, but it was otherwise undeterred. It wasn't going to abandon its piece of American Pie for a wisp of a woman as she floated by. She thought about the Post Office on Canal Street, but that was on the hill, not under it. Now she wished she was a crow, a bird, and not a Native American, or at least wished she had her truck.

She could see a restaurant down the river and people were coming out the door. She thought she caught a glimpse of a woman named Steales, all gussied up in an evening gown, the wife of a Klan member she had seen talking with Slaughter in Ferriday and who brought her children in for haircuts. Emmy ducked behind a bush near the boat ramp; her heart was already racing. "Is he with her? Does she know about me? Why was it that these people are about when there is a mission to run?" Emmy was guided by principal and still thought of the anonymous letters as part of a Civil Rights' Mission, and was trying to figure out how far that role could take her.

Steales had been the pilot of a plane that had crashed, clipping another plane that dived, killing five people, including the attending doctor for Frank Norris. Had he done it on purpose? He claimed that it was the other plane that had touched his wing, only, it was the second plane crash he had survived and that, that looked suspicious by all accounts. She would add him to her list. His brother, another Klan figure suspected of bombing Blacks and Jews, was, like Harper, already dead and she could only count on the Devil to give them Hell. *But who could count on the Devil? And what was the price?* These thoughts had not become conscious. Besides, *just now, just now,* she couldn't let disappointments cloud her mind. She had another mission. "Where did the man in the suit go? Is he hiding from me? Waiting for me?" Emmy looked up and down the street. People from the restaurant were returning to their cars. Taking a sigh of relief at what she thought was a mistake, but keeping an eye out all the same, she waited a few minutes in the long shadow of the Under-the-Hill building until the street was clear.

Wondering if there might be a mailbox on the corner of Silver Street and Biglane (named after the family, and not the size of the street) after most of the cars passed, she decided to take her chances. She was near the intersection where she hoped she would find the mailbox. "Hope is a funny thing," she thought, "it can be used for all kinds of purposes, even against enemies. But what happens if they invoke it as well?" Emmy didn't have an answer, and for now, she felt she had lived without protection from God, or anyone else, for so long, that she shouldn't dwell too long, hoping for divine intervention. She watched a door shut from afar, and felt, for just a moment, that she was involved with a scene that went way beyond herself, but not enough to ask herself *what the Hell she was doing there*. Hearing the motor of Steale's crop-dusting plane getting close overhead, she lowered her head, and dropped on her haunches, behind a bush, until the sound came so close that she realized, even as focused on her mind's makings as she had been, that the motor was a June-bug or other night beetle, droning near her ear. She swatted it away. As she regained her path and hurried down the street, she thought she heard footsteps. Her ears seemed to be playing tricks on her. Turning, she could see no one other than a couple of cats chasing each other, and pressed on to where she thought the mailbox would be ahead.

While Emmy was crouched behind the bushes, before she had moved from her place of waiting, Skizzum realized that she was not seated at her table, drinking her Coke. Even with her three extra beers, and her two-round winning streak, she was preoccupied by her absence. When the bartender asked if the players wanted anything else, she asked if he had seen her friend. He shook his head. "I saw her go into the bathroom about fifteen minutes ago. Look, if you wanna know if she's okay, go see for yourself. I don't wanna go near the ladies' room if she's in there. When I brought her, her drink, she looked at me with killer, *Bette Davis Eyes*, and as it happens, I wanna go home to my wife and kids."

The pool players all laughed. Skizzum knew that what the bartender said was true. If you didn't know, or couldn't remember, her former beauty, all you could see when she focused her eyes on you, was a hatchet-face with sunken dark eyes that appeared to look straight at you from a *Hush, Hush, Sweet Charlotte* film, and from wherever you were standing.

As Emmy's friend, and the person who had brought her there; she was now worried. She thought, "Emmy hasn't been right in her mind. She hasn't been eating or taking care of her home. Confusing dead possums in the guest room with a girl she imagined she kidnapped and starved, is beyond the pale. I should have talked to her about a hospital in Tennessee. I shouldn't have insisted that she come tonight. I wonder if she is still having a breakdown. The list of signs is getting longer and longer. It's worse than when we lived above the dance studio. Has she been sending terrifying letters to Jeremy and the KKK? She might be putting herself in danger... her and anyone else she hangs around with for very long, including me."

Skizzum put her cue down on the table. Her realization was so sudden that she explained nothing to the other players. She ran towards the bathrooms. "Emmy," she called into the stalls. She peered under the doors. No one. She hurried out and saw the back door. Pushing it open, and rushing through the side alley into the street, she saw Emmy as she emerged from the bushes and crossed the street. She ran after her and caught up with her. Emmy whirled around; her weapon pointed once more at her friend. "Emmy!" Skizzum screamed. Emmy stared ahead at the empty street. "Emmy!" Skizzum called out, forcing her voice down a notch. This time, Emmy lowered her arm and put the pistol back into her purse. She turned towards again towards the intersection. Skizzum caught up with her and said, "Emmy, I don't know what is with you, but you have to stop. We can talk about this. It's hurting you." But that was just it. She couldn't talk and kept moving ahead. She didn't know what *it* was. "The time for talkin' is over. Are you gonna rat me out?" The words scoured Emmy's throat as they came out in an accusatory rasp, detached from Skizzum's intentions.

"Oh Emmy," said Skizzum. "No, no, no. Come here," she said, opening her arms as her friend turned around for a second. "Please tell me what is happening. What is going on? I know it isn't easy for you to talk since you were hurt and had those treatments. But I can help you. Whatever it is. Let's leave. We are almost to my car. I'll pay them later." Emmy stood there, her feet firm and holding their ground, one hand on her handbag, the other, ready to pound. Skizzum lowered her arms. The two stood there, like sisters, a sad look growing over their faces, knowing that each of them knew that there was no easy solution to the problems before them.

Without warning, Emmy pulled the gun from her bag, and pulled the trigger. ZZZZZZZZZZZZZZZZZZ. The bullet whizzed by Skizzum's ear in a high-pitched whine. ZZZZZZZZZZZZZZZZZZZZZZZ another bullet. A man fell to the ground, his arms out, holding his own weapon. The man was Wesley Steales. Under the dingy streetlight, Emmy recognized him from the bar. Not the airplane pilot, but his father, another Klansman. "He followed me", thought Emmy, relieved that she had gotten it right and frightened that she had.

Here is where the diamond needle of the new hi-fi gets snatched up and dragged over the LP record and is taken back to the beginning. Cryyyzzzhhhhzzzzzzz, the record shrieks! Not the scream or *funk of forty-thousand years* of dead coming to life in Michael Jackson's *Thriller*. The bullet grazed her ear. Almost. She shot, but the bullet was out front so how did it whiz by? Was time on a motion to Hell like Bee had tried to describe in light-years? Did she shoot just to get out in front of a bullet?

"You could get yourself killed like that," said Skizzum, as if the letters had become animated and were now packing *heavy metal*. It wasn't over. Footsteps resounded on the pavement behind her. Emmy spun around, ready to fire again, but this time Skizzum was faster and grabbed her from behind. She didn't want her friend to kill a person that she recognized and did not fear. She had no firm grasp about what was going on with Emmy and wondered how they had been caught in crossfire, although Jeremy, shaken by the encounter, appeared to be no longer armed, if in fact he had been. As for Emmy, in that instant, she felt she was done-for. With Skizzum restraining her, and her now visible adversary upon them to help, Emmy went limp and collapsed, an unconscious quarry falling into the arms of her target, as if falling into her own mirrored image, her gun clattering on the street, Echo meeting Echo, drowning like Narcissus. It was Jeremy.

"Jeremy! Thank God! It's you! That man tried to kill us, but we can't stay here. We've got to move fast! I'm parked just a few cars down. Help me get her to my car before someone comes." Skizzum picked up Emmy's gun and tucked it into her waistband. "There'll be cops swarming all over the place in five or ten minutes. It won't take long, but I need to get my purse and pay if I can, so we can get out of here, okay. I guess that guy was following her. It was self-defense, but she doesn't need to be mixed up with this." Looking at Jeremy with pleading eyes, she held Emmy's arms, head dangling backwards, and Jeremy took her feet without looking back and without questions.

He had recognized Steales and thought the man had stopped to take aim at him, dodging the bullet while firing his own. He didn't admit any of this to the young woman, but wanted them both out of the way in case there was more trouble. He knew he had killed Steales. He had known someone from the Klan would be coming for him ever since the night near the river. Maybe even since Deputy Crowder had been killed from his truck. They had seen him and he had seen Emmy. He wondered what her role in this was. He did not suspect her of sending the letters, not to him or to anyone else, but thought she might have become the unwilling witness of the Klan's threats to Broderick or some other Klan crime while working at the barbershop. It had happened to him. Because he had been present when the crimes were planned, because he had witnessed some of these, because his father had preceded him in this line of terror; they all thought, and he sometimes thought as well, that he was one of them. "Rover must suspect that I have become an informant. That's the only explanation for Steales' shot," he thought.

"Stay with her until I get back," Skizzum ordered. "Here's the keys in case you hear sirens. I'll meet you up on the bluff if that happens." Jeremy had not spoken a word. Catching the keys, he sat down in the front seat of her car. Skizzum ran up the street to the bar. Looking up and down the otherwise quiet street, Jeremy stared at

Emmy, stretched out behind the seat. "What the Hell are we gonna do with you?" He looked back towards Steales' body. "Ya know, I wouldn't have recognized you. Just look what the prettiest girl of the South has become! You're downright scary-lookin', you know that?" he said, his hairs on his arms now lifting as he was realizing the fate that had almost befallen them. "You must be outta your fuckin' mind if you're messin' with those guys. They some mean sons-of-bitches. They killed a bunch of people. Hell, they might be guilty of participatin' in Kennedy's assassination." Was he repeating something he knew, or just local gossip? Emmy couldn't think. Her terror at having Jeremy touch her and his talking with her had mortified her almost to the point of petrification. Beginning to tremble and struggle with her legs, to shake off the binds of a would-be death's grip or even the one that put her mind in a bench vise, she found that she had no strength, as if she was sinking in an invisible quicksand. She was conscious, but glued to a vision, her eyes unseeing, her ears scorched, shrill sounds jarring her brain along with Jeremy's words, and her mouth filling with unsavory mush.

Skizzum turned to return to the Under-the-Hill Saloon. Not wanting to seem hurried, she walked, trying to catch her breath. It had slowed to the short pant of culpability, not of sin, this was no confessional. Back and forth between short breaths, the decision of responsibility bounced like an eight ball between sockets, before she could sink it, if sink it did. Panicky before she got back to the bar, she knew that she would be questioned at some point, and forced herself to prepare her story.

Hers was the breathlessness or gasp from escaping something greater than herself, put into motion by her own negligence, like a butterfly, lifting its graceful wings, flitting and forlorn, knocking out the power grid in the whole county. Now, she was forced to sit with the guilty, like people who don't want to be involved, so, she did her best to side with them, slapping her hands as if trying to remove pollen or dust. She went through the alley, into the side door, back into the pool room, and grabbed her purse off the chair where she had left it.

"My friend's sick. She'll be alright. I just need to get her home." Holding her breath, she took out a ten and put it on the bar and took a step away. "Keep the change." Taking a few more steps, she waved, calling out to the young men at the pool table, trying to appear natural; "See ya!" They stood there, confused by the abrupt end of the competition and the sensation that they had lost all their chances for the night.

She walked out of the bar, and looked both ways. Not knowing where the next shot might come. Heading towards the bridge, she hurried down Silver Street. A foghorn vociferated its complaint, sounding like a silver-base watermelon harmonica revved up to clear the stage. Jeremy moved over and let her slide in. She turned the engine over, and the motor purred. Pulling out into the street, and glancing over at the Steale's body, she saw it lying in the space between two parallel-parked cars. With his gun lying near him, he now looked more like roadkill than a man in a three-piece suit; blood had unified the outfit. Under the streetlights, across the middle section, the pants, vest, and jacket appeared like one weave, or at least like they had come from the same store, as long as you didn't look below to the blue fabric still covering the legs from the knees down. The shot had not been clean as she had thought. He had lived long enough to pump out a few quarts of blood. Still in the middle of the street, she peered into her rearview mirror, "I gotta get out of here. Do you want me to drop you off?" she asked.

Jeremy, who, all this time, had not said a word to her, opened his mouth. "How 'bout you tell me what is goin' on?" He knew it would take anyone a good three minutes to walk from the bar to the place they were standing and they couldn't judge if the couple had seen the body before driving off. If it came to that, they would be gone before.

"Look, Jeremy, it's not like we have a lot of time or leisure right now to talk, she said, looking in her overhead rearview mirror. "I've gotta get her home. She hasn't been well. Not eating right and spending too much time alone in that house. You can't imagine. I thought it would do her good to get her out, but...I'd like to talk to you, really, I would, but not just now. Tomorrow? How does that sound? You could meet me at Emmy's camp. I've been helping her clean it up so she can rent out those trailers again. How about in the early afternoon? I'll be there. I'll try to bring Emmy along."

Jeremy nodded. "I'll just get out here. I'm parked further down the street. I went to see a movie with a couple of friends and thought I'd join 'em for a beer, but was goin' for my cigarettes in the car when I heard a commotion. I thought she'd taken a shot at you when I saw the man on the ground. She sure got him good. Right through the heart, he bragged. Who was that, do you know? Is she okay?" He continued to pretend that he had not fired a gun, and that Emmy had killed the man, and that she had been the target. It was his usual form of gallantry. Take the credit, take the blame, which could become on occasion; take the credit, not the blame, if you were left hanging with the bill.

"I think so. I don't know who he was, but it sure seemed he was ready to kill us. I have no idea why. Look, you better get goin', too. He got out, calm considering what had happened. He walked around to the driver-side, turned towards her, and bending towards the window, one hand on the roof of the car as if to say something, Skizzum asked, before he had the chance, "Will you be okay?" she asked through the open window. Skizzum was concerned for them all.

He raked his hand through his dark hair, pushing it behind his ear. "Sure. I know the cops. I didn't see nothin', just like I told ya and that's what I'll tell 'em. It was all over when I came runnin' up. At least that is what I'll tell them if they find me on the scene. I ain't armed. I wonder where they at?" And he did wonder. Hadn't anyone in the bar heard the shot? With loud music inside and with gusts of wind twisting the trees and curling over the Mississippi River's lap, he doubted anyone paid attention at this hour of the night. While he figured the Klansman was after him, he had questions as to why the girls thought he could be after them. If Emmy thought she was a target, then why? Was she as crazy as all that? He wanted answers. Since his daughter had been kidnapped, even though she had not been gone long and had been returned with a box of popcorn, and without any ransom, he had questions. His daughter could not answer these, but he knew he had had enough of the wrecking crews before these started up like before. And he wanted out. He didn't want to be involved with these men. He knew what they were capable of doing. Yet, since childhood, he knew he shouldn't flinch. He suspected their involvement with many killings and thought them capable of more, much more, in spite of the changing times.

A couple came out of the saloon and headed up the street in the opposite direction. Before they reached their car, while their backs were turned, he kneeled next to a car that, as a regular Under-the- Hill patron of late, he'd seen parked in the vicinity for what seemed days. Careful to wipe the prints in case it was found, he placed his gun, empty of bullets on the top of the front right tire. If someone drove away, it would fall into the gutter and still buy time. Otherwise, he would pick it up as he left the bar, and throw it in the Mississippi, further down the river, when the coast was clear. Prodding the dead man's knee with his foot, he looked at his face on the ground. His eyes were wide open. "Old man Steales alright. Clean enough shot. Almost instant death anyway. Looks like he been took out by the Grim Reaper and it ain't even Halloween. Didn't live long enough to tell it. She don't need no hood or mask, that girl. I wonder why he felt like he had to kill her. She ain't even Jewish. He could've took me out too. Hell, all three of us. Wonder what he was doin'? If he'd been after me, I would be dead. Lucky, I saw him first." Jeremy muttered to himself as he moved on to the old Saloon, feeling better that he was able to convince himself that he was not the target, but at the same time, feeling that if that was his story, self-defense would not hold. And neither would the theory about Steales not making his shot.

Eating humble pie

A heavy rain had started to fall, oblique and silver. It shifted from one direction to the next. Fat drops splatted on the windshield, like batter in a frying pan, discordant with the wipers, and making it hard to see.

Skizzum slowed the car. She didn't like doing so on this stretch of land between Vidalia and Ferriday, where cars might be stopped for a whim, and where, due to police intervention, some drivers had been lost forever. It was midnight by the time she got home with Emmy. On one hand, she felt relieved for helping Emmy avoid arrest; on the other, she was afraid, not only of what she was mixed up with, but of what seemed more and more to her like a delusional theater where she was given an unwilling role to play.

As she drove, she wondered how she could juggle her upcoming agenda, with her music, and the additional stress of helping Emmy so as to avoid taking her to a hospital. *Talking cures* might work for some, but when someone is so far gone, and can't talk, what can you do? Should she humor her friend, pretend with her that someone was out to get her? *Let's run!* As if they were playing cops and robbers. Stick reality in her face like a dirty sock? *There! There! I told you. It stinks. You need to wash it!* Make Jeremy explain things to her? *Come on, we know what you are up to. Tell the truth.* "*I never wanted to be part of the Klan, but got sucked into with my dad and with work. Then I didn't know how to get away. You know what that is about, don't you. You've been in a cult. You can admit it to me.*" As if anyone could figure that out while they are in one of these groups. Or, *"You're right. We plan to do what has to be done to keep the White race pure."* No.

Perhaps, he was as delusional as she was, but in another way. He would never admit to participating in another group like his father had created, if it were true. "What was he doing there? Sneaking around, hanging out with old White supremacists. He was always such an *as if*, as if he were somebody and it wasn't even *real* pretending. And he wasn't *really* guilty of whatever he did. Couldn't he *pretend* to be a Klingon, and not a *Cling on*? Following us girls around, doing whatever we told him, and getting all mad about it when we all got caught, oh, he was only an edge of a boy, or a vase to fill. *They made me do it. I only went along because they asked me.* Had he become a different man? Why weren't these things clear?" she wondered.

She felt her doubts grow as she searched for ways to appease Emmy. She couldn't save them all. She didn't entertain the most obvious question, *could Emmy, this fragile, fluttering, fallen ephemera, have shot that man?* But how could she know? How could this idea come to her mind? She had no idea of what Emmy considered her mission to expose Klan crime; about how she stirred up cold cases, hoping to make the rats come out of their holes and make the guilty pay. Being from Louisiana, she assumed they all knew how to shoot, Emmy, as much as her mother, as much as Bee, as much as herself.... She had no idea of how this was somehow linked to Jeremy other than through his long dead father. Did he know more than he was letting on, too?

Arriving at Emmy's house, Skizzum had reached a decision. The job was too big for her; she would call her brother, T-Pierre. He and Sandy could come for a few days and help out. Perhaps they would have an idea what could be done for Emmy. They could also talk with Jeremy, or at least help haul off a bunch of junk.

The dream

"The typewriter is burning. The pages of the newspaper are stuck together. They can't be printed. The letters are unreadable. They are blank. I was in an old house that smelled of horse manure, sulfur, and ammonia. Piss? Shit? Death? Rot? All day the animals bray, meow, growl, neigh...the wasps sting and the mosquitoes buzz in my ears. It doesn't hurt. That's how I know it's a dream. At night, I hear church bells ring and count thirteen gongs. That can't be real either. I know it's the bearings, scythes, and chains, hanging in the machine graveyard. I saw them swinging in the dark when I looked for the gun, hiding under the harvester. Who put it there? Jeremy? Me? Jeri-me? M-E? Had it been there a long time?

All at once, I hear electrical impulses. Cryyyzzzzzhhhh. It's the electroshock machine that thinks it's a hi-fi. I wait for it to hurt, but like the wasp stings, nothing happens. The wait is worse the second time because I know what could happen and I try to catch the wasp. It flies back to its nest in the corner. There are more of them now. They are angry because I killed one of their tribes. Why had I been so impatient? I could have waited until they had all left their nest and not used the instant *Death*. I should have whispered to each one of them, told them what would happen if they stayed. Was it reasonable to ask wasps to leave? To threaten them with poison? Some of what I'm thinking is real and some of it is just a dream. It happened, but not all at once and not right now, and not how they say it. I hear my parents whispering. Harper is there. He says he is the Devil. He says he is God. He says he is God-in-the-Devil. I ask, "How can that be?" He says, "Don't ask my child, it is so. If you don't stop arguing now, you will suffer in Hell." He looms over me like a querulous storm. I struggle and try to escape, to leave my body, anything, but my legs are heavy and they have attached me to the bed. He clutches my thigh. It is not unpleasant, but I'm afraid. The second time around is worse because I wait for it, thinking it will hurt like the first time. I know he is dead. So are my parents. This isn't real. It's a dream. Jeremy is there and his daughter is speaking a strange language. I can't understand her. I think she says if I talk, they will know, and they will tear my thoughts out like they did hers. I have to be silent now. I can't talk. I can't tell them. I have to act like I don't know."

"Emmy....Emmy...Wake up. It's me." Skizzum was trying to make her sit. Emmy was in her bed, but didn't remember coming home. "I've made you some tea. Please wake up." But Emmy didn't want to wake up. She wasn't asleep, but she didn't want to move. She wondered if the letters were still in her purse or if they would have somehow disappeared or they would be blank, eaten by the night. Not sure what she wanted, she was afraid to get up and look.

"Emmy," said Skizzum. "I've called T-Pierre and Sandy. I've asked them to come for a few days. They can help. With whatever you need, they can help. They might have new ideas about helping."

Emmy opened her eyes. Although Sandy and Pierre had been open to some of her queries, she wasn't sure how much she should tell them or anyone else. Still, she was overwhelmed and she knew that some bit of something in her mind was getting away from her. It was the buzzing she kept hearing that was the worst. She glanced in the corner to see if the wasp nest had gotten bigger. In daylight, it looked like a piece of wall-paper that had come unglued in the corner. "These must be night-flying wasps," she thought, interpreting her dream. "Unless they are the kind that are disguised in white sheets. *W-A-S-Ps*" She took the cup from Skizzum and sipped.

The diddle in the middle

The couple drove up on their Harleys. Emmy thought this would bring Mrs. Broderick out of her house, but lately, she had been staying indoors, overcome with grief, perhaps, or she had just given up her gossip. Loss encourages people to look over the edge, unless it pushes them off. When her friends rang the doorbell, they were surprised that Emmy opened the door. She appeared to be happy to see them, smiling if not radiant. On the upside of the cliff, looking down, she had not been able to *Keep on the Sunnyside of Life.*

She led them inside. Skizzum asked if they wanted coffee or beer. They both had coffee. This early in the day, they said... Skizzum had a beer. "The trouble is, Emmy wants to help people who have been victims of the Klan. The KKK is still active in the area, and not just huntin' down Black people, or disturbing elections. We were wonderin' if you two had any ideas. And while we're thinkin' about it, thought that we could also help her clean up the house a bit, maybe get it ready to sell or rent, along with the camp. She needs to get out of here and needs to figure out a way to earn money. At least for a while." They looked at Emmy, who began to get worried and stare at the dust-bunnies along the baseboards. She hadn't much thought of taking Skizzum up on her offer to follow her to Tennessee.

After their coffee, they all went over to Emmy's camp. It was an astonishing sight. Kids had filled the oil drums with beer cans and these had overflowed. They had then kicked over the drums, spreading the contents out to form a glistening aluminum *Swan Lake* with napkin birds, performing to gusts of wind instruments, thunder rolls, and lightening clashes. Skizzum, her brother, and her sister-in-law, filled up the truck-bed with the cans to return to the stores for the deposit. Since environmental policy had changed, nothing was guaranteed. If there was no center, the aluminum would all go to shine the topsoil of the local dump, along with the napkin swans and other flapping detritus, some that would find a place to roost in the surrounding trees.

Jeremy showed up about ten, and Emmy, who had been walking with her hands hidden in her arm pits, holding herself tight, already shy about interacting with the group; slunk back, and went into a trailer. After rocking with consideration, she was able to get ahold of herself, a little. "If I can just keep the noise out of my head, this would be the occasion to find out just how much he knows. Skizzum won't say anything she thinks might be one of my secrets. But I don't like hearing his voice. He scares me. He reminds me of his father."

Almost like brother and sister, the two had shared a lot of their childhood together. They weren't twins, not doubles, not like the north and south poles of a magnet, but in some ways, by their differences, almost mirrored images of one another, with opposing genders and symmetry. Tweedle-me and Tweedle-mum. One with a voice and one with none. Hadn't they grown up opposite each other? Hadn't her mother killed his father? But as in the mirror, there isn't only left and right, there is also an overlapping of images. Hadn't they been to the same school and church? Hadn't he been in those awful car rides to the Black part of town? Hadn't they both been mistreated by Harper? Didn't they both go through part of their adolescence without a father? Then, there was that Mardi Gras where Harper had gone too far, and their paths had parted. That was another one of those double-edged blades.

On one hand, she had lost a brother, whether good or bad. On the other, after that and until up until the other night in front of the bar, she had only seen the parts that she hated, and even now, he still had a way of looking at people, judging them by their skin. Didn't he? But something had changed him. Was it the Vietnam War? His empathy with other veterans? The Agent Orange that fell over him in the jungle and left him with a hearing problem and who knows what else? His daughter's disabilities? Her disappearance, however temporary? Had loss taught him compassion; given him a little space to think? Sometimes a small space of doubt leaves enough room to move ideas around like squares in a sliding-block puzzle.

Emmy set to writing, not her usual lampoons meant to infuriate as much as to frighten, but another kind of rhythmic poetry. Without considering herself a poet, she understood paradiddles and five stroke rolls. To lighten her message and make it more mysterious, she wondered about putting a diddle in the middle, and, like a horse, it could lope into a phrase and gallop out of sight; *hiiiiiiiiiiiiiiiiiiiii* whinny, snort, snort, swish of the tail. Here, have a carrot. Neigh. Now, that's a happy sound. Head shake, yes? The gentle beasts grazed no longer in her yard, but she held their sounds, and the olfactive souvenirs to go with them. The *ruade* of her heart hit hard inside her chest. *Hiiiiiiiiiiiiiiiiiiiiii. Whinny. Snort. Snort. Te-dot te-dot te-dot te-dot.* But it had all been true. The crimes in her area had been horrific, and her songs would not be made of saccharin sunshine.

Outside, a March wind was blowing. The sun was warm. A golden light peaked through the trees. The callery pears had all finished blooming and soon, it would be Mardi Gras. Impatience had turned to passion. The others, seated around an old carved up picnic table on the point, close enough to the trailer for Emmy to hear through the open window, if she so chose to listen. Skizzum laughed when she saw the heart with SL and ER. She hadn't forgotten, but it was a one-sided affair, it had always been so. This was true with many other of her impatient adolescent drives. She found another, ER and BL, girl-friendship, she thought. Then an SL and HS, which made her pensive and a little sad. Hiram saw the group and landed his boat. He walked over and said, "I saw y'all was cleanin' up your old camp. Ya need some hep?" All, but Jeremy smiled. He stood up and held out his hand to shake, "Sure," he said, "come on over, brother." Inside, Emmy lifted her head a little. "Was that Jeremy greeting Hiram and treating him like an equal? Like a brother? How can that be?" She had a hard enough time understanding her own inner struggles without considering those of others, or understanding how a dilemma, or a tragedy, might alter one's course. She was composing without her piano.

Been out a while
Listening to dread
Pushed over backwards
Wished I was dead.

Came up fightin'

Couldn't miss a trick
Wrote some letters
For tricky dicks.

Started off nice
Didn't worry a lot
Thought I'd show them

A brand-new slot.
A grave was waitin'
And a devil too
Been beat with sticks
Thrown out of view.

Better take care,
I carry a knife.
Letters taint scary
Might take your life.

Washed out your sheets
Changed White to Blue
Had enough hurtin'
Being kept down too.

We try to rise
You keep pushin' hard
Stick us in jail
Throw us in yards.

Outside they were talking about her. If ears burned when they heard such focused, personal conversation, hers would be flaming by now. Hiram started. "Well, he said, Emmy was real sweet to my kids. She bought 'em candy sometimes, and let the girls comb her hair. But I haven't seen her in months. The wife and I thought she might be sick. But you know, when I think about it, my daughters have 'bout growed up and I don't think they've mentioned her at all in the last two years, busy with high school and cheerleading, I guess. Once in a while, I saw her pick up her boat. From the lake, I couldn't really tell, but she looked poorly. She didn't seem interested in her property. You can see that, I suppose."

Jeremy interrupted. "Gosh, I haven't seen her since we were kids. I wouldn't have recognized her last night if Skizzum hadn't been there." His throat released some of the tension that had developed since Hiram had joined them. Talking about Emmy, however complicated, gave him an excuse to avoid confronting his own quagmires. He hadn't thought about Hiram being Black since the war-time horrors they had shared, where racial differences seemed to matter less than fighting people who were hard to perceive as enemies--until they shot at you. Having a common enemy made them seek a hometown alliance.

Jeremy was surprised to encounter the friendship this man had with the young women. He knew less about the adolescent-love relationship Hiram had shared with Skizzum many years before. He would not have recognized the cleaning lady at the Concordia Parish Courthouse as Hiram's mother. How could he? His family never had shared anything with their closest neighbors outside their clan. No one would have thought about it because it was inconceivable that Blacks and Whites would mix in Ferriday, Louisiana in the sixties, even after the Civil Rights Act was signed. Now he was confronted with what the Ku Klux Klan declared was the worst of evils confronting America; desegregation, and it didn't bother him a bit. Well, it did, in the long run, because he was not the courageous type and, it was hard for him to stand up to any authority figure. Nevertheless, he was becoming more reflective. "Afterall, are they so different from us?"

Emmy made a sigh of relief. "So, Jeremy hadn't seen me when they fried Broderick," she mumbled to herself. Confusion began to bubble along the path of her nerves. She didn't care about how she looked. She had heard him in the car make his jangled remark about how ugly she had become. "Didn't I keep the mirrors and other reminders hidden in the guest room? Hadn't I avoided bathing so I could escape the glares of the one over the sink?"

Emmy didn't have a deformed image of herself. She didn't think of herself as fat or thin. Those things weren't important, she thought. It just made her uncomfortable to look at her reflection and she couldn't say why. It was like in the new video cameras in stores when you caught a glimpse of yourself, or like looking at the bridge from the river in a fog. Blurred and fleeting; sometimes there, sometimes gone.

Jolted out of his moment of contemplation by a second or two of silence, Jeremy continued. "I really don't know how to help with Emmy and all that. I came to talk to you in private, when we're done with this crap." He said to Skizzum as he indicated the pile of trash.

"Jeremy the word burner. Couldn't he just say *when we're done with this cleaning*?" Skizzum thought, nodding. An image of herself grabbing his tongue and holding it, popped into her mind and made her smile. "Couldn't he hold his own tongue?" she thought, speculating more on another level about what he wanted to keep secret. "What's all the silence about, if he thinks we're on the same side? (Which side wasn't yet clear). Does it have something to do with Hiram? Couldn't he talk about the KKK in front of a Black man? Or, was it because he was hiding something? Maybe the man from Under-the-hill wasn't shooting at us after all?" Like a detective in a thriller, she was quick at understanding complexities once things were on the ground and running. What she didn't get is what triggered the shooting in the first place, at least where she was concerned. She knew Emmy was a little skittish. Okay, maybe a lot, but she had seemed frightened before last night. Skizzum remembered her speaking of Jeremy and the Klan. She had meant to ask her for details, but there were so many things happening at once.

Hellbent n' harried
Pull us n' fights
Blow-up decades
Take away rights.

Tain't 'nough whippin'
The strife and blood,
All we tried got
Nipped in the bud.

Better take care,
I carry a knife.
Letters tain't scary
Might take your life.

Inside the trailer, Emmy was finishing her poem, which was beginning to sound like a song. She remembered her parents stomping in songs Cajuns called *complaints*.

Barbara Bonneau

A punctuation mark in a sentence of humanity

Emmy identified more and more with the downtrodden and tortured Black people of Ferriday, and everywhere else. Whether right or wrong, she mistreated the privilege of having moon-pale skin in a White-looking community. Sometimes she couldn't stand it. The life that was afforded to her family and herself in that town had been possible in those days because most of them appeared to be White, or at least whitish. In spite of a larger percentage of Black people, the Whites made all the rules. This schema of favoritism put everyone under scrutiny. No one was ever enough of something, or they were too much of something else. She understood the despair of people whose dark skin was almost like a life-threatening sentence doled out at birth, because she felt akin to it. She had seen Skizzum give up her child, understanding that it would be easier that way, knowing she might never have another. All and all, both had come away from community-based silence and cruelty, and, since her grandmother's death before her fourteenth year, Emmy had grown up alone. "Silence is another kind of violence," she decided.

She tried to be like many Americans who, with mixed origins and missing genealogies, claim only one. But wasn't identity something that went further than the depth of their skins? How could one say when so many had their identities ripped to shreds? "I'm Emmy. Emeline Dufrene-Robichaux," she reminded herself. And that was enough, at least to get her through the day. She was fed up with people talking about how she looked; how porcelain- white she was, how beautiful her skin had been, how sad it was that she had fallen from grace.

"Don't Hiram's daughters have skin like panthers, with a perfect grain, all velvety and smooth? And what if it wasn't so beautiful? We're all more than our skins. Hadn't Mamere known?" She questioned, mumbling to herself.

Her grandmother had been caught up in the fascination of that early-century making, linked to her abandonment by her own parents as much as to the prejudices of the day. Her mother, whom Emmy had only seen in dreams, or couldn't remember, had the vague reputation of being either a gypsy singer, a flame thrower, a long- lived, nimble, circus acrobat, and now, a Mississippi-River-catfish- flamenco-swimmer. Her father, Emmy's great-grandfather, an Irishman and roadside rapist, according to the great-grandmother, was from *who knew where*, ending up as *who knew what*, and had only that baggage for reputation. Speaking of him in those terms did not leave room for a good abode (because nomadic people also have their standards). Mamere took her omens from future projects, forgetting how the past somehow weaves itself into the *Best Laid Plans*, like hope and, like its opposite, despair. "The only successful Black singers," she said, "are whiter than the others. You do more than pass the paper bag test," she had said to her grand-daughter, perhaps in answer to questions about the Creoles in their family.

But Emmy knew. She was neither Black nor White, whether she could sing or not. She was Black and White and Redbone, Cajun.

She was Irish, French, Gypsy, African, American Indian, and *every* other color of the spice rainbow sprinkled on

America. And that was enough. She could not be who she was not and she could not be more or less. Like a punctuation mark in a sentence of humanity, she stood there, silent. Longing for pacification, she was desperate to leave something behind, for her family, for all those who lived before, as a substitute for the child of her blood, a fantasy-child, who would not come later. This tumultuous, hopeless urge was to create a rampart against the irreparable harm of all those who had lost their lives too young, or where entire families, in migrations and genocides, had been wiped out by the powers in place and lost their link in memory's lineage. It was also the base of her determination to stand against personal annihilation. Although she could no longer sing, she needed to communicate with others, if only in sorrow, but she could write songs.

Skizzum began to talk about the group that had formed around Harper in the fifties and on into the sixties. "While I was away, I participated in women's marches and protests against the war in Vietnam. I saw the workings of political machines inside organized groups of young people and caught a glimpse of the same in the political arena. Little by little, I became less resentful of the adults in our community who, in the past, had joined Harper's church and put on blinders as to what was going on with the girls. I couldn't stay angry like that forever." The dissonance she had lived with for years, and that she suspected still troubled Emmy , had dissipated. Had she had learned scrutiny and cynicism, or did the beer she drank envelop the world in a softened, livable haze? "I heard about what had happened in Jonestown, Guyana, with the People's Temple, people drinking poisoned Kool-Aid, under threat of being shot, even little kids. It isn't fair to say that they were all drug addicts or broken vets. Think about it," she said.

"Oh come on, Skizzum, after you left, you sometimes said they were nuts, or idiots," said Pierre.

"I know. Sure, there were those in Harper's group, who, who were children or adolescents, like me," he stammered. "We were captivated by whatever we thought was funny, elsewhere forbidden, or just because he said he loved us. And our parents let us decide. They said it was okay. Children are vulnerable to affection. So are many adults. Give us a gift, a smile or pat on the back and we will have a harder time judging you. It only took a little flattery and enthusiasm to hook us. He reeled us in like willing fish and got us to flop in the bottom of his boat without resistance. Instead of gasping for breath, we repeated everything he said. To adults, to other children, people within or outside the group." She looked at Jeremy to see what he would say. It wasn't often she had a captive audience outside a bar where she played her guitar or shot pool.

"Well, for people like Mérite-Lajoie and Deux Ours, the foot in the door, came in like a foot in the mouth," Jeremy laughed, the others listening.

"What do you mean, *people like Mérite-Lajoie and Deux Ours*?" she started to get angry.

"You know. They were kinda of naïve-like, like they could believe any of his bullshit."

"Really, Jeremy? Coming from you, you think that they got into that because they believed just off the bat? That they, who had been Catholics all their lives, could just drop everything, fall to their knees and crawl around a salt-lick like it was an altar? Do you think you would have been different in their place? I've given this a lot of thought," she said. She opened another beer, forgetting to offer one to the others. Jeremy helped himself.

"Mérite-Lajoie saved Harper's life. That already gave her a choice, a choice of kinds, I think I should say. She could have left him at the hospital and never turned back, but she wanted to understand what had happened. She must have felt some sort of responsibility to him, and loyalty to her beliefs. But isn't the idea of responsibility what attracted most of the adults here? I know it was for the adolescents who came without their parents. It was as if telling them that they were free adults, with the liberty to choose, and each one necessary to protect each other, God and country, was all it took to change our beliefs and follow this man into the proverbial desert. The adults began to believe that if they left him, things would fall apart; that we would lose our freedom, and everyone else would as well. I was old enough to feel that. The idea of community here was not that of a community of sharing. It was the community of giving; giving to him. A community based on his greed. Me, me, me. That's all you'd ever hear from him, even when he talked about God. *God wants me to be the one to lead us. God has chosen me to be his lookalike!* Please. Don't forget that! We could laugh about it if it hadn't happened to us."

"Harper told us all that we were free to go, but if we did, that would also be the beginning of the downfall of family and morality in our community, Hell, the whole country. He said we would lose everything. He made adults sign over their belongings. He asked kids to bring him small offerings. Some of us would steal from our parents to bring him money. That a complaint about any of this would hold up in court or not was another affair. I'm not a lawyer but I can tell you Emmy is lucky not to have had that fight! Had he wanted it, Mérite-Lajoie would have signed the land over to him. There is some reason he didn't ask or else, Deux-Ours reminded her of this limit; don't give away your land to the White man, and she respected it. Everyone else lived on the property and you know as well as I that Harper's wife, your mother I guess, is Mérite-Lajoie's kin. The idea that any of us were free to go, caused them to stay, in a weird way, and to adhere, little by little to his nonsense. We became the glue to our own flypaper," she continued.

"The older the person, the more Harper relied on the identity of the congregation. He knew how to shake personal attachments and make people dependent on him for recognition. Identifying with him and what he called *the Patterns*, or *the Angels* for the girls, created a kind of inescapable cohesion--and a prison. Once committed, it was harder to back out. Now I know I'm missing something here, but not enough to conclude that Emmy, or anyone else, gets stuck in a group like this because of their vulnerability or their beliefs. It's not that simple. We were all manipulated, not because we were vulnerable, but because we are human," Skizzum affirmed.

"Hell, Skizzum. What are you talkin' bout? You got out, and you can still see how vulnerable Emmy is," argued

Jeremy, still finding it hard to admit he had been in a cult, and not even thinking about the one he was dealing with at present.

"I didn't escape. Harper dumped me. I think you all know how distressed that made me and how, had I not found friendship and love elsewhere, I would have died. Died. But that isn't something you expect," she countered, looking from Hiram, to Jeremy. She didn't know if he had known about his father's infidelities. "Surely he must," she thought. "As for Emmy, I don't know how she has managed to survive. It has been hard for her. Hard like you can only begin to imagine; seeing this littered campground and these junked-up trailers," she said. "Harper got rid of all your doubts about life, about God, about everything. You no longer needed to have questions. Now, Emmy seems like she has only questions."

Hearing this, Emmy wondered and her mind began to wander again. This was the first time they had all gotten together since the fire. It wasn't as if this version of the past could shake her out of her state of mind. Her troubles went deeper. Disbelief had shadowed her for years. "Had all that happened? Was it real? Are they talking about me or is this another dream? I know what Skizzum is saying is true. If we had had warnings then, or if anyone of them would have had been disoriented like I was, it would have taken more than a few cautionary sentences to convince any of us to leave. Early on, my parents argued about it and we moved back from the lake lot, into our house. But we couldn't just shake off Harper's hardened grip. At that time, we didn't have the

Jonestown example on our TV screens and if we had had it, who would have made the comparison?"

They would have all said; *that's not like us, we're different.* If the person listening to Harper was not vulnerable before the involvement with their group, then, like Jones, the preacher would manage to create an atmosphere of dependence where it seemed like the member could not survive outside the group. Using his brand of Bibliomancy, he would yell, interpreting the arrival of a storm as a sign of a Jesus' imminent second coming, *the Pentecost, Jesus's disciples were all gathered round when suddenly there came a sound from heaven as that of a powerful hurricane blowin'. The wind filled the house where they were sittin'. And there appeared unto them cloven tongues like fire, and it sat upon each of them. They were all filled with the Holy Ghost and began to speak with other tongues, as God's messenger gave them utterance. He came once, and he is comin' again now I tell you. If you have confessed and you made pure, you've nothin' to fear from the storm.* Once everyone was captive, he continued, *the world is a dangerous place. We don't have to flee from hurricanes and the like. There are those out there who would like to shut us down. That, friends, is the only danger we have to face.* And where there was no danger, he managed to create one and implant it in their hearts and minds.

This was the colorful language of fear--fear of change, fear of the other, fear of death; fear that paled when he put it into words. How could they ask for help when he called out: *White light! White light! Everybody, take cover!* And from the small campsite with less than ten trailers, or from the church with perhaps a hundred souls, they would all run for the woods and stay there until Harper said it was okay; the danger had dissipated with the rain.

But just then Emmy, inspired and writing, no longer thought about this personal shared past. Perhaps thinking that there were those, worse off than yourself, whose bad luck was unending, that made a difference. For some, hearing of the starving children, of genocide, of illness, or oppression has no effect. But just now, she was turning her rage with her pen, and it was becoming social.

See that Black man?

See that Black man?
Got blood on him.
Run down and over,
can't come again.

See those Black men,
Buried and dead
Bombed in a car
All God's children.

See that Black man?
Been burned alive
Deputy's boots
Has kicked his can.

See those Black men?
Hangin' in a tree
Been called strange fruit,
Mississippi sin.

See that Black man?
Been shot and burnt
Drivin' his car,
T' escape the Klan.

See that Black man?
Under water,
Cain't swim 'way from a

Barbara Bonneau

Mississippi plan.

Louisiana was as much to blame, but here, Mississippi was the word, for the river, from the song, for the crimes that had been solved and unsolved. She thought about the writer, Abel Meerpol and the singer, Billie Holiday. He could write with tears from the heart, from inside a skin as white as her own and share these with the people whose voices had been silenced for so long and whose souls poured out from the singer's rich voice.

Ain't that kind of a cult?

Outside, she heard Hiram interrupt. "Jeremy," he said. "Was he calling him out?" Emmy wondered. "I know you ain't gonna like it. And I don't wanna get into trouble for sayin' it. But wadn't your daddy in the Klan? Ain't that kind of a cult?"

Jeremy turned red, with anger and embarrassment. He remained silent, thinking. It was a quick reaction of those forced to meet with the raw hot blade of reality. Even before his involvement with the guys at work, he had picked up the silver dollar from his father's corpse. He knew. Oh, yes, he knew alright. He was ready to hem and haw and make excuses, but, in his wild thoughts of running for the woods, he wondered if they had seen his father's silver dollar. Of course they hadn't, but there was still no escape. "I cain't run from the truth. I cain't hide it from them," he thought as he lowered his head and nodded a *yes* to both questions, realizing that it was Hiram, a Black man, perhaps the only Black man he cared about who brought the truth out of him.

After a few seconds of silence, he offered, "I'm through with those men, done with hidin', done with anything that connects me to them. I ain't never harmed a Black person since I've been grow'd up. Sure, I been to the KKK meetin"s, said a lot of shit that I regretted as soon as it came out of my mouth. I've enough of David Ducal's crazy arguments about Black people and Jews," he confessed, submitting to their judgement more than he had ever before been able to do. He didn't think the Klan wanted him anyway, and perhaps, they had it out for him now since he had carried out an unauthorized mission. Did they know? He wasn't sure.

At least, he wanted all of it to be over. "But I killed a man. And the girls know. They were witnesses, weren't they?" Jeremy's mind hesitated while the others stared at him, expecting him to continue, but he couldn't share more. "True," he continued in his mind, "Old Man Steales was no angel. He had killed, tried to kill, and had ordered killings. He had raised two sons who were worse and who killed even more people. He had tried to kill me, hadn't he?" Jeremy wasn't sure anymore what was happening and was beginning to think that his only solution was to take his family far away from Ferriday, far away from Natchez, far away from the Klan. To run.

The tension was high. It bounced like hot popcorn on an open fire. But if there was a fire; there was no trial by fire, no madman forcing anyone to talk. Jeremy was coming to terms with his past in presence of people who knew a lot more of the Truth than his truth could tell. It was an admission of sorts. He said at last, "I know I been a sorry neighbor and grew up to be somebody that ain't very nice. I never was. I ain't too smart, but I knowed it for a long time. I ain't gonna shame myself worse by makin' excuses. Too much has been goin' on lately for me to sort it all out. I got a wife, a handicapped daughter, and two other kids to think about. I don't think nobody here in danger with the Klan today, 'cept maybe my oldest boy lookin' like he's a little too interested in Ducal. I'm a curious though, about Emmy, and what she was doin' on the street last night in Natchez. I don't know if it was an accident or not, and to tell you the truth, just now, I don't wanna know. If you can get her away from here soon, it would surely be better for all of us, especially her. She don't look too good. I know a few cops, and word gets 'round fast. People are talkin' about Steales and some drug deals. Somebody said something about a cold case he was involved in in the sixties, and there might be revenge for that, but I don't know if there will be much of an investigation now that he's dead. Goddamit, I wish she would come out here and talk to us."

Hiram, Pierre, and Sandy looked around the table. "What did she do?" they asked in unison. But no one answered their question.

"She can't talk, Jeremy. Didn't you know that? She doesn't have a voice and has been ill since the church burned."

Jeremy hung his head again. "Yeah, I heard about all that, or kinda. Rumors I guess, but I guess some of it was true. Some people said she took drugs. Said she had a meth lab, but I don't think anyone believed it. People make up shit to try to look interestin' I guess. Look, I ain't my old man. I might have tried to be like him, at least for a while. It seemed like he had a lot of pride and self-assurance. He had talents I ain't got, and for some reason, women liked him, men, too. That has an effect on a boy. But today, well, mostly, I just try to get by and just livin' 'round him, was like..." He didn't want to think of all the times he tried to be like some man or another. Men who talked tough, and were feared. He thought if he could be like them, doors would open. He had tried to teach his boys in the same way. Now his face burned. He had never thought that the killings he had been mixed up in were much more than a Saturday afternoon double feature at the Arcade. The murder of two Klan members who had been thought to have been informers for the Klan were recent, but for some reason, those deaths seemed distant from him. This was a chapter he wanted left out of his discussion with Skizzum and her friends. He had only accidently mentioned Emmy's name, as if it had to come out and be put on the table.

Pierre then asked the question he had hoped to avoid answering, "Jeremy, how involved are you with the KKK?"

Jeremy sighed, "It would be better if you didn't know."

"You see, I was wondering if you knew something about Ducal's plans for the LSU former student body president? There again, rumors are floating about all the way from Ferriday to Baton Rouge and back." Pierre was far removed from his own fears and didn't understand the different turns of the conversation.

"I'm not in on any of his plans. He mostly just throws his weight around and stirs up crowds. He gambles here and there. I think the Klan in Concordia Parish, most of them older, are confused about his projects to go after Jews. And most of them are keeping a lid on what happened in the past. They got away with it. At least the law ain't stopped 'em. Some of 'em been accused of bein' informants and writin' letters and shit. This makes 'em insecure and dangerous. With 'em I see more and more that, bein' in a group like that, havin' loyalties don't mean ya got friends. And ya got no hope either. Sure, they invite you to fish fries and shit like that, but that's just like *Big Brother*. It's hard not to answer their invitations because ya have this kind of desire to know what's goin' on. It's like ya can feel the truth hoverin' 'bout, and ya go, just to find out if ya will learn it this time. But instead of havin' hope, even 'bout goin' and bein' there, ya still feel in the dark. Instead of hope, ya feel angry and that gives ya energy to move forward. They tell ya that you're angry because ya know the truth and if ya do their biddin', you'll feel better. But it don't get no better. And you don't know the Truth. And ya just feel worse because of the awful things happenin' around ya, and the fear ya got 'cause they might accuse ya' of tellin'. A lot of us don't ask when it will start gettin' better. All this gets mixed up with union talk at work too and it's hard to keep it all straight."

Jeremy was afraid to reveal himself or to buddy up to anyone. He talked as if he knew everyone felt like him. But he also knew he could still get called out as an informer, especially if someone saw him talking to a Black man or people who they thought came from out of town. He was also afraid one of them might turn on him for his admission about his presence last night. He had one idea, and that was to get out of there. "Why did I come," he wondered. The table wasn't visible from the road, but their vehicles were there to see for anyone who came over the levee or who came to the camp to put their boat in. He didn't know who used the camp.

Sandy was quiet the whole time. She was wondering what was going on with Emmy. They had put the information about Ducal and the Klan together. Was Jeremy in on one of these lists? "Where's the bathroom?" she asked. It was an old trick, seen in every detective show or thriller movie. She was playing the role of cop, or the curious cat. Like a feline, she tiptoed around the back of the table and towards the front of the trailer where Emmy was working.

Emmy's head jerked up when she heard the door open. She covered her writing and stood. Sandy asked, "Emmy, how are you doing with those charts? Can I see?"

Emmy shook her head. It was more of a, *I'm not working on those anymore*, or, *I don't know what you're talking about*, than a refusal to show Sandy the work they had done. "That was so long ago," Emmy thought.

"Why not?" Sandy persisted. Emmy grabbed a paper and pen.

"I'm not working on that. I'm writing songs and stuff." Emmy wasn't sure that Sandy believed her. Sandy was a sweet girl, but Emmy had a hard time being with anyone and was worried that Jeremy might also come in.

"Can I see?" she asked.

Emmy wrote. "Maybe later. Maybe when I'm done. I'm just trying some new things."

Of course, Sandy had no idea of Emmy's project of the past five years and had never seen the anonymous letters. Until a few days ago, Emmy had no idea five years had passed. She had been living in a bubble, a scary, deflated bubble, like inside a piece of chewing gum, folded over, stuck, and forgotten, on the bottom of a desktop. Sometimes she was near others, somewhat folded up themselves, but she was unable to interact with them, or to scrape herself off and go somewhere else. She had been concentrating on revenge, and rebuilding herself, on what she still thought of as her contribution to the Civil Rights Movement.

"Why don't you join us outside. He's okay. Jeremy, I mean. He seems like he's making an effort. Even Hiram talks to him."

Emmy shook her head, annoyed. She thought that if Jeremy knew that she had taken his daughter that day, he wouldn't be sitting outside talking with her friends. This thought gave her an idea. "Why don't you ask him about his family?" she wrote. She was still unsure about the truth, and when she slept, tenebrous clouds seeped into her soul.

"Okay," she answered. "I'll try to get him to talk more about himself. I'm not sure he'll talk more about Ducal."

A sad relic

January weather was unpredictable, often cold and wet, but today, the sun was out. The shadows were shortening towards noon. When Sandy came back outside, the young people were still seated around the picnic table. Everyone, except her, began to complain of their empty stomachs, and the trailer park still needed work. Skizzum said she would go get some chicken at the local fast-food chain, because now, after the installation of a Walmart, and the closure of local diners and the Sandwich Bar, Ferriday had one, all of its own. Everyone chipped in for the meal. Before leaving, she checked on Emmy.

Again, she started when someone opened the door. When she saw Skizzum, she smiled. It was a smile of relief. She didn't hide her writing this time.

Skizzum looked at her friend's paper. She read the last poem. They exchanged glances like two sisters who understand something deeper than themselves. Skizzum put her hand on Emmy's shoulder and gave it a soft squeeze. "Emmy," she said, "I have to go get us something to eat. Do you want to come with me ?"

It was a simple question, but again Emmy was worried. She didn't want to see the others. It was as if as long as she and Jeremy didn't cross paths, she would be alright. She gathered her papers, came outside with Skizzum, and locked the door to the trailer. She thought she might ask Skizzum to take her home.

Since Jeremy had showed up, they had cleared away some of the brush. The beer can pond had dried up and the swans had flown away to another dump. The young women got into Emmy's truck, and were at the levee pass when another truck met them in front. Skizzum gave a short honk. It was Rover with another man and his boat. He didn't back away, thinking he would be allowed passage with the boat and trailer. Emmy stared straight in front. Skizzum looked at her. She didn't understand Emmy's anxiety, but saw she had written on a paper. *The camp is closed.*

Skizzum got out of the truck and walked up to Rover. He had a cigar in his mouth and the window opened. She didn't know the other man. "The camp and boat landing are closed for clean-up and repairs," she said. "She might sell it for the right price."

Rover laughed as if he thought that was a joke. "Listen here young lady. I've been puttin' my boat in here since before you was born. I don't need no permission."

Back at the camp, both Jeremy and Hiram were nervous. Hiram said to the others, "I think that honk was my cue. I gotta git goin'. Tell Skizzum and Emmy bye. Good to see ya, man," he said shaking Jeremy's hand again. And with that he ran over to his boat, lifted the rope off the piling, jumped in and paddled out into the lake. Hiram had seen Rover put his boat in there and tried to stay clear of these men. He knew nothing about their Klan activities, but had witnessed Rover's enraged outbursts. Jeremy, having come by car couldn't leave. He looked at Pierre and Sandy. Not knowing whose car was on the other side of the levee, his thoughts went wild. "I should've never come. Maybe I could take one of their motorcycles and escape," he thought, although, there was nothing strange about his being at his father's old encampment. But he had seen how Hiram jumped, wide-eyed, as if he knew who might be there. Wild images of Steve McQueen in the film, *The Great Escape*, came into his mind. He felt that he was no hero, in spite of what he let Emmy and Skizzum think about the night in front of the Under-the-Hill Saloon. Although he had spent close to ten years living at the campsite with his family, he hadn't gone there in years, and didn't think of it as home anymore. Guilt feelings were tickling his nose, causing him to sneeze, to expel feelings that he might have lied, or hadn't fulfilled the Klan's pledge. *Why had he taken it?* Wiping his nose, he shored up as much courage as he could and walked up to the entrance to assist Skizzum, come what may.

As he neared the vehicles, he saw Rover and the other man. The old flag *AUSSI INEBRANLABLE QUE L'ECREVISE* was flying nearby. For some reason, it caught his eye. What did it mean? He never had much of an understanding of French, but knew what the flag had said, and that it had stood for courage and resolve. He saw that many of the letters had faded. For an instant, he thought he caught the word; N-E-B-U-L-I-S-E, the British spelling for nebulize, and remembered their *Star Trek* playing days and the even more recent film he had watched. Was that close to dematerialize, disintegrate even? Was he supposed to take this riddle as some sort of message? To accept his end as inevitable as with all things? As if to show it to the flag, whether as a threat or as a form self-reassurance (and perhaps there was no difference between the two), he raised his gun in the air.

"I got my gun in case you's tryin' to predict me a short future. I'm a man, and I ain't gonna disappear into dust just yet." In truth, if he could know his deep-down Truth, he sometimes wished he could become one of the fine powders he worked with and be lifted by the breeze.

The wind was up enough where he could see the crawfish claw, which had prevailed on one side, over the cult-leader's imposed painted hand, pinching the remaining hand. Was it a warning; its gesture reminding him that *he could harm himself or the others*? Was it recalling that *yes, this was happening*, it was really happening. Just pinch yourself. One of the evilest Klan members of all times was just there in front of them and he was about to tell him to remove himself from the premises. After their past difficulties, he couldn't imagine that a standoff would end there. He didn't know the other man in the truck, and that worried him even more. "Euhhhhh, he groaned, letting out a long sigh, "it don't look too good."

He raised his hand in a subdued greeting, but also to signal a stop, and walked over to the driver's side. Rover could have a surprise prepared for him, but as with the magician, the eyes should be kept on the eyes, not the hands, which are, if not quicker, at least trickier. "Hey," he said. "The boat landing and camp are closed today for cleanup and repairs. Y'all will have to go up to Mallard's landing or someplace else to put your boat in the water. Sorry about that."

Now Rover didn't know much about the relationship between Jeremy and the Cajuns, but he knew that they had all lived there. He knew that Jeremy's father had been a minister of a church that had been there.

"We can just put our boat in and we won't be any trouble after that," Rover suggested, trying to be cordial and get what he wanted all the same.

"No that won't do. You see, we've got it fixed up so we can patch some holes," replied Jeremy, hoping that Rover couldn't tell that he was lying and thinking that now, instead of leaving, he was going to have to make good on the claim.

Rover rolled his eyes over to his passenger and then back to Jeremy. Skizzum was standing beside him, equal to him in size and stature. Emmy was still in the truck. Because of the glint of the sun off the windshield, the driver could only see the sun shining like a halo over the truck and not who was inside it. In an attempt to frighten them, Rover squinted his eyes, as if that would help him see what was behind their front of secrecy. He put the truck in reverse, backed up before turning around and squealing his tires on the Lake Road, going north. Jeremy and Emmy didn't think that that would be the end of it. Without consolidating their thoughts, they both knew of Rover's tenacity and his hatred. They wondered if he had something other in mind. In this part of the country, people carried weapons in their trucks to settle accounts with poisonous snakes, alligators, or other perceived or imagined threats. This habit was as much of a sad relic of pioneer days where lawlessness had reigned as needed to supplement one's diet with wild game.

In spite of the no trespassing signs around the full property, and not just the campsite, Emmy wondered if they might come in from elsewhere. "Is he after me? Are he and Jeremy after me for shooting Steales?" Each understood the shooting of this elder Klan member differently. "Didn't I kill Steales?" wondered Emmy.

"Did she really kill Steales?" Skizzum, queried to herself, somehow unable to process it all. "Did I have too many beers that night? Could Emmy do something that crazy? Who was that guy anyway? Why would he be after Emmy , unless this had something to do with her letters?"

"I know I killed Steales," thought Jeremy, "but, what if the Klan finds out that I did? Do they suspect me of being an informant? What did I do wrong? Why does Emmy think she did it? Doesn't she realize that two shots were fired? And Skizzum?" He had no idea about Emmy's letters. In spite of all, she had been careful. Memory's triangle connected them and weighed on all three, as had much of the past. Three stories. Three versions of the same memory. But three, that kept the conclusion from being mirrored back from one another and becoming fatal to anyone of them.

Emmy put her pistol back into the glove compartment. Minutes before, she had taken it and was holding it, pointed in the direction of Rover. It was a wild thought. It was more likely that the bullet would ricochet inside the truck than pierce the windshield in the right way and find its target out front. Still, she felt better holding it, in spite of all warnings from everyone, both friend and foe, dead and alive. It wasn't safe for any of them. Jeremy decided he would pull his truck into the breach in the levee after Skizzum and Emmy left. Neither of the women had seen him do it. Would blocking the entrance be enough if the men decided to come back?

Camp Coonass

Rover drove along the Lake Road. When they got to Mallard's Landing, they backed the trailer down the ramp, and launched the fishing boat. It was a nicer model than Emmy's had been. It had a motor. With the boat, they could go back towards the point, and the inlet located just before it, to fish, like they were accustomed to doing. And they could also see what was up with the landing at *Camp Coonass*, as they were beginning to call it, based on the once unpleasant descriptive of the Cajuns.

Nowadays, many Cajuns, proud of their ancestry, don't mind this nickname, or some others, and their children don't mind being called *Radbwah* (a kind of woodrat or possum), or *grenouille* (frog), even though they understood well enough what those creatures looked like and what they ate. Cajuns' feelings about being called *Coonasses* changed in the same way with the term, *Redbone*, which for years had angered many, as had the words *Cajun* and *Creole*, generations before. These slur words had seemed abject to the Acadians, and before, to the French, who were called *Acadians*, upon their encounter with the British some five hundred years before. These derivative denominations may have been the fact of differences in language and mispronunciations. Perhaps another reason that Cajuns were not a recognized minority, is that the derogatory terms were attached to a race component. Racial differences were not as recognizable as with some other peoples because most of the Cajuns had seemed, well, seemed white. With lineages from Africa as well as France, combined with those of the not so new continent, it is perhaps, with this lighter skin, along with the willingness to integrate the once abject denominations as being a sort of distinguished identity, that Cajuns found themselves included in other populations. As long as they didn't open their mouths and start speaking unknown tongues, or insist on their religious or food differences, no one much questioned their beginnings. However, the idea of enduring abuse can only get one out the back door. Black people had been forced to accept everything and bearing mockery had not helped them as far as anyone could tell. Consciousness of what it meant to be a slave or to hold slaves was not raised by lack of opposition. No one was ever heard by remaining silent and waiting for tyrants to stop being tyrannical. In some places, racial equality and use of a native language comes from fighting out front. In others, it comes only in the grave, as all bones are white, at least at first, before they turn gray and then, to dust.

But can territory be claimed *post mortem*, so to speak? If burial grounds are sacred because of the dust they contain, who owns the dirt that houses the sanctified remains? In Louisiana, it is difficult to contest that apart from the Native Americans, the French touched ground there before other Europeans. Still, equal footing against fortunate and armed adversaries had to be hacked out and reformed as much as forest trees and swamp critters.

What goes around, comes around

On the way to the fast-food store, Skizzum stopped to buy drinks at the PicQuick. When she got back in the car, after a usual once over and sermon from Mrs. Gosset, she asked Emmy, "Have you ever thought about songwriting? I'm not talking about blues or writing classical music. I'm talking about music that people are starting to listen to today; like rap or hip hop. A lot of those songs have some sort of social implications; like, speaking out against police violence towards Blacks or political riffs. I think those poems you are working on might work for that."

Emmy looked at her. She was too frightened by what she had just witnessed and thought that Skizzum had seemed unaware that Rover might come back. She didn't seem to know who he was or why he might be there, other than to put his boat in the water.

"What's goin' on?" Skizzum asked. Emmy, who did not try to talk often because of the side effects from her shock treatments, croaked. "The man in the truck is Rover. He is KKK. The man I killed, too," coughing as she finished her sentence. It wasn't much to go on, other than to realize that Emmy was nervous about why the men had come and at first had refused to leave. Emmy got on her knees and looked behind the seat of her truck. She found her twenty-two rifle and her pouch with enough bullets to take care of a whole army division, if necessary. Of course, unless Jeremy and Skizzum would help her, that wouldn't do much good, not against Rover and his clan of killers if they showed up to start trouble again.

Skizzum braked when she saw Emmy move the gun towards the front of the truck. "What are you doing, Emmy! You can't fight these men! Do you want to end up in prison like your mother? We don't even know what happened to that guy the other night or who he was!"

Emmy figured she knew. Because she hadn't seen anything in the news about it, she thought that someone, perhaps Jeremy, had told the Klan, or perhaps the attending cop had been a Klan member, and that they had taken care of Steales' body. Although it seemed unlikely to her, she thought that Jeremy could have even dragged the man down the boat ramp, and rolled him into the river. End of story, at least until his body bobbed up like a cork or an unleashed buoy, somewhere between Baton Rouge and New Orleans.

This wasn't far from the truth. While Jeremy was in the bar, three other Klansmen who had been present at the restaurant with Steales, and who were not his sons, had been the first to arrive on the scene after the departure of all three of the living protagonists. They had been assigned to remove a body, but didn't know it would be Steales. They had assumed that Steales would be the shooter, and someone else would be the victim. Still, they took assignments as they came. One of them was a Natchez police officer. The two others, were from the Mississippi White Knights. While the police officer stood watch, the two other men wrapped the body in a tarp, and carried it into the Mississippi River where it floated an instant before it was swept off by the swirling waters and sank in a watery grave without a sepulture. Like so many others before him, both Black and White, now equal in death, he became another nameless corpse.

Steales had failed in his mission, but the men could have believed that his shooting was the fruit of a successful enterprise to eliminate an informer. As with the unknowns between Emmy, Skizzum, and Jeremy, these men didn't fully understand why they had to remove Steales' body instead of allowing a police investigation. They were told to do it; and they obeyed.

Emmy's glare hardened. "What didn't Skizzum get? This was not a barbecue or Sunday picnic they were headed to. These men might fish, but it was their way of keeping an eye on the inhabitants of the lake," she thought. "They might be here for me."

"Emmy's state of mind is so entwined with her delusions that she might even see enemies where there are none," thought Skizzum. Desperate to hold on to their new-found calm, she was trying to figure out something else to do before returning to the camp. "Emmy," she said. "Why don't we stop by your house and we can think this out. Make a plan. In the meantime, I'll go get the others and we can have lunch here." Even as she said it, she knew that this wouldn't work. Emmy wouldn't allow that Jeremy come into her house.

To her surprise, Emmy nodded, "Ok."

Emmy got out of her truck, taking her ammunition with her. Although the camp was in walking distance, Skizzum drove back across the Lake Road. She called to them, "Chicken's waitin'. The table's set. If y'all are hungry, come and get it. We'll finish up later."

By now, Jeremy was worried. He got on the back of Pierre's bike and rode over to Emmy's with Sandy following them. "'bout now," he thought, Rover will show up, walk across the levee, or come by boat, and see I ain't filled no pot holes in the landing. Well, I cain't do much about that 'til it happens." He tried to talk himself out of a future he could not control, and that he would have to face when the time came, if it came.

While they were away, Emmy had stored her guns and ammunition in her trailer office. She also opened the shed and was trying to pull out a table and lawn chairs when the others arrived. The weather was still cool, but not cold. She wanted them to sit outside and not be bothered in her home. Skizzum ran over and called Pierre and Sandy to help. The three of them set up the table and chairs for an outdoor meal on the side yard where Mérite- Lajoie had once had her horses.

"Emmy," called Sandy. "Why don't you come out and eat with us?"

Skizzum gave a half smile. No one believed she would come, so she brought Emmy some chicken. She didn't think she would eat it alone either, even if her eating had improved to the point, she could chew meat and swallow. She sat down beside her friend and began to talk. She didn't tell Emmy what she should or shouldn't do about the other people. Emmy was in her home and Skizzum would not advise her. "Emmy," she began, "I want you to come back to Nashville with me. Your poems seem more like hip hop or rap. I mean what they say could interest people who work in that field. Nashville is mostly country, and a little rock. There are blues people too. But I have contacts in Memphis. There are people in the music field who cross over to different kinds of music and I could get them to look at your songs if you wanted?"

Emmy just stared out the window towards the farm equipment cemetery, or spaceship star-craft-zone, her state of mind dictating the ultimate twilight. She seemed like she was about to leave the planet again on one of the former make-believe Enterprise spaceships. "I'm leaving this food for you," Skizzum continued, sighing. "I hope that you will eat some of it before I come back."

Emmy was already gone in her mind and in just seconds, before the door closed behind Skizzum, she was out the door, recovering her weapons from the trailer. She walked behind it, and out across the lot, crossing the Lake Road, north of the early encampment. Deciding that being anonymous was a way of just being anyone and everyone at the same time, she thought she understood at last why Mérite-Lajoie shot Harper in front of a crowd. "She was doing it for me, and for herself. She wanted everyone to know that she couldn't tolerate what he had done to me, and to her way of thinking, only she could show that it was intolerable to her, whatever the consequences. Not a sheriff, not a judge, not anyone else in the community or outside of it could give her back what Harper had taken."

She was still on her mother's property; near the place where many years before, Mérite-Lajoie, had had her unfortunate meeting with Harper. It was near the trail marker tree, left there by Native Americans, years before. Something moved in the bushes and she shivered, pointing her gun in the direction of the noise. "You can't kill spirits," she murmured. Continuing north, she moved with caution. Mallard's landing was not far. The men could have left their truck there and continued on foot, or by boat, towards her property. Suddenly, Emmy saw something wavering with the moss. It seemed to her for an instant that a man had been there, and had slipped behind the trees. She crouched down for a minute near the ground. In the distance, she could hear the water lapping the shore, and the whir of car's engine on the Lake Road. With these came the drifts of algae and dried grass, a mixture that smelled like a badly put-together soup. Her nose burned with something like sulfur, and her ears, like when she heard a scratched record. She wasn't sure she could write rap songs, unless they got some musicians on board with her. Her senses rolled together without distinction.

Voices came in from the area not far from where the bootlegged whiskey had once been made. She wondered if the buried cistern was empty and if she could open the top. She couldn't tell if it was Rover who was talking, or someone else. They kept their voices low, and were moving near the lake. Perhaps they were in a boat. Emmy stopped moving, and listened again.

Skizzum and the others had finished their meal. When she brought the trash back into the house, she saw that Emmy's food was untouched. Sighing, she put it in the refrigerator and walked out to the office. Knocking, she called out to Emmy at the same time. No answer. She opened the door and called again, but Emmy was not there. Realizing that this could only mean that Emmy had gone back to the camp alone, and on foot, she ran to find the others. "She's gone back to the camp," she cried. Pierre and Sandy didn't understand the anxiety in Skizzum's voice. Jeremy didn't know about the guns, but knew that Emmy could be in danger if the men had come back for him.

They all jumped into Emmy's truck, and drove back across the road. Jeremy's truck was still blocking the entrance so they got out and ran up over the levee. Jeremy stopped and grabbed his gun from his truck.

Once they arrived at the camp, they realized Emmy was absent. Skizzum called out to her. Jeremy said, "shhhhh," putting his finger in front of his mouth. He tried the trailer door. It had been forced open. Papers were strewn about the room and furniture overturned. They looked in the other trailers. The other doors had been forced too. Emmy was nowhere to be seen. Their faces wore frantic features as they looked around the site. Pierre and Sandy didn't know what to do. They all stood around the picnic area and began to discuss her possible whereabouts in low voices.

"Anything could have happened to her," said Skizzum, alarmed. "I shouldn't have let her eat alone. I should have confiscated her guns."

Pierre and Sandy raised their eyebrows together, as if in a single stroke of a paint-brush vow. "She has guns!" they exclaimed, looking at each other. The last time they had spent time with Emmy, she had seemed determined to carry out a mission, and even seemed paranoid. Sandy wondered if mission and paranoia were one in the same. Jeremy wasn't surprised about the guns, because he had seen her with one the other night. He had warned Skizzum to get rid of it. Had she missed Steale, intentionally or because her shooting wasn't what it once was ?

Emmy was watching for signs of movement. Hearing the scrunch and bristle of the weeds behind her, she jerked away. It was Rover. She ran into the Indian trees where she had heard the sounds before. She had less fear of spirits than of these men. Now, she thought she was being tracked. "He saw me. He knows it was me. Now he will..." She heard another noise, and turned around pointing her gun. Her ears were playing tricks on her. There was no one there. She went further into the forest and towards the lake. There she found the empty boat. The men were on her property, trespassing.

Circling back, she heard them whispering again. "I saw her run. She's around here somewhere. The Harper kid must be here too. We should split up."

"No, said Rover. "Let's just find her and see what she knows. We could fool around with her. Scare her a little." He laughed. "She's deaf you know. And dumb. Maybe a little retarded. It's not like she's gonna talk. I seen her at the barbershop. The last time was a couple of years ago. They took her broom and told her to go home. She smelled like a tramp. Hadn't taken a bath in who knows how long. I think she's got moths in her head, like her mother."

Emmy knew not to move. She had hunted with her mother before getting too involved with Harper's church. She kept hearing someone talk behind her and wondered if Mamere had come back, but no one was there. She got up to move and suddenly, there was Rover, in front of her pointing his gun in her direction. She pointed her gun and did not hesitate. She fired. Ross fell. He hadn't expected her to shoot. A man tried to grab her from behind and she managed to pull her gun back, hitting him in the stomach. She ran towards the lake. Briars tore at her ankles and she tripped over a branch. She caught herself before falling to the ground. When she got there, she found their boat and slipped out in it, pulling into a cove. She paddled twenty-five yards, got out again, and moved back into the cover of the woods. She needed to find the man before he found her, or the others. They may have heard the shot. Quiet as a doe who knows her fawn is in danger, she circled back to the place where Rover had fallen, but he was no longer there.

There in his place was an old possum with a gun-shot wound, still breathing. Remembering her mother's story about her meeting with Harper, and how she thought she had shot Harper along with a possum; she didn't understand how she had shot it. She hadn't used a shotgun. She could not have shot both Rover and the possum. She picked up a rock, and hit it against its head. She didn't want it to suffer from the wound, and she was afraid because of stories about how the Devil could turn into a beast, or vice versa, come out of an animal. "Isn't that what had happened to Harper?" she asked herself. "Were those Biblical stories about the pigs jumping off the cliff true? Had her mother lied? In ending the possum's pain, perhaps I prevented our own?"

There was something in her gest that reminded her of what had happened the night of the church fire, too.

"How had she learned to kill like that?" Even if it was a mercy killing, it confused her to know how she knew. Then, deep inside herself, where memories had seemed to disappear with nightmares, while she stood, hypnotized by the flames lighting up and licking piano keys in hieroglyphic formations, paralyzed by the words of the pyromancer, waiting for it all to disappear so she could wake up; Jeremy had taken her by the hand and forced her away. As he pushed her outside in front of him, she stumbled over Grits, Harper's gelded dog, now, with his head bashed in.

Jeremy had said, "Get up and run, he won't hurt you no more. Someone done him in with a can. Ma did, I guess. She's gone nuts. Maybe set the church on fire, and is after somebody else, but not to save them. Unless it was Dad? Now get up and run."

She got up, but she couldn't run. She had seen. Before Jeremy had pulled her by the arm, she had stood there just inside the door of the church, staring as Harper had bashed in the dog's head and left her to burn in the church. She remembered now. He told her to go back inside so she would be cleansed, purified by the fire. "That is how girls become real Angels," he said, kissing her forehead. Now, she looked at the dead dog wondering why Jeremy had forced her outside. Trying to hear, to hear what her tooth was telling her. It said, she had swallowed the seed of the Devil and her skin would turn black in Hell. She could never ever be an angel.

She had stood there, staring at the dead dog and the fire, trying to find the courage to return to burn in a church fire and escape Hell as Harper had promised, as her tooth was telling her, until someone picked her up and taken her to her grandmother's trailer? Now as she thought about it, Emmy knew Harper had killed the dog. She had seen him as a rapist and as a murderer of dogs and realized now what her mind would not let her understand then. He wanted her to die with the secret he knew she could not keep. She didn't have to tell. Everyone would know. At the time, she couldn't think at all, not enough to save her own life. Her mind, as well as her body, had turned in circles, almost like now, repeating and remembering what she had or had not done. Does the body know? Or does the mind? The tooth talked a lot but could not know more than the rest of them what to do when it came to the Devil. It heard Harper, whispering with his forked tongue, telling her to stay in the church and burn, but it just told her that is how she would be a sister to the other Angels and it smiled, with the other teeth.

Jeremy couldn't get close to Grits while he was alive. The dog had mistrusted him since he had used the rubber bands. If he had seen the fire, until the dog was dead, he couldn't get past him. But the dog had yelped and choked on its own blood. It had saved her life by its curdled yowl. Then Jeremy, had pulled her from the flames. Now, more than once. Once from the fire, once from gun-fire. And now, she remembered.

She heard more noise in the briars and slipped away towards the lake again. The other man was nowhere to be found and neither was the boat. "He must have taken Rover. Maybe he isn't dead?" Emmy was frightened. Afraid of the violence within her, she had never intended to kill anyone, not even a half-dead, suffering possum.

Now she had shot two men, and been the cause of the death of at least five. "How many others will I have to kill, now ?" she murmured, thinking of her poison pen list. There was Hogden. He would have to wait. Her act had removed her anonymity, at least in part. Wasn't that what she had decided would be best? Maybe it *was* time that she left Ferriday.

Skizzum and Jeremy arrived at the sight where they found Emmy in a state of dazed fright. They took the weapons and held her up as she staggered away from the Lake's shore. "Emmy, said Skizzum, trying to sooth her friend. "It's okay."

"But how could it be okay ?" thought Emmy, leaning on Skizzum, she whispered. "I shot a man. I think I killed him, but he's gone. The only good thing is that they are both gone. Are they gone? Please tell me they're gone. I'm so tired. I can't keep going. My blood has stopped flowing. Like Mama, I'm cut off from the world. Kin to no one." Trembling, her feet like molten lead, she could not stand.

The friends helped her back to her camp and to Jeremy's truck. "Did I just hear her say something? Jeremy asked. Skizzum shook her head, and gave him a look that meant, *let's not talk about it now.* They took her home while the others continued to clean, to get the place ready for sale or for rent. At this point it was hard to think of anything other than helping their friend get out of there. Law enforcement wouldn't help them. Sandy and Pierre thought that she needed to go to a hospital. Jeremy and Skizzum thought that she would be better off somewhere else far, far away.

The man who had been with Rover was the other Steale, the surviving brother and airplane pilot. Rover had a chest wound and was not dead. He was bleeding, mostly internally. Steale got him to the boat and motored him to Mallard's landing. From there, he took him to the Concordia Parish Hospital where he was treated. Declaring he had been involved in a hunting accident, he survived his wounds, but the pain would remind him of the score, every day for the rest of his short life.

Although the Sheriff was somewhat suspicious, having been a deputy years before when a certain Harper, injured in the same area, declared he had also been involved in a hunting accident; it was nevertheless, the right season. There were hunting accidents every year. So, there were no further questions. Rover knew better than to involve the cops more than that, whether the Sheriff's office, where newcomers who were not Klan members now reigned when Slaughter was out, or the police department. He was thinking one thing and one thing only when he told Steale, the son and pilot "we need to get that girl and make her talk. She knows something. I don't think she was there with her gun to shoot birds." Rover had a punctured lung and could not smoke his cigars any more than go after Emmy or anyone else. This made him madder than Hell. He told Steale, "get Slaughter. He's the one for the job." As he said it, he hoped that Slaughter would also go down for sending the anonymous letter to him about Broderick and the ants. "He's brave enough with girls, but in the end, a pussy when it comes to real men," he added.

The gunshot wound to Rover's chest was healing, but before winter was over, before anyone would catch up with Jeremy or even Emmy, he caught a case of pneumonia in his good lung, and died.

The man for the job

Besides torturing Blacks in the Ferriday jail, and other Klan members on ant hills and in wash basins, Slaughter beat members of the Congress of Racial Equality (CORE) and extracted money from local bars and brothels. He was a big, brutal man. "I ain't no pussy, Rover. Screw you," he said. He would not hesitate to do as much with Emmy if she refused to tell him what he wanted to know: "What were you doin' Under-the-Hill last weekend? Why are you hangin' out with that no-good, Jeremy Harper? Do you know what he was up to that night?" Of course, he would need to check with Ross, as he always had, to know in what order to put his questions. Not much could be said about the girl's shooting Rover. The men had been on her property and accident or not, Rover had aimed at her. He had to be careful to avoid talking about the Klan unless she said something first.

He spilled his coffee on his khaki uniform as he pulled up in the Sheriff's Office-car in front of the trailer at the Sportsman's camp. "Shiiiittt. Goddammit, shit!" he muttered, wiping away the coffee with his hand. "I'm too old for this shit." He was thinking he didn't want to end up in prison for a second term. He got out of the car, walked over to the door and knocked. Skizzum answered. Slaughter was surprised to see her and asked, "Er, uh, is Miss Robichaux here?"

Skizzum, knowing full well who Slaughter was, but propped up from her adolescent cat-shit prank, was not afraid in the least. "She's here, but isn't seeing anyone."

"Young lady, do you know who I am?" said Slaughter, getting out his badge.

"Sure, I know you, but unless you got a warrant, you cain't talk to her. Besides, in case you didn't know, she cain't talk." Skizzum had a stern look on her face. "She's been ill for years and got something wrong with her voice." Emmy was lying in bed, in the other room. They had come back over to the camp to clean up the mess Rover and his man had made, overturning drawers and cabinets, looking for who knows what. Emmy's anonymous letters had all been sent, and the scraps burned behind her house. Emmy heard Slaughter, and was frightened. After witnessing what he had done to Broderick, she had never gotten around to writing to him. She had hoped Rover would take care of him, but that had not gone as planned. As is often is the case, things were not as she imagined them to be. Rover had been a witness like herself. No one else would tie him to the ant-fire. What had started as an angry pebble in a pool of anxiety, rippled and waved into a revolt inside her.

Worrying that her letters might be just another sign of dithering resolve, like the hated ones from people who said that they wanted to help and did nothing, she sat up in the bed and swung her long legs over the side. She had been eating better and her body didn't ache as much. Her skin did not burn like it had. Putting on her jeans, she tucked a pistol into the back waistband. They had not been able to keep the weapons from her. These had been around her since she was a child and she argued that she needed them for protection. Without understanding why, her friends had to recognize the facts. There were threats, and they seemed to be directed at Emmy. Skizzum knew part of the reason but couldn't tell Jeremy or anyone else.

Skizzum scowled at Emmy when she saw her come out of the bedroom. Refusing her friend's protective measures, she stood in the door, in front of Slaughter. "I want you to come with me," he said. She looked at him like she didn't understand. Skizzum said, asking without asking, "See what I mean? She cain't talk." Slaughter didn't ask how she had known he was at the door. He shook his head and told Skizzum, "I gotta look around the property. I know she won't mind, unless she's got somethin' to hide. Y'all aint makin' no moonshine over there, are you?" he snickered, knowing that they weren't. "What about meth?"

"You ain't got no warrant," said Skizzum. "You ain't even said what's your business here."

Slaughter shook his head again. He said, "Oh come on. You both know there was a huntin' accident over here a few weeks ago and the survivor told me where it was, and how it happened. Now I gotta verify all that."

Skizzum started to argue, but decided to let him go ahead. "Do whatever you want. We got nothin' to do with that." Then she closed the door looking towards Emmy. "Damnit," she said. "How does she do it?" Emmy was no longer in the room. Skizzum had no doubt that she had followed Slaughter. She ran out the door and all the way to Emmy's house to call Jeremy. He wasn't home. She left a message with Shelley, not sure his wife would tell him. "Please ask him to get over here. I need him to help. It's an emergency." She hung up without explaining and ran back in the house to find Emmy's rifle. It was in the cabinet where she had locked it up. Her car was still out front so she got in and drove back to the camp.

Skizzum wasn't like Bee or Emmy. She hadn't explored the woods behind the camp like they had. It was getting late, but it wasn't dark yet. The sky was lavender and gray over the lake when she pushed Emmy's new boat off from the peer. She had a flashlight, and the rifle, but hoped that she wouldn't have to shoot. Rounding the point and rowing as fast as she could, she found the dirt landing back in the cove. At least thirty minutes had passed, she thought. She pulled the boat onto the shore and listened. The crickets and frogs who had been starting to chirp fell silent as she walked. She tried not to make noise, but they heard her and the broken insect noise seemed as bad as crashing through the brush. Noisy silence. She picked up a stick and rubbed it against the rifle. The ridges made sounds that could fool a person into thinking the crickets, or some other insects, were still chirping, if not the frogs.

"Hell, this might even fool the crickets," she thought, also considering it might make a good musical addition.

She pressed on. She didn't know where she was going or where the dangers might be. She tripped over the top of what seemed like buried sewage tank, hidden beneath the brush. It had a handle. Not knowing what this was, she pulled until the top lifted. The fumes from the whiskey mash were strong. She had already smelled the makings of moonshine before. She wondered who made it here on Emmy's property and thought her friend must not know about it. There had to be a fine for moonshine these days. If not, why were those kids always sitting out in a chair on the roadside of Highway 61? You could see them when you drove to Baton Rouge. Weren't they there to warn someone if a curious driver stopped? There was a noise in the trees and she looked up to see Emmy pointing a pistol in Slaughter's direction.

Slaughter was backing towards her. Skizzum moved away to one side. She motioned to Emmy, pointing to the cistern. Emmy didn't flinch. "Now look, young lady." Slaughter was trying to talk her out of whatever he thought her plan was. Emmy thought he would try to charge her at some point. He was waiting for his chance. He was thinking anything could happen. "Why is she trying to get me into the clearing." He saw Jeremy running up behind Emmy. He lowered his arms, "You little son-of-a-...."

Out of the corner of his eye he saw Skizzum to his right, and lost his balance, tripping backwards over into the cistern. He didn't have time to cry out. He was already a goner. He had not drowned his sorrow in whiskey, but he nevertheless fell into it. Anyone with a brain who has ever made any kind of alcohol knows about asphyxiation or in this case, hypoxia, although they might not call it by the scientific or medical name. Carbon dioxide poisoning in whiskey mash, floating just above the liquid, colorless and odorless, hiding behind an aromatic curtain. He had hit his head, but the toxic gas is what killed him. No one could have saved him. They didn't bother replacing the cover. The shiners would find him. It was a death too easy for someone who had orchestrated the death of Frank Norris and had beaten and killed many more. At least he was gone. As for the moonshine, with a body floating in it, it would be hard to recover. But they might try. Afterall, aren't rattlesnakes sometimes left in tequila bottles?

They wiped down the cover of the fermenting tun to get rid of any prints, dusted it with dirt, and left in a hurry by boat. The Sheriff department's car was parked on the same gravel road, in the same place, that Mérite-Lajoie had parked, when she had first met Harper, and had loaded him into her truck to take him to the nearby hospital. It would stay there, empty of assailants, cult or Klan members, as well as void of the innocent who had so often occupied its back seats on their last ride for eternity. It would stay there as part of a crime scene, for another day or two, until someone else found it and Slaughter's death was investigated. Other than Hogden, and Steale, whom she had learned about much later, he was the last one on Emmy's list. On the way home, no one said a word.

Reconciliation

Emmy had been taught by her parents to forgive the unforgiveable. This was a necessary part of reconciliation for the crime of genocide. Native Americans, as well as the African Americans, had been targets of genocide, as had the Jews her parents sought to protect in World War II.

Emmy, herself, the victim of crimes, still unnameable to herself, wanted a reckoning for all the families hurt by crimes of hate. She had been focused on revenge, englobing her suffering with that of others, not realizing that a reckoning went before and beyond the act of homemade justice. In doing so, already with her anonymous letters, she didn't realize she was becoming a criminal herself. Emmy could forgive those who had harmed her; not those who had harmed the people and causes she cared about. Her kin had also been victims of forcible assimilation and other crimes. News of recognition of Cajuns as a minority group and attempts to preserve their language came late, too late for her. But her path of retribution, if it was misguided and sometimes made of pure folly, ultimately brought her back to her beginnings and to its building blocks; her identity, her songs, her languages, her words.

A childhood event had tied the sins of the son to the father in her memory, but it was not until she could sever these binds that she could understand that he was a victim like she was, like they all were who prostrated before Harper, were there, ready to do his bidding, looking for love, identity, and recognition.

Jeremy had mixed feelings about his father. Even as he loved him and had wanted to be loved by him, he didn't know if he could forgive him. He understood that the man's actions had taken his children down with him, and understood now more than ever, why Mérite-Lajoie did what she had done. As a youth, he had tried to honor his memory, tried to forgive himself for a childish petty crime, but in doing so, he found himself entrapped in another cultlike situation, that spread over his life like a spilled vat of toxic chemicals, infecting his friendships, his job, his home. Jeremy left the paper mill and took his family to Tennessee, on the river near Memphis. He was able to break free of his old chains with the help of the girls, whom he now thought of as friends, whether or not they agreed.

Emmy had not carried out her first mission, a revenge transferred to her tormenter's son. In her eyes, he had managed to repurchase his soul, because if nothing else, with his limited means, he had saved her life more than once, and wanted nothing more than an end to the strife and anxiety he had known. Consciousness, or at least with regrets for his past, came for him in the form of fear for himself and for his family. Emmy forgave him, at least in part, because she was not without reproach. Having kidnapped an innocent child, whether thus had been her intention or not, she was no longer an innocent herself. "I'll have to keep an eye on that one," she murmured.

Skizzum returned to Nashville and was having some success as a blues musician. She was doing what she had always done, living each day as it came, using music to deal with her anxiety, in addition to her self-medication.

Her health was damaged when she went too far. At first, she and Emmy lived together until Skizzum moved in with a girl with whom she had fallen in love. She tried to watch over Emmy, pulling her back from the brink when needed, nursing her back to health. She was learning to do yoga and eating healthy food. Emmy had her own agenda, but sometimes she needed someone to be there for her. Who doesn't need love?

They would have to wait for many years to hear of the undoing of Steale and of Hogden. Steales was ratted out to the FBI by one of his own for the drowning of two young men, still in their teens, in an old branch of the Mississippi River near the Homochitto National Forest. He was the only member of the Silver Dollar Group of the KKK to have been condemned for murder, more than forty years after the crime. As for Hogden, a source reported to *The Concordia Post*'s new editor, that the former deputy had had hallucinations of Joseph Edouard in his last months, as he finished his days in a nursing home. Skizzum and Jeremy wondered if these visions from Hell were caused by an inkling of guilt or if someone had slipped him a poison pen letter with its edges dipped in *Strynos toxifera*, or some other fatal poison or hallucinogen.

Had the slaves in the graveyard found peace? No one knew. The last of the farm equipment had been moved away and perhaps some of the graves transferred to another cemetery. No one knew how many slaves had been buried there. Their tormentors, as well as the modern-day versions of these, would rot in Hell--their crimes of blood having cut them off from all humanity. Mamere, however, seemed to have been allowed a long-deserved rest. Harper's wife, being Mérite-Lajoie's cousin, was her niece, meaning that Jeremy was her great-nephew. Had Mamere come to repair the conflict that Harper had caused between cousins? Emmy had not seen or talked to her since she had played the guitar in her bedroom, singing the adagio of "The Roses of Aranjuez." Perhaps, like Jeremy's little girl, after delivering her message, she just left the scene and never came back. Emmy was left to deal with the mess she alone, had created. Perhaps, inside the labyrinths of her mind, she had somehow acquired a little of her grandmother's wisdom, whatever that was. Only those who have passed can possess the faith and the clairvoyance of the whole picture, delimited and framed by death.

Emmy's poems were no longer vengeful rhymes, but songs about social unrest. Now with a not new, but properly tuned piano, she added music to her songs about police violence, political unrest, of protests and riots, of unbridled capitalism, of nostalgia, and sadness. Celebrating the life of Klan victims, she chanted in whispers their story-songs like the griots. Skizzum sent Emmy's songs to music editors and performers to see if she could help her break in as a songwriter.

The Sportsman's camp was now managed by another family and Emmy collected a small rent. She sold her family's house on Iowa Street. Outside her songs, she never spoke of the Klan. With the help of a speech therapist, she began to recover her voice. Not a full singing voice, but at least a speaking voice that did not cause pain when she used it. Encouraged by Skizzum, she considered whispering her own songs in public, as her grandmother had done in a music that belonged more to nomads than to stationary peoples, and she worked on these every day. During one of her of *crises de nerfs*, someone asked her if she had heard about Hogden's demise and the new investigations into the Silver Dollar Klan crimes. "Poison is a woman's weapon," she told her friends. She smiled an inward smile, as she remembered deviling the Devil.

Epilogue

After Slaughter had breathed his last breath, before
Rover had taken his, and before the other Klan members
were dead or dying, Emmy, Skizzum, and Jeremy went
back to the trailers in the campground. They looked
around, making sure all was in order. At last, they went
to the trailer Jeremy had lived in as a boy, with his
brothers, his mother, and his father who had been simply
called, Harper, even though it was not his real name.
Skizzum had almost finished cleaning it, but had not
explored every corner. "Hey, come in here and help me
with this box," she called out. Emmy and Jeremy came
into the room. They brought down a box from the top of
the closet. Emmy opened it and a cloud of moths flew
into the room. They all peered inside over her shoulder.
There, facing them, was the lycanthropic-possum mask
Harper had worn at the Mardi Gras festival, the very
night he had violated Emmy and the church had burned.

Emmy had a moment of recoil, and stopped. Harper had
been the one to unite them, and to devastate their lives to
the point of near destruction. They had all wanted in
some way to murder him. Beyond the grave could he still
perpetrate fear and control to ruin their lives? Push them
to violence and to crime? He had said a lot of words that
could not be erased, but only rearranged in their minds.
How could they be rid of him forever?

Taking the mask with both hands, Emmy stared. There
was something ridiculous about its face. But what is any
face if not a reflection of the feelings we have for the one
who wears it, and of the words we use to express the
love, or distaste we have for that person? Still holding the

mask, she turned towards her friend and her cousin. All three took it into their hands and held it as its gossamer fur came unglued in patches, the *paper mâché* muzzle cracked, and the teeth fell out, by clumps, then, one by one, onto the trailer floor. All three stared at the bits and pieces covered by years of mold and mildew. And just like that, he was gone, and with him, his certitudes, as well as the attention with which these were bestowed. He could no longer shape their lives, no longer stir their blood. Emmy picked up a dust bin, swept up the remains, and threw them into the garbage.

The end

Barbara Bonneau

Acknowledgements

First and foremost, I want to thank my family for their precious encouragements and patience over the years. My heartfelt thanks to my friends, Leonard Feiss, Tom Wells, Andy Smyser, Jim Fuchs, Lisa Muller, Gary Keith, and Jennifer Duval for their patient reading, encouragements and/or advice in preparing this novel. Applauses to Bashar Lulua for his musical expertise and advise on finding and using classical music in writing. I would also like to thank "The Copyright Alliance" and "Rightsclick" for information on preparing this book for copyright, as well as the group, "Authors and Writers Helping Each Other Grow", the title hinting to the purpose. All mistakes must be attributed to me.

About the Author

Barbara Bonneau has published articles and two books about body image, language, mental disorders, and destructive cults. *Deviling the Devil* is her third novel, preceded by *White Light Yoga* and *These Beans Have Too Much Salt*.

Barbara Bonneau spent most of her youth in Ferriday, Louisiana and attended both Louisiana State University and The University of Texas at Austin. She obtained her doctorate degree in psychopathology from the Université de Paris, Denis Diderot in 2001, now called l'Université de Paris. She currently shares her time between Burgundy, France and Austin, Texas, and works with children who have special needs.

About the novel:

The work here is entirely fictive. Any references to real people, living or dead, real events, businesses, organizations, political movements, churches, and localities are intended only to give the fiction a sense of reality and authenticity. All names, characters and incidents are either the product of the author's imagination or are used fictitiously, and their resemblance, if any, to real-life counterparts is entirely coincidental.

The work here is entirely fictive; however, Barbara Bonneau grew up in Ferriday, Louisiana, and was not much younger than the character, Emmy, when her house burned on Virginia Avenue, just a few blocks away from where Frank Morris was burned alive in his shoe shop, murdered by the Ku Klux Klan, during the same year. As a child, she saw the ruins of the building and was informed by her parents of the probable cause. This cold case was brought to light by the work of Pulitzer Prize finalist, Stanley Nelson, and can be read about in his documentary book, *Devils Walking, Klan Murders along the Mississippi*, 2016, Louisiana University Press.

Barbara Bonneau expressed a desire to write about these crimes early on, in a letter to her sister about the first novel, but did not know much about the truth behind these crimes until Stanley Nelson's work was published. Inhibited by the idea of writing about such suffering and what it could mean for the families of the victims and the sensitivity needed to write about them, she waited until she could resolve her question. It is hard to observe the suffering of others. Yet, if we close our eyes, who will uncover the truth, if not writers? Natchez neighbor and novelist, Greg Isles, equally wrote a thriller about Klan crimes in the area in 2015 based on Stanley Nelson's research.

Nevertheless, it was essential for Barbara Bonneau, if she could not understand the crimes, to at least understand how victims dealt with trauma, to the point of disbelieving what has happened to them. Her own house fire provided first-hand experience of this moment of disbelief, although certainly not to the degree that the victims of racial violence had suffered at the hand of the Klan. Having a racially mixed family, and having some idea of the devastation racial crime causes, she felt it was necessary to write about these crimes.

The characters, Emmy, Skizzum, Jeremy (called Charlie in *White Light Yoga* (©2022), Bee, Mamere, Mérite-Lajoie, Deux Ours, and Harper, are all present in *These Beans Have Too Much Salt* ©2015- 2016, and were in part, created in the first drafts of this novel, *Porcelain Hands* © 2005, then *Sweetbriar*©2008, then *Sweetbriar Cajun* ©2013. This stand-alone novel is a character development, which speaks to Emmy's years of solitude, following the 1963 condemnation of her mother, Mérite-Lajoie, for the murder of Harper, before her mother's encounter with Bee in prison. The information about cults, necessary for the development of these characters, is provided in *These Beans Have Too Much Salt.*

www.ingramcontent.com/pod-product-compliance
Lightning Source LLC
Chambersburg PA
CBHW030630020726
47493CB00006B/1645